AMERICAN BORN CHINESE

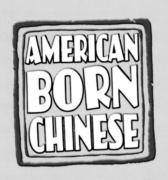

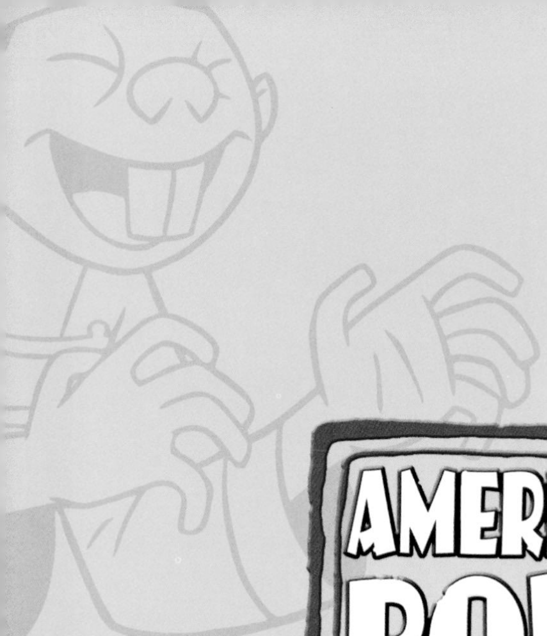

AMERICAN BORN CHINESE

Gene Luen Yang

Color by Lark Pien

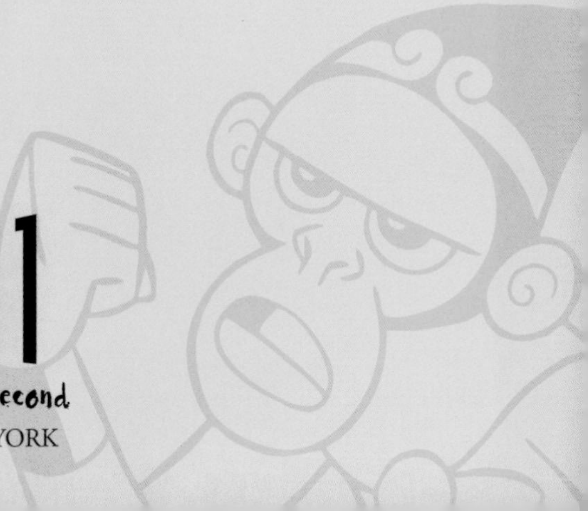

:01
First Second
NEW YORK

To Ma,
for her stories of the Monkey King

And Ba,
for his stories of Ah-Tong, the Taiwanese village boy

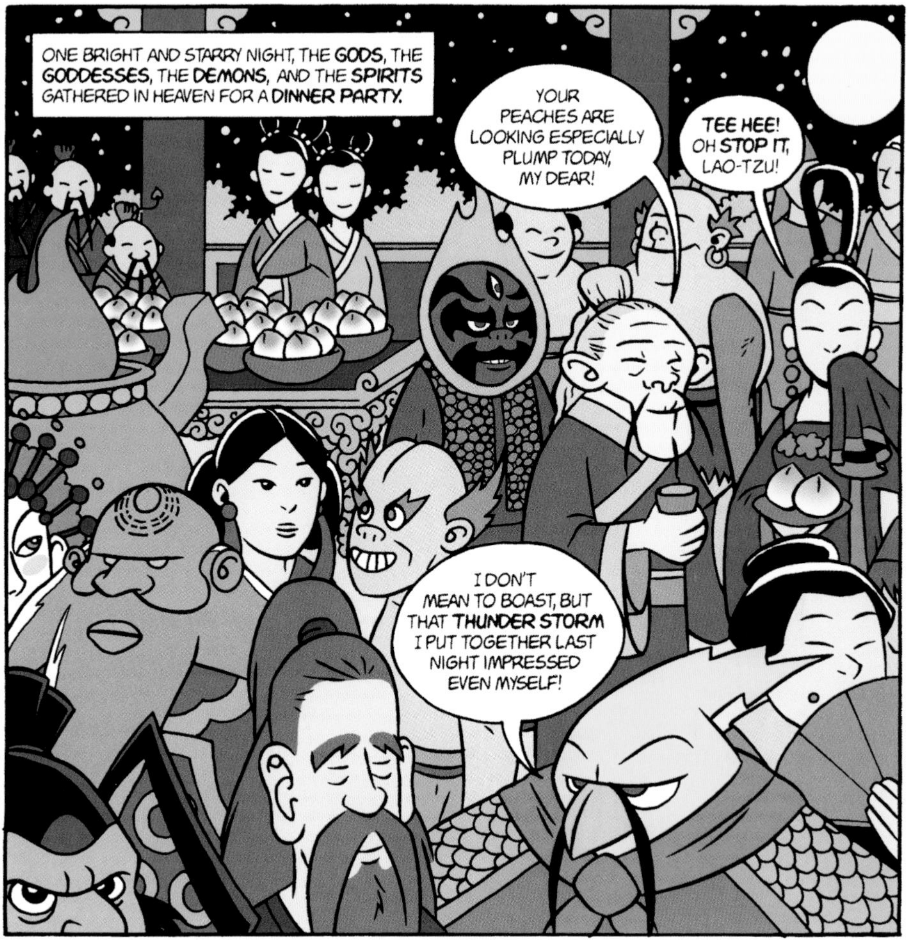
ONE BRIGHT AND STARRY NIGHT, THE GODS, THE GODDESSES, THE DEMONS, AND THE SPIRITS GATHERED IN HEAVEN FOR A DINNER PARTY.
YOUR PEACHES ARE LOOKING ESPECIALLY PLUMP TODAY, MY DEAR!
TEE HEE! OH STOP IT, LAO-TZU!
I DON'T MEAN TO BOAST, BUT THAT THUNDER STORM I PUT TOGETHER LAST NIGHT IMPRESSED EVEN MYSELF!

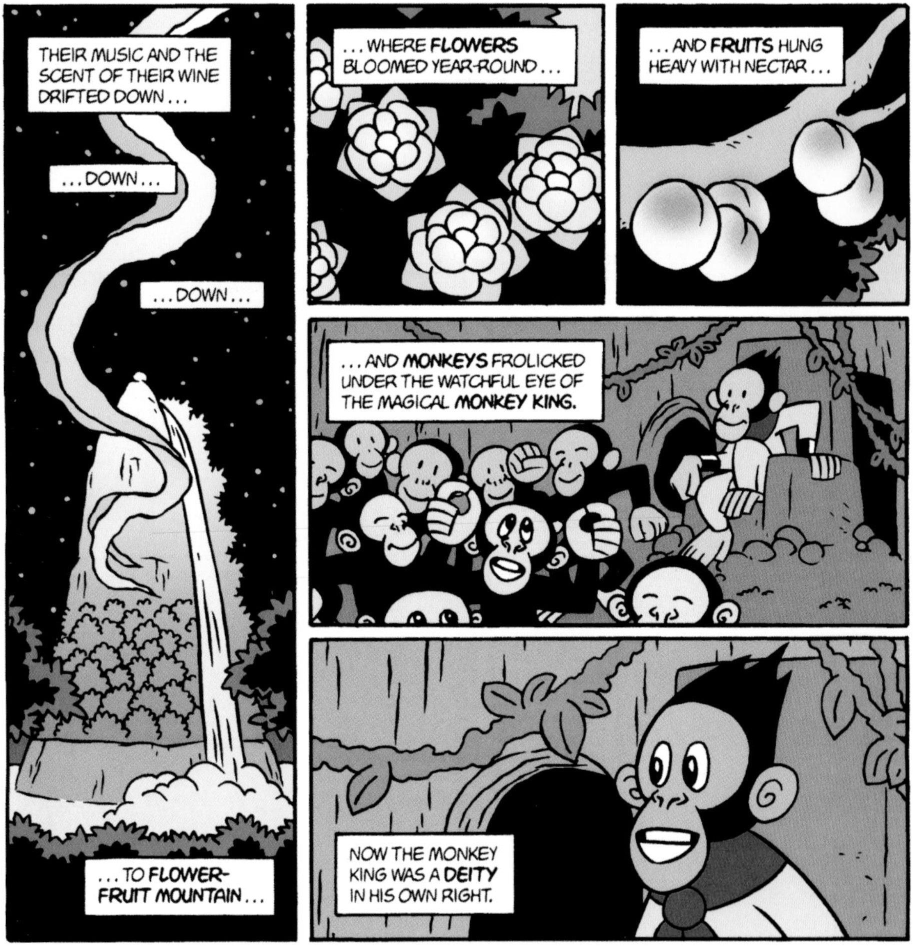
THEIR MUSIC AND THE SCENT OF THEIR WINE DRIFTED DOWN . . .
. . . DOWN . . .
. . . DOWN . . .
. . . TO FLOWER-FRUIT MOUNTAIN . . .
. . . WHERE FLOWERS BLOOMED YEAR-ROUND . . .
. . . AND FRUITS HUNG HEAVY WITH NECTAR . . .
. . . AND MONKEYS FROLICKED UNDER THE WATCHFUL EYE OF THE MAGICAL MONKEY KING.
NOW THE MONKEY KING WAS A DEITY IN HIS OWN RIGHT.

LEGEND HAD IT THAT LONG AGO, LONG BEFORE ALMOST ANY MONKEY COULD REMEMBER, THE MONKEY KING WAS BORN OF A **ROCK**.

KRAK!

WHEN HIS EYES FIRST OPENED, THEY FLASHED **RAYS OF LIGHT** DEEP INTO THE SKY.

ALL OF HEAVEN TOOK NOTICE.

WHAT THE-?

SOON AFTER, HE PURGED **FLOWER-FRUIT MOUNTAIN** OF THE **TIGER- SPIRIT** THAT HAD HAUNTED IT FOR CENTURIES.

HE ESTABLISHED HIS **KINGDOM** AND MONKEYS FROM THE FOUR CORNERS OF THE WORLD **FLOCKED** TO HIM.

9

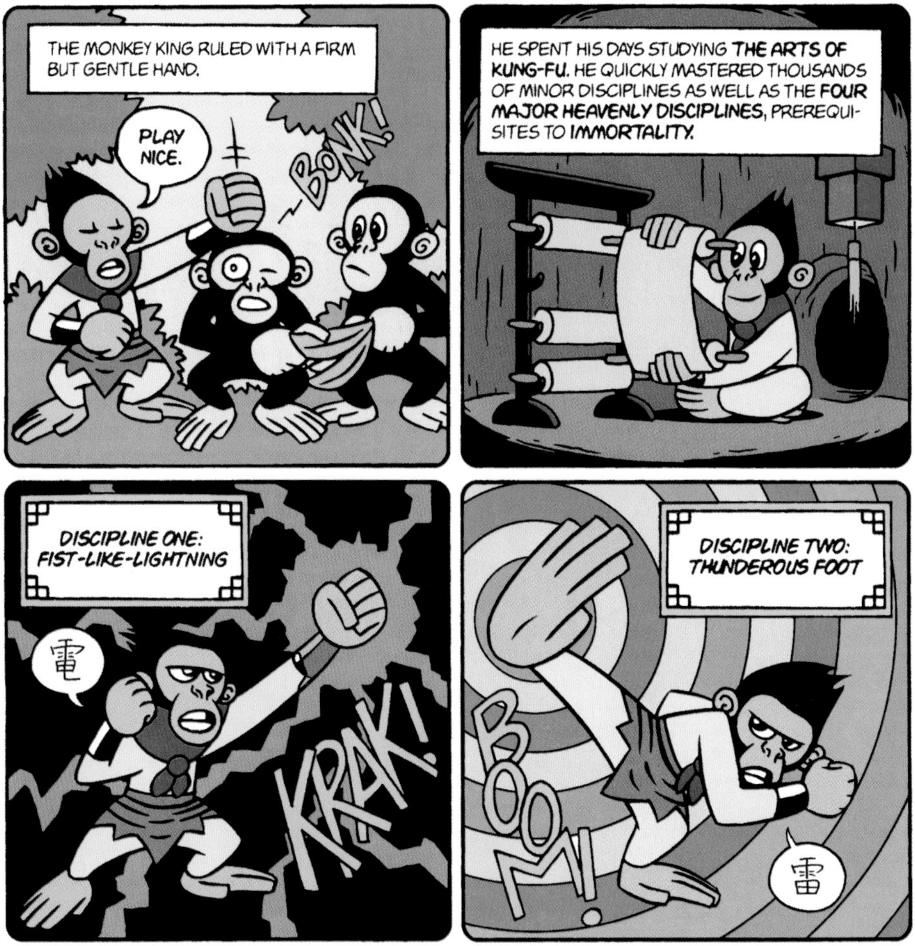
THE MONKEY KING RULED WITH A FIRM BUT GENTLE HAND.
PLAY NICE.
BONK!
HE SPENT HIS DAYS STUDYING **THE ARTS OF KUNG-FU.** HE QUICKLY MASTERED THOUSANDS OF MINOR DISCIPLINES AS WELL AS THE **FOUR MAJOR HEAVENLY DISCIPLINES,** PREREQUISITES TO **IMMORTALITY.**
DISCIPLINE ONE: FIST-LIKE-LIGHTNING
電
KRAK!
DISCIPLINE TWO: THUNDEROUS FOOT
BOOM!
雷

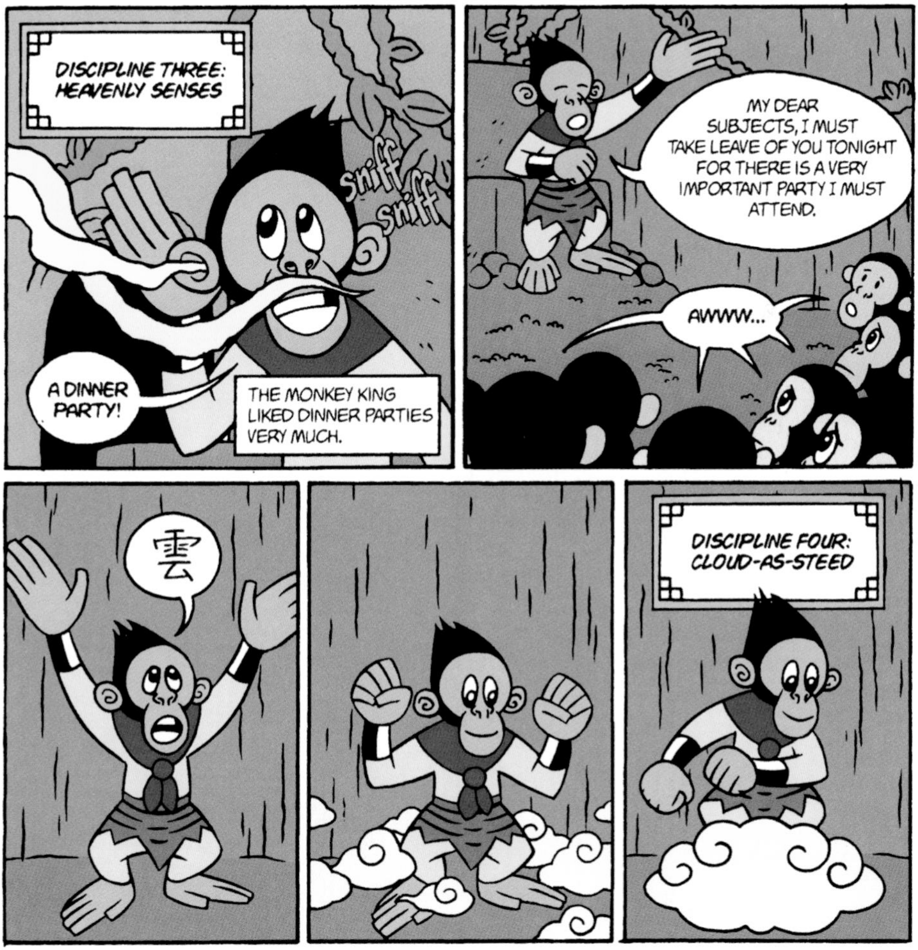
DISCIPLINE THREE: HEAVENLY SENSES
sniff sniff
A DINNER PARTY!
THE MONKEY KING LIKED DINNER PARTIES VERY MUCH.
MY DEAR SUBJECTS, I MUST TAKE LEAVE OF YOU TONIGHT FOR THERE IS A VERY IMPORTANT PARTY I MUST ATTEND.
AWWW...
雲
DISCIPLINE FOUR: CLOUD-AS-STEED

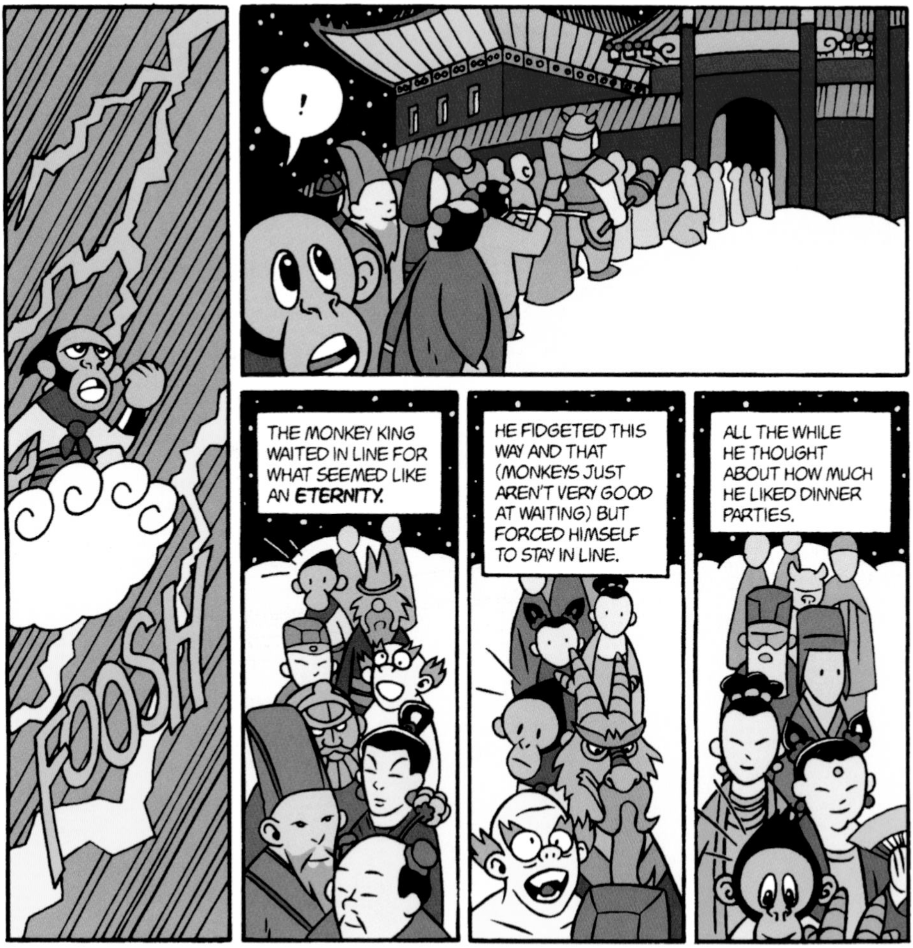
FOOSH
!
THE MONKEY KING WAITED IN LINE FOR WHAT SEEMED LIKE AN **ETERNITY.**
HE FIDGETED THIS WAY AND THAT (MONKEYS JUST AREN'T VERY GOOD AT WAITING) BUT FORCED HIMSELF TO STAY IN LINE.
ALL THE WHILE HE THOUGHT ABOUT HOW MUCH HE LIKED DINNER PARTIES.

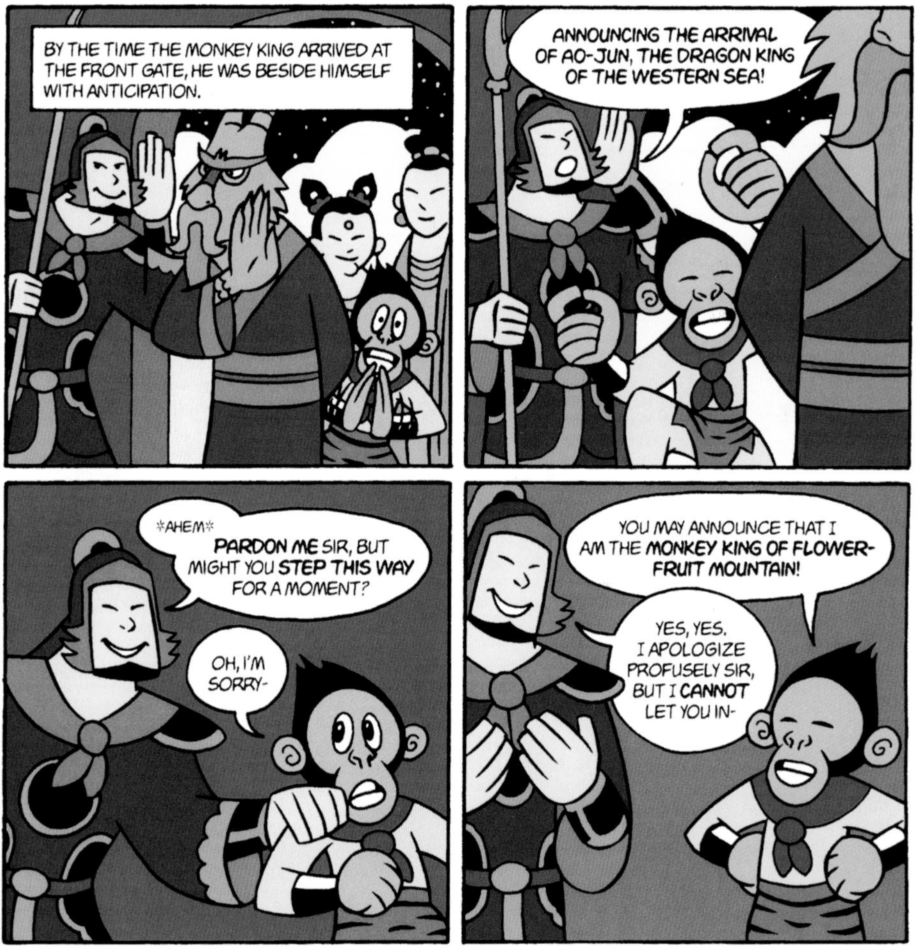
BY THE TIME THE MONKEY KING ARRIVED AT THE FRONT GATE, HE WAS BESIDE HIMSELF WITH ANTICIPATION.
ANNOUNCING THE ARRIVAL OF AO-JUN, THE DRAGON KING OF THE WESTERN SEA!
AHEM PARDON ME SIR, BUT MIGHT YOU STEP THIS WAY FOR A MOMENT?
OH, I'M SORRY-
YOU MAY ANNOUNCE THAT I AM THE MONKEY KING OF FLOWER-FRUIT MOUNTAIN!
YES, YES. I APOLOGIZE PROFUSELY SIR, BUT I CANNOT LET YOU IN-

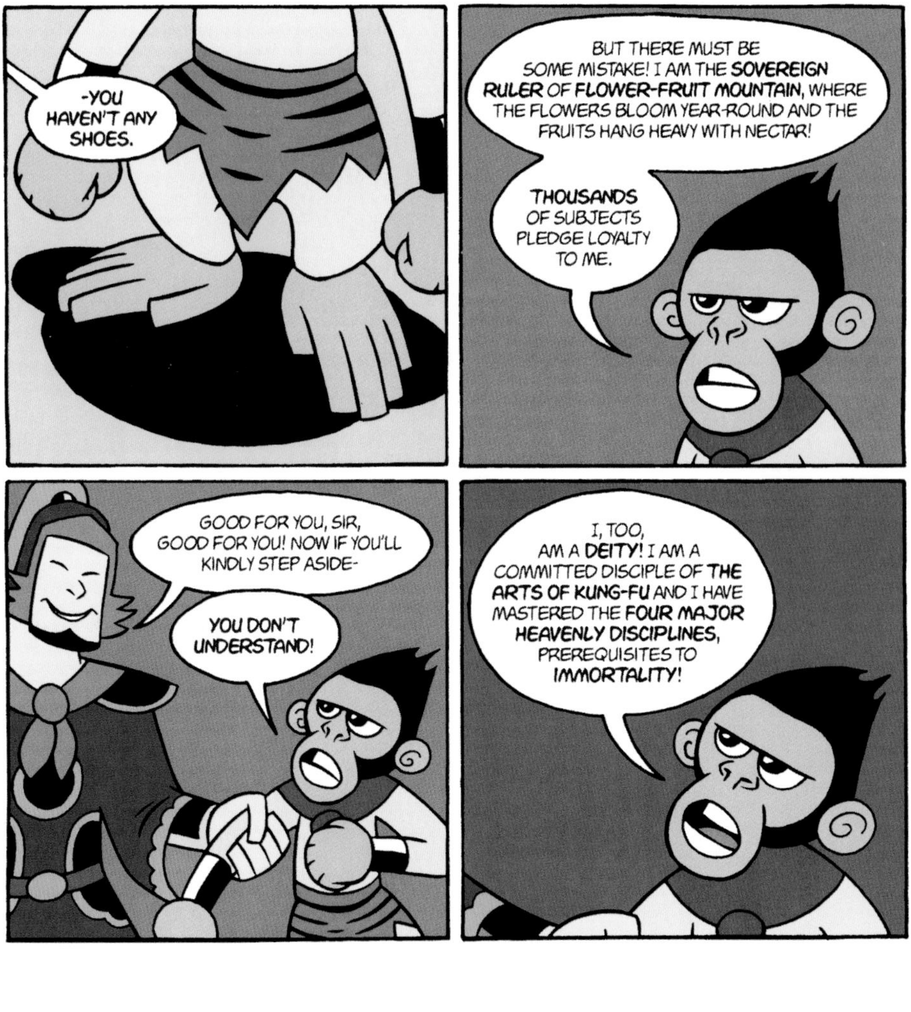
-YOU HAVEN'T ANY SHOES.
BUT THERE MUST BE SOME MISTAKE! I AM THE SOVEREIGN RULER OF FLOWER-FRUIT MOUNTAIN, WHERE THE FLOWERS BLOOM YEAR-ROUND AND THE FRUITS HANG HEAVY WITH NECTAR!
THOUSANDS OF SUBJECTS PLEDGE LOYALTY TO ME.
GOOD FOR YOU, SIR, GOOD FOR YOU! NOW IF YOU'LL KINDLY STEP ASIDE-
YOU DON'T UNDERSTAND!
I, TOO, AM A DEITY! I AM A COMMITTED DISCIPLE OF THE ARTS OF KUNG-FU AND I HAVE MASTERED THE FOUR MAJOR HEAVENLY DISCIPLINES, PREREQUISITES TO IMMORTALITY!

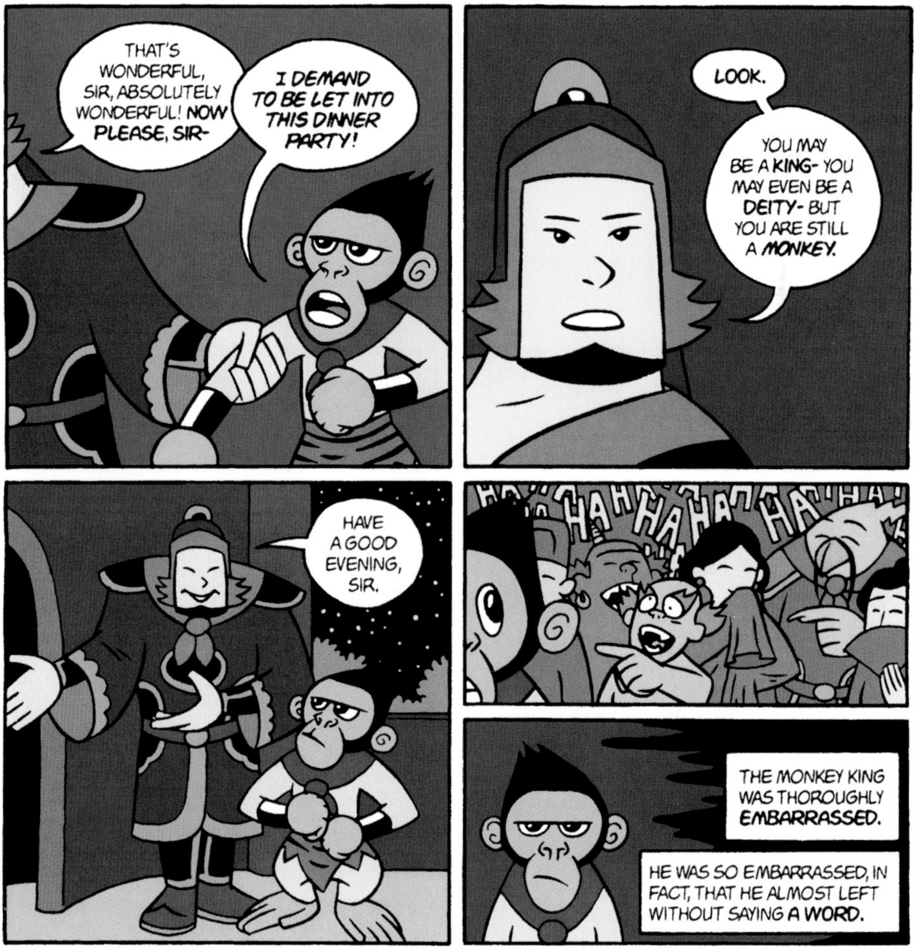
THAT'S WONDERFUL, SIR, ABSOLUTELY WONDERFUL! NOW PLEASE, SIR-
I DEMAND TO BE LET INTO THIS DINNER PARTY!
LOOK.
YOU MAY BE A KING- YOU MAY EVEN BE A DEITY- BUT YOU ARE STILL A MONKEY.
HAVE A GOOD EVENING, SIR.
HA HA HA HA HA HA
THE MONKEY KING WAS THOROUGHLY EMBARRASSED.
HE WAS SO EMBARRASSED, IN FACT, THAT HE ALMOST LEFT WITHOUT SAYING A WORD.

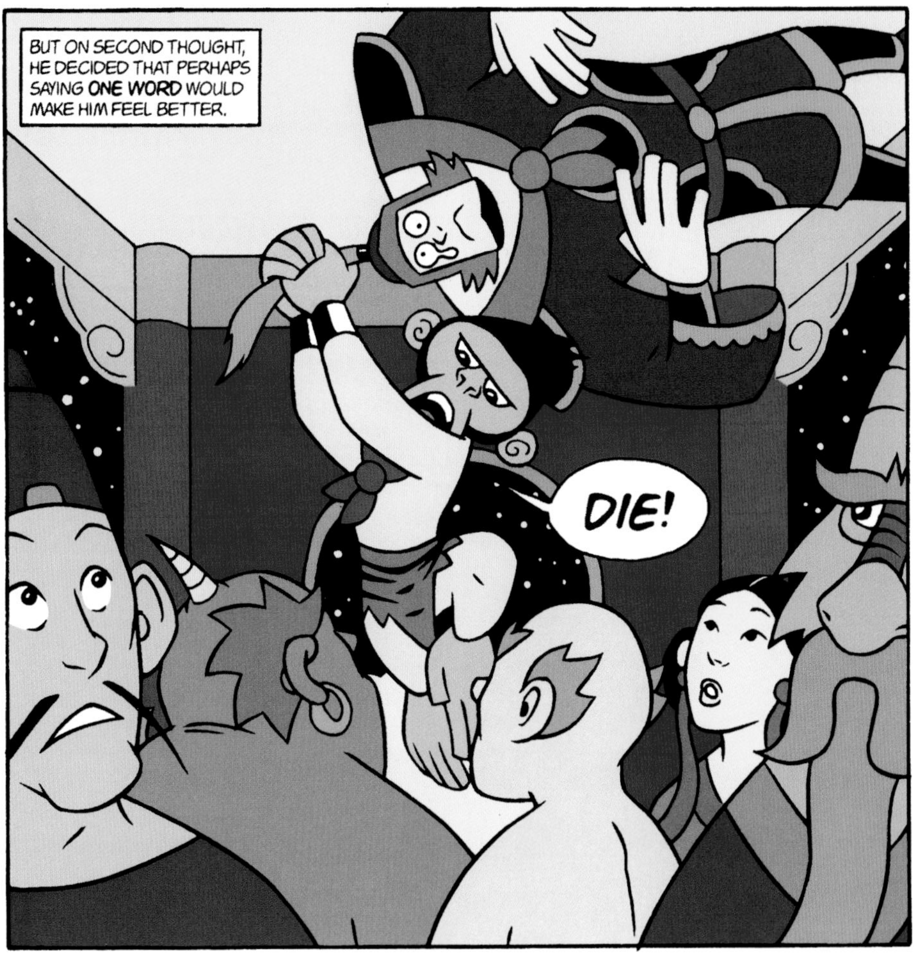
BUT ON SECOND THOUGHT, HE DECIDED THAT PERHAPS SAYING **ONE WORD** WOULD MAKE HIM FEEL BETTER.
DIE!

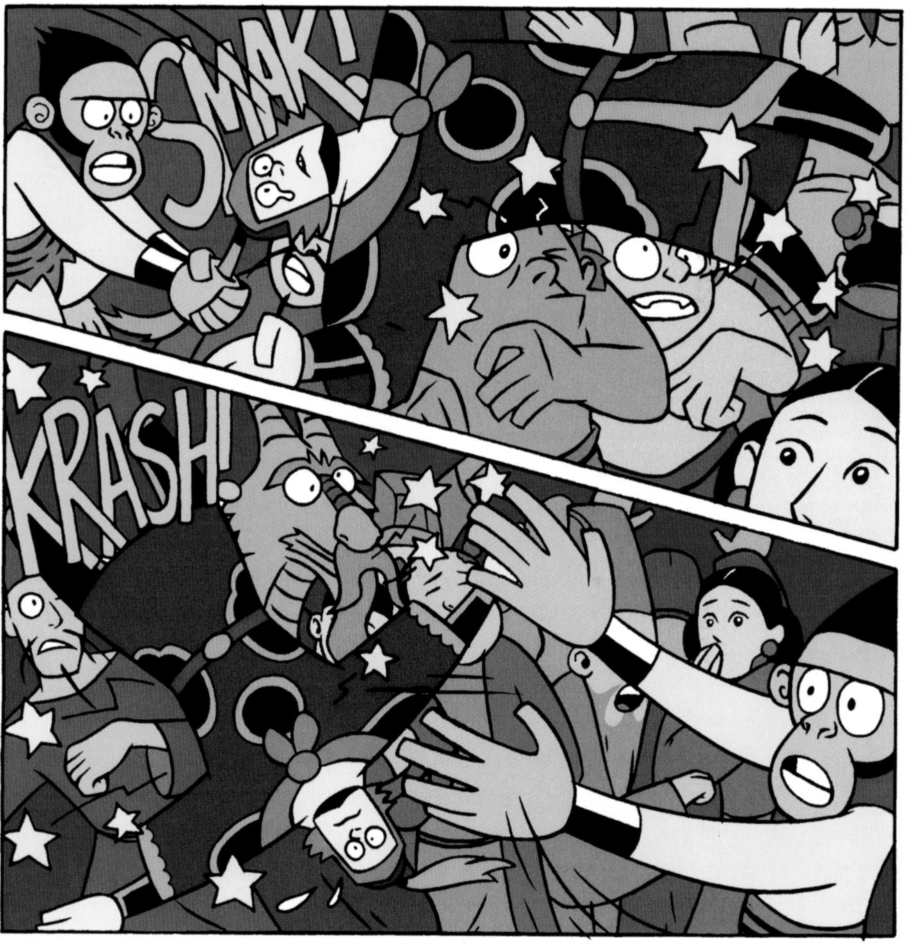
SMAK!
KRASH!

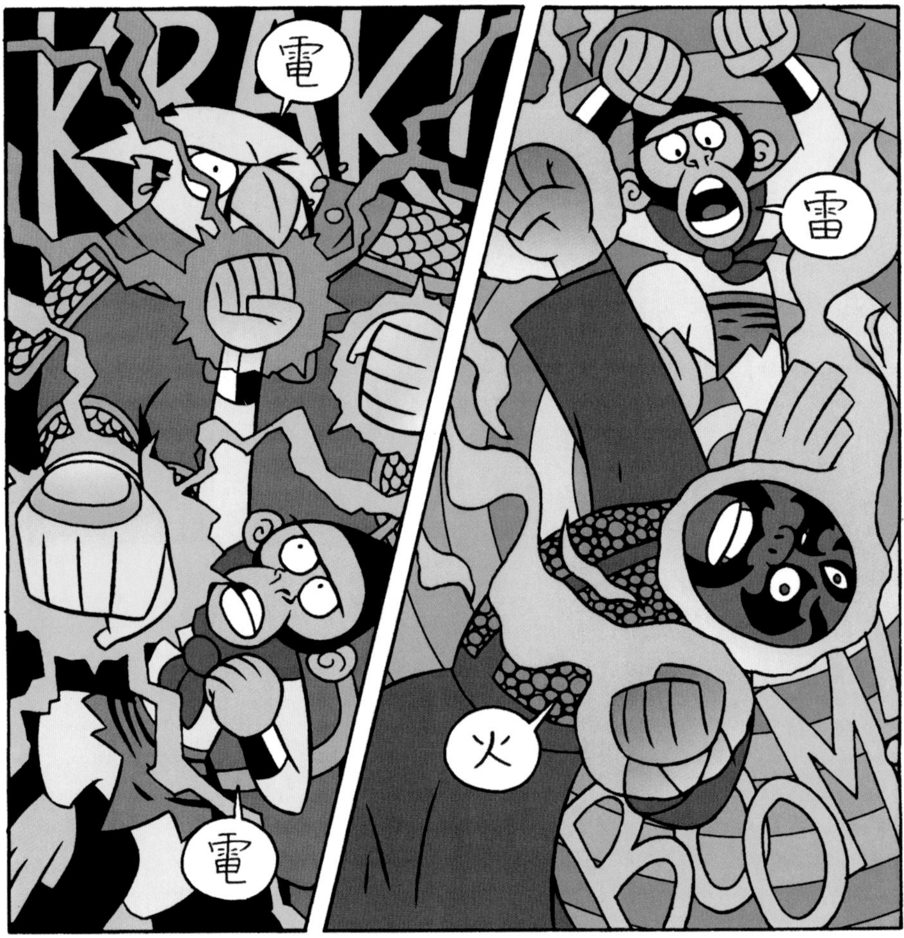
KRAK!
電
電
雷
火
BOOM!

THE MONKEY KING COULDN'T STOP SHAKING AS HE DESCENDED ON **FLOWER-FRUIT MOUNTAIN.**

WHEN HE ENTERED HIS ROYAL CHAMBER, THE THICK SMELL OF **MONKEY FUR** GREETED HIM.

HE'D NEVER NOTICED IT BEFORE.

HE STAYED AWAKE FOR THE REST OF THE NIGHT THINKING OF WAYS TO GET RID OF IT.

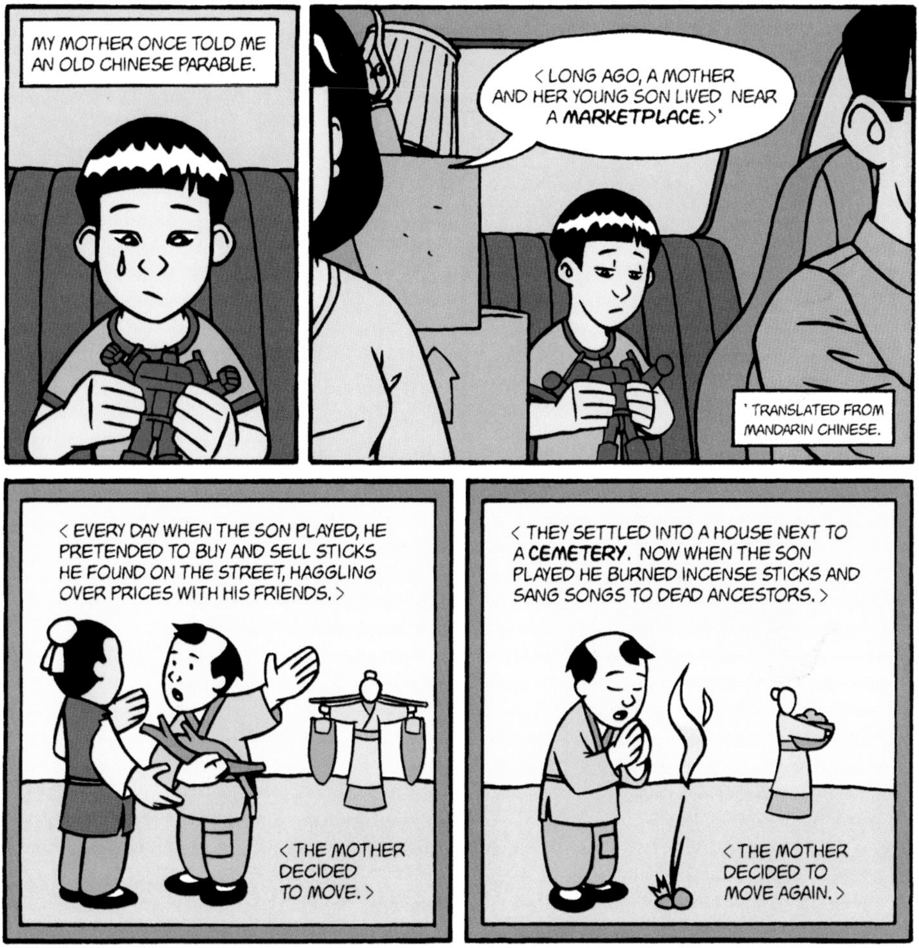
MY MOTHER ONCE TOLD ME AN OLD CHINESE PARABLE.
< LONG AGO, A MOTHER AND HER YOUNG SON LIVED NEAR A **MARKETPLACE**. >*
* TRANSLATED FROM MANDARIN CHINESE.
< EVERY DAY WHEN THE SON PLAYED, HE PRETENDED TO BUY AND SELL STICKS HE FOUND ON THE STREET, HAGGLING OVER PRICES WITH HIS FRIENDS. >
< THE MOTHER DECIDED TO MOVE. >
< THEY SETTLED INTO A HOUSE NEXT TO A **CEMETERY**. NOW WHEN THE SON PLAYED HE BURNED INCENSE STICKS AND SANG SONGS TO DEAD ANCESTORS. >
< THE MOTHER DECIDED TO MOVE AGAIN. >

< SHE FOUND A HOME ACROSS THE ROAD FROM A **UNIVERSITY**. THE SON NOW SPENT ALL HIS FREE-TIME READING BOOKS ABOUT MATHEMATICS, SCIENCE, AND HISTORY. >

< THE MOTHER AND HER SON STAYED THERE FOR A LONG, LONG TIME. >

SHE FINISHED THE STORY AS WE PULLED UP TO OUR NEW HOUSE.

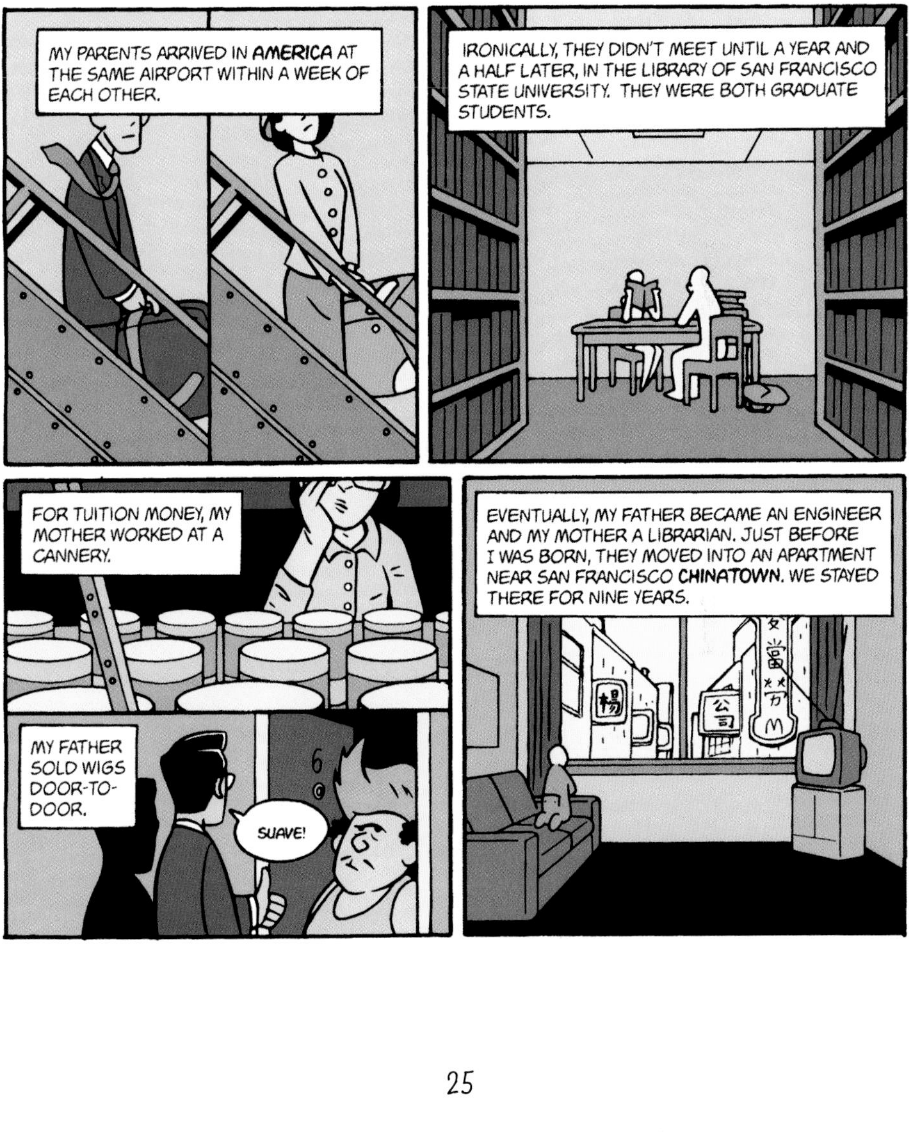
MY PARENTS ARRIVED IN **AMERICA** AT THE SAME AIRPORT WITHIN A WEEK OF EACH OTHER.
IRONICALLY, THEY DIDN'T MEET UNTIL A YEAR AND A HALF LATER, IN THE LIBRARY OF SAN FRANCISCO STATE UNIVERSITY. THEY WERE BOTH GRADUATE STUDENTS.
FOR TUITION MONEY, MY MOTHER WORKED AT A CANNERY.
MY FATHER SOLD WIGS DOOR-TO-DOOR.
SUAVE!
EVENTUALLY, MY FATHER BECAME AN ENGINEER AND MY MOTHER A LIBRARIAN. JUST BEFORE I WAS BORN, THEY MOVED INTO AN APARTMENT NEAR SAN FRANCISCO **CHINATOWN**. WE STAYED THERE FOR NINE YEARS.

THERE WAS A GROUP OF BOYS AROUND MY AGE THAT LIVED IN THE SAME COMPLEX.

THEY CAME OVER ON SATURDAY MORNINGS TO WATCH CARTOONS. (OUR APARTMENT, BEING ON THE TOP FLOOR, HAD THE BEST RECEPTION.)

⟨NO, MEGATRON!⟩

⟨DON'T DO IT!⟩

AFTERWARDS, WE WOULD STAGE EPIC BATTLES THAT LEFT OUR TOYS SMELLING LIKE SPIT.

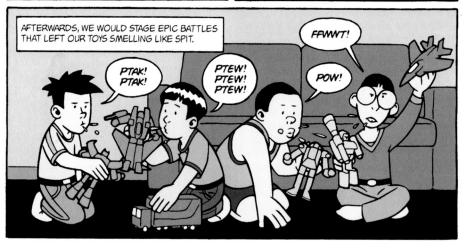

PTAK! PTAK!

PTEW! PTEW! PTEW!

FFWWT!

POW!

26

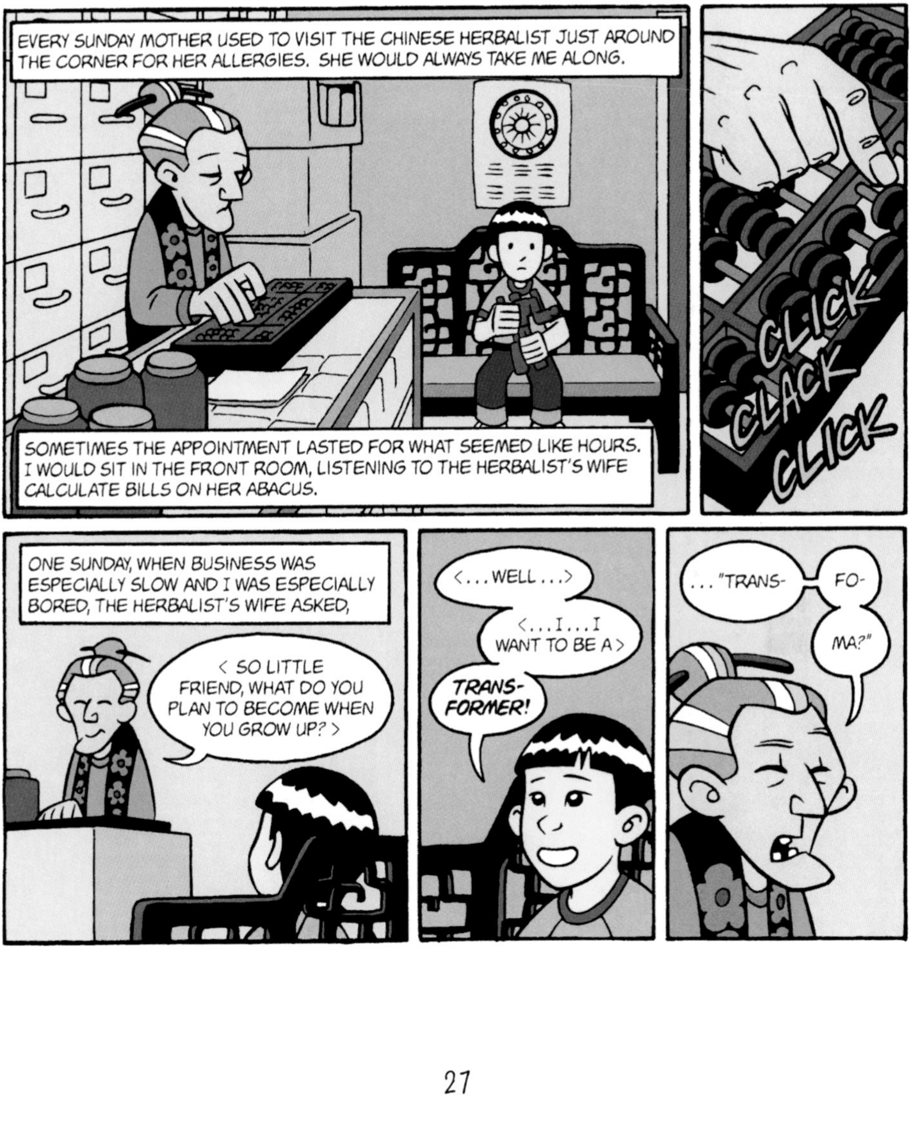
EVERY SUNDAY MOTHER USED TO VISIT THE CHINESE HERBALIST JUST AROUND THE CORNER FOR HER ALLERGIES. SHE WOULD ALWAYS TAKE ME ALONG.
SOMETIMES THE APPOINTMENT LASTED FOR WHAT SEEMED LIKE HOURS. I WOULD SIT IN THE FRONT ROOM, LISTENING TO THE HERBALIST'S WIFE CALCULATE BILLS ON HER ABACUS.
CLICK
CLACK
CLICK
ONE SUNDAY, WHEN BUSINESS WAS ESPECIALLY SLOW AND I WAS ESPECIALLY BORED, THE HERBALIST'S WIFE ASKED,
< SO LITTLE FRIEND, WHAT DO YOU PLAN TO BECOME WHEN YOU GROW UP? >
<. . . WELL . . .>
<. . . I . . . I WANT TO BE A >
TRANS-FORMER!
. . . "TRANS-
FO-
MA?"

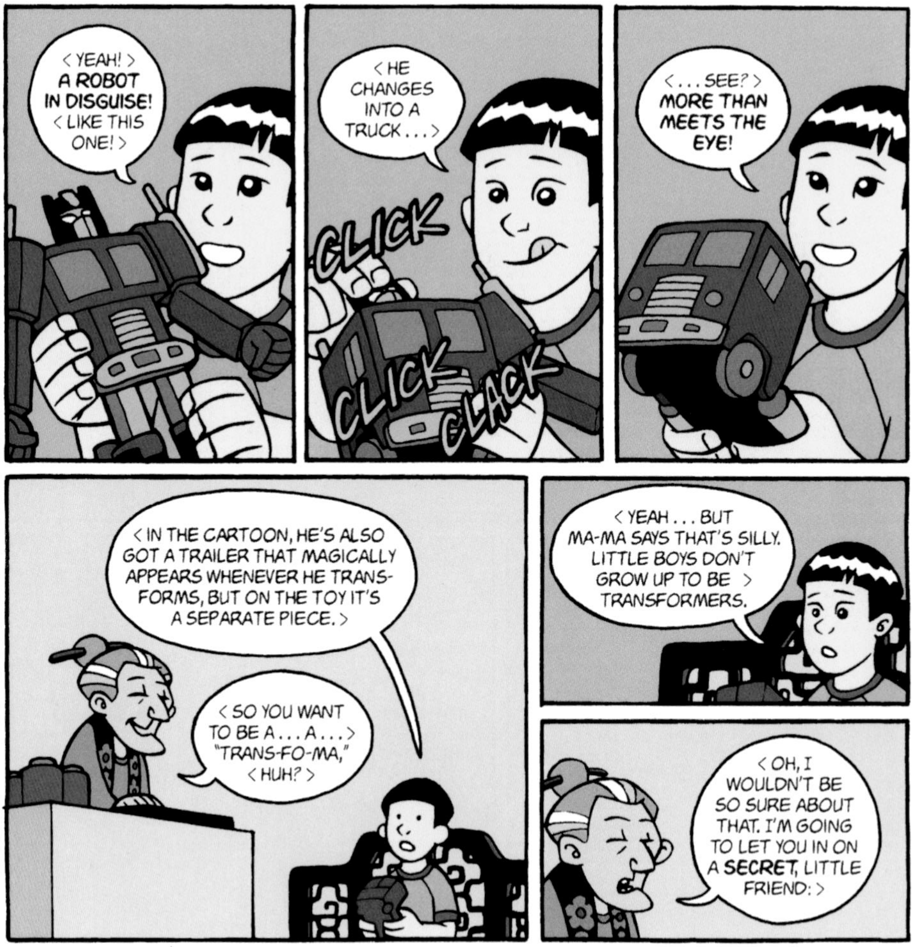
< YEAH! > A ROBOT IN DISGUISE! < LIKE THIS ONE! >
< HE CHANGES INTO A TRUCK . . . >
CLICK
CLICK
CLACK
< . . . SEE? > MORE THAN MEETS THE EYE!
< IN THE CARTOON, HE'S ALSO GOT A TRAILER THAT MAGICALLY APPEARS WHENEVER HE TRANS-FORMS, BUT ON THE TOY IT'S A SEPARATE PIECE. >
< SO YOU WANT TO BE A . . . A . . . > "TRANS-FO-MA," < HUH? >
< YEAH . . . BUT MA-MA SAYS THAT'S SILLY. LITTLE BOYS DON'T GROW UP TO BE > TRANSFORMERS.
< OH, I WOULDN'T BE SO SURE ABOUT THAT. I'M GOING TO LET YOU IN ON A SECRET, LITTLE FRIEND: >

<IT'S EASY TO BECOME ANYTHING YOU WISH...>
<...SO LONG AS YOU'RE WILLING TO *FORFEIT YOUR SOUL.*>
CLICK
CLACK
CLICK
CLACK

ON THE MORNING AFTER WE ARRIVED, WITH THE SCENT OF OUR OLD HOME STILL LINGERING IN MY CLOTHES, I WAS SENT OFF TO MRS. GREEDER'S THIRD GRADE AT MAYFLOWER ELEMENTARY SCHOOL.

CLASS, I'D LIKE US ALL TO GIVE A WARM MAYFLOWER ELEMENTARY WELCOME TO YOUR NEW FRIEND AND CLASSMATE JING JANG!

JIN WANG.

JIN WANG!

HE AND HIS FAMILY RECENTLY MOVED TO OUR NEIGHBORHOOD ALL THE WAY FROM CHINA!

SAN FRAN-CISCO.

SAN FRAN-CISCO!

YES, TIMMY.

MY MOMMA SAYS CHINESE PEOPLE EAT DOGS.

NOW BE **NICE**, TIMMY!

I'M SURE JIN DOESN'T DO THAT!

IN FACT, JIN'S FAMILY PROBABLY STOPPED THAT SORT OF THING AS SOON AS THEY CAME TO THE UNITED STATES!

THE ONLY OTHER ASIAN IN MY CLASS WAS **SUZY NAKAMURA**.

WHEN THE CLASS FINALLY FIGURED OUT THAT WE WEREN'T RELATED, RUMORS BEGAN TO CIRCULATE THAT SUZY AND I WERE ARRANGED TO BE MARRIED ON HER THIRTEENTH BIRTHDAY.

WE AVOIDED EACH OTHER AS MUCH AS POSSIBLE.

WHAT THE **HELL** IS ***THAT?!***
DUMPLINGS.
sniff sniff
HMPH. STAY AWAY FROM MY **DOG.**
HA!
HEY **BE COOL,** MAN.

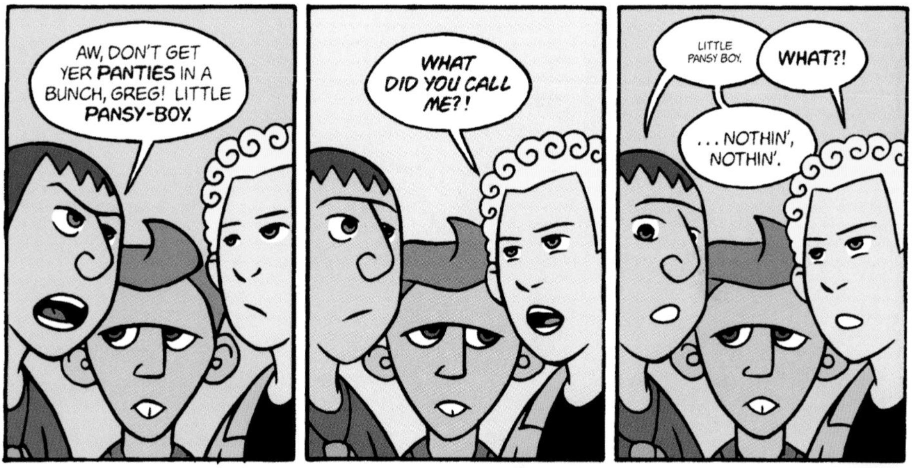
AW, DON'T GET YER PANTIES IN A BUNCH, GREG! LITTLE PANSY-BOY.
WHAT DID YOU CALL ME?!
LITTLE PANSY BOY.
WHAT?!
. . . NOTHIN', NOTHIN'.
COME ON. LET'S LEAVE BUCKTOOTH ALONE SO HE CAN ENJOY LASSIE.
HA HA! "BUCK-TOOTH!"

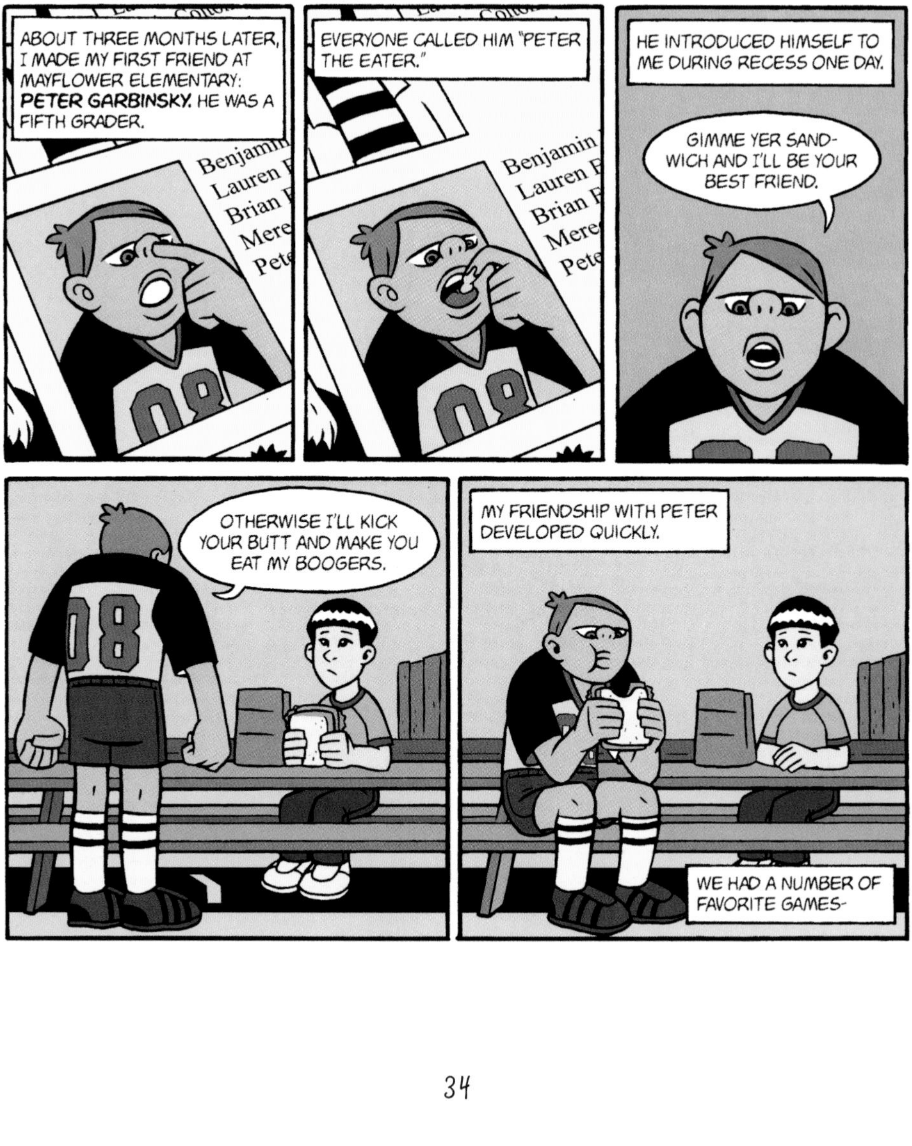
ABOUT THREE MONTHS LATER, I MADE MY FIRST FRIEND AT MAYFLOWER ELEMENTARY: **PETER GARBINSKY.** HE WAS A FIFTH GRADER.
Benjamin
Lauren
Brian
EVERYONE CALLED HIM "PETER THE EATER."
Benjamin
Lauren
Brian
HE INTRODUCED HIMSELF TO ME DURING RECESS ONE DAY.
GIMME YER SANDWICH AND I'LL BE YOUR BEST FRIEND.
OTHERWISE I'LL KICK YOUR BUTT AND MAKE YOU EAT MY BOOGERS.
MY FRIENDSHIP WITH PETER DEVELOPED QUICKLY.
WE HAD A NUMBER OF FAVORITE GAMES-

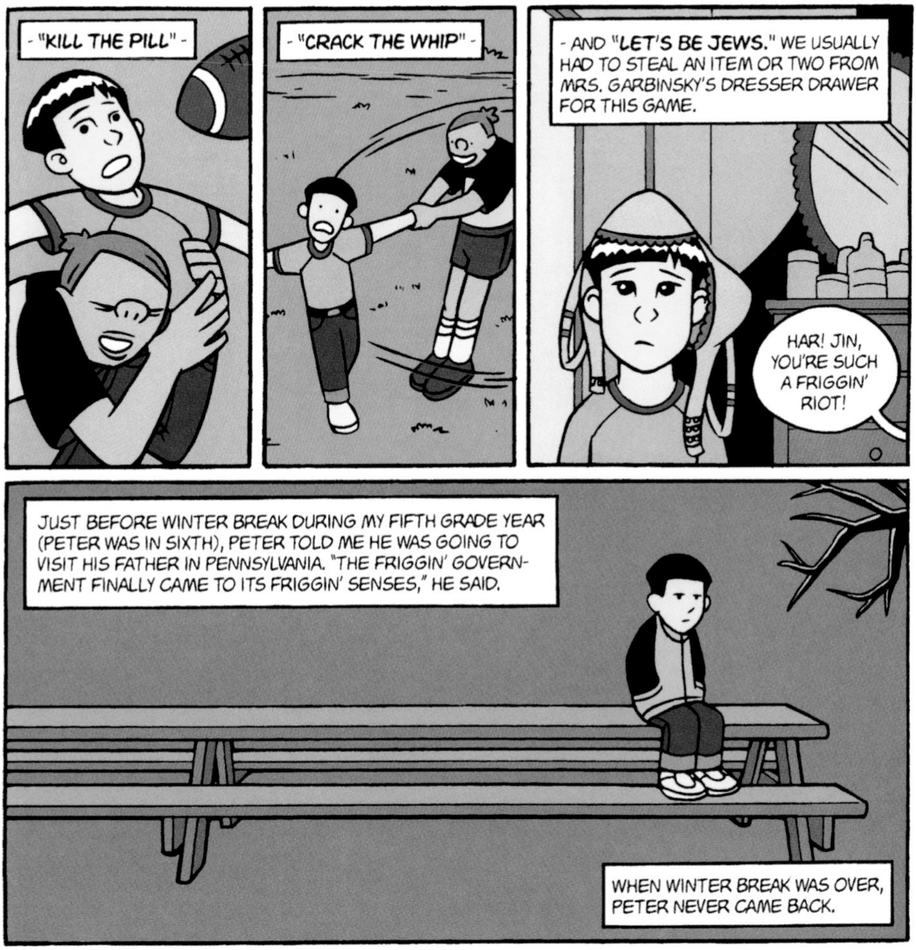
- "KILL THE PILL" -
- "CRACK THE WHIP" -
- AND "LET'S BE JEWS." WE USUALLY HAD TO STEAL AN ITEM OR TWO FROM MRS. GARBINSKY'S DRESSER DRAWER FOR THIS GAME.
HAR! JIN, YOU'RE SUCH A FRIGGIN' RIOT!
JUST BEFORE WINTER BREAK DURING MY FIFTH GRADE YEAR (PETER WAS IN SIXTH), PETER TOLD ME HE WAS GOING TO VISIT HIS FATHER IN PENNSYLVANIA. "THE FRIGGIN' GOVERNMENT FINALLY CAME TO ITS FRIGGIN' SENSES," HE SAID.
WHEN WINTER BREAK WAS OVER, PETER NEVER CAME BACK.

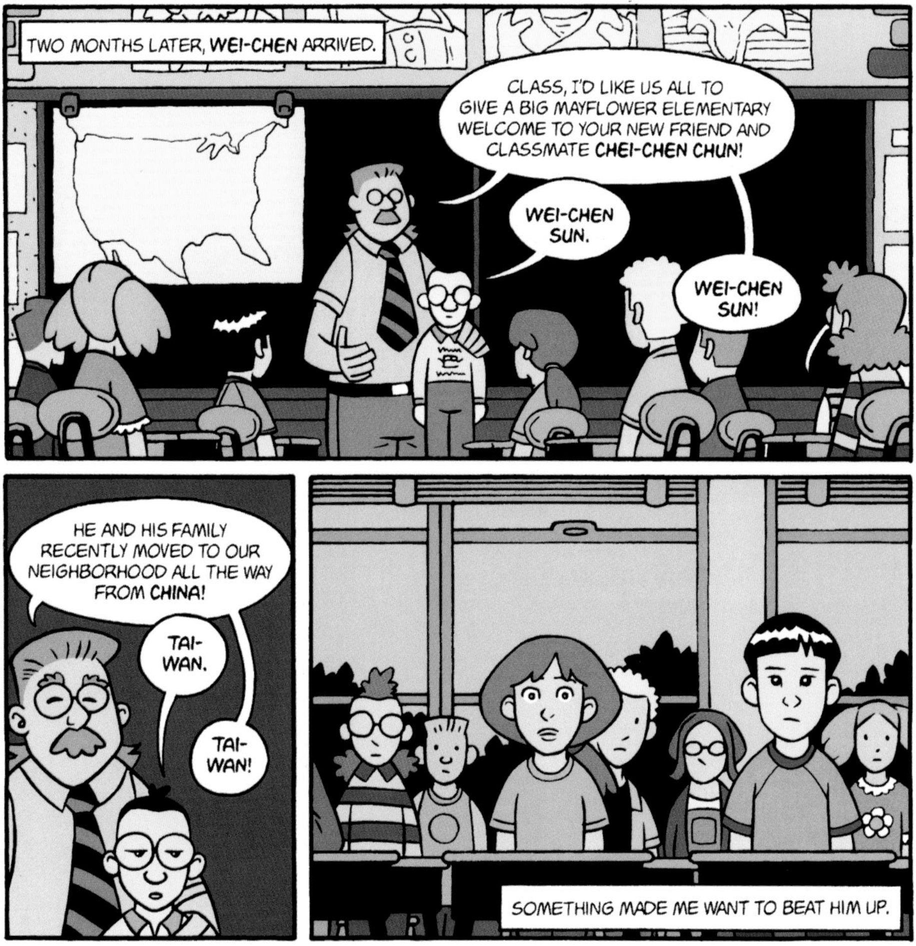
TWO MONTHS LATER, WEI-CHEN ARRIVED.
CLASS, I'D LIKE US ALL TO GIVE A BIG MAYFLOWER ELEMENTARY WELCOME TO YOUR NEW FRIEND AND CLASSMATE CHEI-CHEN CHUN!
WEI-CHEN SUN.
WEI-CHEN SUN!
HE AND HIS FAMILY RECENTLY MOVED TO OUR NEIGHBORHOOD ALL THE WAY FROM CHINA!
TAI-WAN.
TAI-WAN!
SOMETHING MADE ME WANT TO BEAT HIM UP.

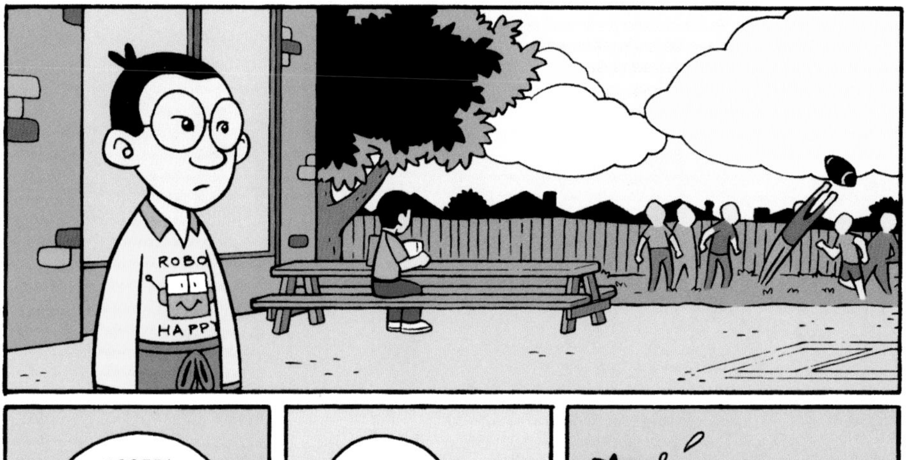

< SORRY TO BOTHER YOU, BUT YOU'RE CHINESE, AREN'T YOU? >
YOU'RE IN **AMERICA.**
SPEAK **ENGLISH.**
...EH...
...YOU- YOU- CHINESE PERSON?
YES.

...EH... WE-B-BE FRIEND?
I HAVE ENOUGH FRIENDS.
...SORRY? REPEAT, PLEASE?
I *HAVE ENOUGH FRIENDS.*
...EH ... WHO?
THEM.
OH.

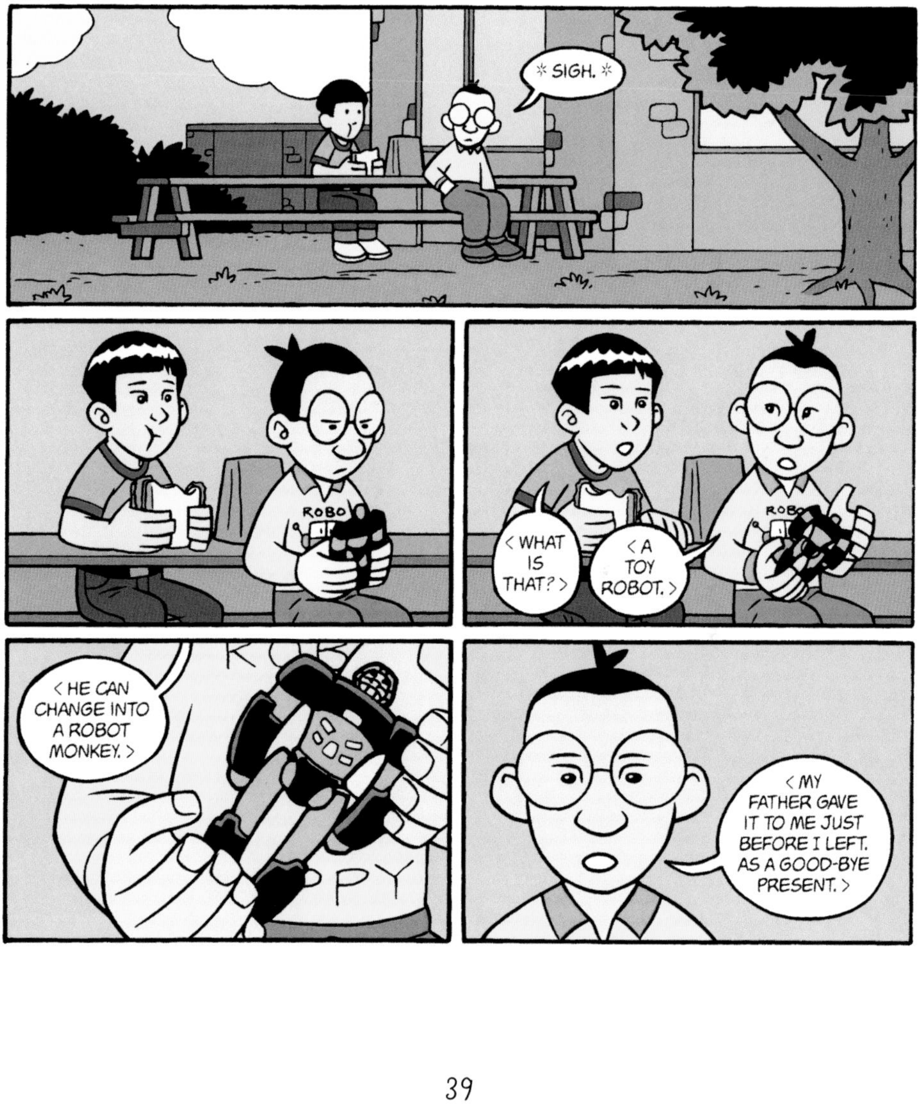

✲ SIGH. ✲
< WHAT IS THAT? >
< A TOY ROBOT. >
< HE CAN CHANGE INTO A ROBOT MONKEY. >
< MY FATHER GAVE IT TO ME JUST BEFORE I LEFT. AS A GOOD-BYE PRESENT. >

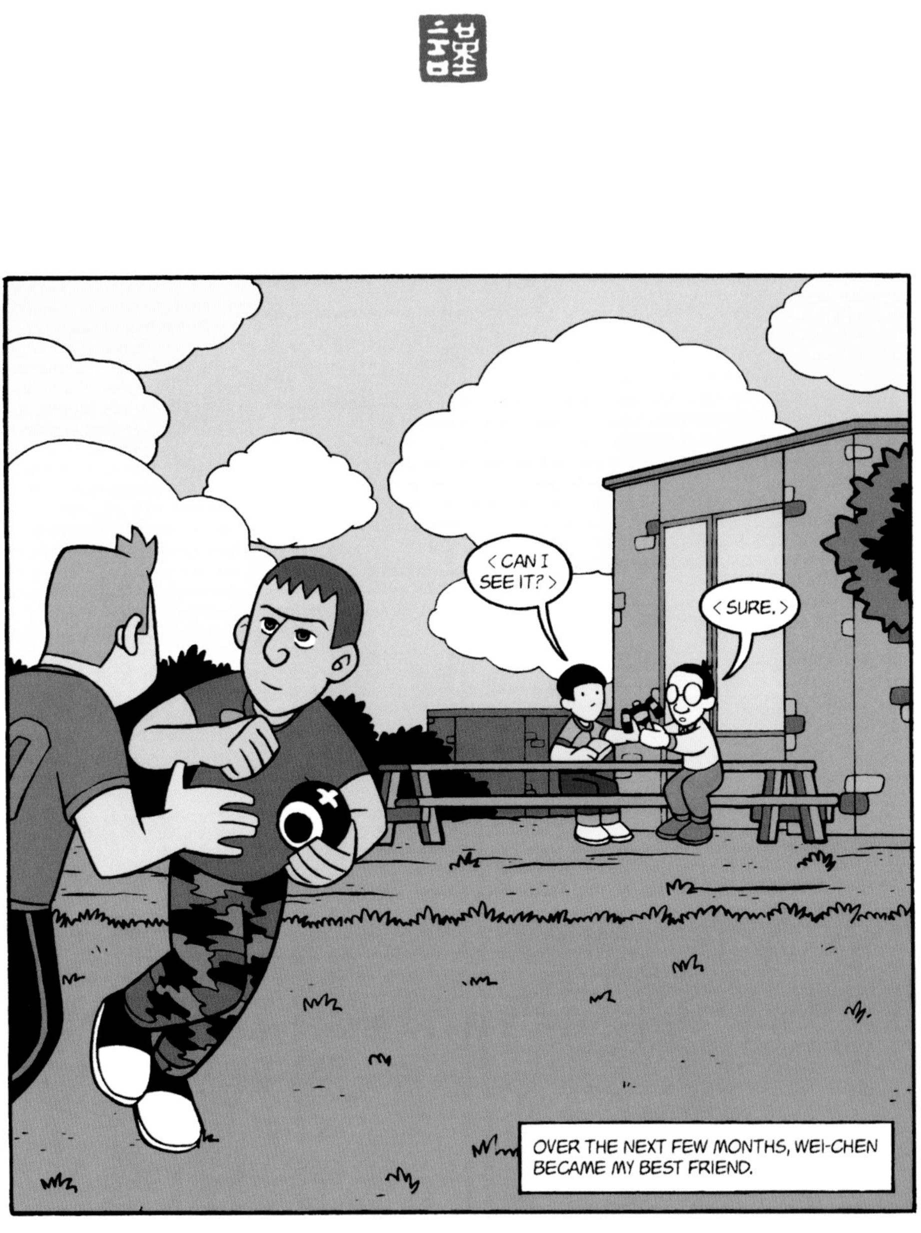
< CAN I SEE IT? >
< SURE. >
OVER THE NEXT FEW MONTHS, WEI-CHEN BECAME MY BEST FRIEND.

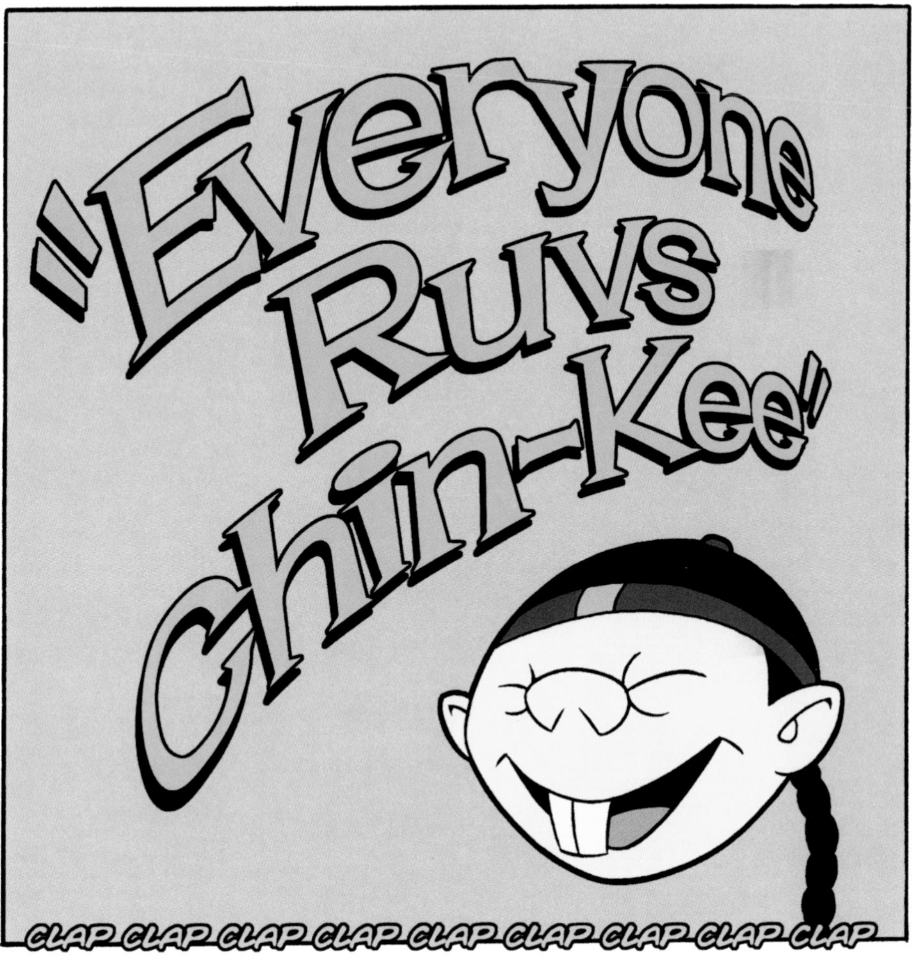
"Everyone Ruvs Chin-Kee"
CLAP CLAP CLAP CLAP CLAP CLAP CLAP CLAP CLAP

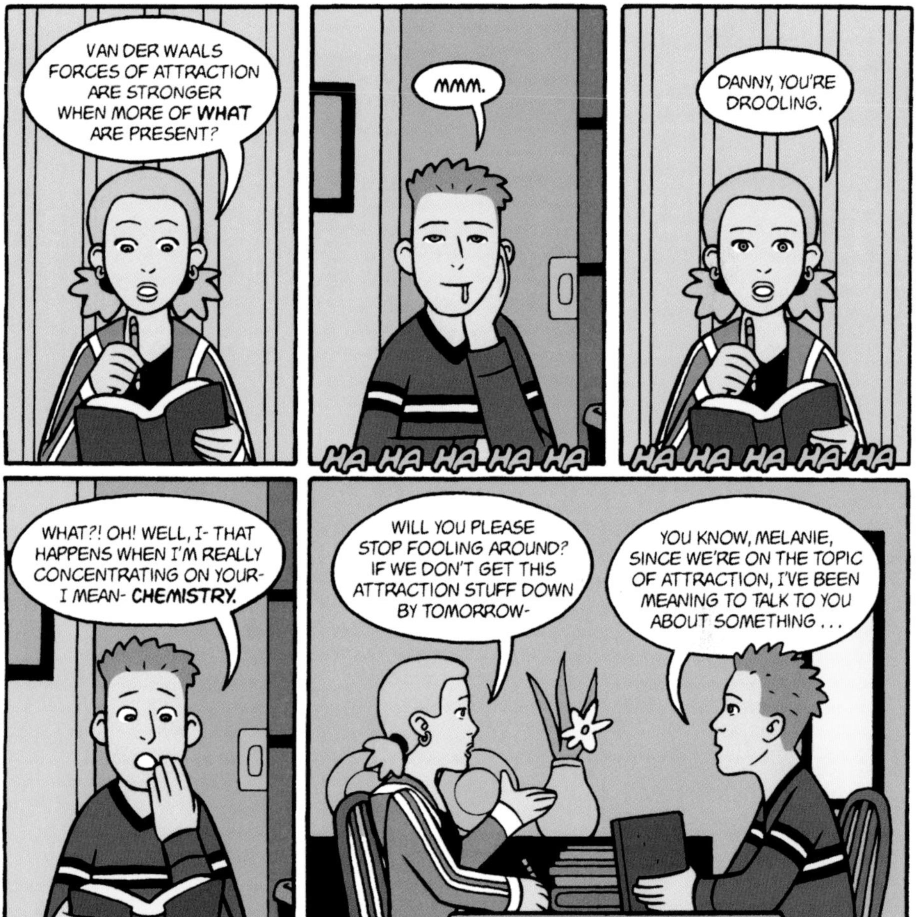
VAN DER WAALS FORCES OF ATTRACTION ARE STRONGER WHEN MORE OF **WHAT** ARE PRESENT?
MMM.
HA HA HA HA HA
DANNY, YOU'RE DROOLING.
HA HA HA HA HA
WHAT?! OH! WELL, I- THAT HAPPENS WHEN I'M REALLY CONCENTRATING ON YOUR- I MEAN- **CHEMISTRY.**
HA HA HA HA HA
WILL YOU PLEASE STOP FOOLING AROUND? IF WE DON'T GET THIS ATTRACTION STUFF DOWN BY TOMORROW-
YOU KNOW, MELANIE, SINCE WE'RE ON THE TOPIC OF ATTRACTION, I'VE BEEN MEANING TO TALK TO YOU ABOUT SOMETHING . . .

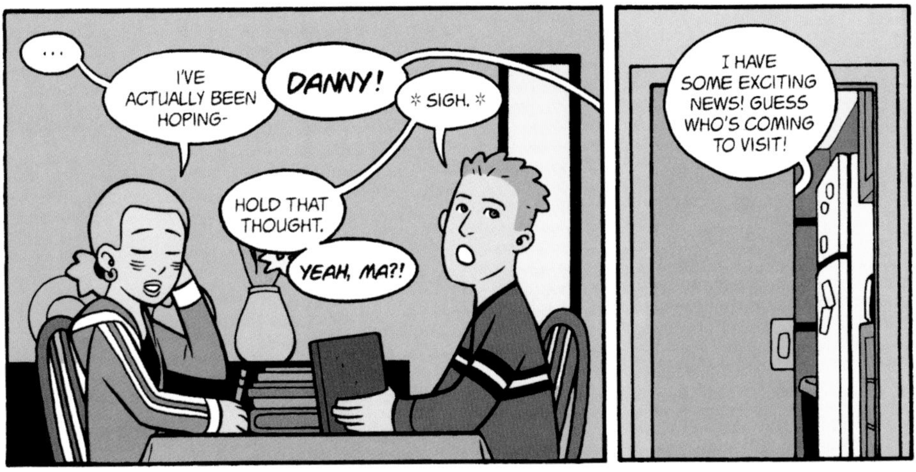
...
I'VE ACTUALLY BEEN HOPING-
DANNY!
* SIGH. *
HOLD THAT THOUGHT.
YEAH, MA?!
I HAVE SOME EXCITING NEWS! GUESS WHO'S COMING TO VISIT!
WHO?
YOUR COUSIN CHIN-KEE!

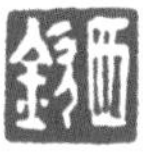

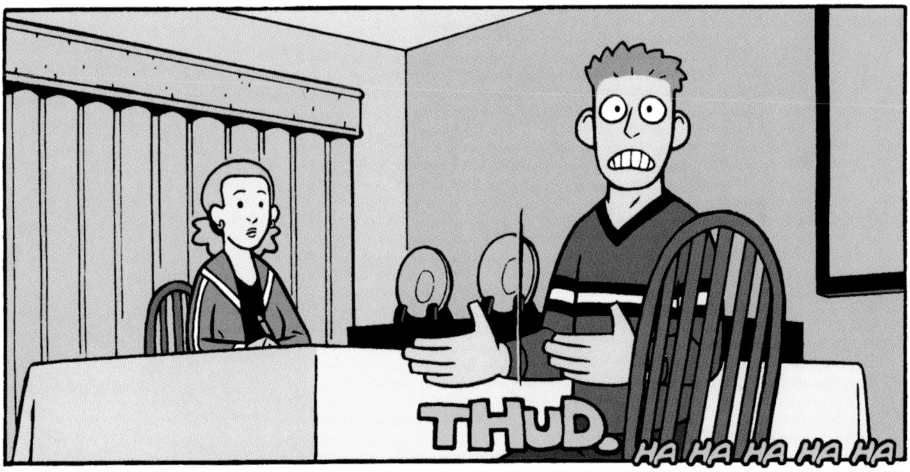
THUD.
HA HA HA HA HA
I KNEW YOU'D BE EXCITED!
YOUR FATHER WENT TO GO PICK HIM UP AT THE AIRPORT! HE SHOULD BE HERE ANY MINUTE NOW!
DANNY, WHO'S COUSIN CHIN-KEE?

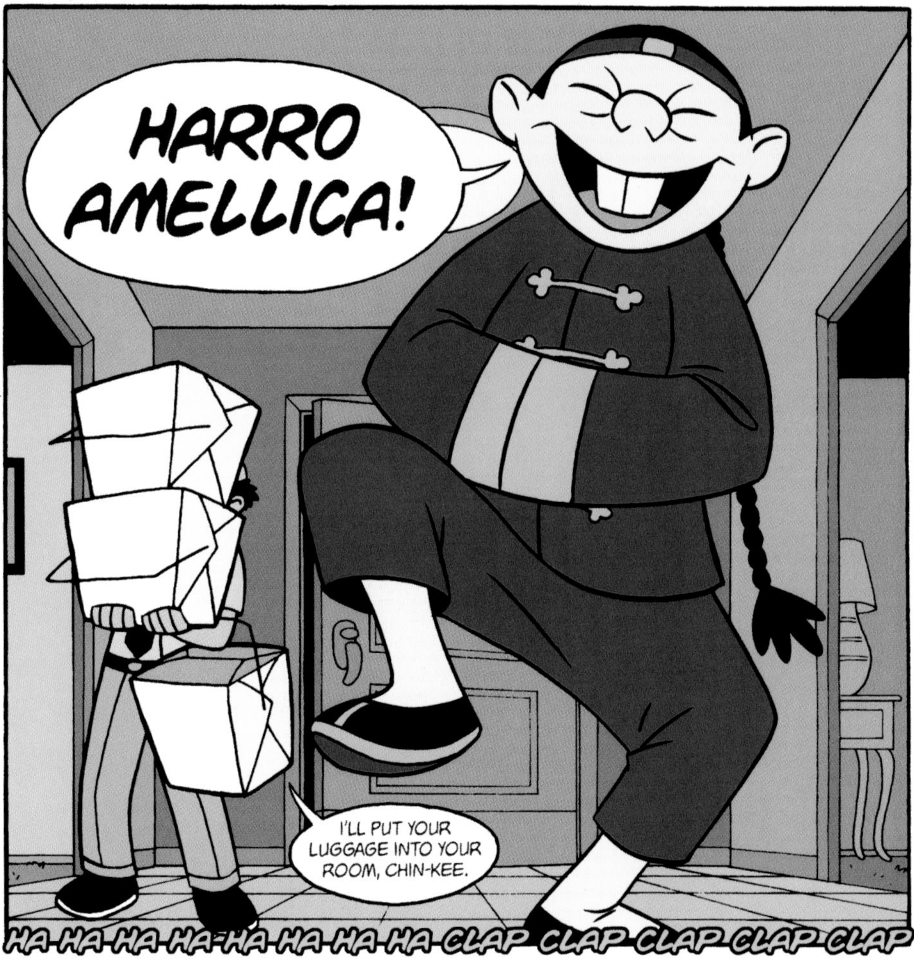
HARRO AMELLICA!
I'LL PUT YOUR LUGGAGE INTO YOUR ROOM, CHIN-KEE.
HA HA HA HA HA HA HA HA CLAP CLAP CLAP CLAP CLAP

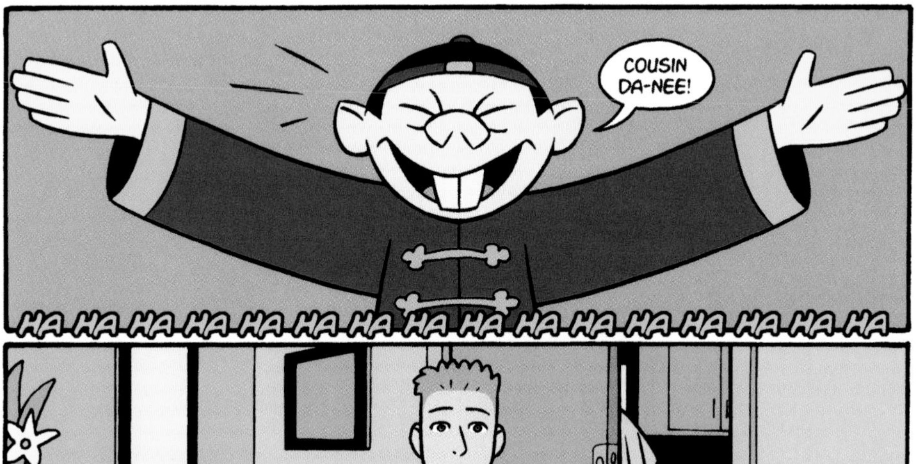
COUSIN DA-NEE!
HA HA HA HA HA HA HA HA HA HA HA HA HA HA HA HA
RONG TIME NO SEE! CHIN-KEE HAPPY AS GINGER ROOT PRANTED IN NUTRITIOUS MANURE OF WELL-BRED OX!
...
HI CHIN-KEE.
HA HA HA HA HA HA HA HA HA HA HA HA HA HA HA HA

WHA--?! CONFUCIUS SAY, "HUBBA-HUBBA!"
HA HA HA HA HA HA HA HA HA HA
SUCH PLETTY AMELLICAN GIRL WIFF BOUNTIFUL AMELLICAN BOSOM! MUST BIND FEET AND BEAR CHIN-KEE'S CHILDREN!
HA HA HA HA HA HA HA HA HA HA HA HA HA HA HA HA

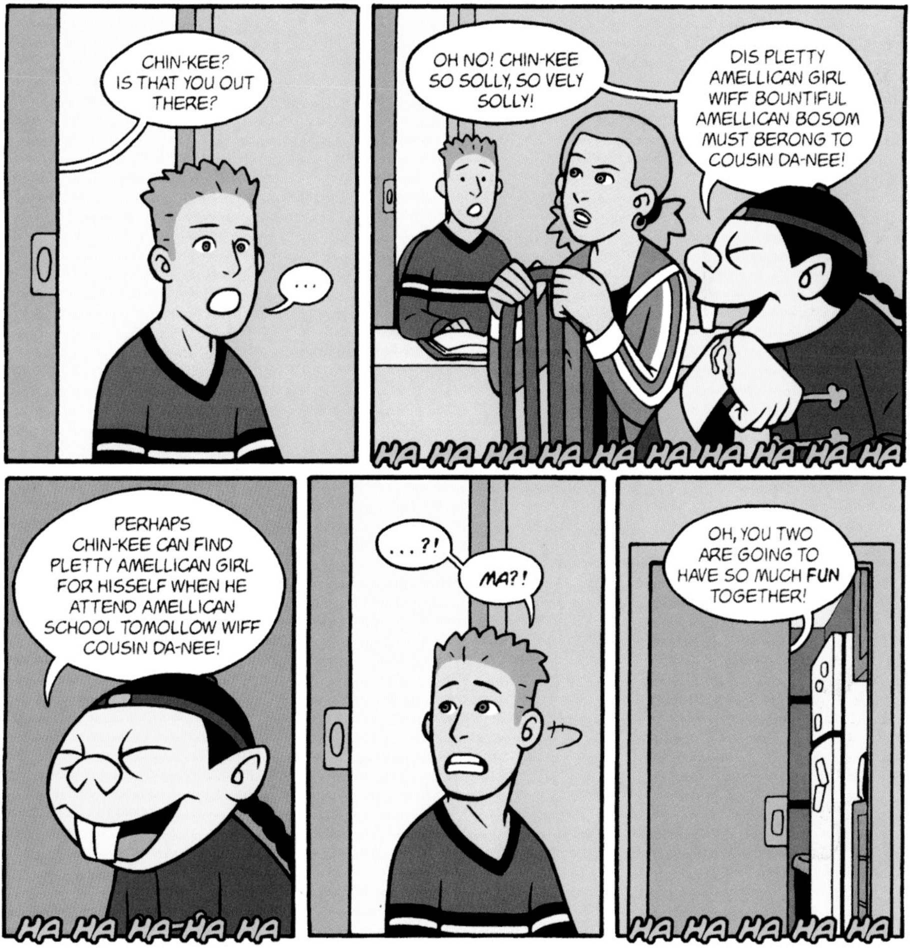
CHIN-KEE? IS THAT YOU OUT THERE?
...
OH NO! CHIN-KEE SO SOLLY, SO VELY SOLLY!
DIS PLETTY AMELLICAN GIRL WIFF BOUNTIFUL AMELLICAN BOSOM MUST BERONG TO COUSIN DA-NEE!
HA HA HA HA HA HA HA HA HA HA
PERHAPS CHIN-KEE CAN FIND PLETTY AMELLICAN GIRL FOR HISSELF WHEN HE ATTEND AMELLICAN SCHOOL TOMOLLOW WIFF COUSIN DA-NEE!
HA HA HA HA HA
...?!
MA?!
OH, YOU TWO ARE GOING TO HAVE SO MUCH **FUN** TOGETHER!
HA HA HA HA HA

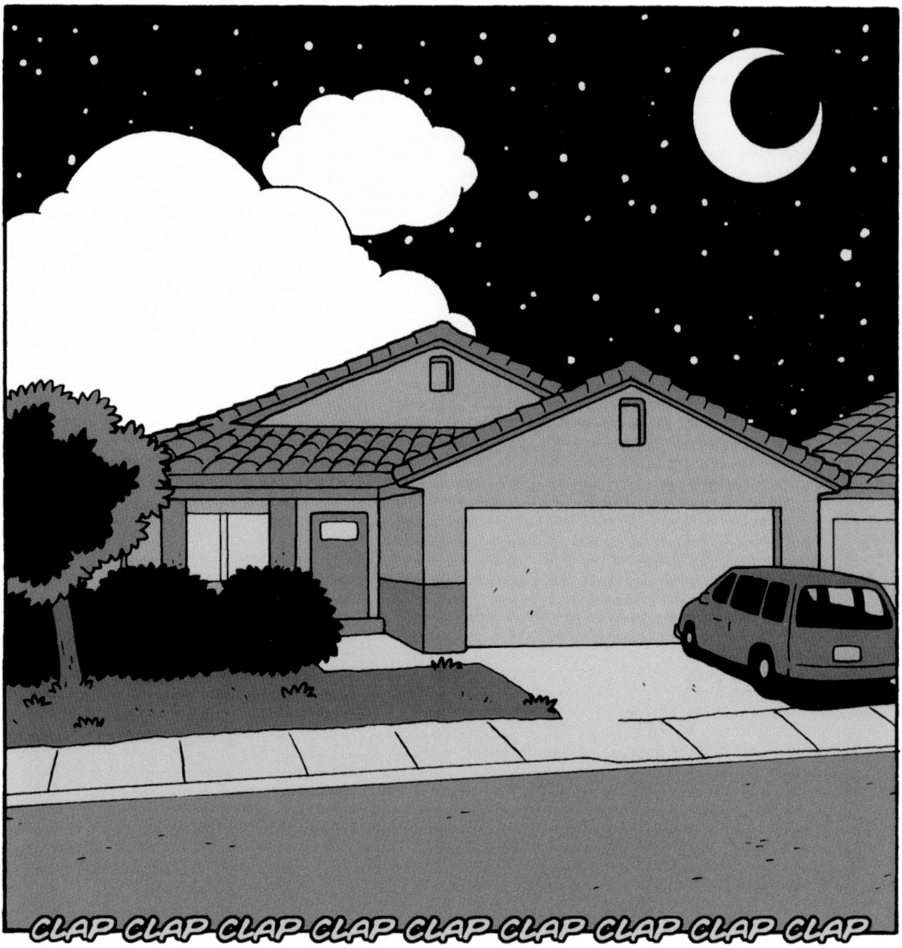
CLAP CLAP CLAP CLAP CLAP CLAP CLAP CLAP CLAP

孫

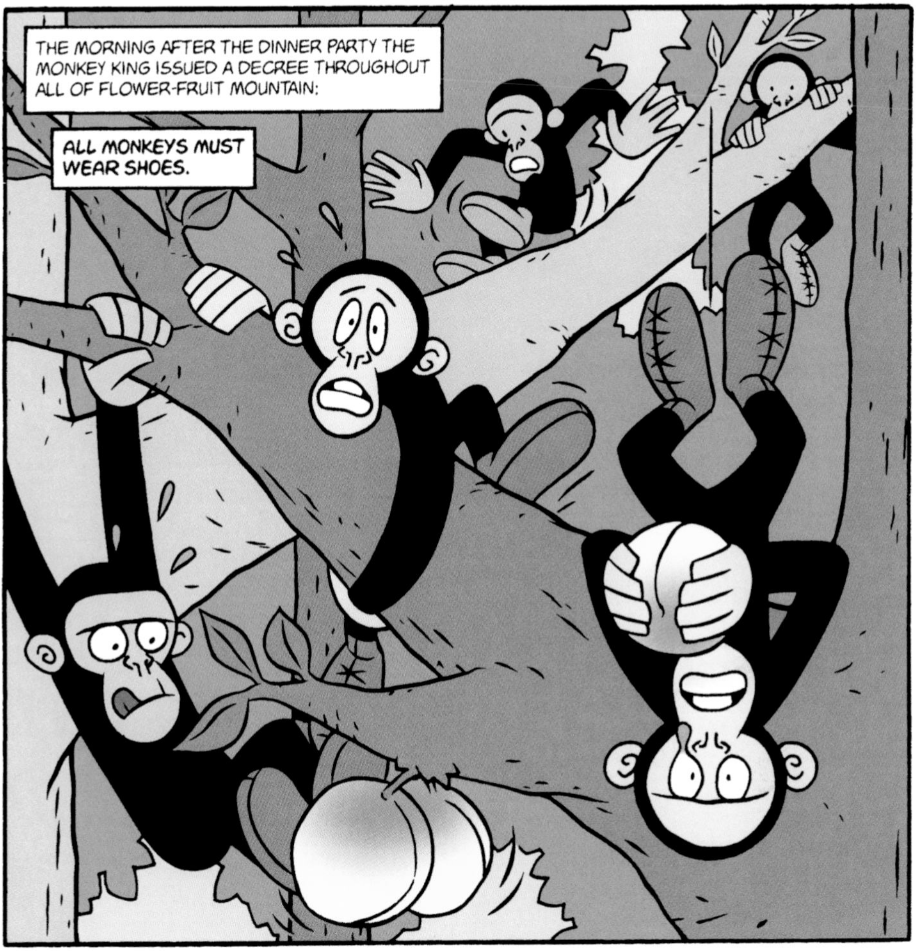
THE MORNING AFTER THE DINNER PARTY THE MONKEY KING ISSUED A DECREE THROUGHOUT ALL OF FLOWER-FRUIT MOUNTAIN:
ALL MONKEYS MUST WEAR SHOES.

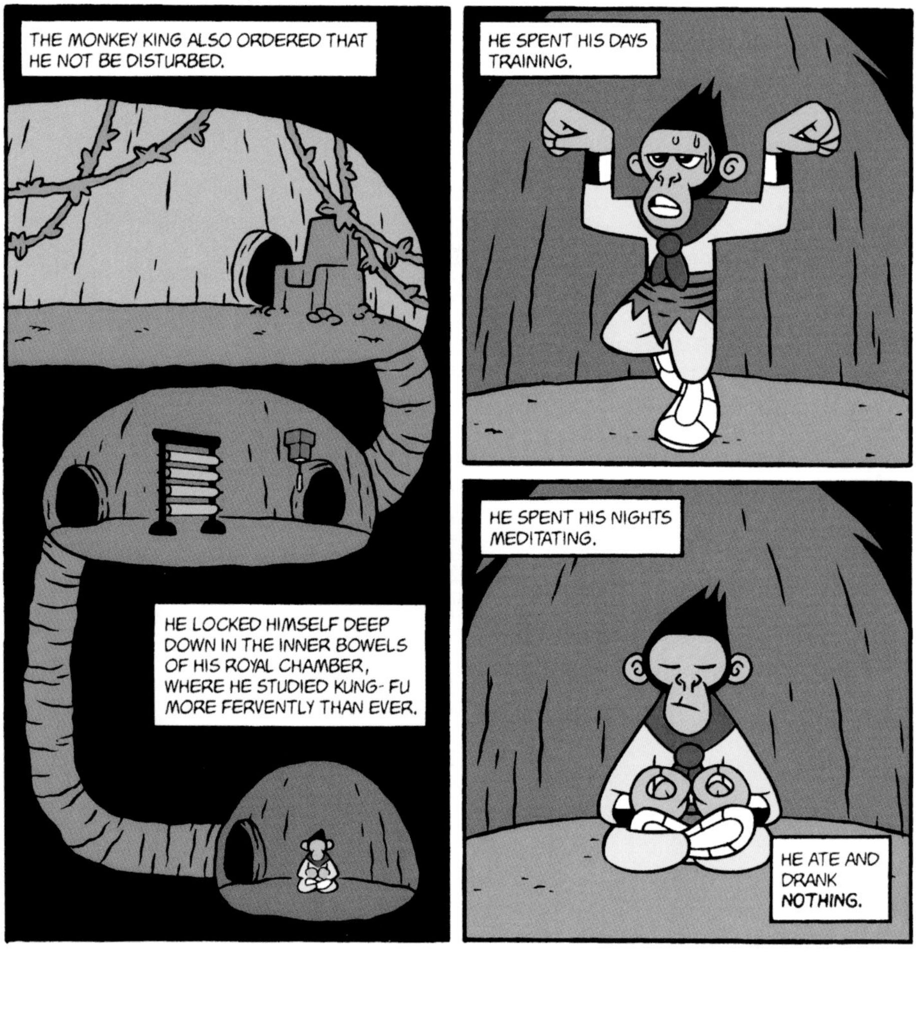
THE MONKEY KING ALSO ORDERED THAT HE NOT BE DISTURBED.
HE LOCKED HIMSELF DEEP DOWN IN THE INNER BOWELS OF HIS ROYAL CHAMBER, WHERE HE STUDIED KUNG-FU MORE FERVENTLY THAN EVER.
HE SPENT HIS DAYS TRAINING.
HE SPENT HIS NIGHTS MEDITATING.
HE ATE AND DRANK **NOTHING.**

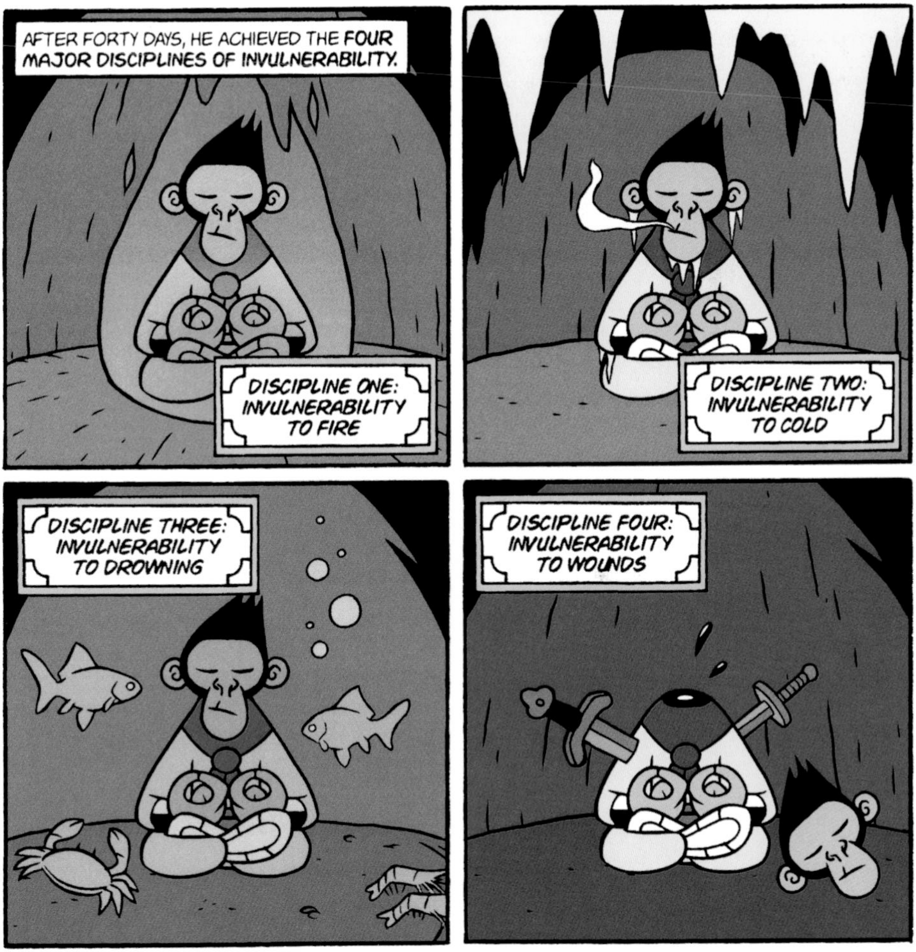
AFTER FORTY DAYS, HE ACHIEVED THE FOUR MAJOR DISCIPLINES OF INVULNERABILITY.
DISCIPLINE ONE: INVULNERABILITY TO FIRE
DISCIPLINE TWO: INVULNERABILITY TO COLD
DISCIPLINE THREE: INVULNERABILITY TO DROWNING
DISCIPLINE FOUR: INVULNERABILITY TO WOUNDS

AFTER ANOTHER FORTY DAYS, HE ACHIEVED THE FOUR MAJOR DISCIPLINES OF BODILY FORM.
大
DISCIPLINE ONE: GIANT FORM
DISCIPLINE TWO: MINIATURE FORM
小
DISCIPLINE THREE: HAIR-INTO-CLONES
㚉
變
DISCIPLINE FOUR: SHAPE SHIFT

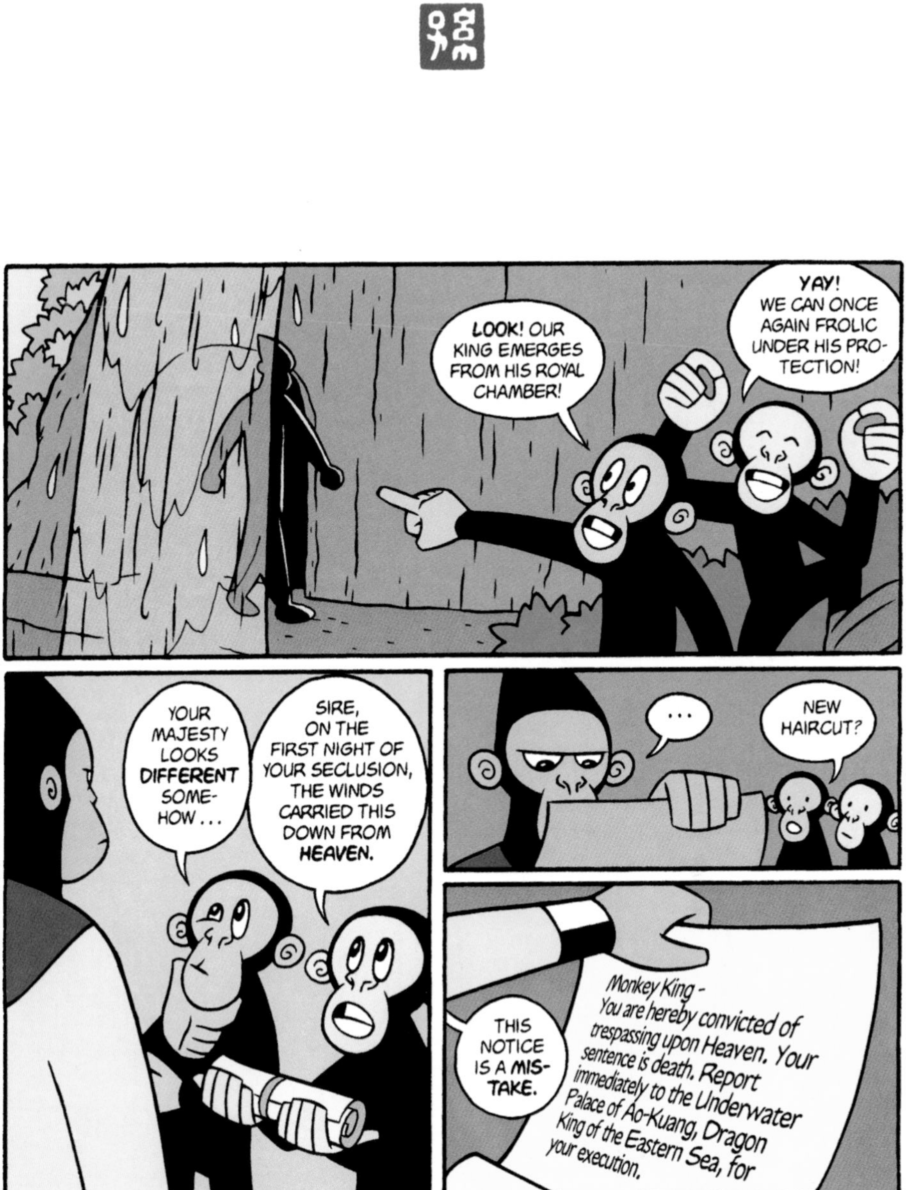
LOOK! OUR KING EMERGES FROM HIS ROYAL CHAMBER!
YAY! WE CAN ONCE AGAIN FROLIC UNDER HIS PRO-TECTION!
YOUR MAJESTY LOOKS DIFFERENT SOME-HOW...
SIRE, ON THE FIRST NIGHT OF YOUR SECLUSION, THE WINDS CARRIED THIS DOWN FROM HEAVEN.
...
NEW HAIRCUT?
Monkey King - You are hereby convicted of trespassing upon Heaven. Your sentence is death. Report immediately to the Underwater Palace of Ao-Kuang, Dragon King of the Eastern Sea, for your execution.
THIS NOTICE IS A MIS-TAKE.

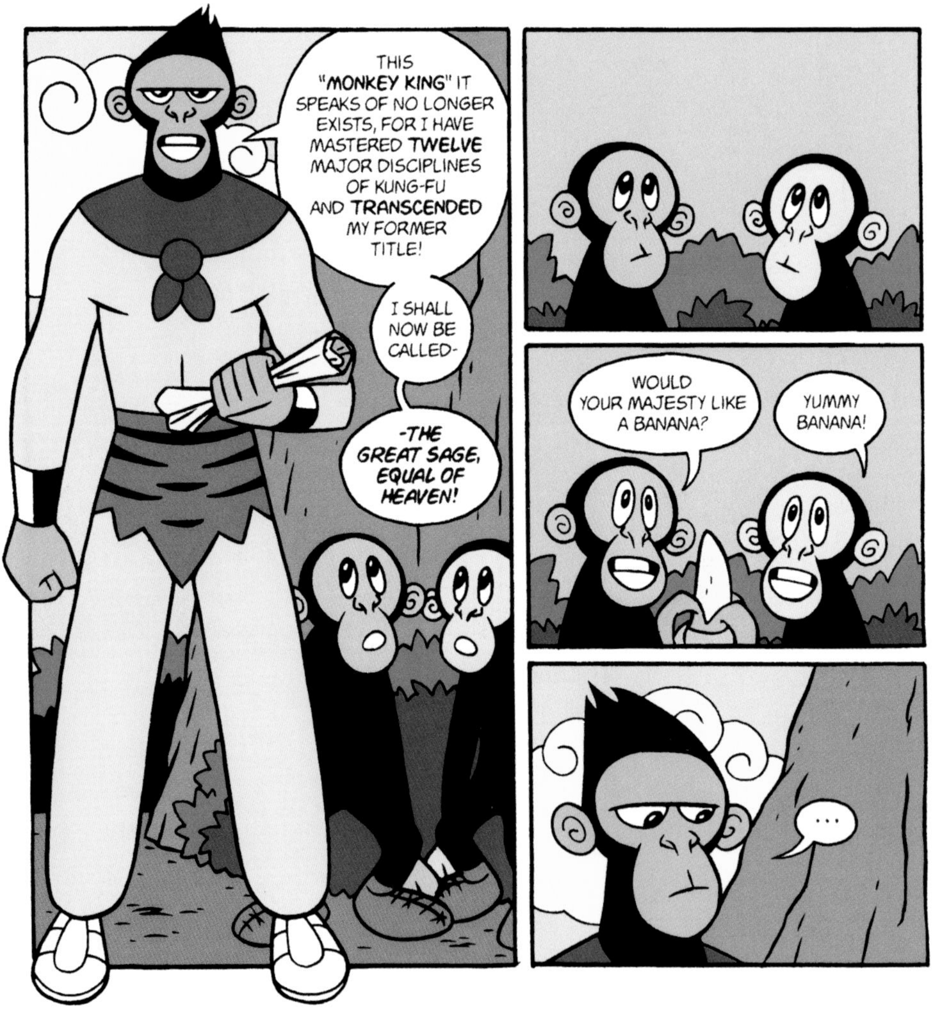
THIS "MONKEY KING" IT SPEAKS OF NO LONGER EXISTS, FOR I HAVE MASTERED TWELVE MAJOR DISCIPLINES OF KUNG-FU AND TRANSCENDED MY FORMER TITLE!
I SHALL NOW BE CALLED-
-THE GREAT SAGE, EQUAL OF HEAVEN!
WOULD YOUR MAJESTY LIKE A BANANA?
YUMMY BANANA!
...

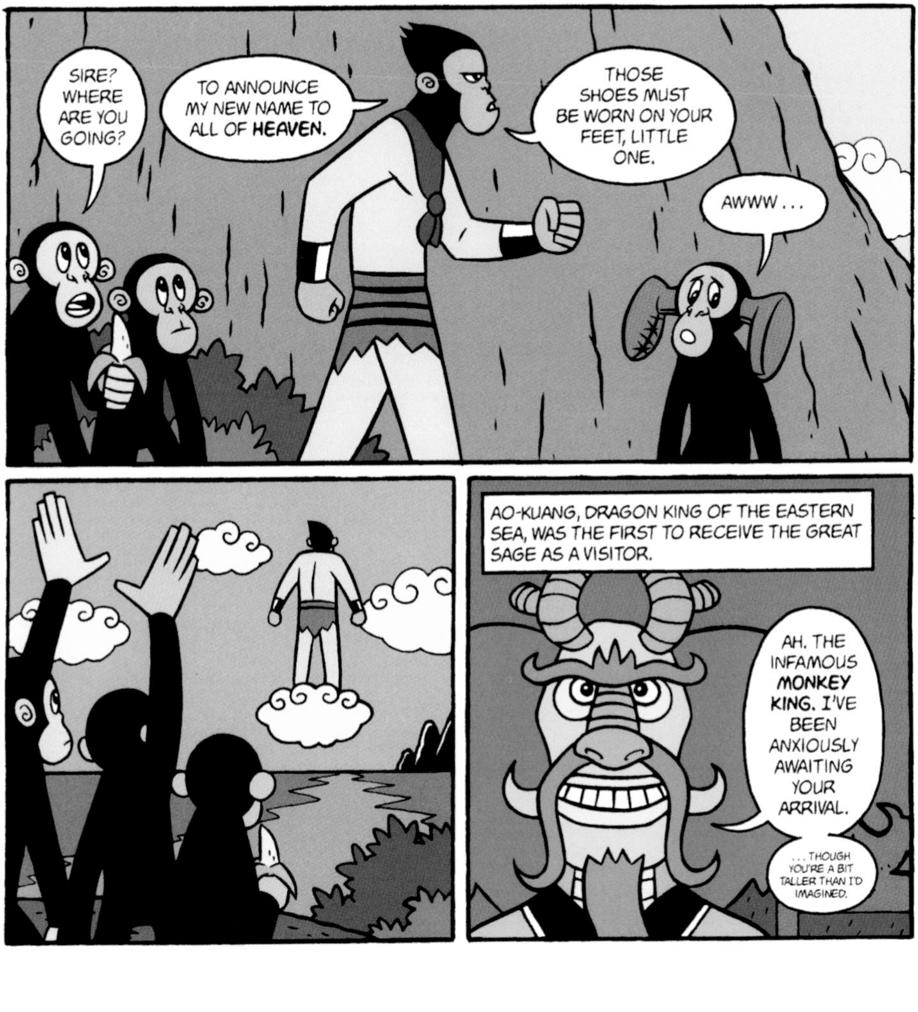
SIRE? WHERE ARE YOU GOING?
TO ANNOUNCE MY NEW NAME TO ALL OF **HEAVEN.**
THOSE SHOES MUST BE WORN ON YOUR FEET, LITTLE ONE.
AWWW . . .
AO-KUANG, DRAGON KING OF THE EASTERN SEA, WAS THE FIRST TO RECEIVE THE GREAT SAGE AS A VISITOR.
AH. THE INFAMOUS **MONKEY KING.** I'VE BEEN ANXIOUSLY AWAITING YOUR ARRIVAL.
. . . THOUGH YOU'RE A BIT TALLER THAN I'D IMAGINED.

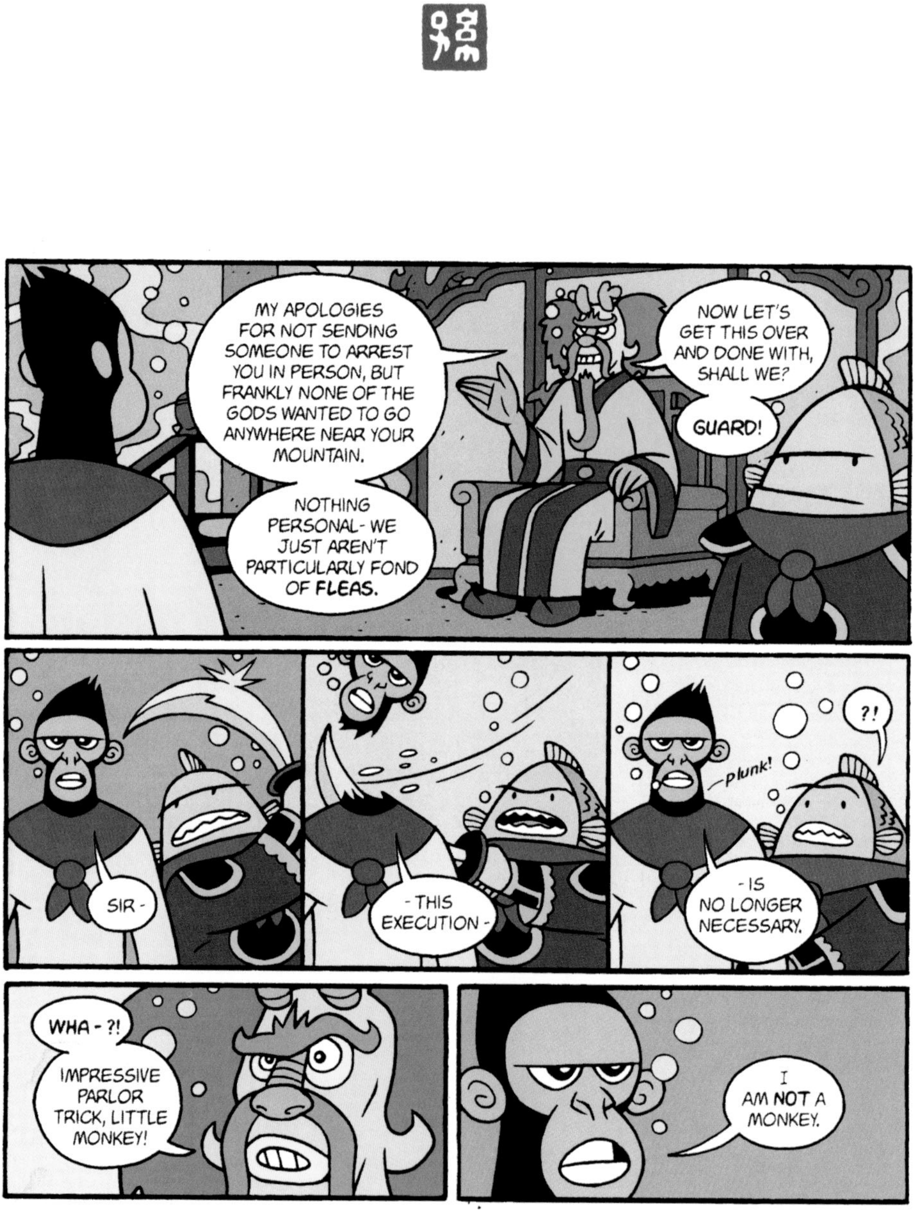
MY APOLOGIES FOR NOT SENDING SOMEONE TO ARREST YOU IN PERSON, BUT FRANKLY NONE OF THE GODS WANTED TO GO ANYWHERE NEAR YOUR MOUNTAIN.
NOTHING PERSONAL- WE JUST AREN'T PARTICULARLY FOND OF FLEAS.
NOW LET'S GET THIS OVER AND DONE WITH, SHALL WE?
GUARD!
SIR-
-THIS EXECUTION-
-plunk!
?!
-IS NO LONGER NECESSARY.
WHA-?!
IMPRESSIVE PARLOR TRICK, LITTLE MONKEY!
I AM NOT A MONKEY.

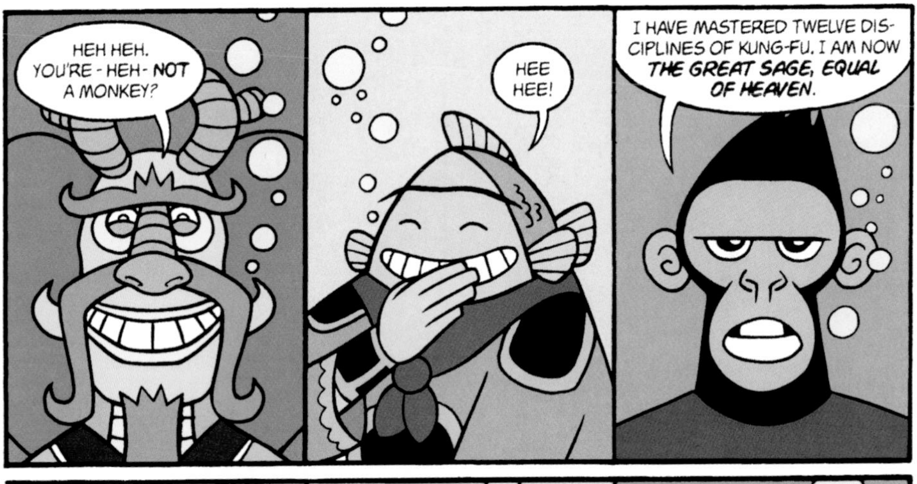
HEH HEH. YOU'RE - HEH - NOT A MONKEY?
HEE HEE!
I HAVE MASTERED TWELVE DISCIPLINES OF KUNG-FU. I AM NOW THE GREAT SAGE, EQUAL OF HEAVEN.
HA HA HA!
BWA HA HA!
THE DRAGON KING NEEDED SOME CONVINCING.

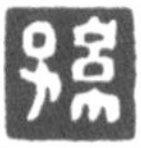

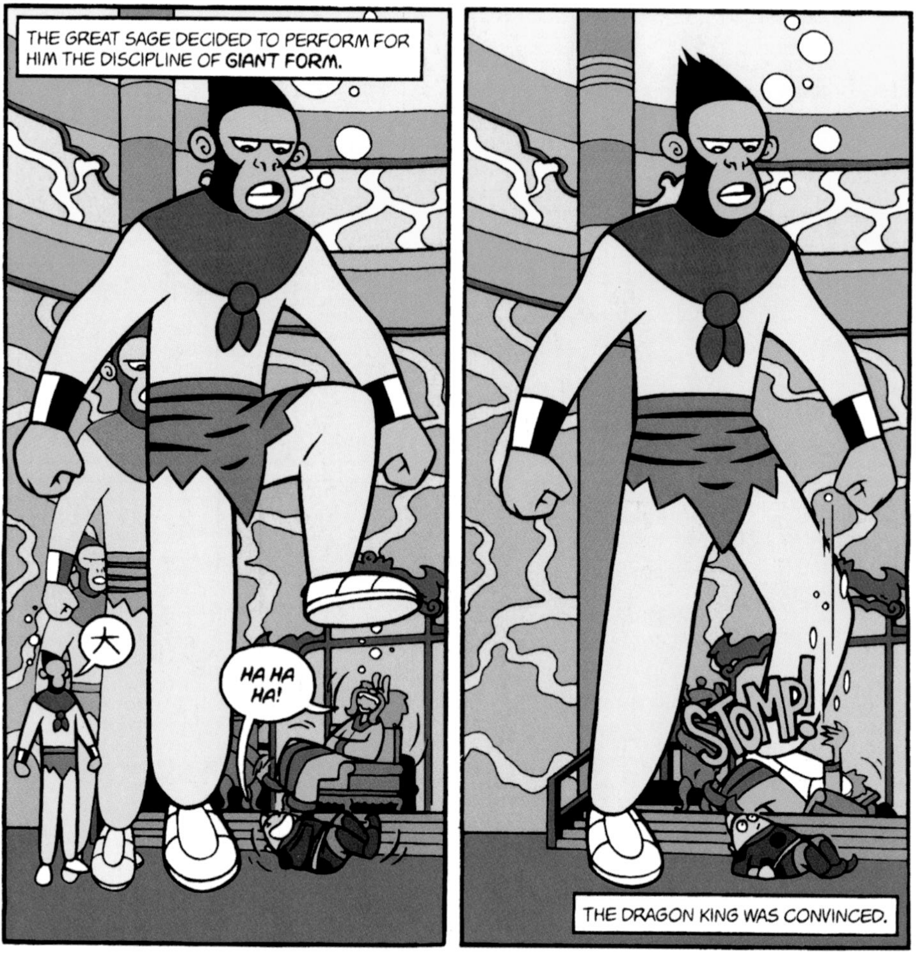
THE GREAT SAGE DECIDED TO PERFORM FOR HIM THE DISCIPLINE OF **GIANT FORM.**
大
HA HA HA!
STOMP!
THE DRAGON KING WAS CONVINCED.

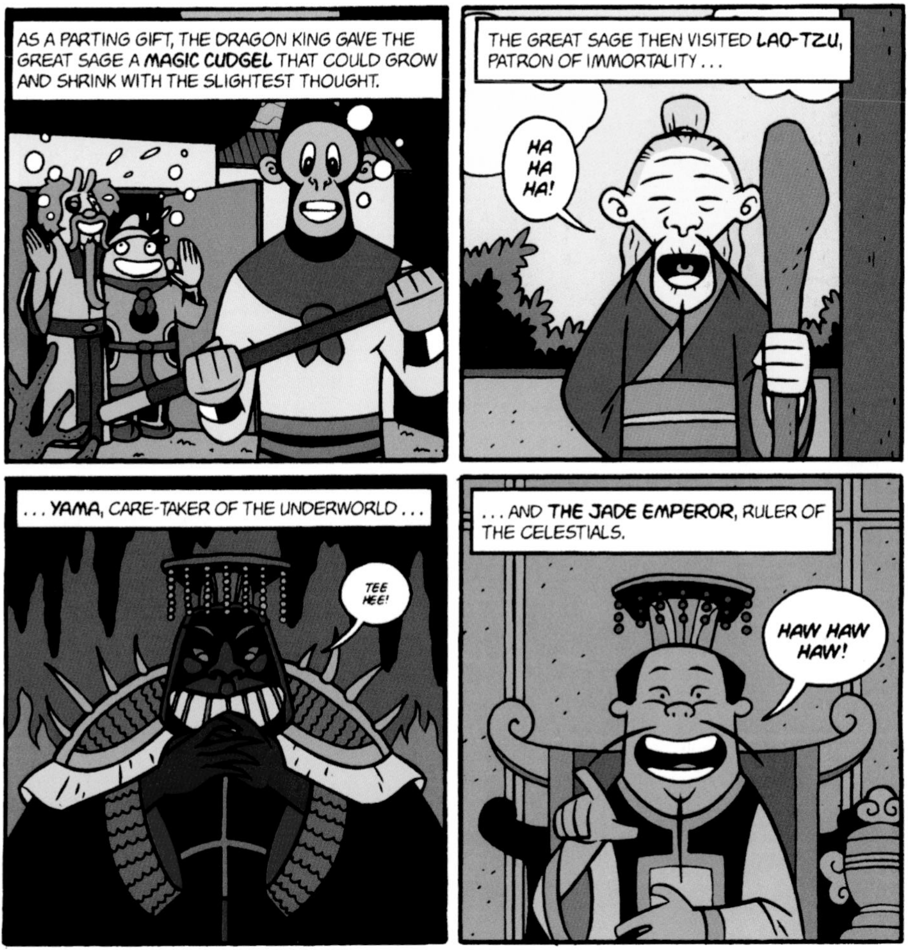
AS A PARTING GIFT, THE DRAGON KING GAVE THE GREAT SAGE A MAGIC CUDGEL THAT COULD GROW AND SHRINK WITH THE SLIGHTEST THOUGHT.
THE GREAT SAGE THEN VISITED LAO-TZU, PATRON OF IMMORTALITY . . .
HA HA HA!
. . . YAMA, CARE-TAKER OF THE UNDERWORLD . . .
TEE HEE!
. . . AND THE JADE EMPEROR, RULER OF THE CELESTIALS.
HAW HAW HAW!

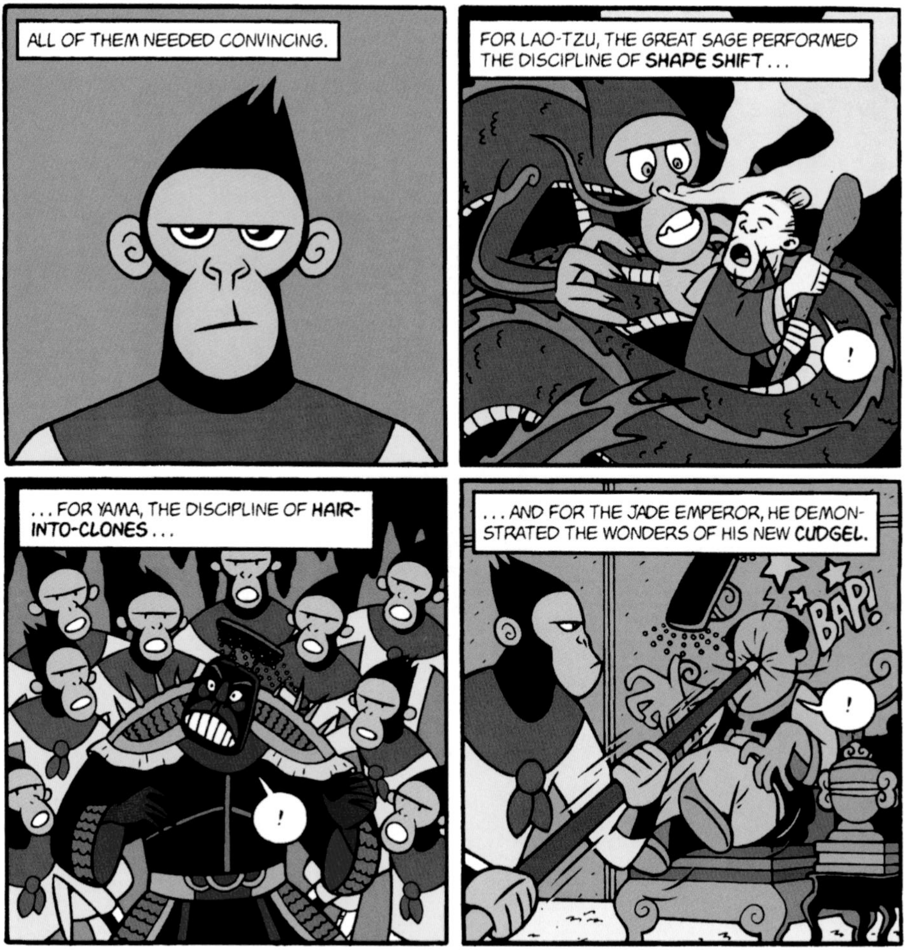
ALL OF THEM NEEDED CONVINCING.
FOR LAO-TZU, THE GREAT SAGE PERFORMED THE DISCIPLINE OF SHAPE SHIFT . . .
!
. . . FOR YAMA, THE DISCIPLINE OF HAIR-INTO-CLONES . . .
!
. . . AND FOR THE JADE EMPEROR, HE DEMONSTRATED THE WONDERS OF HIS NEW CUDGEL.
BAP!
!

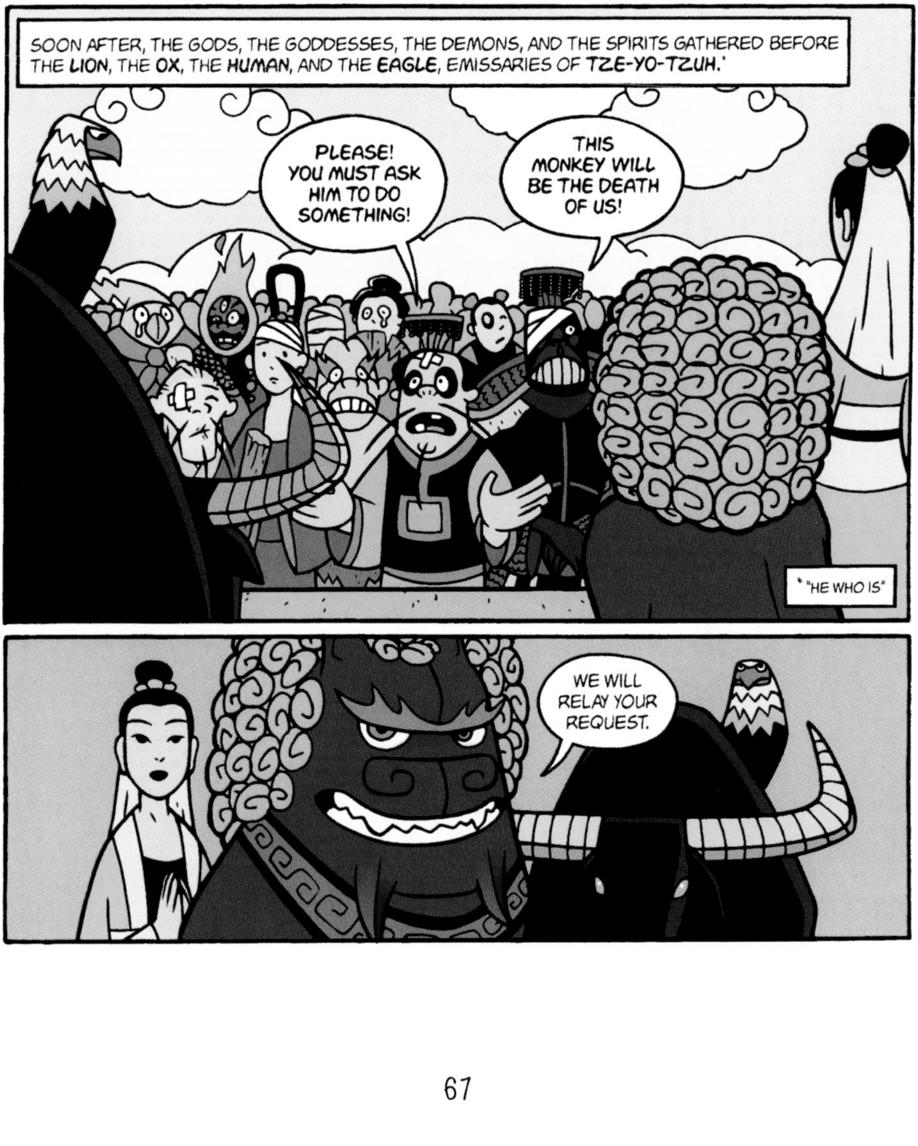
SOON AFTER, THE GODS, THE GODDESSES, THE DEMONS, AND THE SPIRITS GATHERED BEFORE THE LION, THE OX, THE HUMAN, AND THE EAGLE, EMISSARIES OF TZE-YO-TZUH.*
PLEASE! YOU MUST ASK HIM TO DO SOMETHING!
THIS MONKEY WILL BE THE DEATH OF US!
* "HE WHO IS"
WE WILL RELAY YOUR REQUEST.

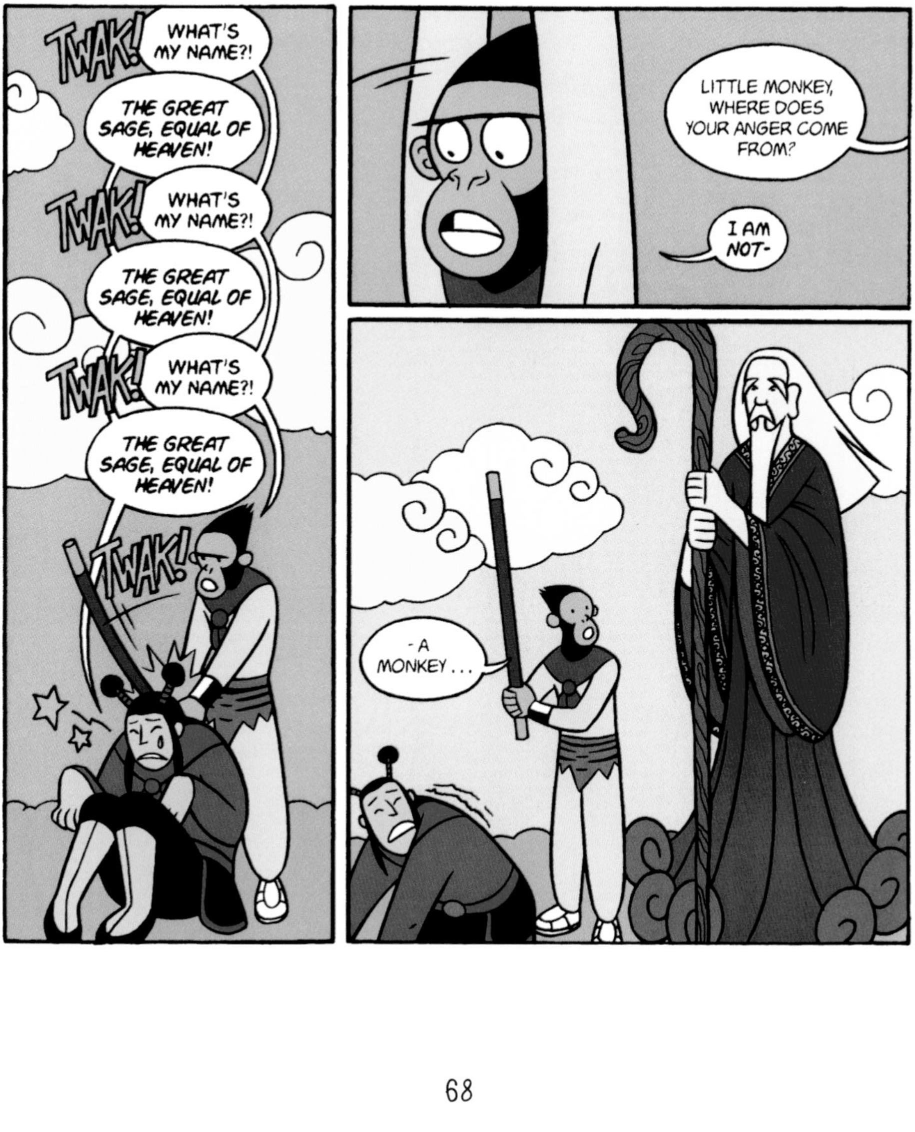
TWAK!
WHAT'S MY NAME?!
THE GREAT SAGE, EQUAL OF HEAVEN!
TWAK!
WHAT'S MY NAME?!
THE GREAT SAGE, EQUAL OF HEAVEN!
TWAK!
WHAT'S MY NAME?!
THE GREAT SAGE, EQUAL OF HEAVEN!
TWAK!
LITTLE MONKEY, WHERE DOES YOUR ANGER COME FROM?
I AM NOT-
- A MONKEY . . .

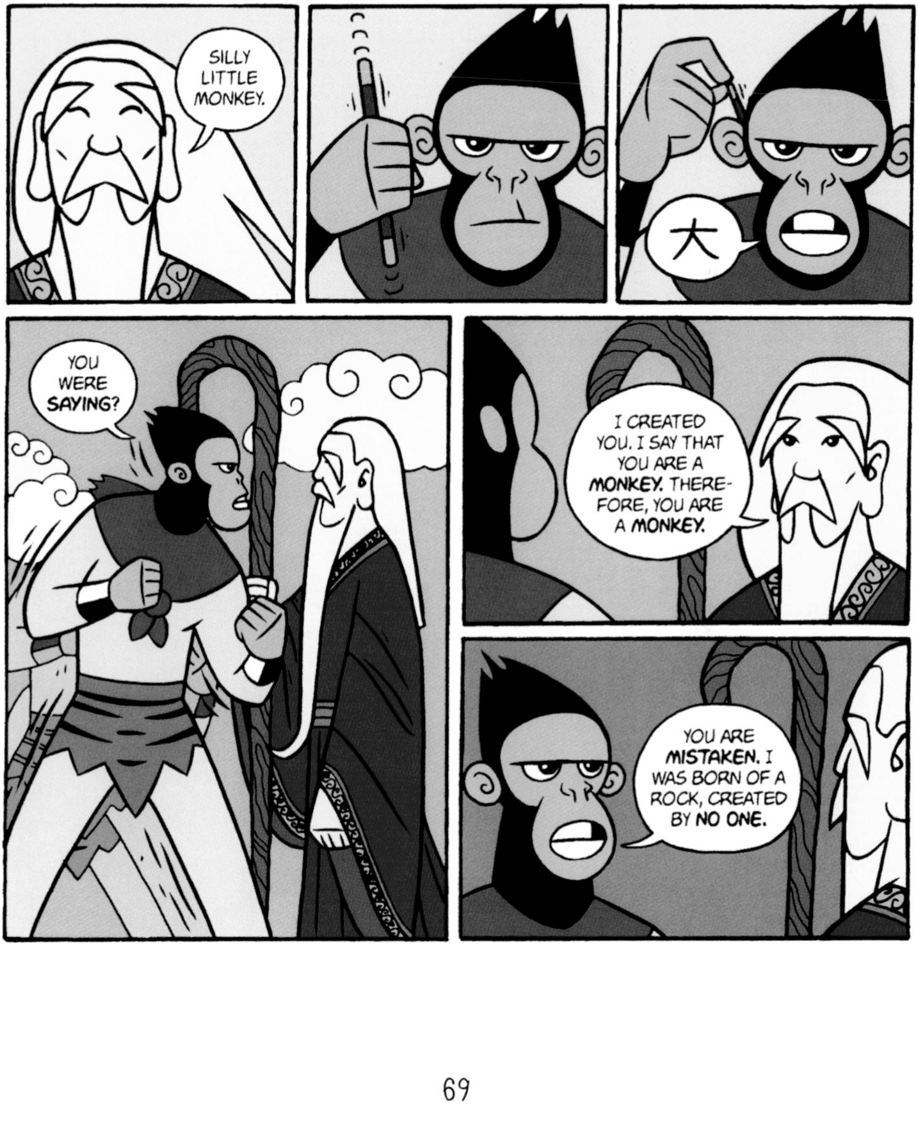
SILLY LITTLE MONKEY.
大
YOU WERE SAYING?
I CREATED YOU. I SAY THAT YOU ARE A MONKEY. THEREFORE, YOU ARE A MONKEY.
YOU ARE MISTAKEN. I WAS BORN OF A ROCK, CREATED BY NO ONE.

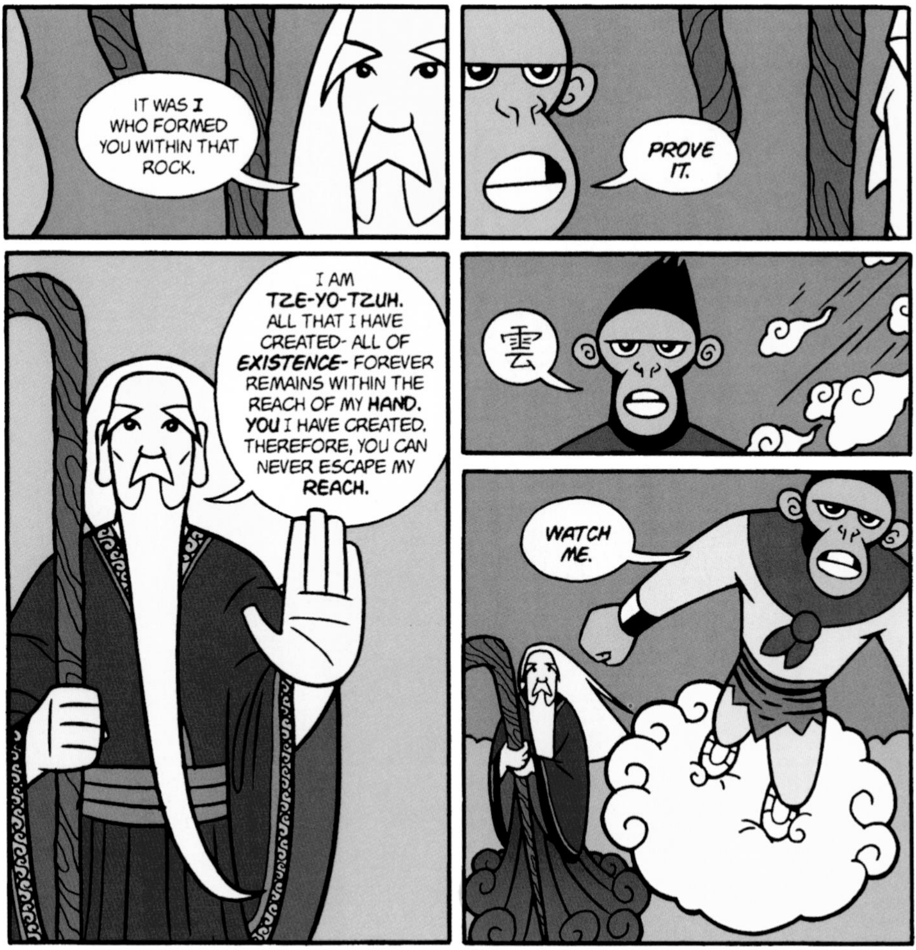
IT WAS I WHO FORMED YOU WITHIN THAT ROCK.
PROVE IT.
I AM TZE-YO-TZUH. ALL THAT I HAVE CREATED- ALL OF EXISTENCE- FOREVER REMAINS WITHIN THE REACH OF MY HAND. YOU I HAVE CREATED. THEREFORE, YOU CAN NEVER ESCAPE MY REACH.
雲
WATCH ME.

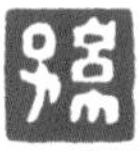

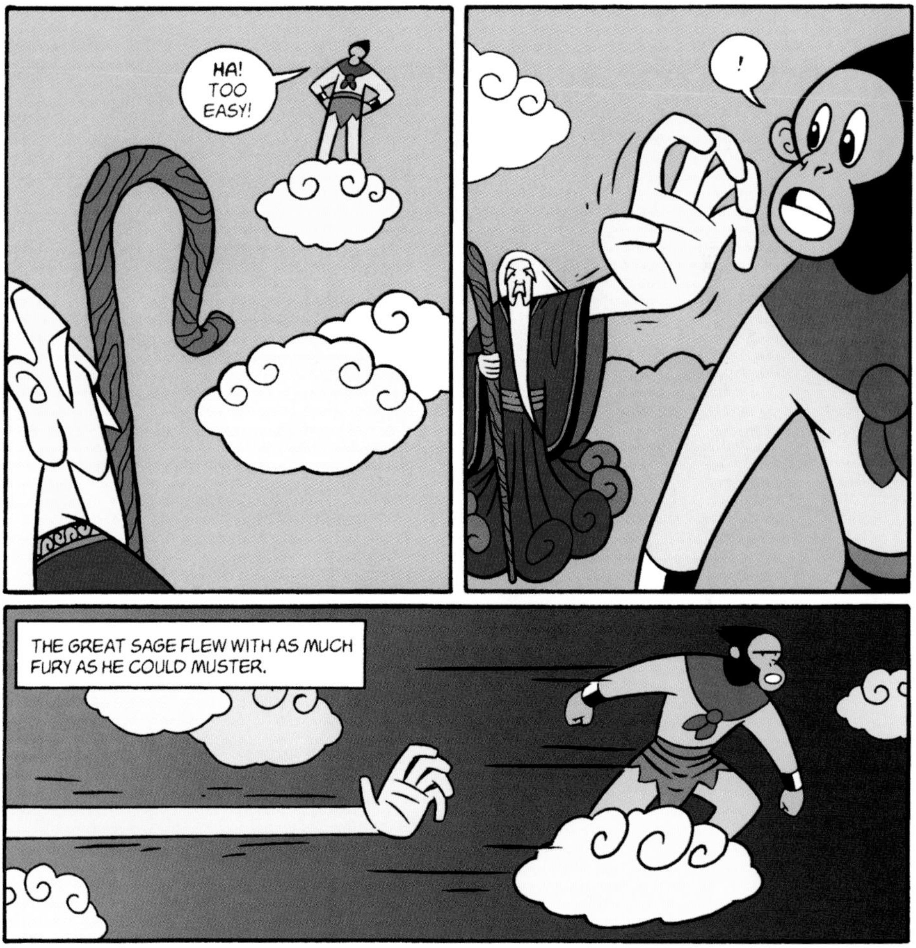
HA! TOO EASY!
!
THE GREAT SAGE FLEW WITH AS MUCH FURY AS HE COULD MUSTER.

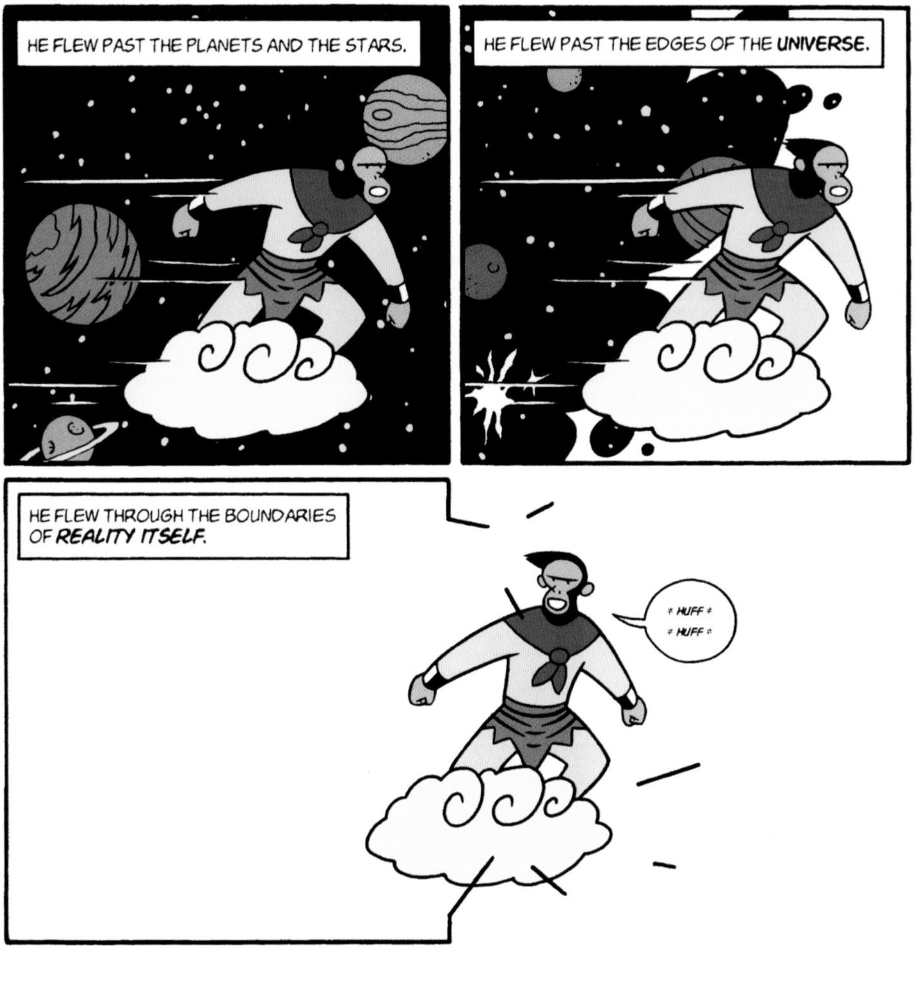
HE FLEW PAST THE PLANETS AND THE STARS.
HE FLEW PAST THE EDGES OF THE UNIVERSE.
HE FLEW THROUGH THE BOUNDARIES OF REALITY ITSELF.
* HUFF * * HUFF *

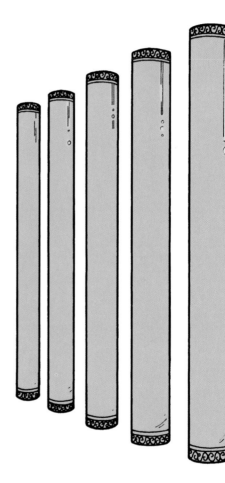

THERE, AT THE END OF ALL THAT IS, THE GREAT SAGE CAME UPON **FIVE PILLARS OF GOLD.**

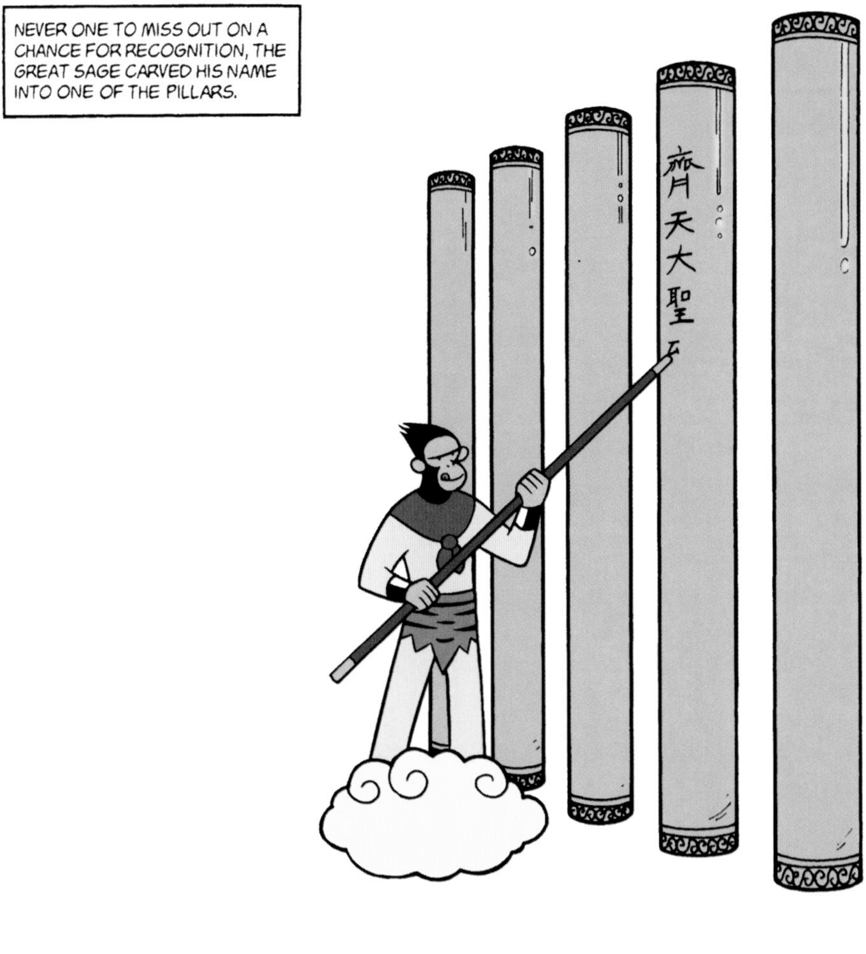
NEVER ONE TO MISS OUT ON A CHANCE FOR RECOGNITION, THE GREAT SAGE CARVED HIS NAME INTO ONE OF THE PILLARS.
齊天大聖

THEN HE RELIEVED HIMSELF.
(IT HAD BEEN AN AWFULLY
LONG TRIP.)

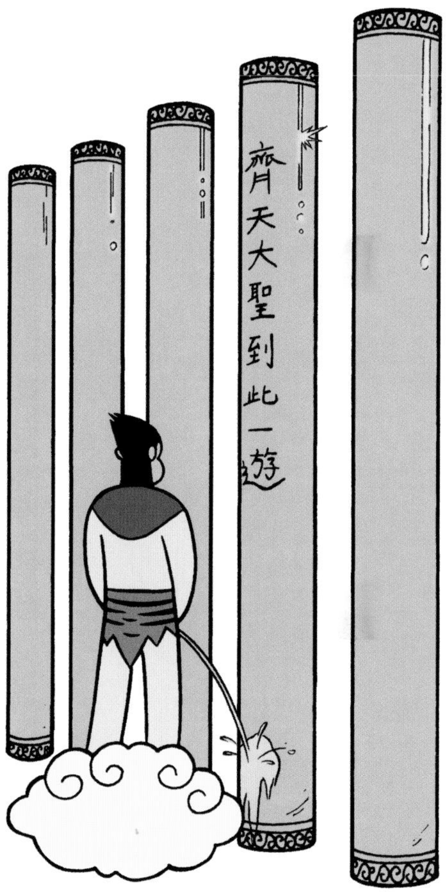
齊天大聖到此一遊

齊天大聖到此一遊

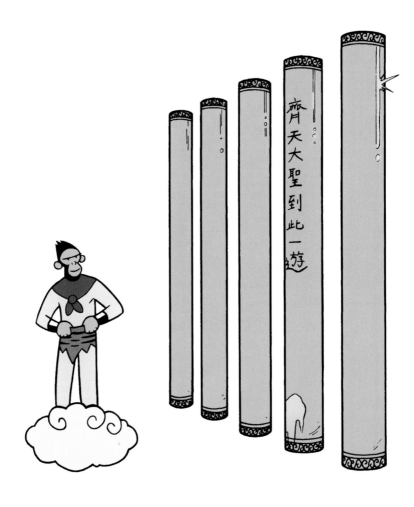

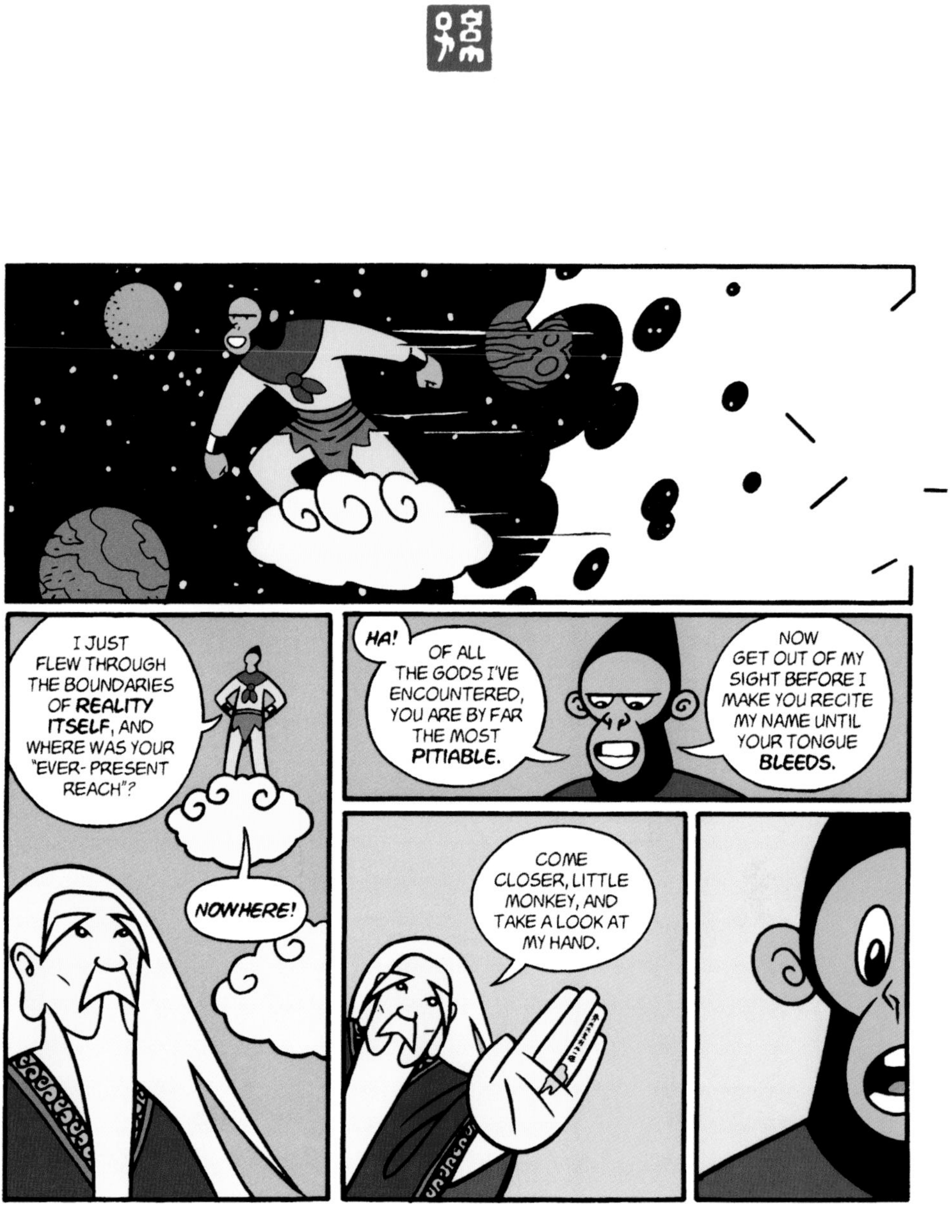
I JUST FLEW THROUGH THE BOUNDARIES OF REALITY ITSELF, AND WHERE WAS YOUR "EVER-PRESENT REACH"?
NOWHERE!
HA!
OF ALL THE GODS I'VE ENCOUNTERED, YOU ARE BY FAR THE MOST PITIABLE.
NOW GET OUT OF MY SIGHT BEFORE I MAKE YOU RECITE MY NAME UNTIL YOUR TONGUE BLEEDS.
COME CLOSER, LITTLE MONKEY, AND TAKE A LOOK AT MY HAND.

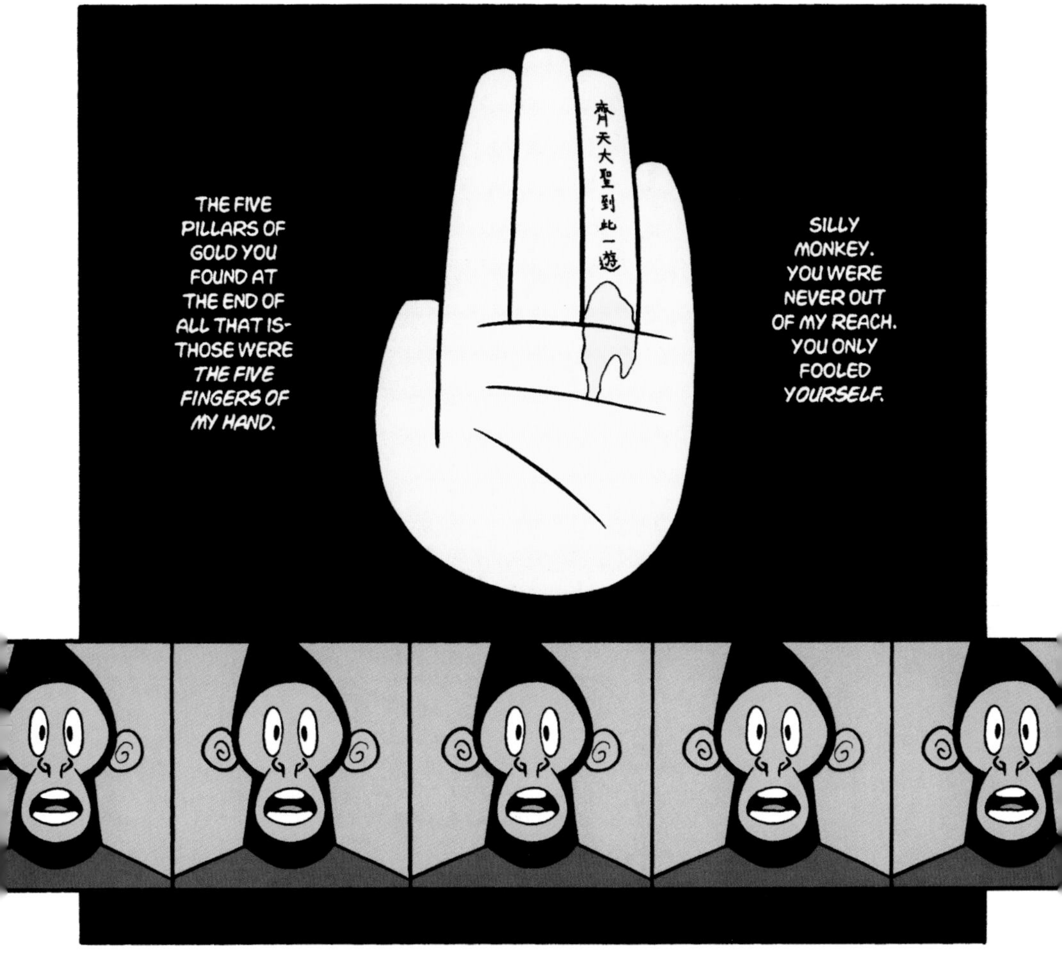
THE FIVE PILLARS OF GOLD YOU FOUND AT THE END OF ALL THAT IS- THOSE WERE *THE FIVE FINGERS OF MY HAND.*
齊天大聖到此一遊
SILLY MONKEY. YOU WERE NEVER OUT OF MY REACH. YOU ONLY FOOLED *YOURSELF.*

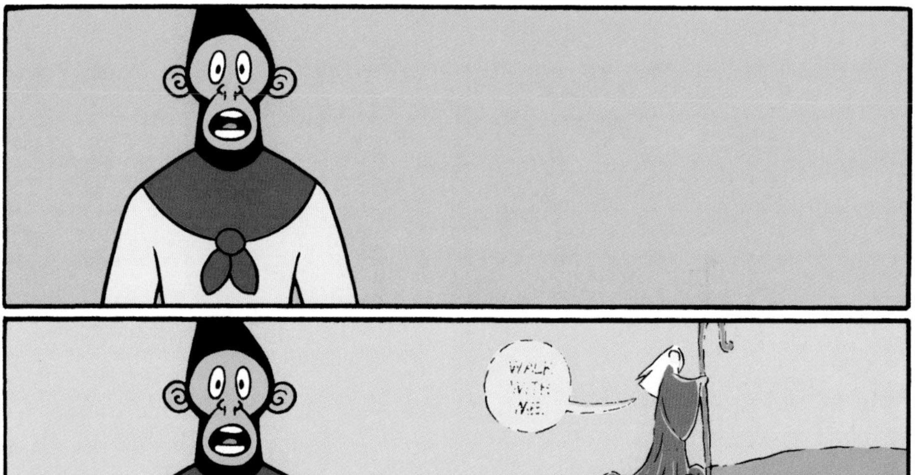
WALK WITH ME.
WALK WITH ME.

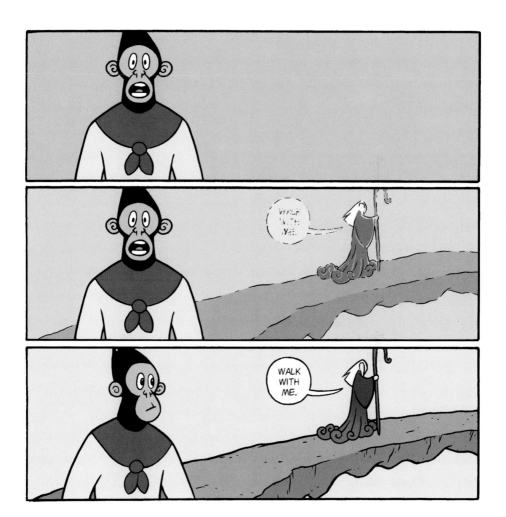

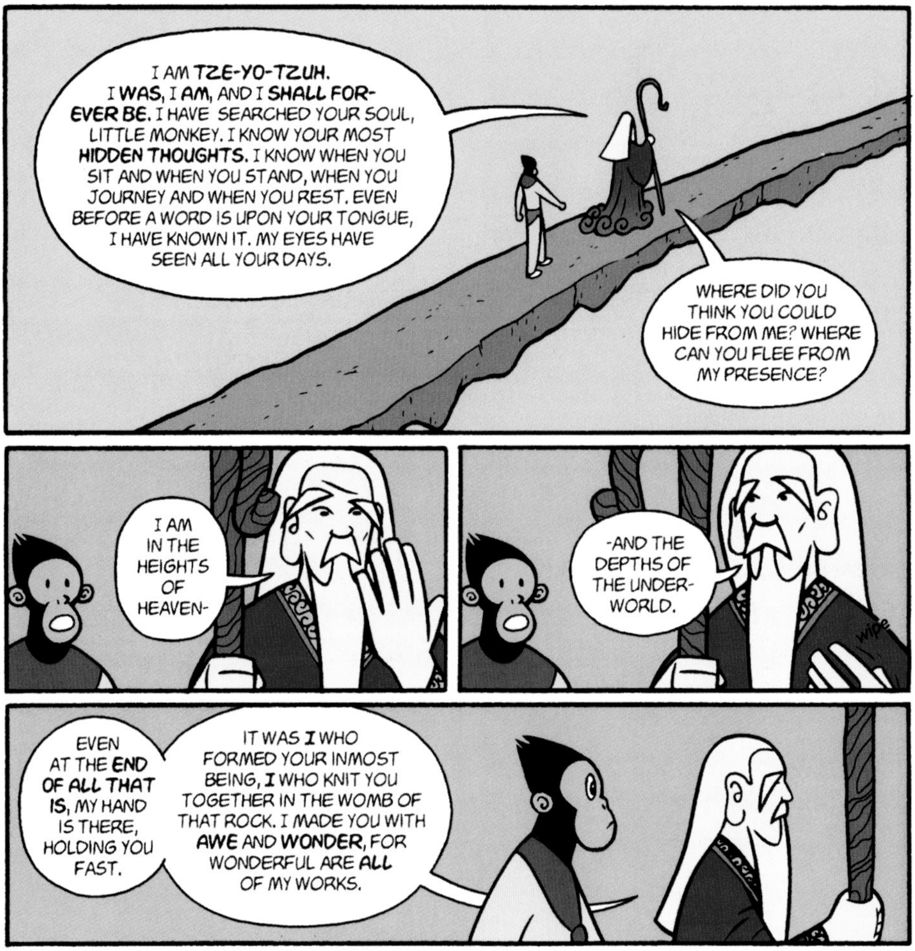
I AM TZE-YO-TZUH. I WAS, I AM, AND I SHALL FOREVER BE. I HAVE SEARCHED YOUR SOUL, LITTLE MONKEY. I KNOW YOUR MOST HIDDEN THOUGHTS. I KNOW WHEN YOU SIT AND WHEN YOU STAND, WHEN YOU JOURNEY AND WHEN YOU REST. EVEN BEFORE A WORD IS UPON YOUR TONGUE, I HAVE KNOWN IT. MY EYES HAVE SEEN ALL YOUR DAYS.
WHERE DID YOU THINK YOU COULD HIDE FROM ME? WHERE CAN YOU FLEE FROM MY PRESENCE?
I AM IN THE HEIGHTS OF HEAVEN-
-AND THE DEPTHS OF THE UNDERWORLD.
wipe
EVEN AT THE END OF ALL THAT IS, MY HAND IS THERE, HOLDING YOU FAST.
IT WAS I WHO FORMED YOUR INMOST BEING, I WHO KNIT YOU TOGETHER IN THE WOMB OF THAT ROCK. I MADE YOU WITH AWE AND WONDER, FOR WONDERFUL ARE ALL OF MY WORKS.

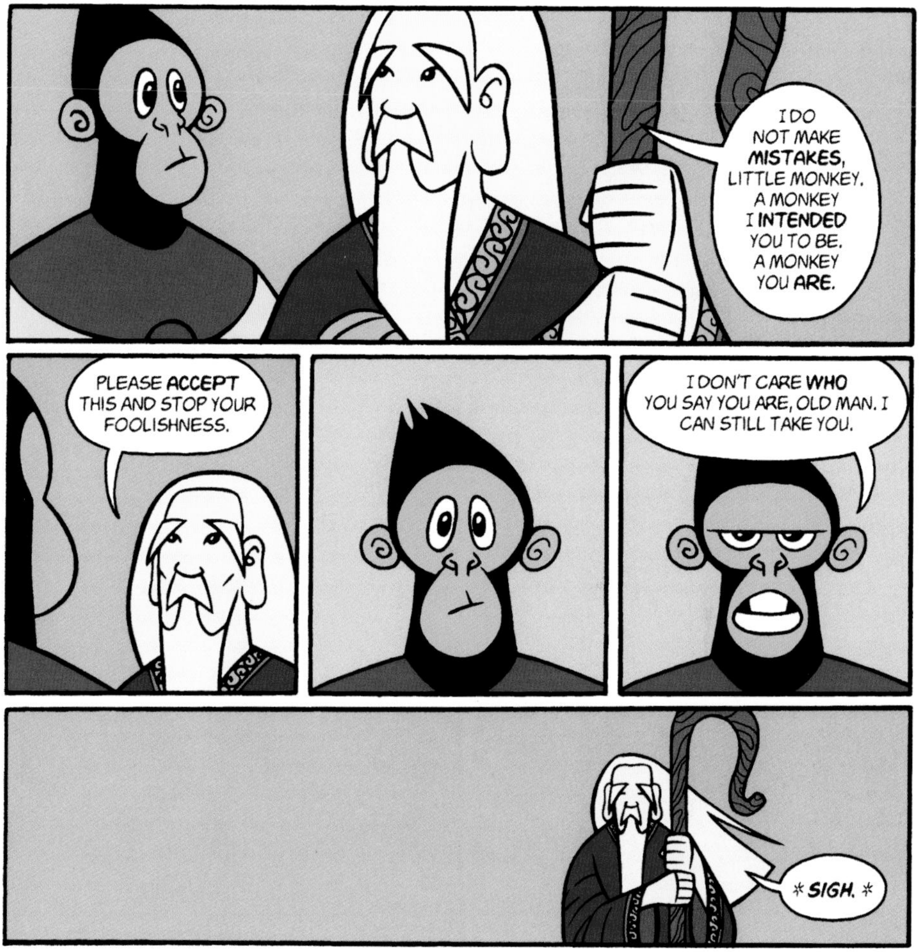
I DO NOT MAKE **MISTAKES,** LITTLE MONKEY. A MONKEY I **INTENDED** YOU TO BE. A MONKEY YOU **ARE.**
PLEASE **ACCEPT** THIS AND STOP YOUR FOOLISHNESS.
I DON'T CARE **WHO** YOU SAY YOU ARE, OLD MAN. I CAN STILL TAKE YOU.
* **SIGH.** *

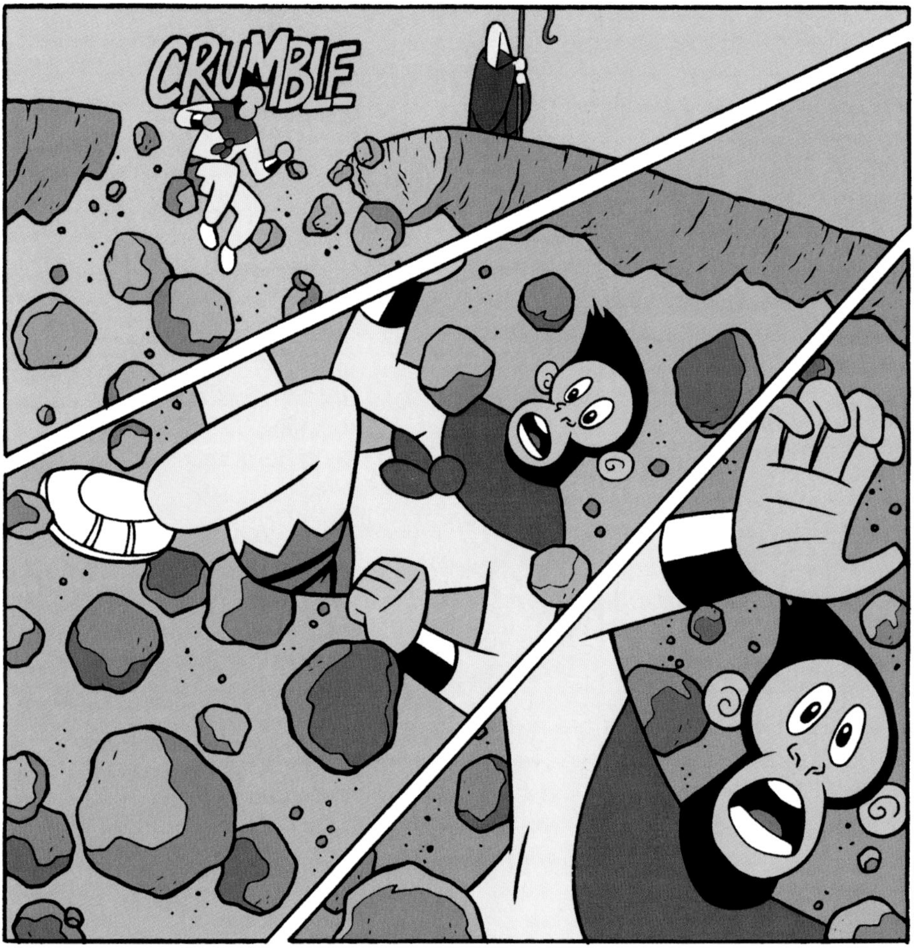
CRUMBLE

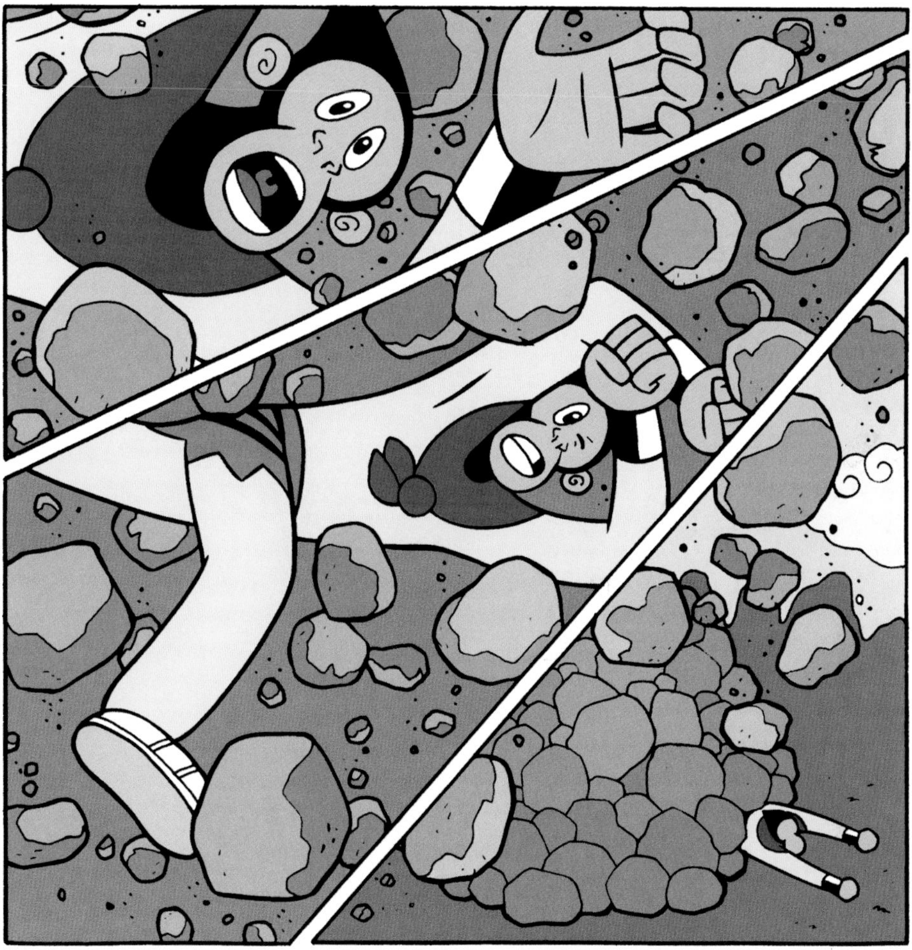

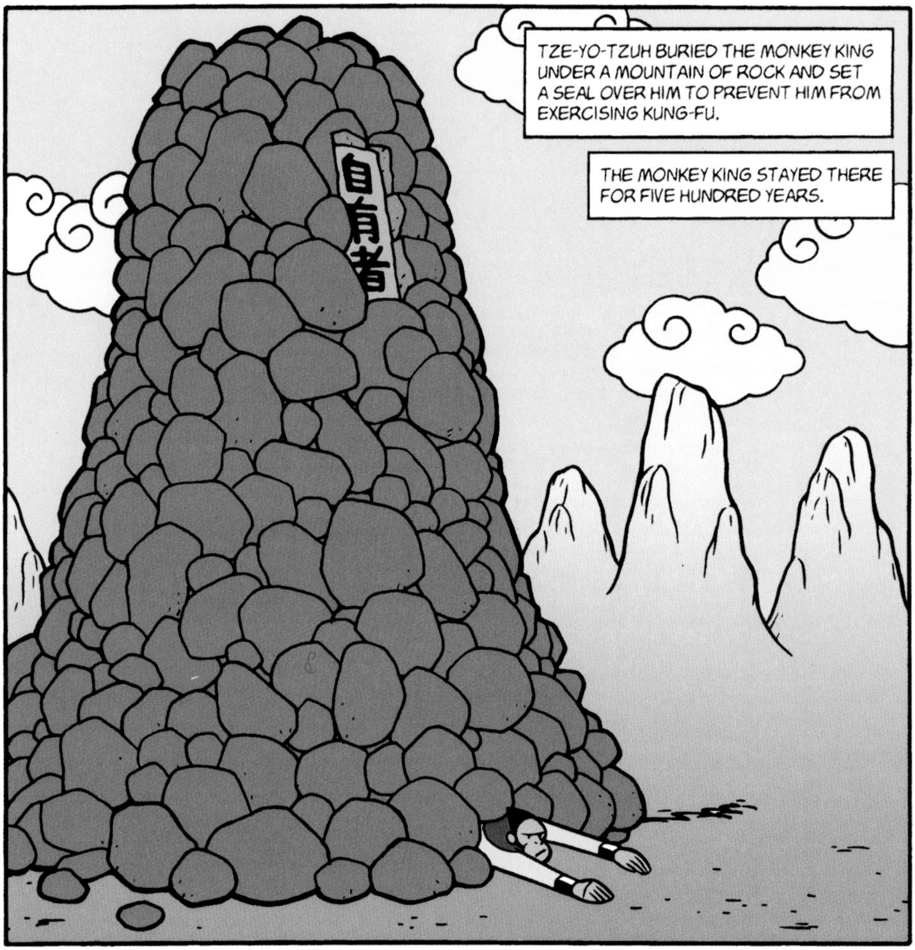
TZE-YO-TZUH BURIED THE MONKEY KING UNDER A MOUNTAIN OF ROCK AND SET A SEAL OVER HIM TO PREVENT HIM FROM EXERCISING KUNG-FU.
THE MONKEY KING STAYED THERE FOR FIVE HUNDRED YEARS.

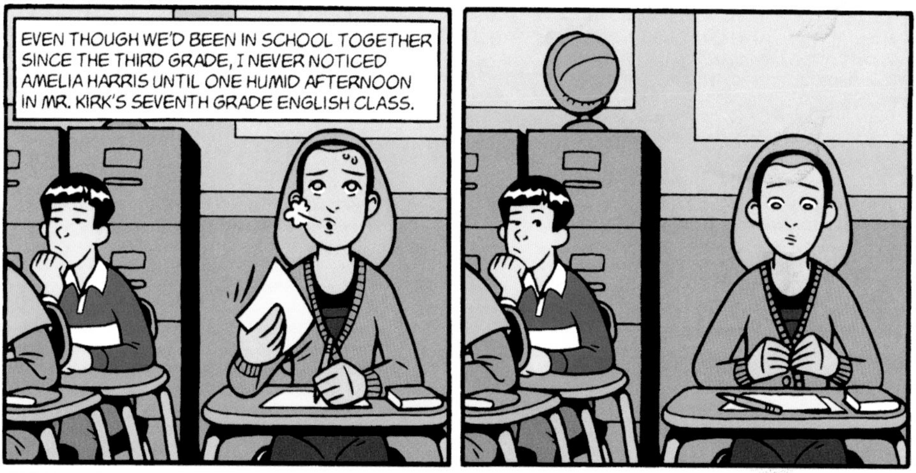
EVEN THOUGH WE'D BEEN IN SCHOOL TOGETHER SINCE THE THIRD GRADE, I NEVER NOTICED AMELIA HARRIS UNTIL ONE HUMID AFTERNOON IN MR. KIRK'S SEVENTH GRADE ENGLISH CLASS.
zing!
LIFE WAS NEVER QUITE THE SAME AGAIN.

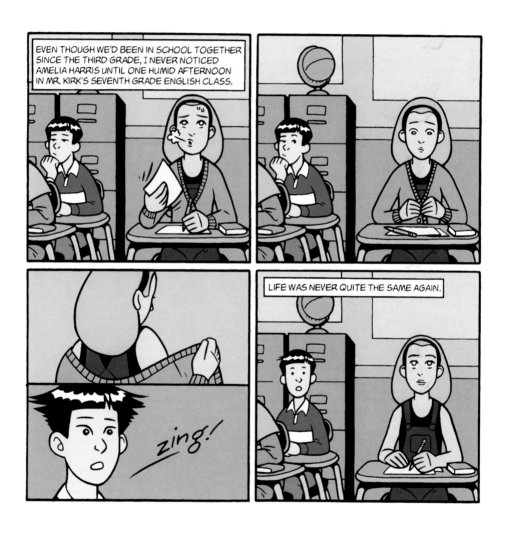

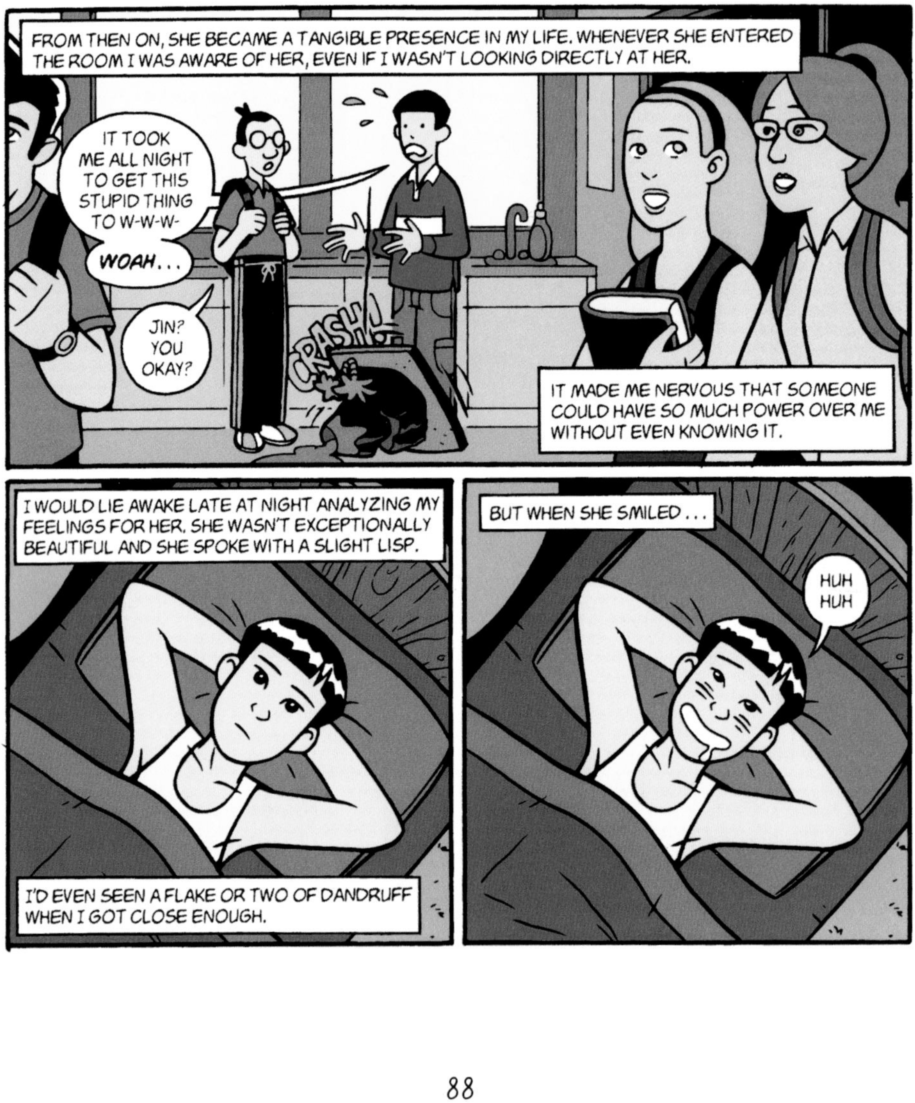
FROM THEN ON, SHE BECAME A TANGIBLE PRESENCE IN MY LIFE. WHENEVER SHE ENTERED THE ROOM I WAS AWARE OF HER, EVEN IF I WASN'T LOOKING DIRECTLY AT HER.
IT TOOK ME ALL NIGHT TO GET THIS STUPID THING TO W-W-W-
WOAH...
JIN? YOU OKAY?
CRASH!
IT MADE ME NERVOUS THAT SOMEONE COULD HAVE SO MUCH POWER OVER ME WITHOUT EVEN KNOWING IT.
I WOULD LIE AWAKE LATE AT NIGHT ANALYZING MY FEELINGS FOR HER. SHE WASN'T EXCEPTIONALLY BEAUTIFUL AND SHE SPOKE WITH A SLIGHT LISP.
I'D EVEN SEEN A FLAKE OR TWO OF DANDRUFF WHEN I GOT CLOSE ENOUGH.
BUT WHEN SHE SMILED...
HUH HUH

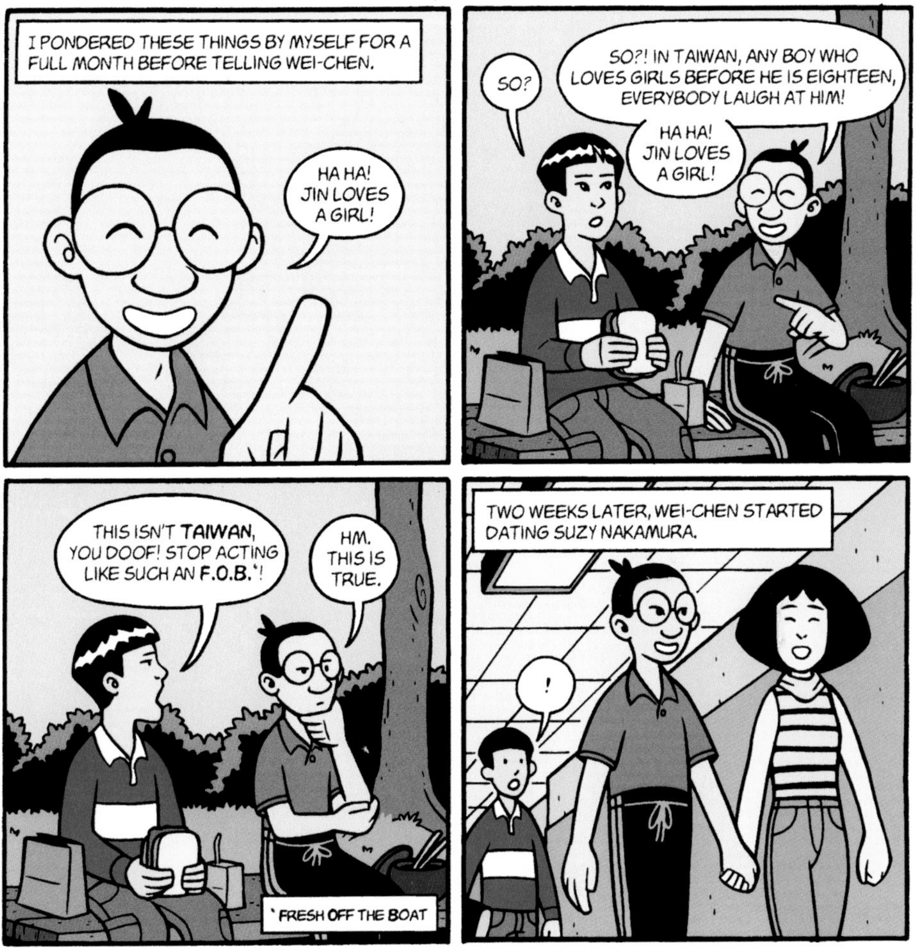
I PONDERED THESE THINGS BY MYSELF FOR A FULL MONTH BEFORE TELLING WEI-CHEN.
HA HA! JIN LOVES A GIRL!
SO?
SO?! IN TAIWAN, ANY BOY WHO LOVES GIRLS BEFORE HE IS EIGHTEEN, EVERYBODY LAUGH AT HIM!
HA HA! JIN LOVES A GIRL!
THIS ISN'T **TAIWAN**, YOU DOOF! STOP ACTING LIKE SUCH AN **F.O.B.***!
HM. THIS IS TRUE.
*FRESH OFF THE BOAT
TWO WEEKS LATER, WEI-CHEN STARTED DATING SUZY NAKAMURA.
!

LOOK AT ITS EYES . . . SO COLD AND STILL . . . ALMOST LIFELESS.

I'VE NAMED HER **CLARISSA**, AFTER MY EX-WIFE.

HA HA

CLARISSA AND HER FRIENDS ARE ON LOAN TO US FROM BABELENE COSMETICS, INC. THIS IS A TRULY WONDERFUL AND UNEXPECTED LEARNING OPPORTUNITY FOR US, CLASS!

I HOPE YOU ALL TAKE ADVANTAGE OF IT!

MABEL, YOU REALLY MUST SAY THANK YOU AGAIN TO YOUR MOTHER.

WILL DO, MR. GRAHAM!

NOW, FOR THE DURATION OF THEIR VISIT CLARISSA AND COMPANY WILL NEED TWO STUDENT CARETAKERS. YOUR DUTIES WILL INCLUDE STAYING AFTER SCHOOL TO FEED THEM AND CHANGE THEIR WATER.
THERE WILL, OF COURSE, BE EXTRA CREDIT INVOLVED. ANY VOLUNTEERS?
THANK YOU, AMELIA.
ANYONE ELSE?
WHAT FOR, AMELIA? YOU CAN PET MY LIZARD ANY TIME YOU WANT.
TIMMY- !
I DON'T KNOW, TIMMY. YOU DO A PRETTY GOOD JOB OF THAT YOURSELF.
HA HA!

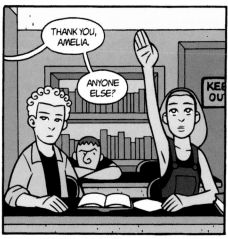

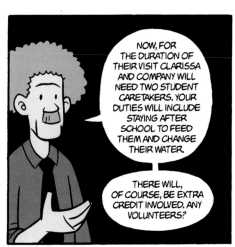

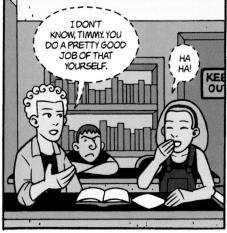

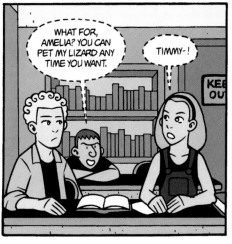

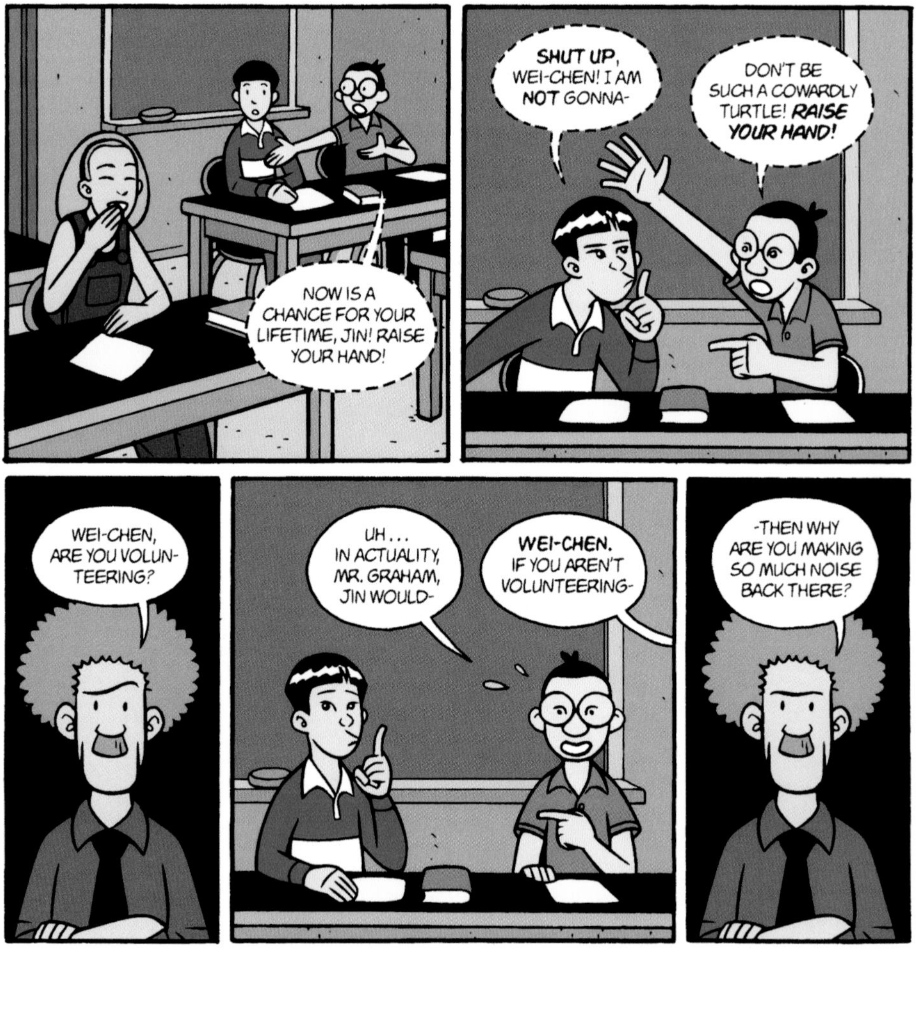
NOW IS A CHANCE FOR YOUR LIFETIME, JIN! RAISE YOUR HAND!
SHUT UP, WEI-CHEN! I AM **NOT** GONNA-
DON'T BE SUCH A COWARDLY TURTLE! ***RAISE YOUR HAND!***
WEI-CHEN, ARE YOU VOLUNTEERING?
UH... IN ACTUALITY, MR. GRAHAM, JIN WOULD-
WEI-CHEN. IF YOU AREN'T VOLUNTEERING-
-THEN WHY ARE YOU MAKING SO MUCH NOISE BACK THERE?

* SIGH. *
YES, MR. GRAHAM. I WOULD LOVE VERY MUCH TO VOLUNTEER.
THANK YOU, WEI-CHEN.
KEEP OUT

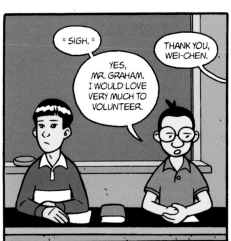

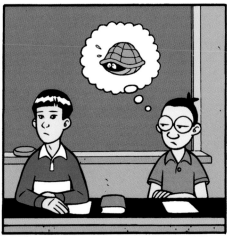

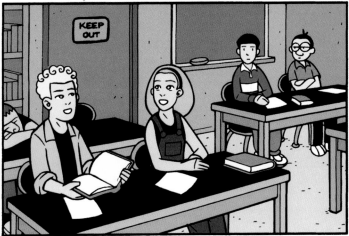

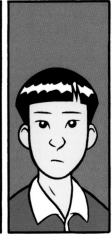

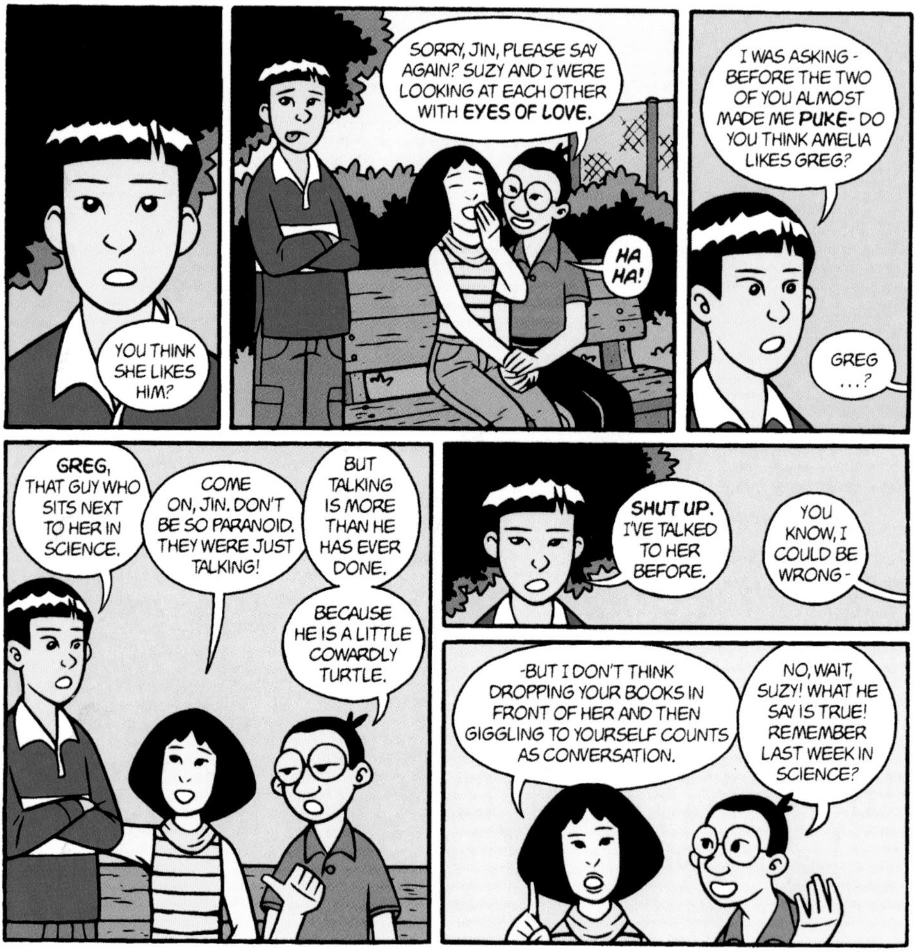
YOU THINK SHE LIKES HIM?
SORRY, JIN, PLEASE SAY AGAIN? SUZY AND I WERE LOOKING AT EACH OTHER WITH EYES OF LOVE.
HA HA!
I WAS ASKING - BEFORE THE TWO OF YOU ALMOST MADE ME PUKE- DO YOU THINK AMELIA LIKES GREG?
GREG ...?
GREG, THAT GUY WHO SITS NEXT TO HER IN SCIENCE.
COME ON, JIN. DON'T BE SO PARANOID. THEY WERE JUST TALKING!
BUT TALKING IS MORE THAN HE HAS EVER DONE.
BECAUSE HE IS A LITTLE COWARDLY TURTLE.
SHUT UP. I'VE TALKED TO HER BEFORE.
YOU KNOW, I COULD BE WRONG -
-BUT I DON'T THINK DROPPING YOUR BOOKS IN FRONT OF HER AND THEN GIGGLING TO YOURSELF COUNTS AS CONVERSATION.
NO, WAIT, SUZY! WHAT HE SAY IS TRUE! REMEMBER LAST WEEK IN SCIENCE?

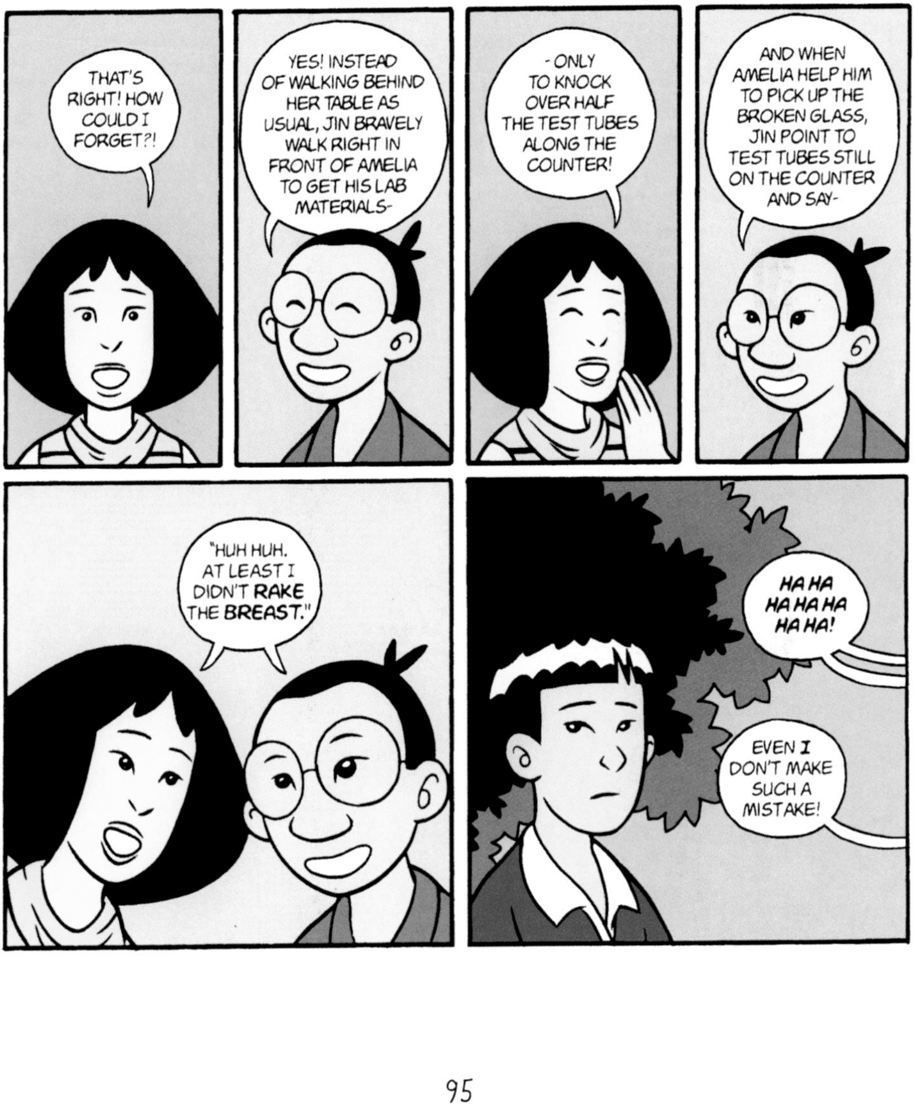
THAT'S RIGHT! HOW COULD I FORGET?!
YES! INSTEAD OF WALKING BEHIND HER TABLE AS USUAL, JIN BRAVELY WALK RIGHT IN FRONT OF AMELIA TO GET HIS LAB MATERIALS-
-ONLY TO KNOCK OVER HALF THE TEST TUBES ALONG THE COUNTER!
AND WHEN AMELIA HELP HIM TO PICK UP THE BROKEN GLASS, JIN POINT TO TEST TUBES STILL ON THE COUNTER AND SAY-
"HUH HUH. AT LEAST I DIDN'T **RAKE** THE **BREAST**."
HA HA HA HA HA HA HA!
EVEN **I** DON'T MAKE SUCH A MISTAKE!

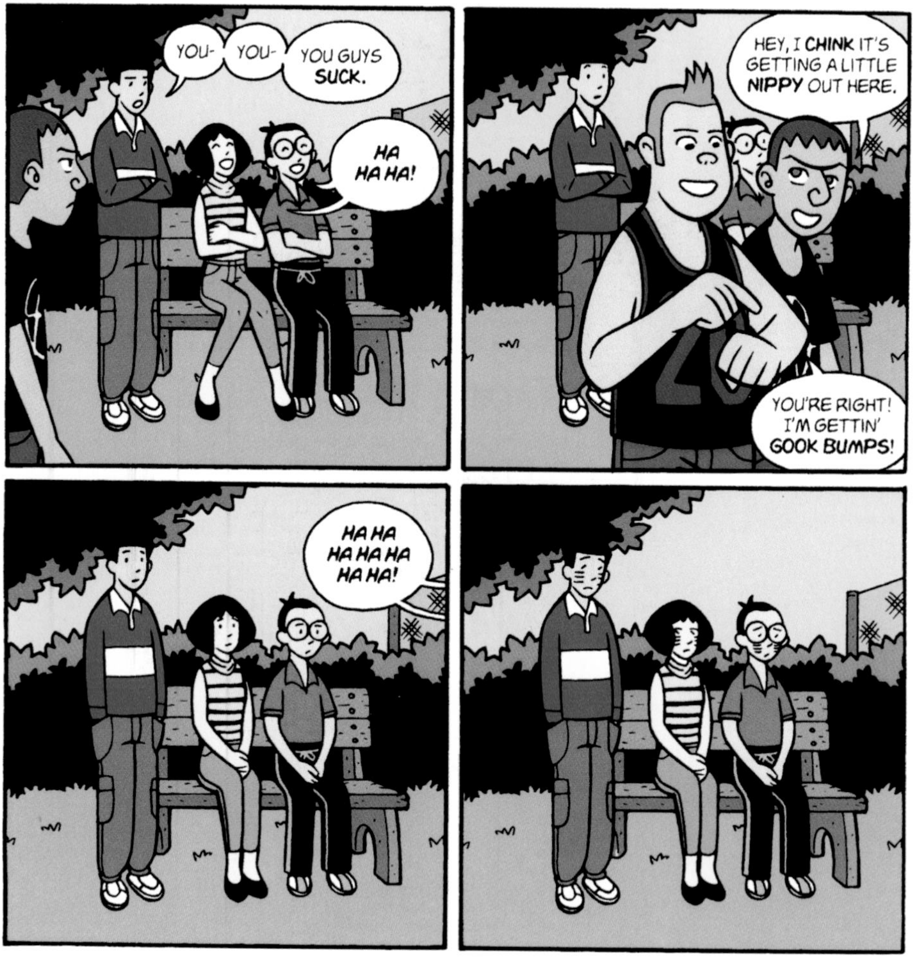
YOU-
YOU-
YOU GUYS SUCK.
HA HA HA HA!
HEY, I CHINK IT'S GETTING A LITTLE NIPPY OUT HERE.
YOU'RE RIGHT! I'M GETTIN' GOOK BUMPS!
HA HA HA HA HA HA HA!

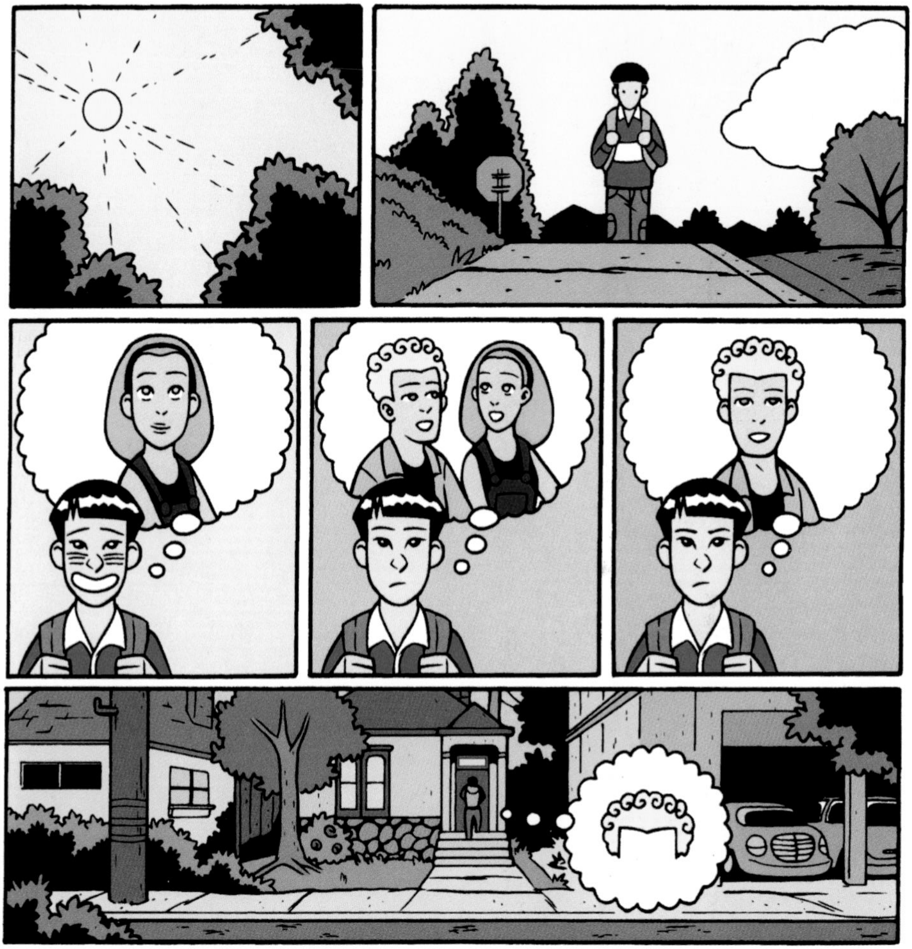

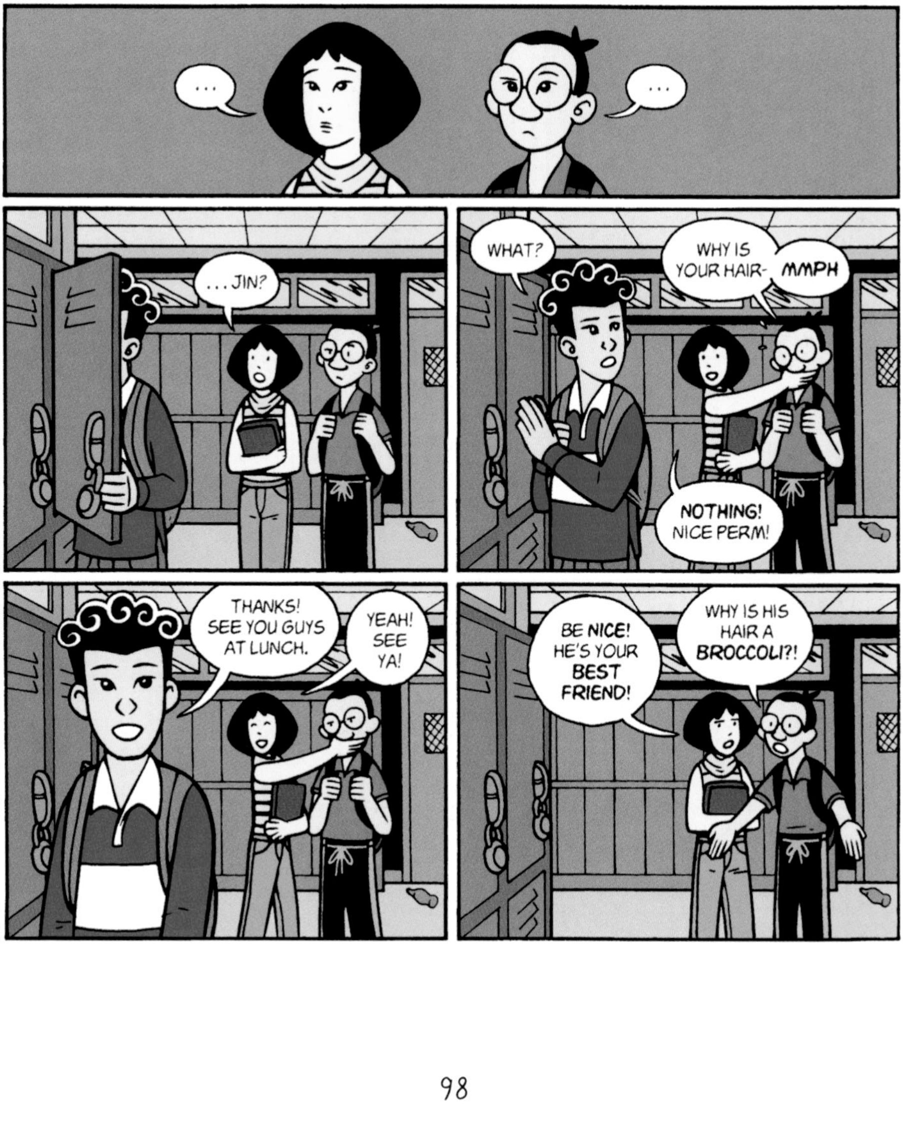
. . .
. . .
. . . JIN?
WHAT?
WHY IS YOUR HAIR-
MMPH
NOTHING! NICE PERM!
THANKS! SEE YOU GUYS AT LUNCH.
YEAH! SEE YA!
BE NICE! HE'S YOUR BEST FRIEND!
WHY IS HIS HAIR A BROCCOLI?!

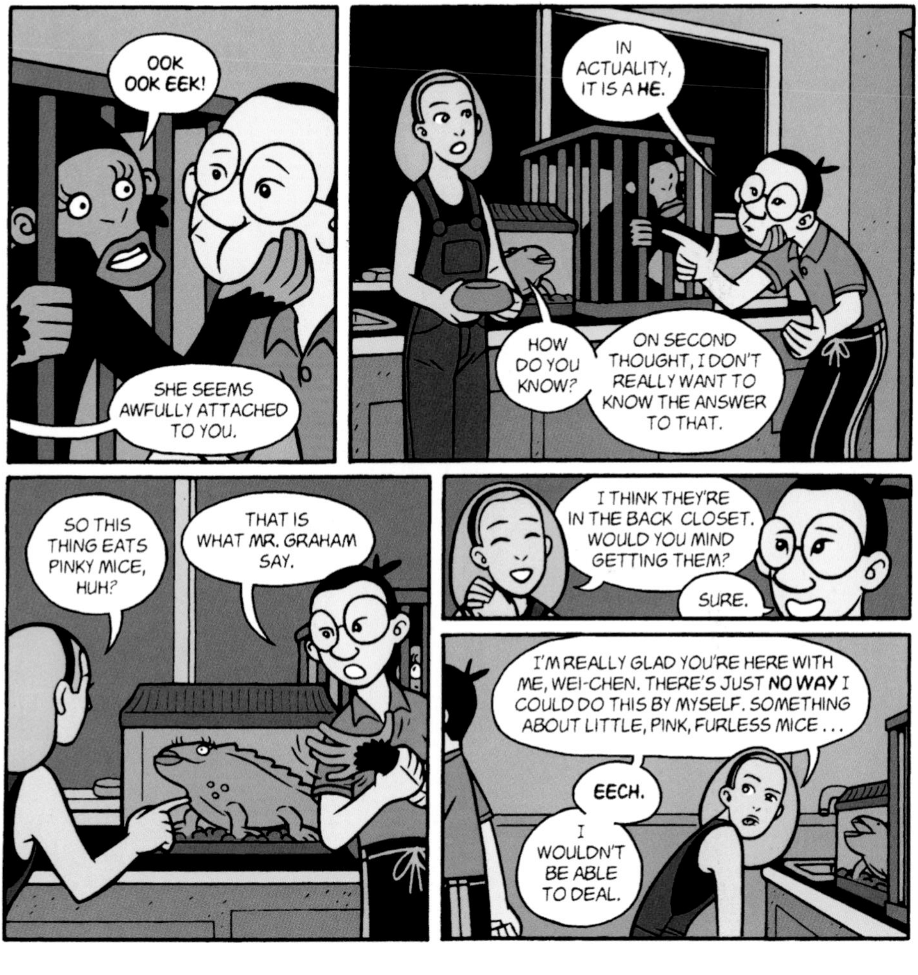
OOK OOK EEK!
SHE SEEMS AWFULLY ATTACHED TO YOU.
IN ACTUALITY, IT IS A **HE**.
HOW DO YOU KNOW?
ON SECOND THOUGHT, I DON'T REALLY WANT TO KNOW THE ANSWER TO THAT.
SO THIS THING EATS PINKY MICE, HUH?
THAT IS WHAT MR. GRAHAM SAY.
I THINK THEY'RE IN THE BACK CLOSET. WOULD YOU MIND GETTING THEM?
SURE.
I'M REALLY GLAD YOU'RE HERE WITH ME, WEI-CHEN. THERE'S JUST **NO WAY** I COULD DO THIS BY MYSELF. SOMETHING ABOUT LITTLE, PINK, FURLESS MICE . . .
EECH.
I WOULDN'T BE ABLE TO DEAL.

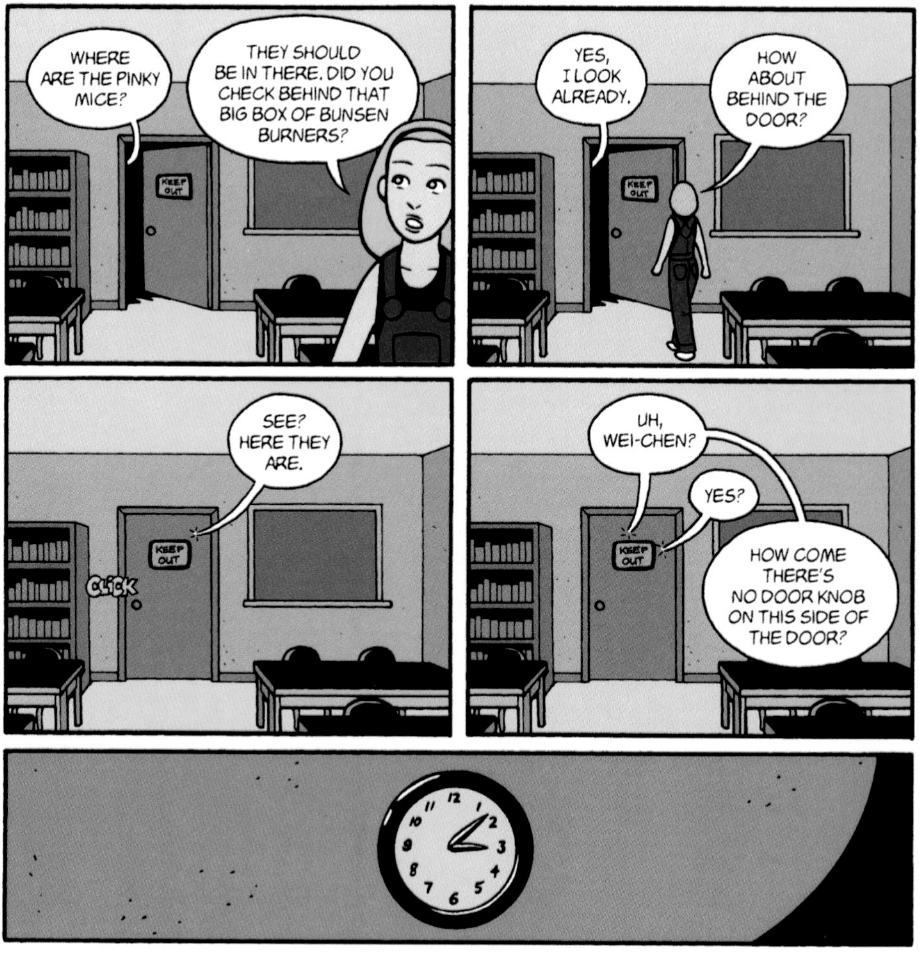
WHERE ARE THE PINKY MICE?
THEY SHOULD BE IN THERE. DID YOU CHECK BEHIND THAT BIG BOX OF BUNSEN BURNERS?
YES, I LOOK ALREADY.
HOW ABOUT BEHIND THE DOOR?
KEEP OUT
SEE? HERE THEY ARE.
CLICK
UH, WEI-CHEN?
YES?
HOW COME THERE'S NO DOOR KNOB ON THIS SIDE OF THE DOOR?

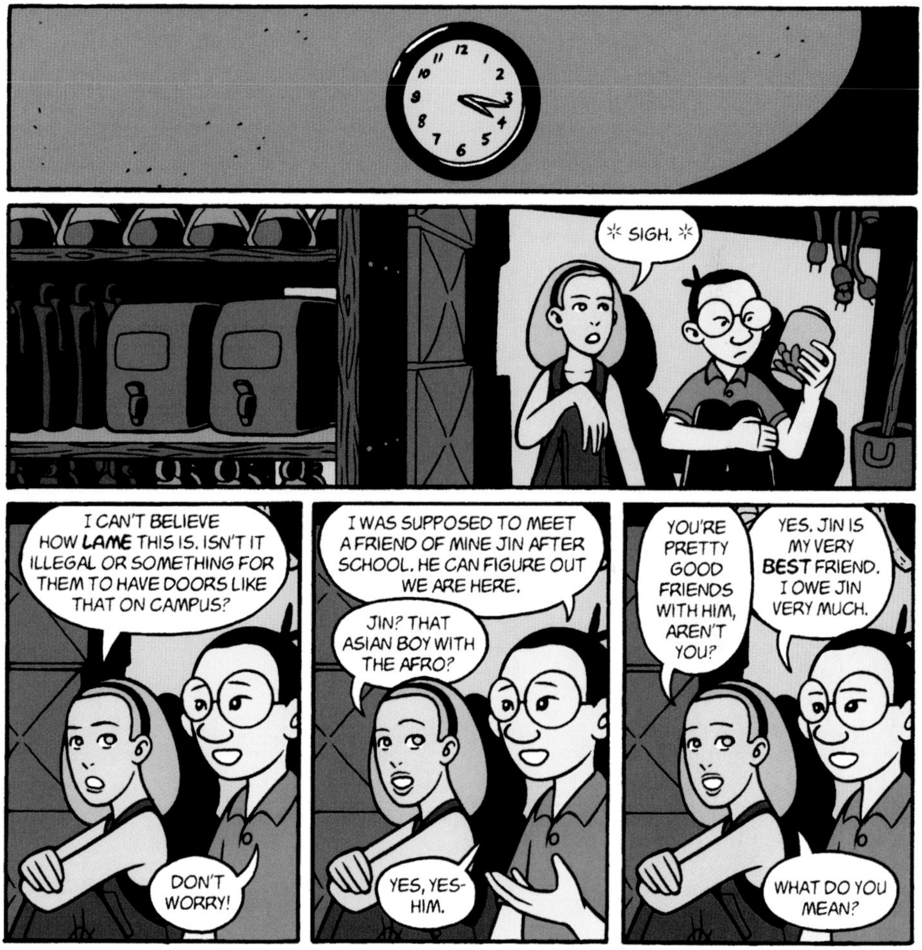
* SIGH. *
I CAN'T BELIEVE HOW LAME THIS IS. ISN'T IT ILLEGAL OR SOMETHING FOR THEM TO HAVE DOORS LIKE THAT ON CAMPUS?
DON'T WORRY!
I WAS SUPPOSED TO MEET A FRIEND OF MINE JIN AFTER SCHOOL. HE CAN FIGURE OUT WE ARE HERE.
JIN? THAT ASIAN BOY WITH THE AFRO?
YES, YES- HIM.
YOU'RE PRETTY GOOD FRIENDS WITH HIM, AREN'T YOU?
YES. JIN IS MY VERY BEST FRIEND. I OWE JIN VERY MUCH.
WHAT DO YOU MEAN?

WHEN I MOVE HERE TO AMERICA, I WAS AFRAID NOBODY WANTS TO BE MY FRIEND. I COME FROM A DIFFERENT PLACE. MUCH, MUCH DIFFERENT.

BUT MY FIRST DAY IN SCHOOL HERE I MEET JIN. FROM THEN I KNOW EVERY-THING'S OKAY. HE TREAT ME LIKE A LITTLE BROTHER, SHOW ME HOW THINGS WORK IN AMERICA. HE HELP WITH MY ENGLISH. HE TEACH ME HIP ENGLISH PHRASE LIKE "DON'T HAVE A COW, MAN" AND "WORD OF YOUR-" NO, NO . . .

"WORD TO YOUR MOTHER." HA HA. HE TAKE ME TO McDONALD'S AND BUY ME FRENCH FRIES. I THINK SOMETIMES MY ACCENT EMBARRASS HIM, BUT JIN STILL WILLING TO BE MY FRIEND. IN ACTUALITY, FOR A LONG, LONG TIME MY ONLY FRIEND IS HIM.

YES, I OWE JIN VERY MUCH. HE HAS A GOOD SOUL.

IF HE WAS NOT HERE, I DON'T KNOW. I WOULD HAVE BEEN SO LONELY.

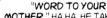

CAN I ASK YOU SOMETHING, WEI-CHEN?

SHOOT AWAY.

I'VE ALWAYS GOTTEN THIS WEIRD VIBE FROM JIN . . .

DOES HE . . . LIKE ME OR SOME-THING?

HA HA! YOU YOURSELF ASK HIM!

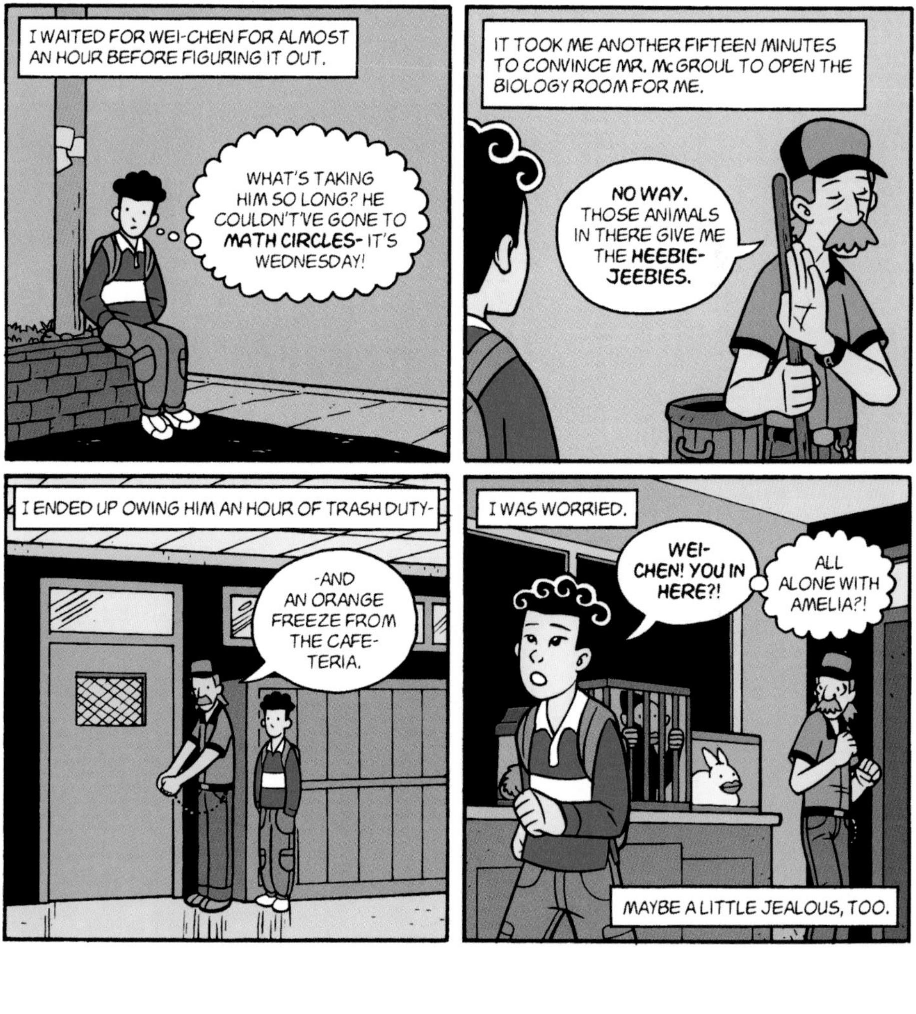
I WAITED FOR WEI-CHEN FOR ALMOST AN HOUR BEFORE FIGURING IT OUT.
WHAT'S TAKING HIM SO LONG? HE COULDN'T'VE GONE TO MATH CIRCLES- IT'S WEDNESDAY!
IT TOOK ME ANOTHER FIFTEEN MINUTES TO CONVINCE MR. McGROUL TO OPEN THE BIOLOGY ROOM FOR ME.
NO WAY. THOSE ANIMALS IN THERE GIVE ME THE HEEBIE-JEEBIES.
I ENDED UP OWING HIM AN HOUR OF TRASH DUTY-
-AND AN ORANGE FREEZE FROM THE CAFETERIA.
I WAS WORRIED.
WEI-CHEN! YOU IN HERE?!
ALL ALONE WITH AMELIA?!
MAYBE A LITTLE JEALOUS, TOO.

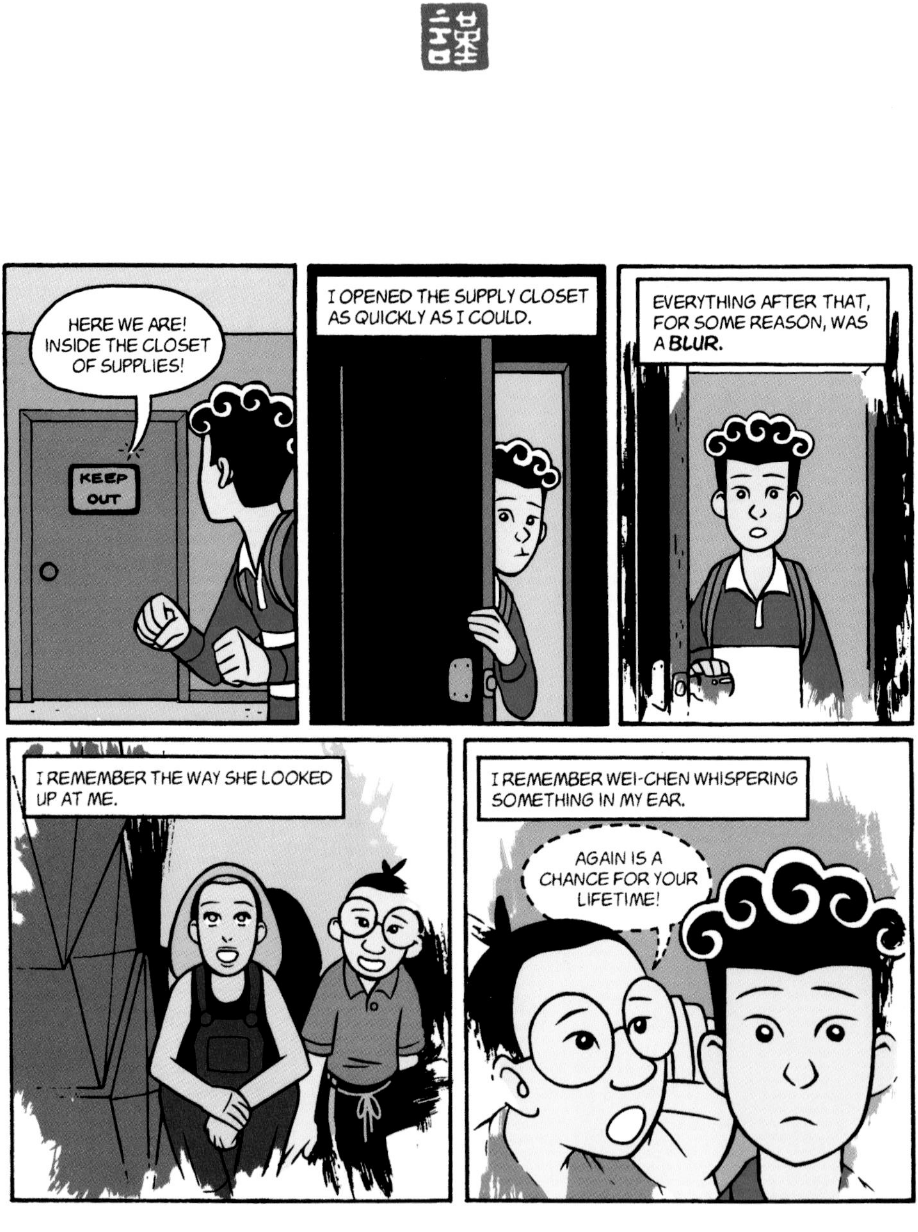
HERE WE ARE! INSIDE THE CLOSET OF SUPPLIES!
KEEP OUT
I OPENED THE SUPPLY CLOSET AS QUICKLY AS I COULD.
EVERYTHING AFTER THAT, FOR SOME REASON, WAS A BLUR.
I REMEMBER THE WAY SHE LOOKED UP AT ME.
I REMEMBER WEI-CHEN WHISPERING SOMETHING IN MY EAR.
AGAIN IS A CHANCE FOR YOUR LIFETIME!

I REMEMBER A JOLT OF CONFIDENCE,
ZZZT!
A STILTED QUESTION,
HANG OUT...
WITH ME...
SOME-TIME?
AND A WORD FROM HER LIPS...
YES.
YES.
YES.

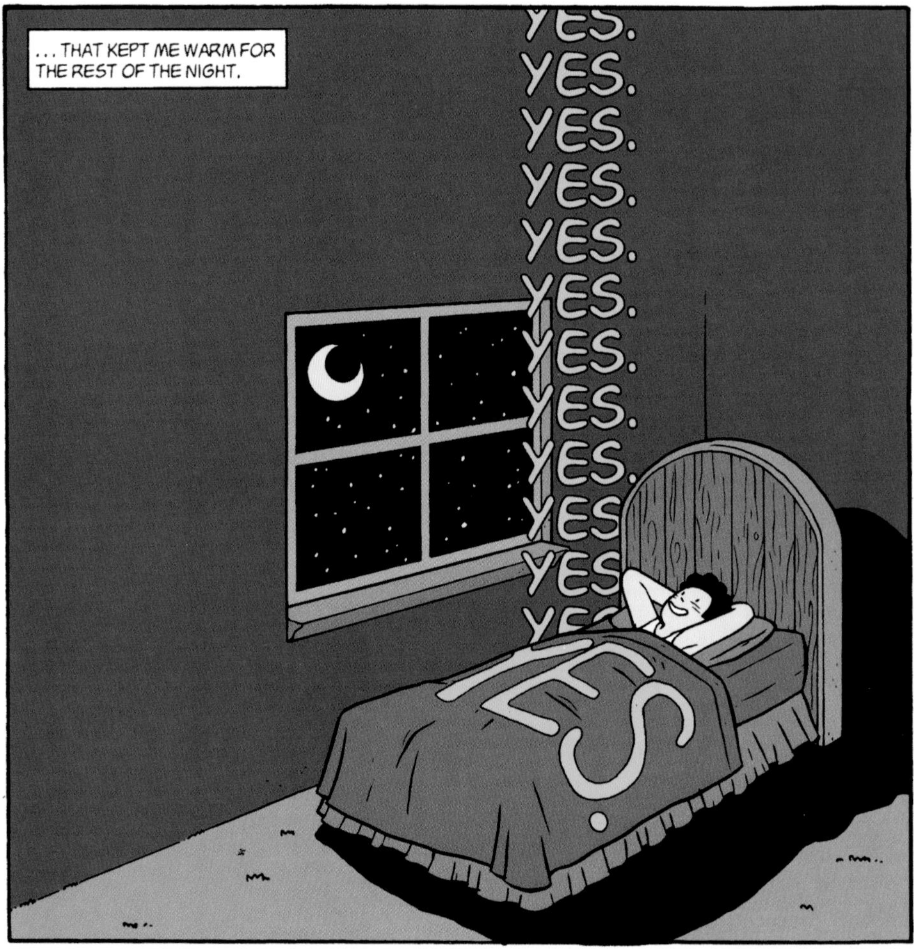
... THAT KEPT ME WARM FOR THE REST OF THE NIGHT.
YES.
YES.
YES.
YES.
YES.
YES.
YES.
YES.
YES.
YES.

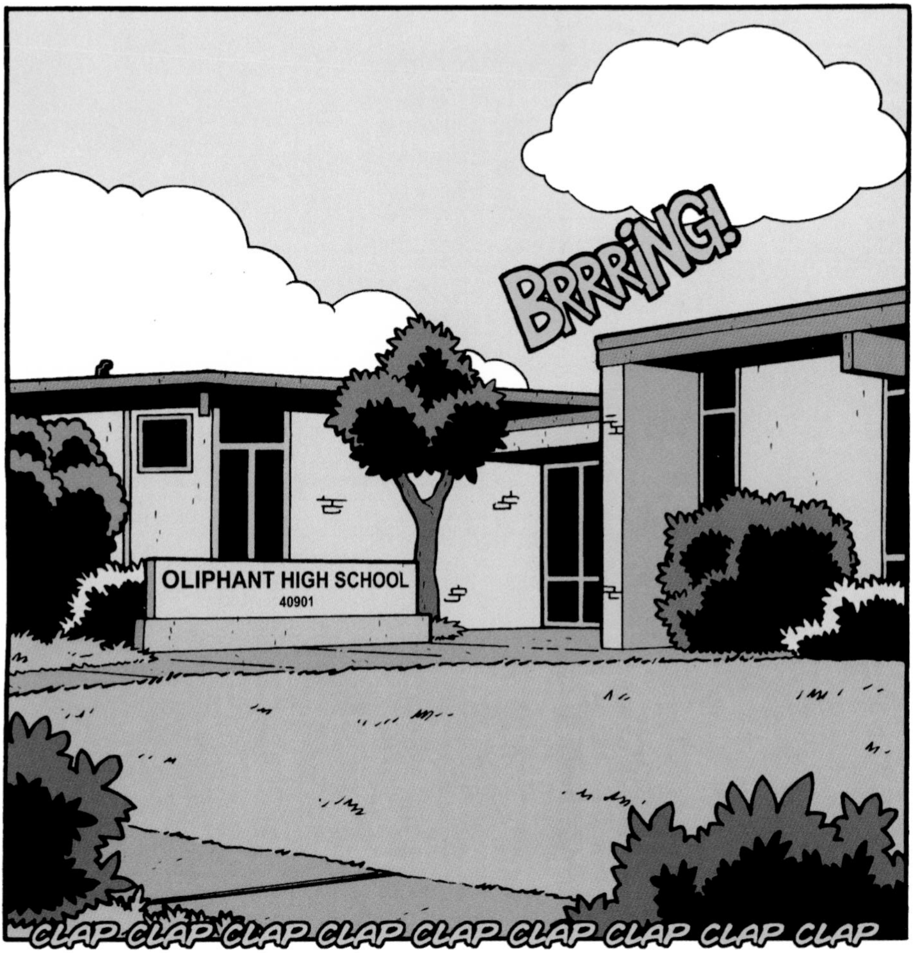
BRRRING!
OLIPHANT HIGH SCHOOL
40901
CLAP CLAP CLAP CLAP CLAP CLAP CLAP CLAP CLAP

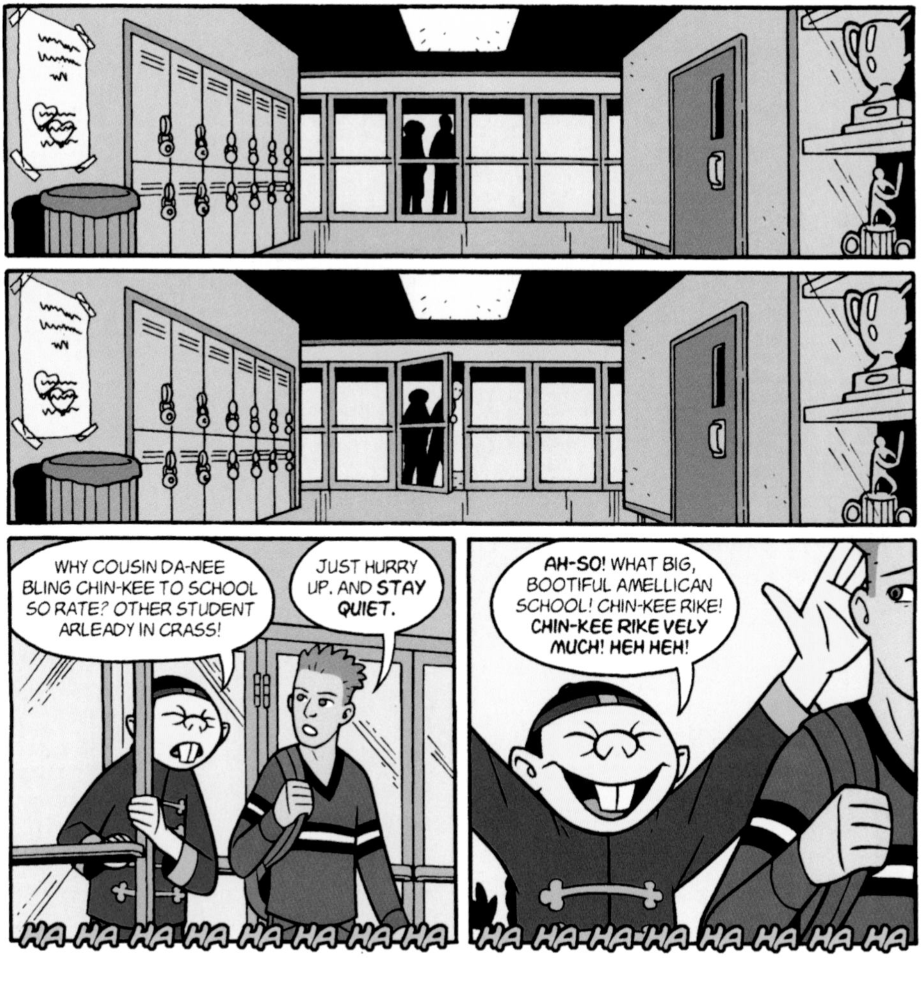
WHY COUSIN DA-NEE BLING CHIN-KEE TO SCHOOL SO RATE? OTHER STUDENT ARLEADY IN CRASS!
JUST HURRY UP. AND STAY QUIET.
HA HA HA HA HA HA HA HA
AH-SO! WHAT BIG, BOOTIFUL AMELLICAN SCHOOL! CHIN-KEE RIKE! CHIN-KEE RIKE VELY MUCH! HEH HEH!
HA HA HA HA HA HA HA HA

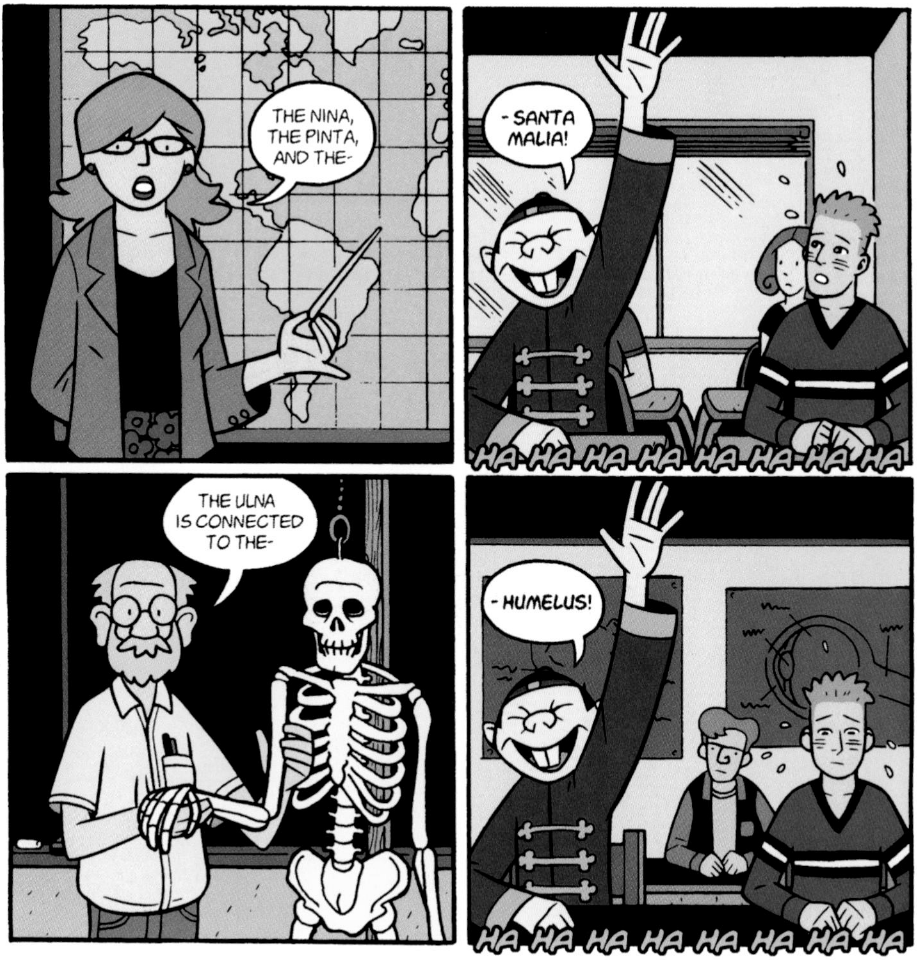
THE NINA, THE PINTA, AND THE-
- SANTA MALIA!
HA HA HA HA HA HA HA HA
THE ULNA IS CONNECTED TO THE-
- HUMELUS!
HA HA HA HA HA HA HA HA

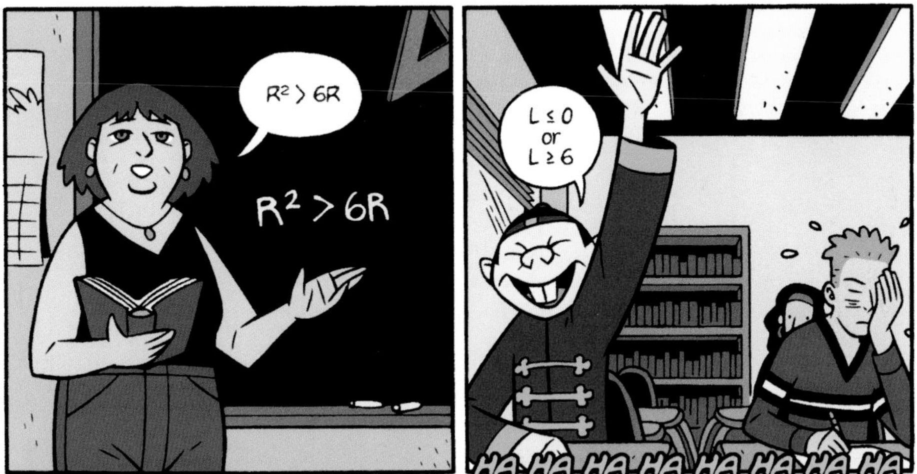
$R^2 > 6R$
$R^2 > 6R$
$L \le 0$ or $L \ge 6$
HA HA HA HA HA HA HA HA
EN ESTA HISTORIA, EL PERRO DE JOSÉ ES-
ESPAÑA
-BRANCO Y MUY GLANDE!
¡MUY BIEN¡
HA HA HA HA HA HA HA HA

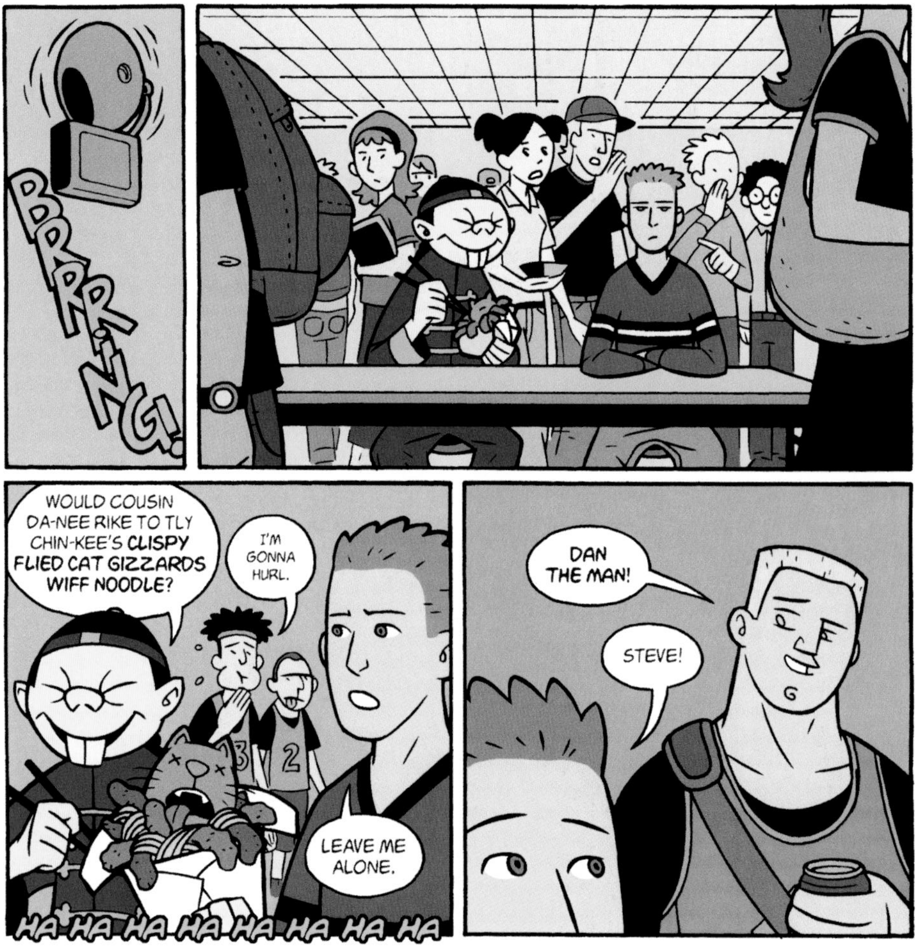
BRRRING!
WOULD COUSIN DA-NEE RIKE TO TLY CHIN-KEE'S CLISPY FLIED CAT GIZZARDS WIFF NOODLE?
I'M GONNA HURL.
LEAVE ME ALONE.
HA HA HA HA HA HA HA HA
DAN THE MAN!
STEVE!

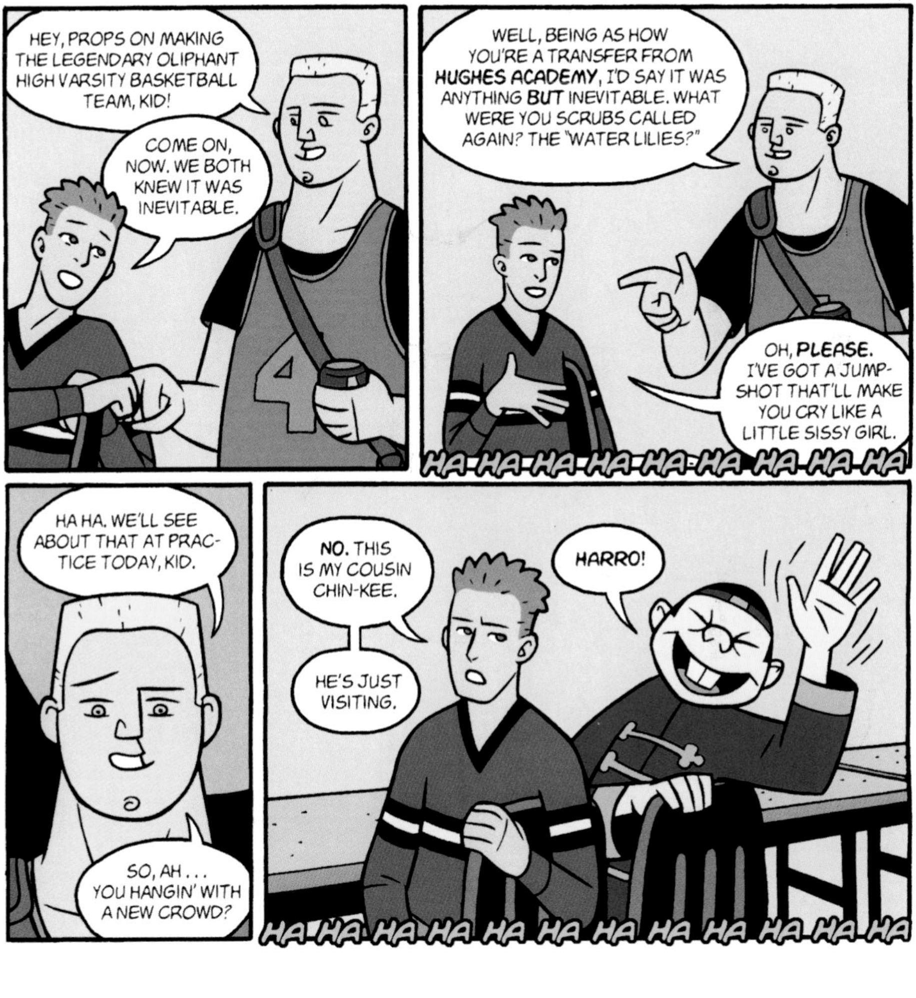
HEY, PROPS ON MAKING THE LEGENDARY OLIPHANT HIGH VARSITY BASKETBALL TEAM, KID!
COME ON, NOW. WE BOTH KNEW IT WAS INEVITABLE.
WELL, BEING AS HOW YOU'RE A TRANSFER FROM HUGHES ACADEMY, I'D SAY IT WAS ANYTHING BUT INEVITABLE. WHAT WERE YOU SCRUBS CALLED AGAIN? THE "WATER LILIES?"
OH, PLEASE. I'VE GOT A JUMP-SHOT THAT'LL MAKE YOU CRY LIKE A LITTLE SISSY GIRL.
HA HA HA HA HA HA HA HA HA
HA HA. WE'LL SEE ABOUT THAT AT PRAC-TICE TODAY, KID.
SO, AH . . . YOU HANGIN' WITH A NEW CROWD?
NO. THIS IS MY COUSIN CHIN-KEE.
HE'S JUST VISITING.
HARRO!
HA HA HA HA HA HA HA HA HA HA HA HA

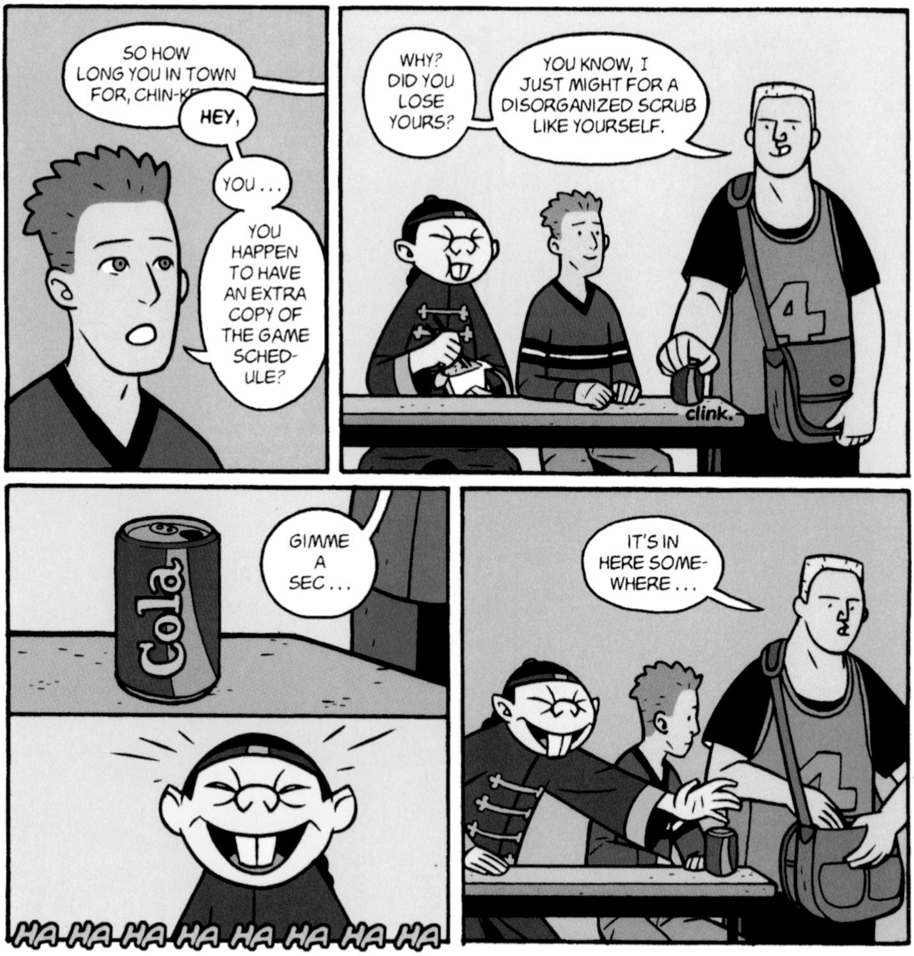
SO HOW LONG YOU IN TOWN FOR, CHIN-K
HEY,
YOU . . .
YOU HAPPEN TO HAVE AN EXTRA COPY OF THE GAME SCHED-ULE?
YOU KNOW, I JUST MIGHT FOR A DISORGANIZED SCRUB LIKE YOURSELF.
WHY? DID YOU LOSE YOURS?
clink.
Cola
GIMME A SEC . . .
HA HA HA HA HA HA HA HA
IT'S IN HERE SOME-WHERE . . .

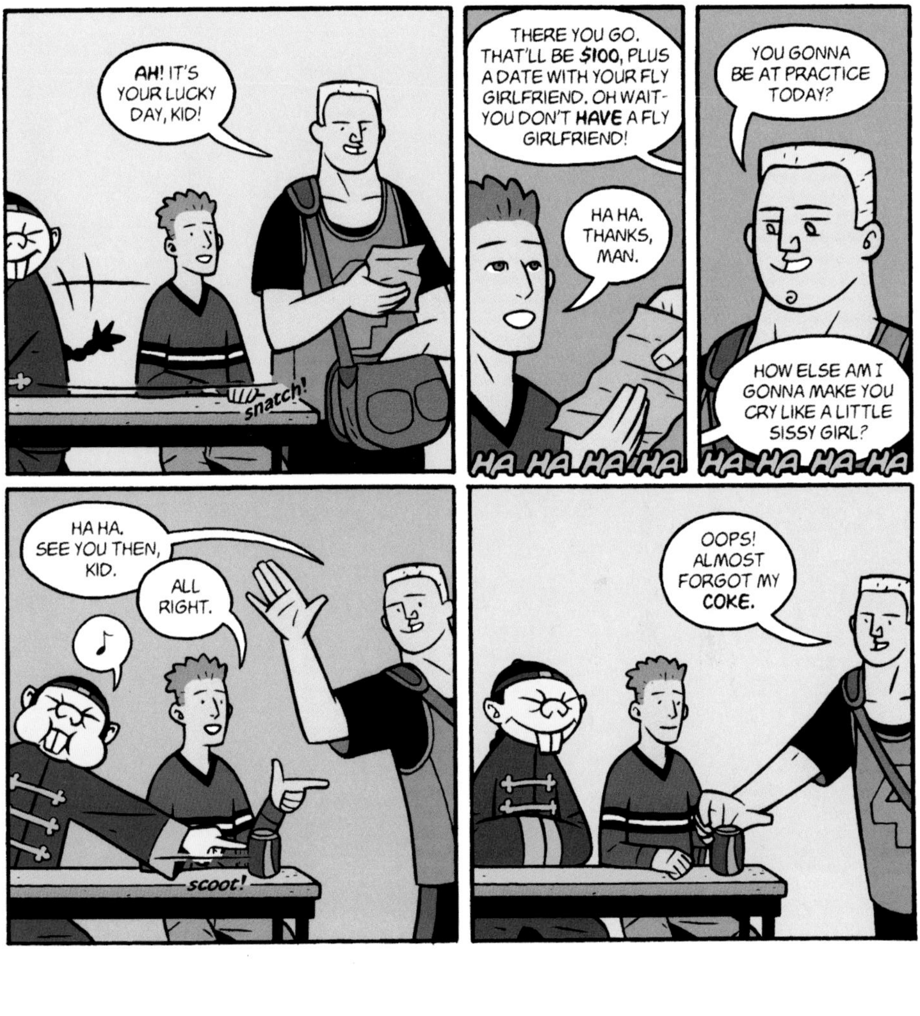
AH! IT'S YOUR LUCKY DAY, KID!
snatch!
THERE YOU GO. THAT'LL BE $100, PLUS A DATE WITH YOUR FLY GIRLFRIEND. OH WAIT- YOU DON'T HAVE A FLY GIRLFRIEND!
HA HA. THANKS, MAN.
HA HA HA HA
YOU GONNA BE AT PRACTICE TODAY?
HOW ELSE AM I GONNA MAKE YOU CRY LIKE A LITTLE SISSY GIRL?
HA HA HA HA
HA HA. SEE YOU THEN, KID.
ALL RIGHT.
♪
scoot!
OOPS! ALMOST FORGOT MY COKE.

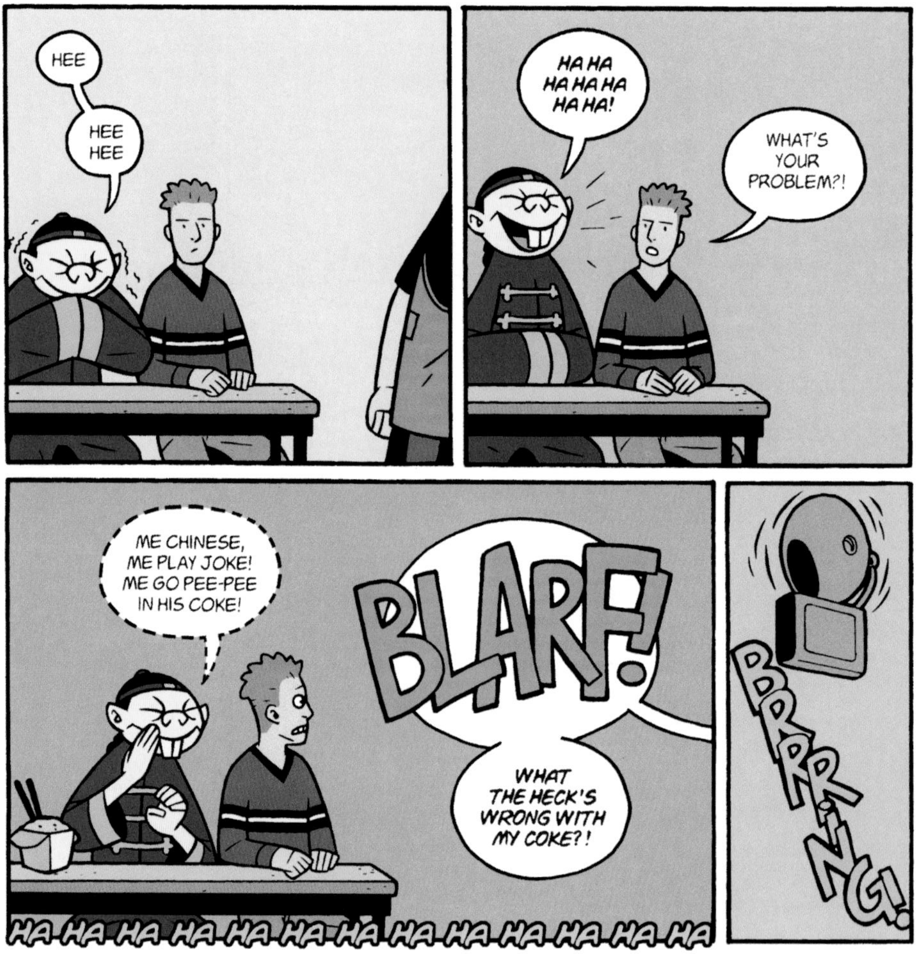
HEE
HEE HEE
HA HA HA HA HA HA HA!
WHAT'S YOUR PROBLEM?!
ME CHINESE, ME PLAY JOKE! ME GO PEE-PEE IN HIS COKE!
BLARF!
WHAT THE HECK'S WRONG WITH MY COKE?!
HA HA HA HA HA HA HA HA HA HA HA HA HA
BRRRING!

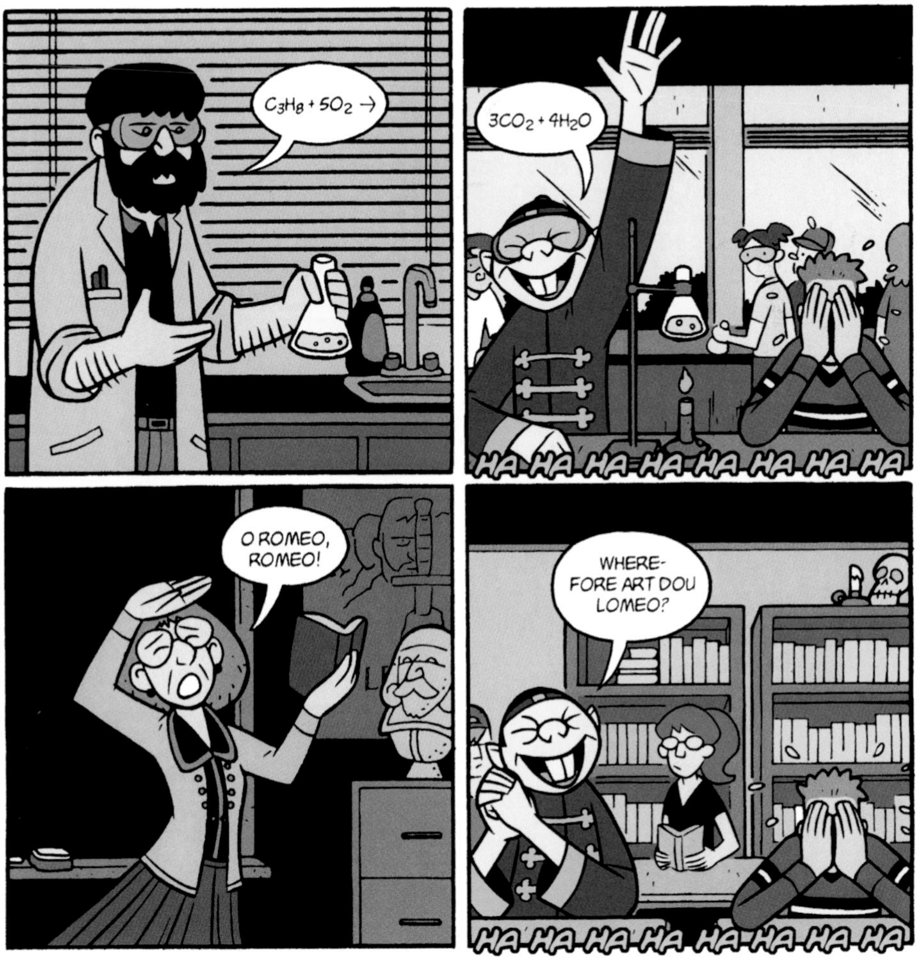
$C_3H_8 + 5O_2 \rightarrow$
$3CO_2 + 4H_2O$
HA HA HA HA HA HA HA HA
O ROMEO, ROMEO!
WHERE-FORE ART DOU LOMEO?
HA HA HA HA HA HA HA HA

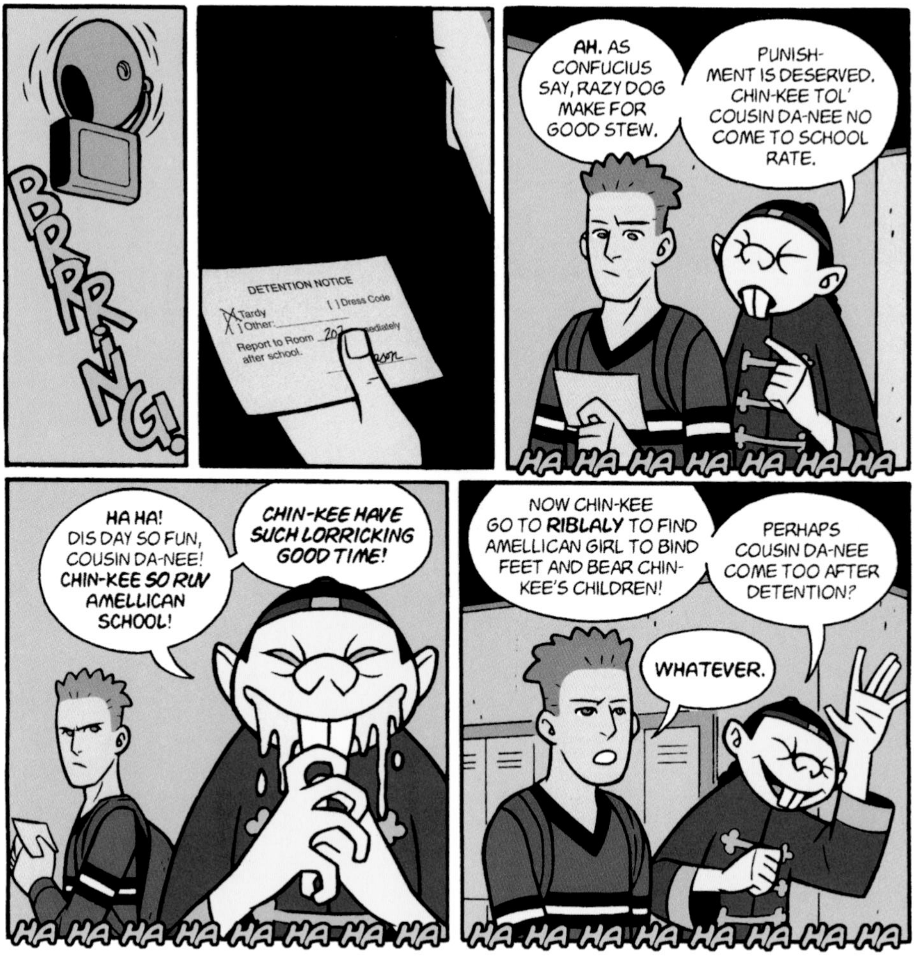
BRRRiNG!
DETENTION NOTICE
Tardy
[ ] Dress Code
Other:
Report to Room
after school.
AH. AS CONFUCIUS SAY, RAZY DOG MAKE FOR GOOD STEW.
PUNISHMENT IS DESERVED. CHIN-KEE TOL' COUSIN DA-NEE NO COME TO SCHOOL RATE.
HA HA HA HA HA HA HA
HA HA! DIS DAY SO FUN, COUSIN DA-NEE! CHIN-KEE SO RUV AMELLICAN SCHOOL!
CHIN-KEE HAVE SUCH LORRICKING GOOD TIME!
HA HA HA HA HA HA HA HA
NOW CHIN-KEE GO TO RIBLALY TO FIND AMELLICAN GIRL TO BIND FEET AND BEAR CHIN-KEE'S CHILDREN!
PERHAPS COUSIN DA-NEE COME TOO AFTER DETENTION?
WHATEVER.
HA HA HA HA HA HA HA HA

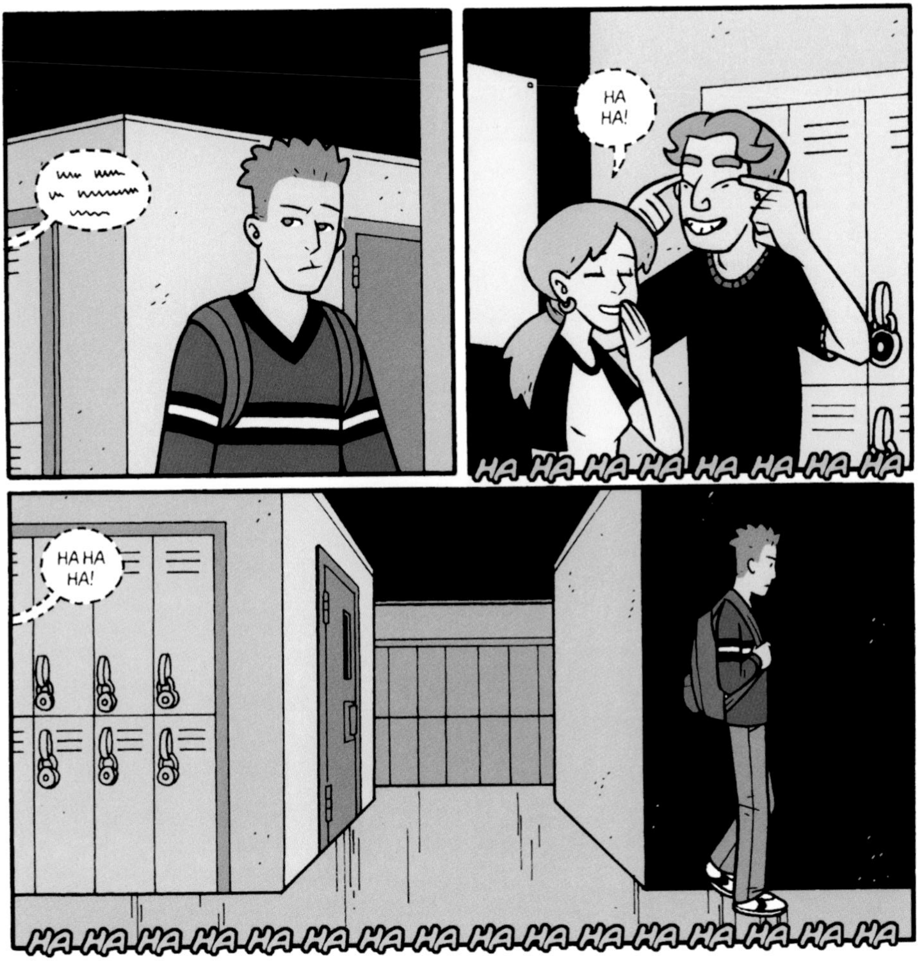
HA HA!
HA HA HA HA HA HA HA HA
HA HA HA!
HA HA HA HA HA HA HA HA HA HA HA HA HA HA HA HA

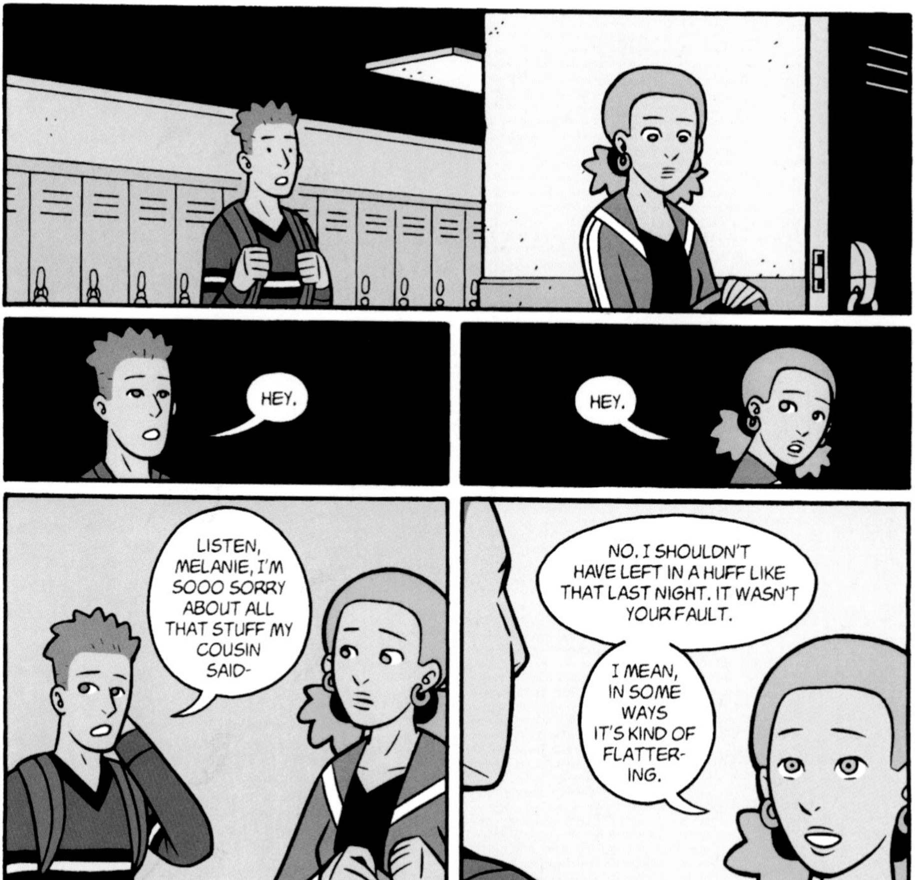
HEY.
HEY.
LISTEN, MELANIE, I'M SOOO SORRY ABOUT ALL THAT STUFF MY COUSIN SAID-
NO. I SHOULDN'T HAVE LEFT IN A HUFF LIKE THAT LAST NIGHT. IT WASN'T YOUR FAULT.
I MEAN, IN SOME WAYS IT'S KIND OF FLATTER-ING.
HA HA HA HA HA HA HA HA

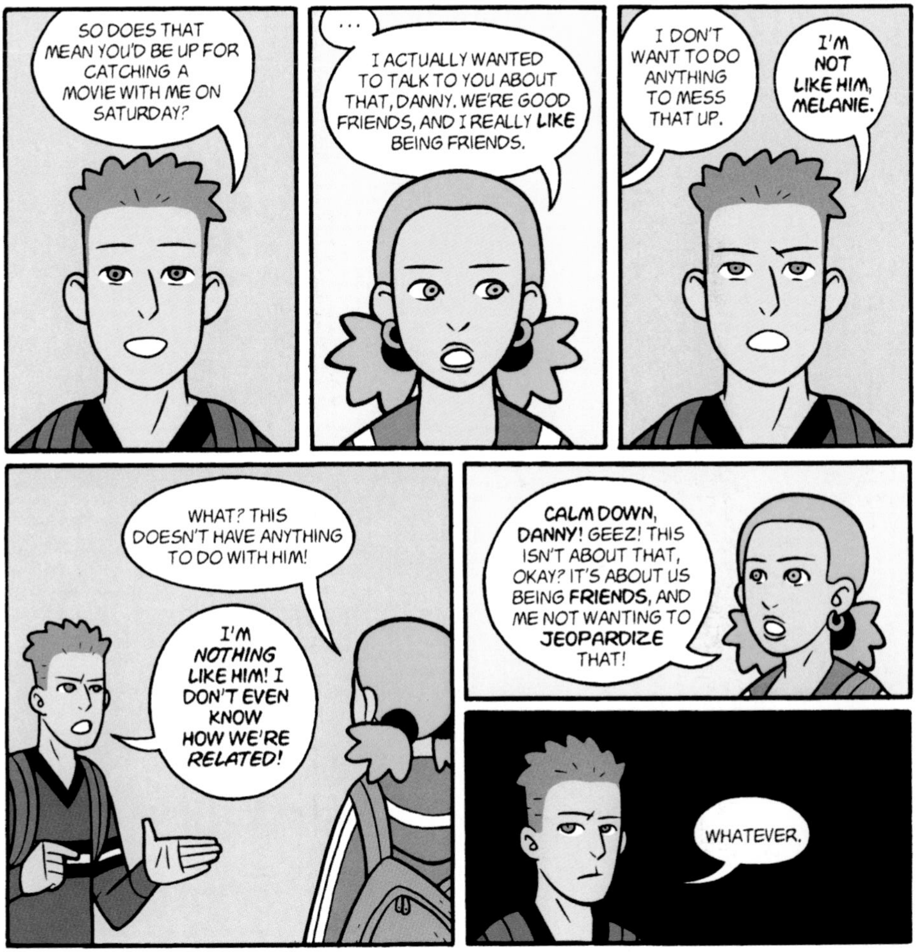

SO DOES THAT MEAN YOU'D BE UP FOR CATCHING A MOVIE WITH ME ON SATURDAY?
...
I ACTUALLY WANTED TO TALK TO YOU ABOUT THAT, DANNY. WE'RE GOOD FRIENDS, AND I REALLY LIKE BEING FRIENDS.
I DON'T WANT TO DO ANYTHING TO MESS THAT UP.
I'M NOT LIKE HIM, MELANIE.
WHAT? THIS DOESN'T HAVE ANYTHING TO DO WITH HIM!
I'M NOTHING LIKE HIM! I DON'T EVEN KNOW HOW WE'RE RELATED!
CALM DOWN, DANNY! GEEZ! THIS ISN'T ABOUT THAT, OKAY? IT'S ABOUT US BEING FRIENDS, AND ME NOT WANTING TO JEOPARDIZE THAT!
WHATEVER.

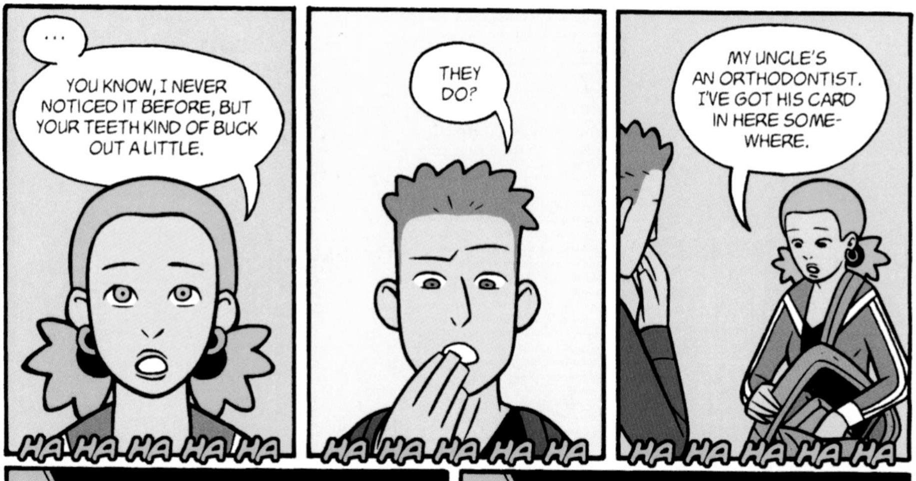
...
YOU KNOW, I NEVER NOTICED IT BEFORE, BUT YOUR TEETH KIND OF BUCK OUT A LITTLE.
HA HA HA HA HA
THEY DO?
HA HA HA HA HA
MY UNCLE'S AN ORTHODONTIST. I'VE GOT HIS CARD IN HERE SOME-WHERE.
HA HA HA HA HA
GIVE HIM A CALL. HE'LL BE ABLE TO HELP YOU OUT.
HA HA HA HA HA HA HA HA
I'LL SEE YOU AROUND, OKAY?

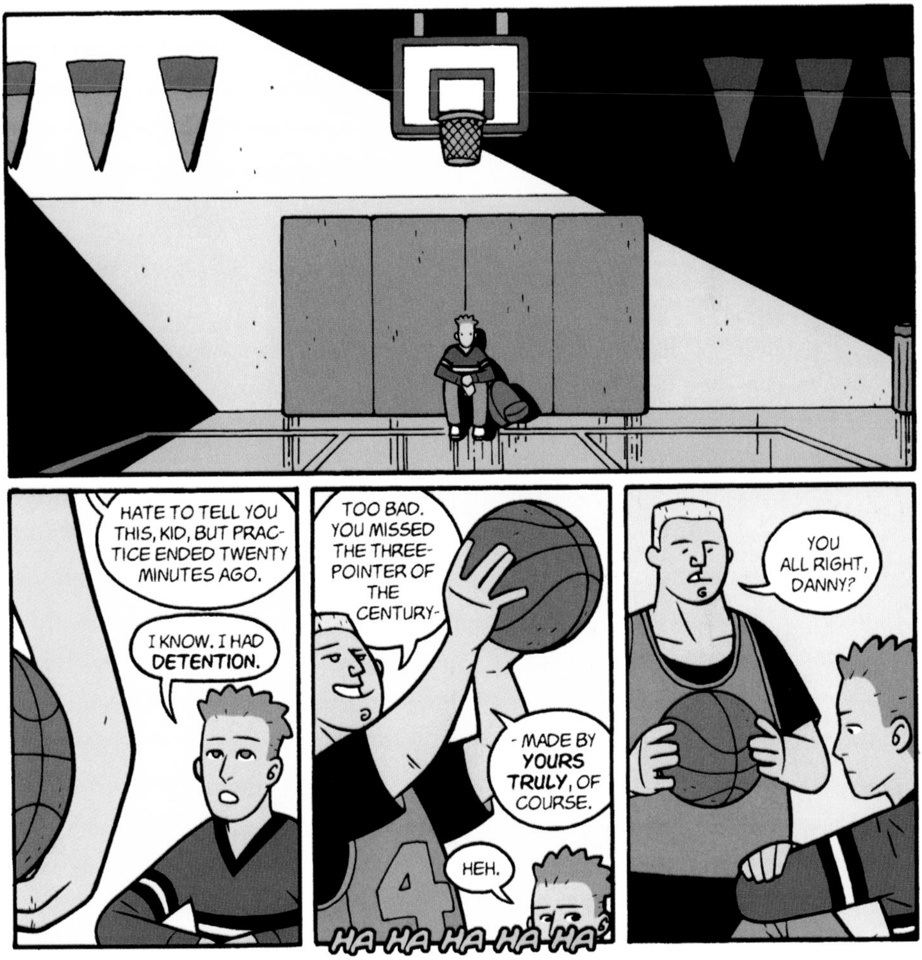
HATE TO TELL YOU THIS, KID, BUT PRAC-TICE ENDED TWENTY MINUTES AGO.
I KNOW. I HAD DETENTION.
TOO BAD. YOU MISSED THE THREE-POINTER OF THE CENTURY-
- MADE BY YOURS TRULY, OF COURSE.
HEH.
HA HA HA HA HA
YOU ALL RIGHT, DANNY?

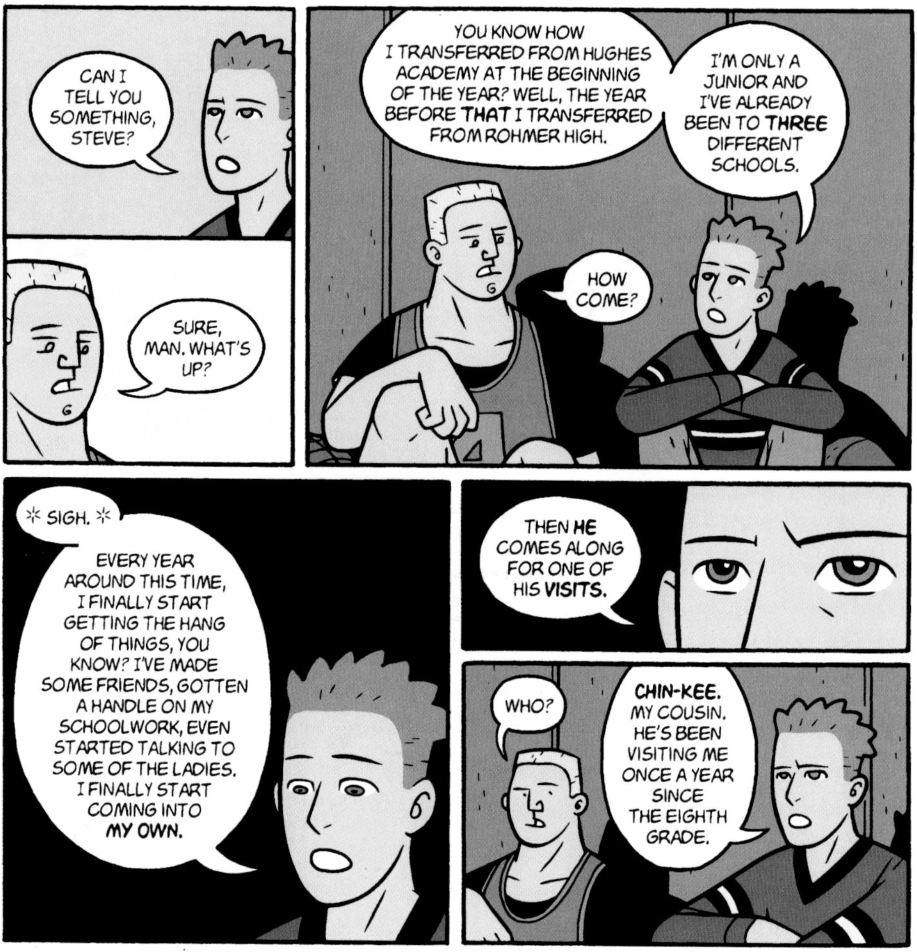
CAN I TELL YOU SOMETHING, STEVE?
SURE, MAN. WHAT'S UP?
YOU KNOW HOW I TRANSFERRED FROM HUGHES ACADEMY AT THE BEGINNING OF THE YEAR? WELL, THE YEAR BEFORE THAT I TRANSFERRED FROM ROHMER HIGH.
I'M ONLY A JUNIOR AND I'VE ALREADY BEEN TO THREE DIFFERENT SCHOOLS.
HOW COME?
SIGH.
EVERY YEAR AROUND THIS TIME, I FINALLY START GETTING THE HANG OF THINGS, YOU KNOW? I'VE MADE SOME FRIENDS, GOTTEN A HANDLE ON MY SCHOOLWORK, EVEN STARTED TALKING TO SOME OF THE LADIES. I FINALLY START COMING INTO MY OWN.
THEN HE COMES ALONG FOR ONE OF HIS VISITS.
WHO?
CHIN-KEE. MY COUSIN. HE'S BEEN VISITING ME ONCE A YEAR SINCE THE EIGHTH GRADE.

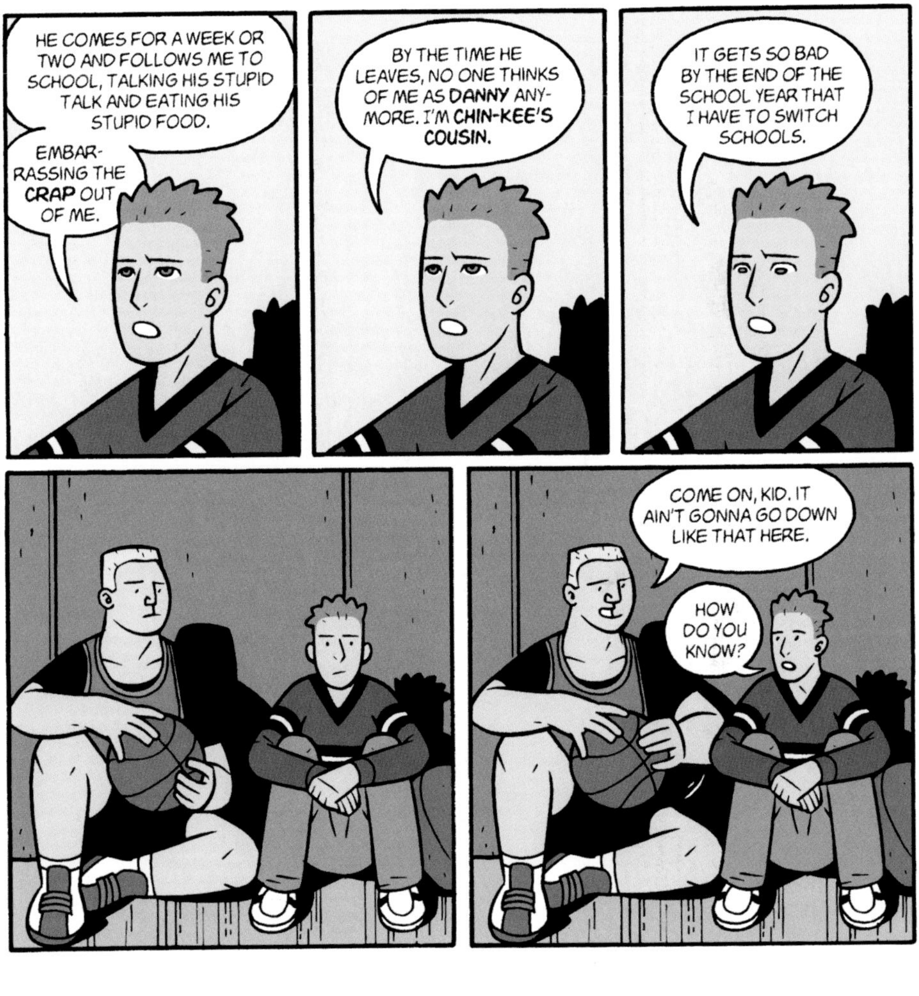
HE COMES FOR A WEEK OR TWO AND FOLLOWS ME TO SCHOOL, TALKING HIS STUPID TALK AND EATING HIS STUPID FOOD.
EMBAR-RASSING THE **CRAP** OUT OF ME.
BY THE TIME HE LEAVES, NO ONE THINKS OF ME AS **DANNY** ANY-MORE. I'M **CHIN-KEE'S COUSIN.**
IT GETS SO BAD BY THE END OF THE SCHOOL YEAR THAT I HAVE TO SWITCH SCHOOLS.
COME ON, KID. IT AIN'T GONNA GO DOWN LIKE THAT HERE.
HOW DO YOU KNOW?

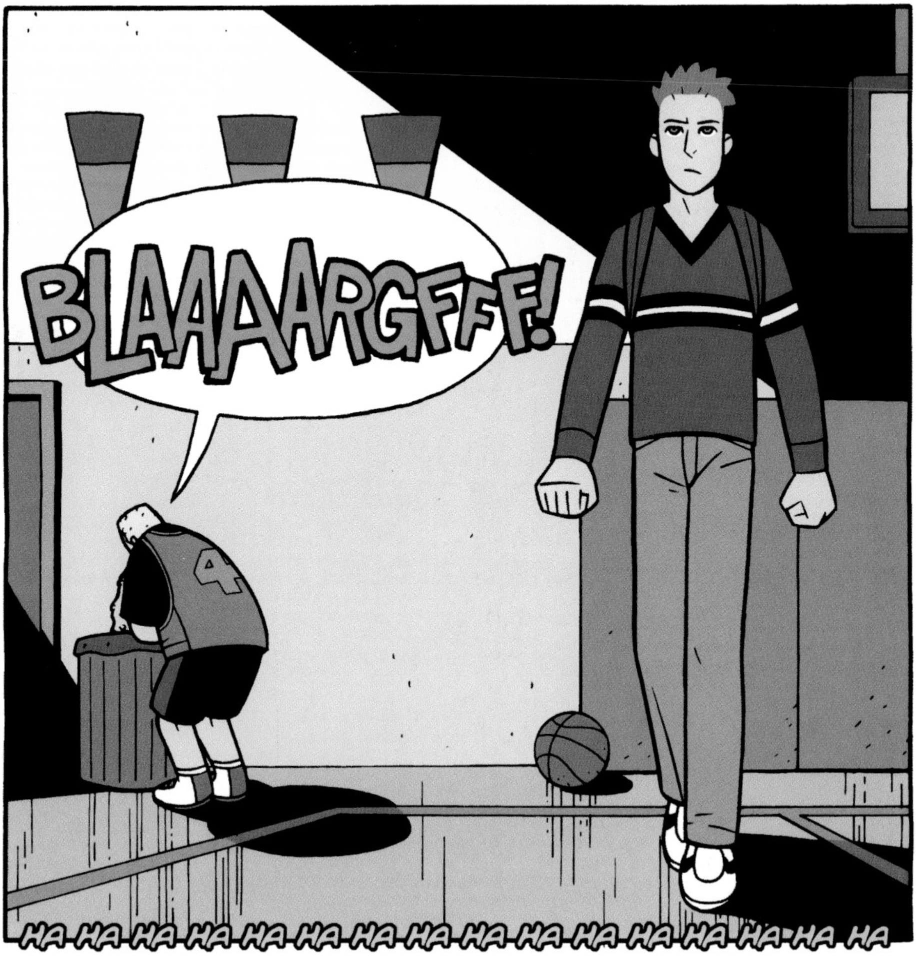
BLAAAARGFFF!
HA HA HA HA HA HA HA HA HA HA HA HA HA HA HA HA

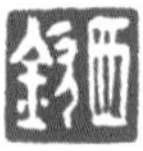

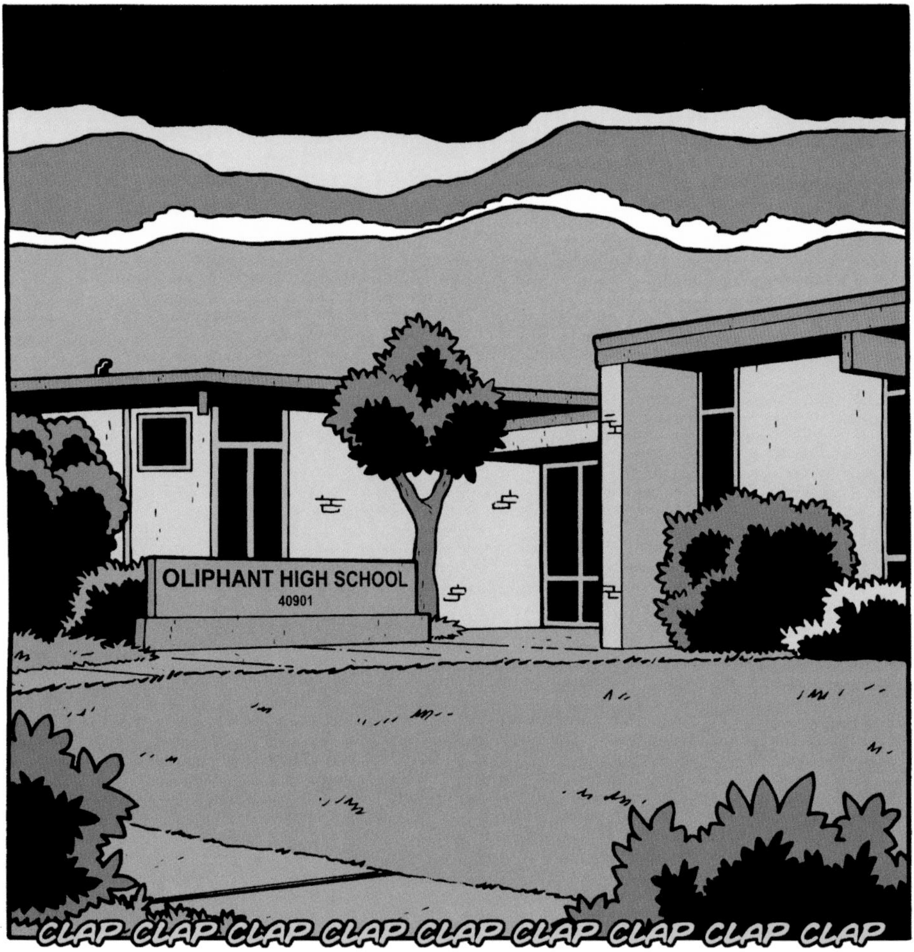
OLIPHANT HIGH SCHOOL
40901
CLAP CLAP CLAP CLAP CLAP CLAP CLAP CLAP CLAP

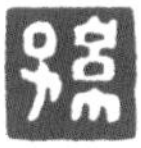

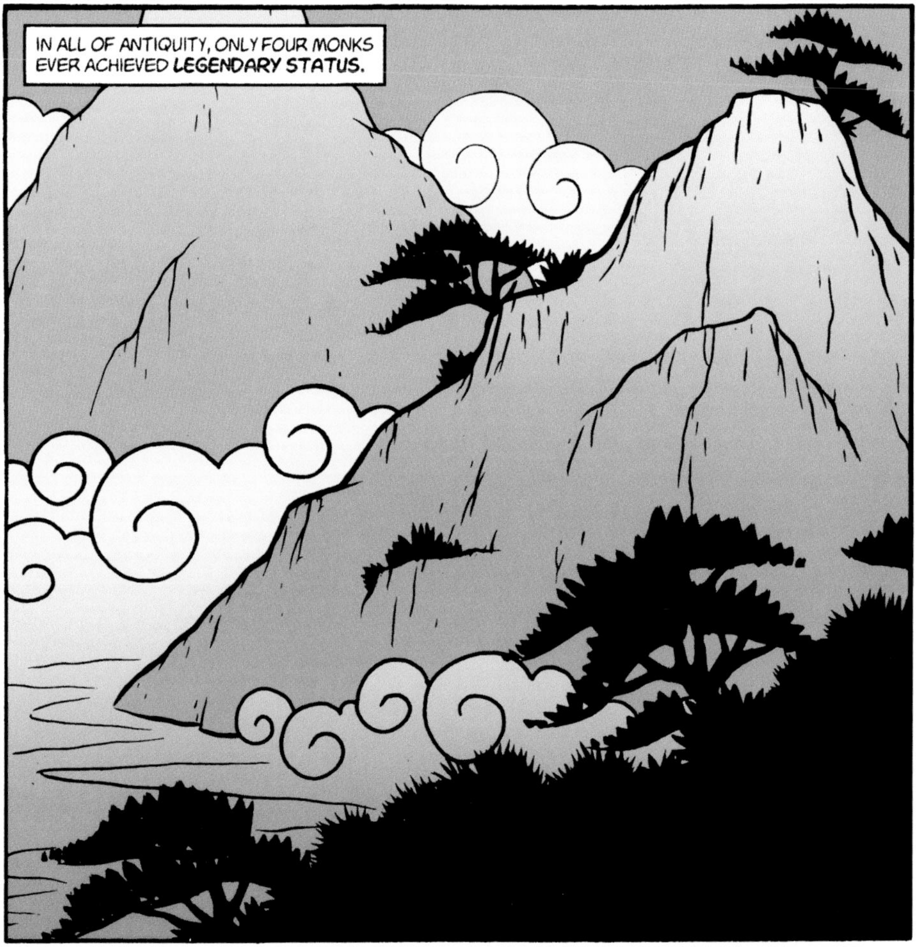
IN ALL OF ANTIQUITY, ONLY FOUR MONKS EVER ACHIEVED LEGENDARY STATUS.

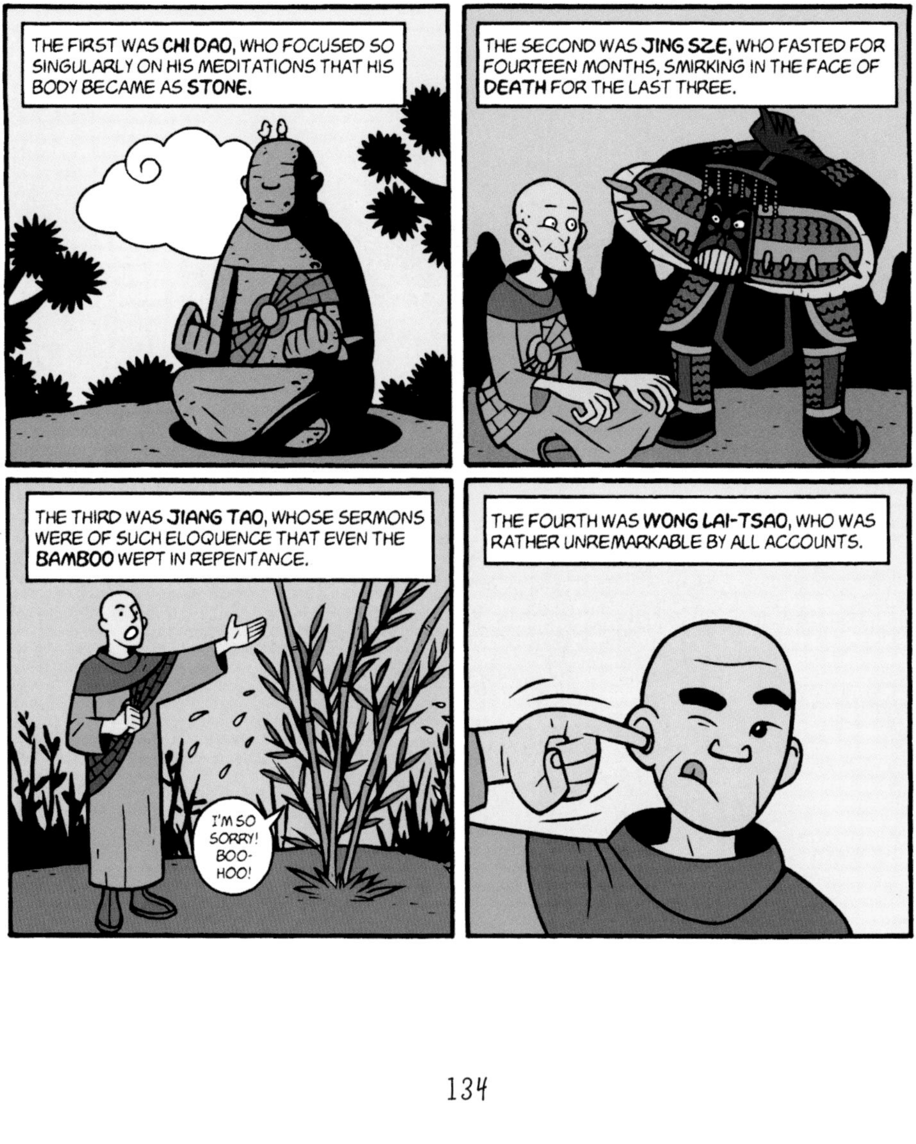
THE FIRST WAS CHI DAO, WHO FOCUSED SO SINGULARLY ON HIS MEDITATIONS THAT HIS BODY BECAME AS STONE.
THE SECOND WAS JING SZE, WHO FASTED FOR FOURTEEN MONTHS, SMIRKING IN THE FACE OF DEATH FOR THE LAST THREE.
THE THIRD WAS JIANG TAO, WHOSE SERMONS WERE OF SUCH ELOQUENCE THAT EVEN THE BAMBOO WEPT IN REPENTANCE.
I'M SO SORRY! BOO-HOO!
THE FOURTH WAS WONG LAI-TSAO, WHO WAS RATHER UNREMARKABLE BY ALL ACCOUNTS.

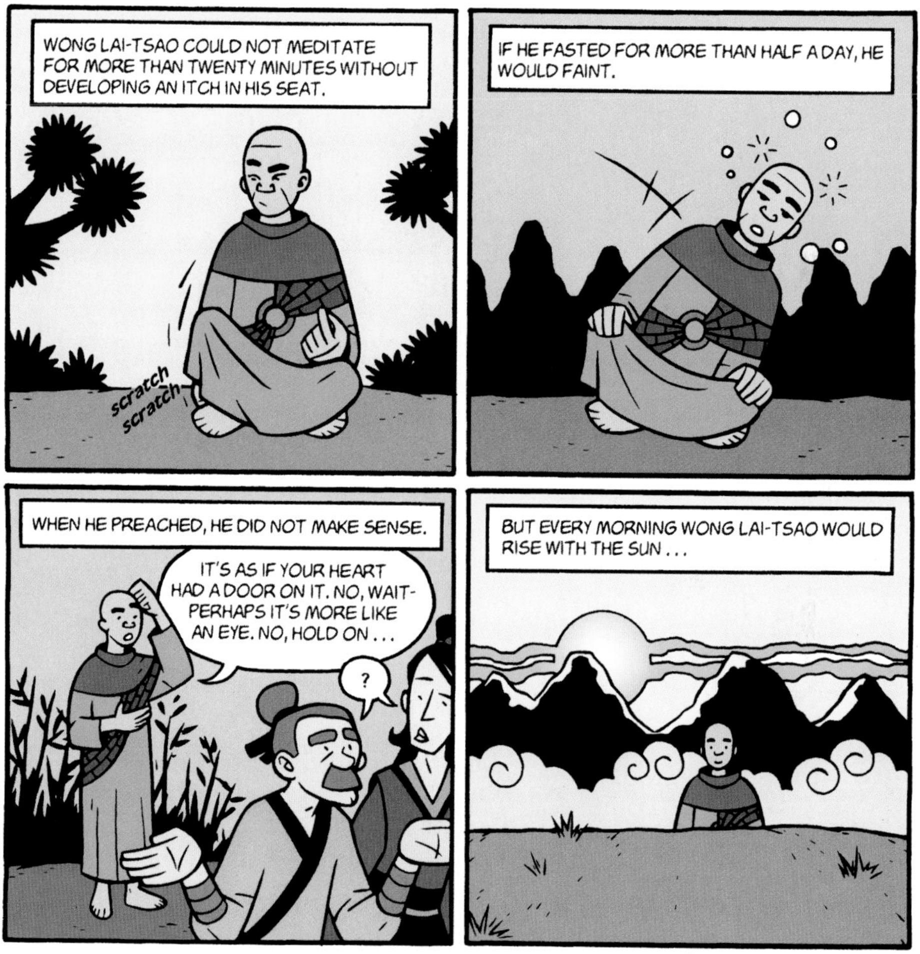
WONG LAI-TSAO COULD NOT MEDITATE FOR MORE THAN TWENTY MINUTES WITHOUT DEVELOPING AN ITCH IN HIS SEAT.
scratch scratch
IF HE FASTED FOR MORE THAN HALF A DAY, HE WOULD FAINT.
WHEN HE PREACHED, HE DID NOT MAKE SENSE.
IT'S AS IF YOUR HEART HAD A DOOR ON IT. NO, WAIT- PERHAPS IT'S MORE LIKE AN EYE. NO, HOLD ON . . .
?
BUT EVERY MORNING WONG LAI-TSAO WOULD RISE WITH THE SUN . . .

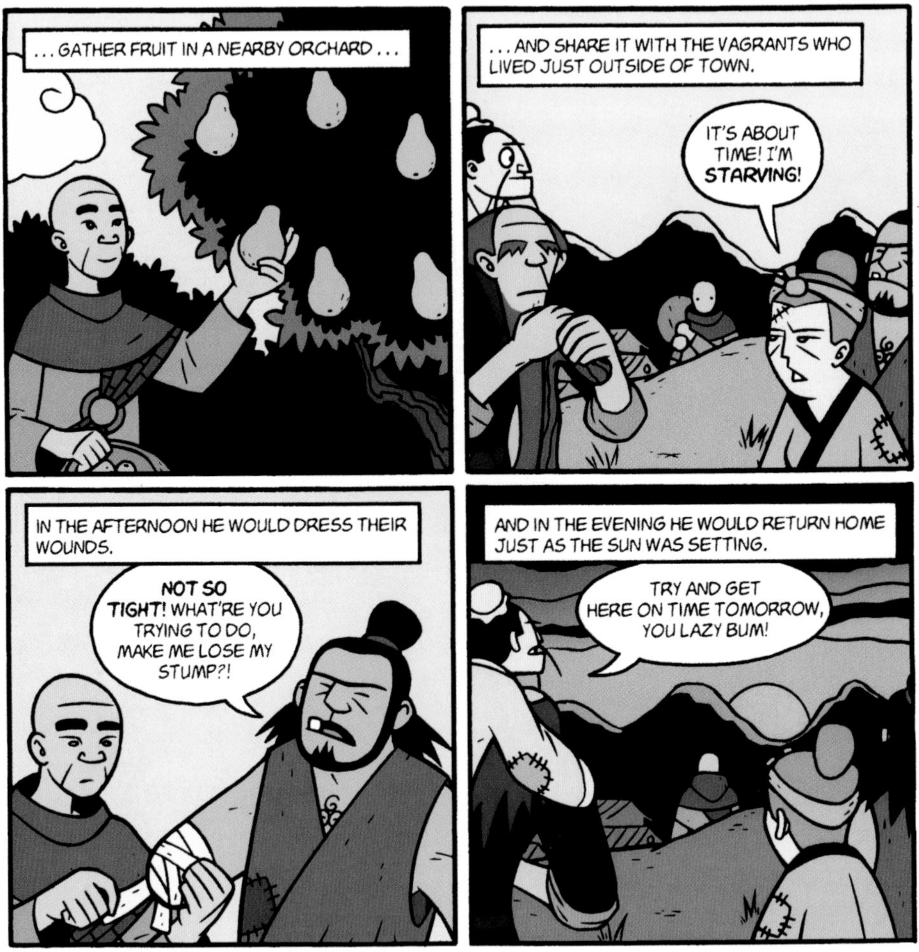

. . . GATHER FRUIT IN A NEARBY ORCHARD . . .
. . . AND SHARE IT WITH THE VAGRANTS WHO LIVED JUST OUTSIDE OF TOWN.
IT'S ABOUT TIME! I'M **STARVING**!
IN THE AFTERNOON HE WOULD DRESS THEIR WOUNDS.
NOT SO TIGHT! WHAT'RE YOU TRYING TO DO, MAKE ME LOSE MY STUMP?!
AND IN THE EVENING HE WOULD RETURN HOME JUST AS THE SUN WAS SETTING.
TRY AND GET HERE ON TIME TOMORROW, YOU LAZY BUM!

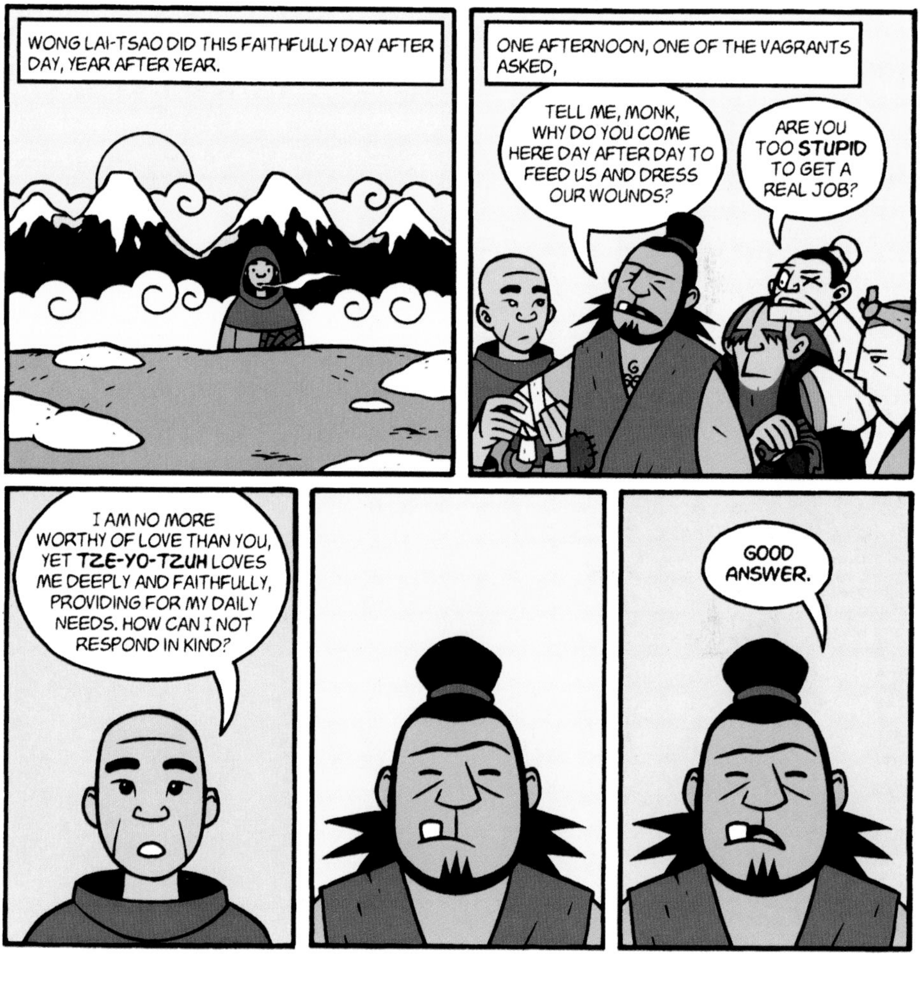
WONG LAI-TSAO DID THIS FAITHFULLY DAY AFTER DAY, YEAR AFTER YEAR.
ONE AFTERNOON, ONE OF THE VAGRANTS ASKED,
TELL ME, MONK, WHY DO YOU COME HERE DAY AFTER DAY TO FEED US AND DRESS OUR WOUNDS?
ARE YOU TOO STUPID TO GET A REAL JOB?
I AM NO MORE WORTHY OF LOVE THAN YOU, YET TZE-YO-TZUH LOVES ME DEEPLY AND FAITHFULLY, PROVIDING FOR MY DAILY NEEDS. HOW CAN I NOT RESPOND IN KIND?
GOOD ANSWER.

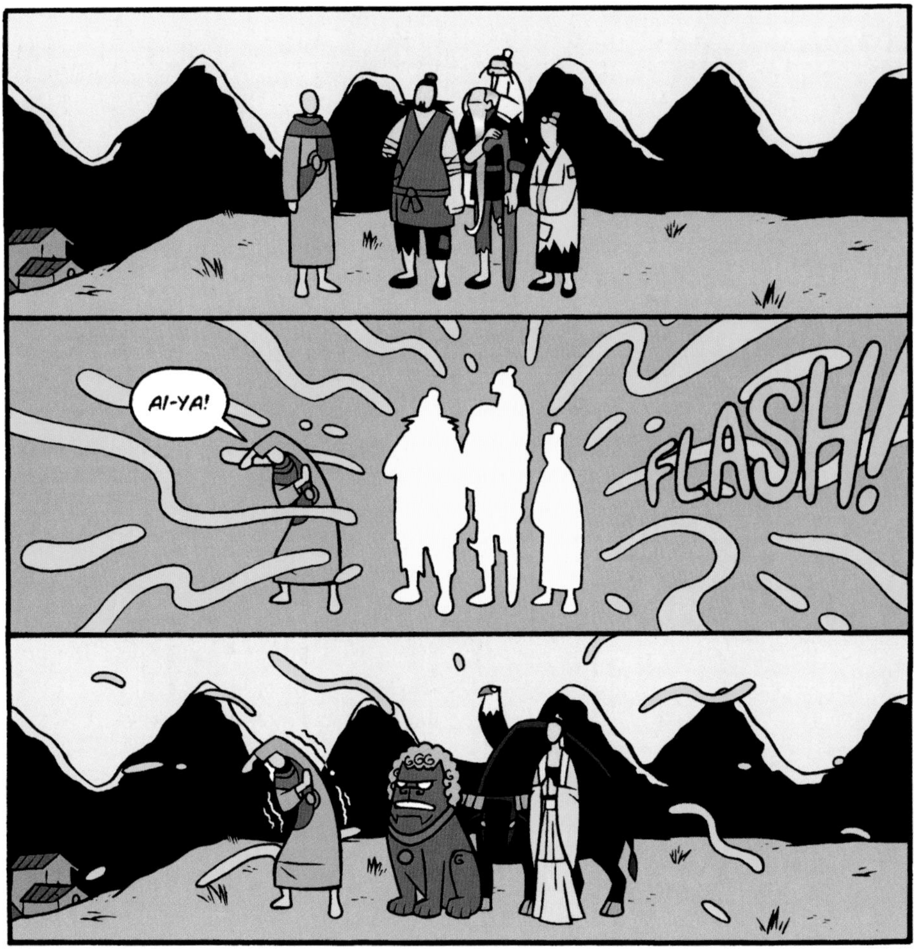
AI-YA!
FLASH!

DO NOT BE **AFRAID**, WONG LAI-TSAO!

WE ARE EMISSARIES OF **TZE-YO-TZUH**, HE WHO WAS, IS, AND SHALL FOREVER BE. TZE-YO-TZUH HAS FOUND FAVOR WITH YOU.

HE HAS CHOSEN YOU FOR A **MISSION**.

YOU SHALL DELIVER THREE PACKAGES TO THE **WEST**. A STAR SHALL GUIDE YOUR WAY.

YOUR JOURNEY WILL NOT BE WITH-OUT PERIL.

IT IS AN OLD WIVES' TALE AMONG DEMONS THAT THE FLESH OF A HOLY MAN CAN GRANT ETERNAL LIFE. ONCE YOU ARE IN THE WILDERNESS, MANY WILL TRY TO EAT YOU.

DO YOU ACCEPT THIS MISSION, WONG LAI-TSAO?

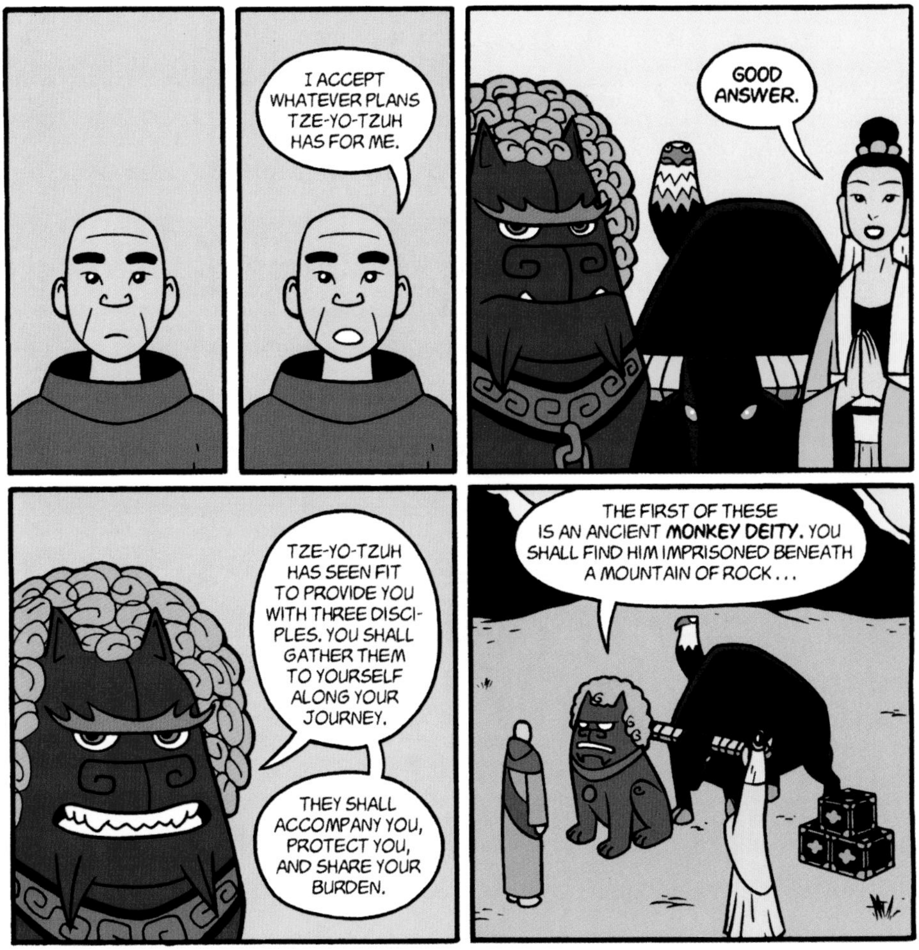
I ACCEPT WHATEVER PLANS TZE-YO-TZUH HAS FOR ME.
GOOD ANSWER.
TZE-YO-TZUH HAS SEEN FIT TO PROVIDE YOU WITH THREE DISCI-PLES. YOU SHALL GATHER THEM TO YOURSELF ALONG YOUR JOURNEY.
THEY SHALL ACCOMPANY YOU, PROTECT YOU, AND SHARE YOUR BURDEN.
THE FIRST OF THESE IS AN ANCIENT **MONKEY DEITY.** YOU SHALL FIND HIM IMPRISONED BENEATH A MOUNTAIN OF ROCK . . .

THE NEXT MORNING, WONG LAI-TSAO ROSE WITH THE SUN AND SET OFF ON HIS MISSION.

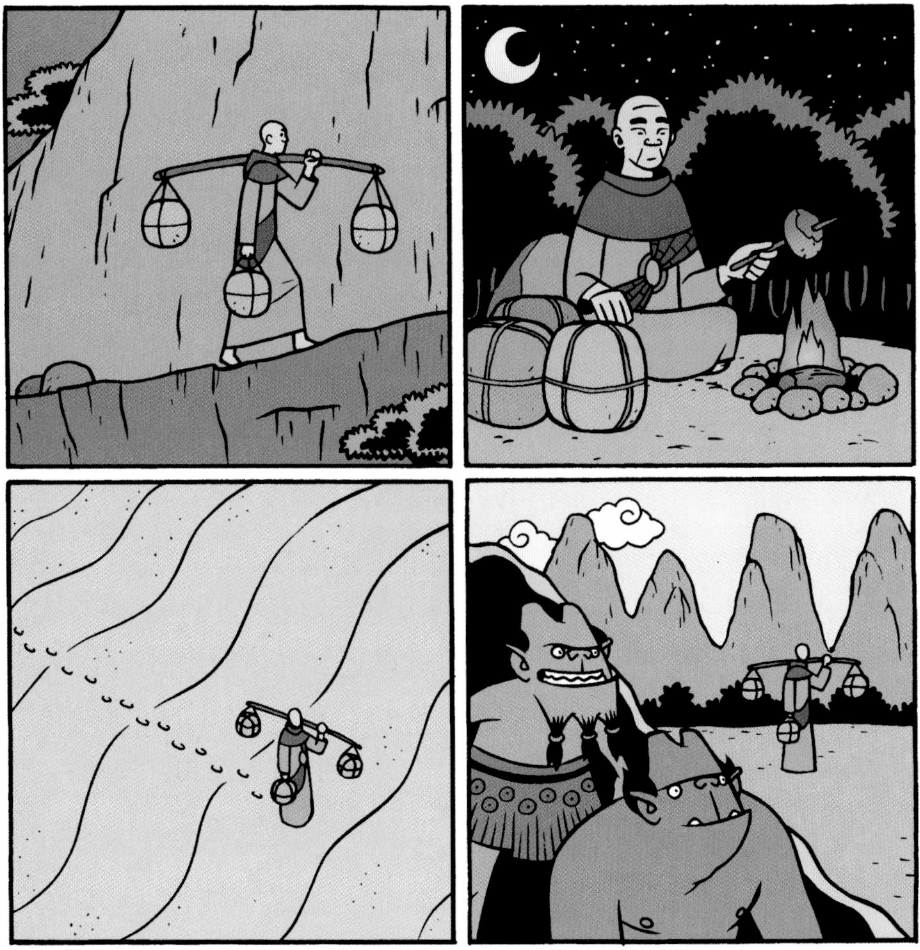

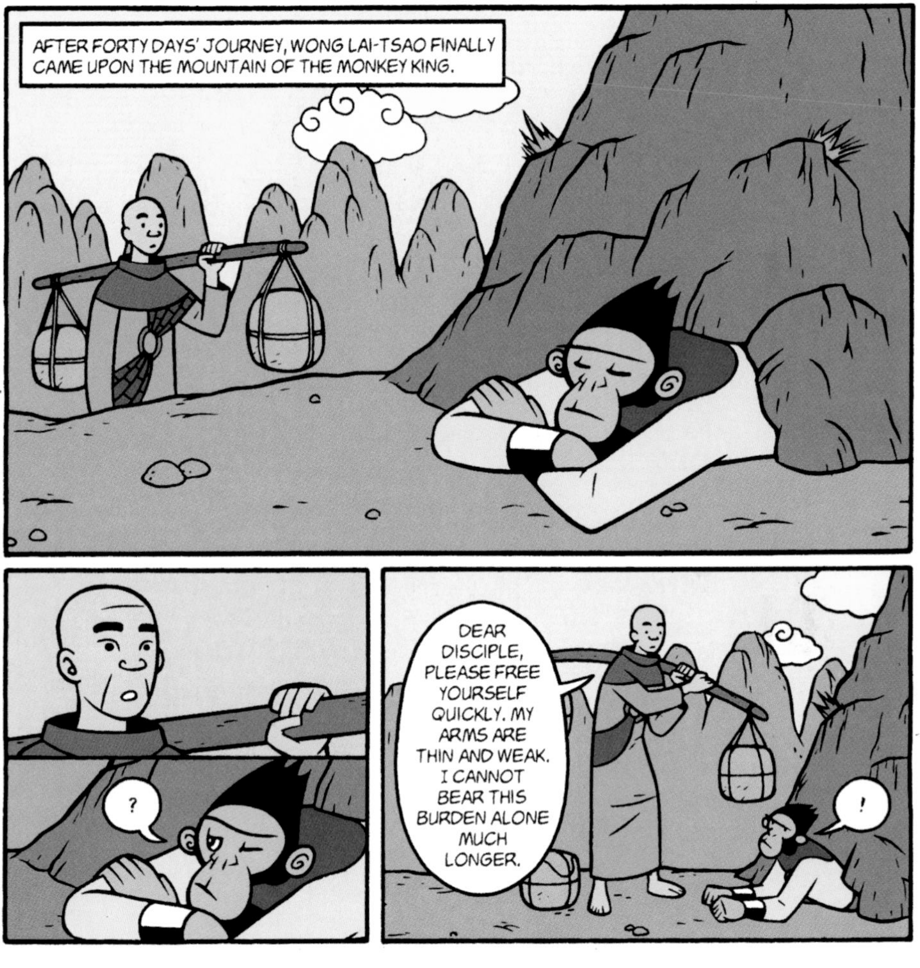
AFTER FORTY DAYS' JOURNEY, WONG LAI-TSAO FINALLY CAME UPON THE MOUNTAIN OF THE MONKEY KING.
?
DEAR DISCIPLE, PLEASE FREE YOURSELF QUICKLY. MY ARMS ARE THIN AND WEAK. I CANNOT BEAR THIS BURDEN ALONE MUCH LONGER.
!

145

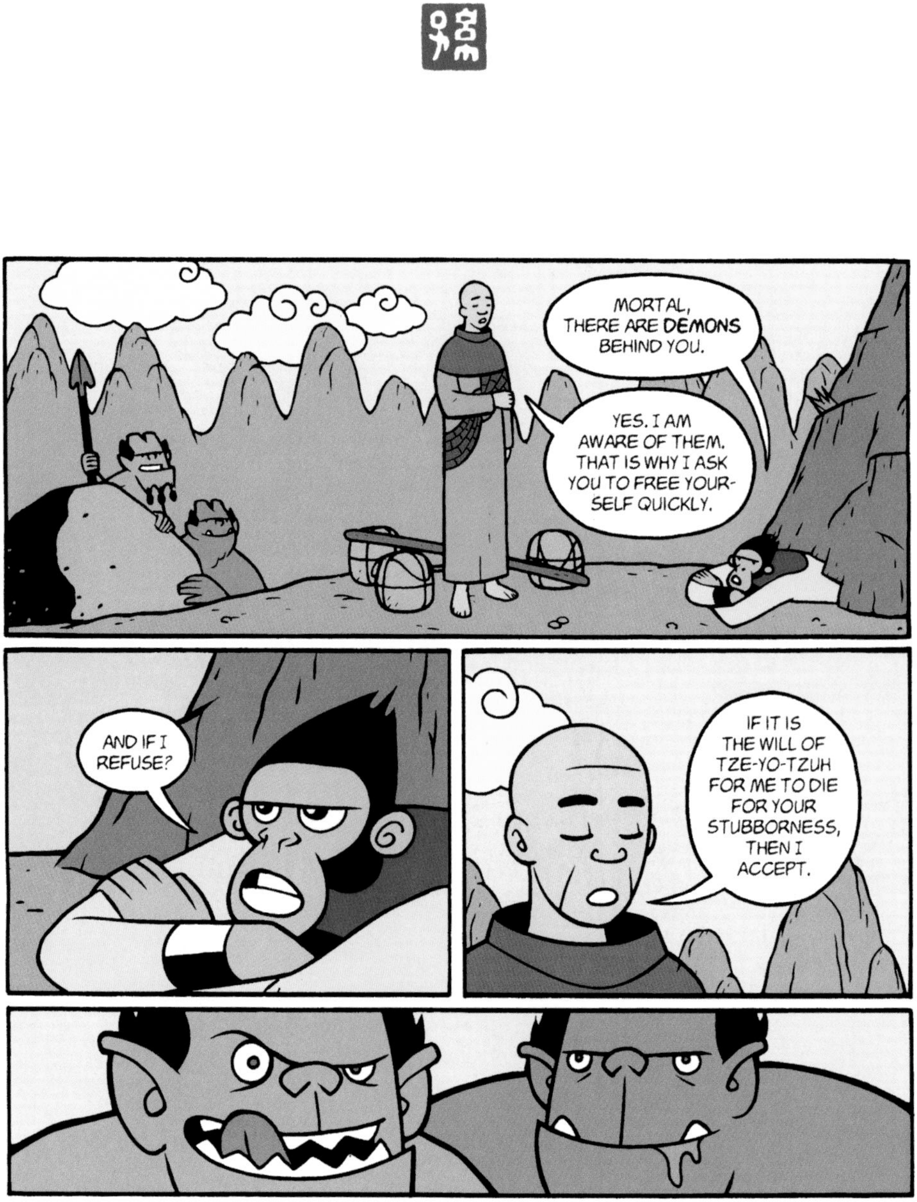
MORTAL, THERE ARE **DEMONS** BEHIND YOU.
YES. I AM AWARE OF THEM. THAT IS WHY I ASK YOU TO FREE YOUR-SELF QUICKLY.
AND IF I REFUSE?
IF IT IS THE WILL OF TZE-YO-TZUH FOR ME TO DIE FOR YOUR STUBBORNESS, THEN I ACCEPT.

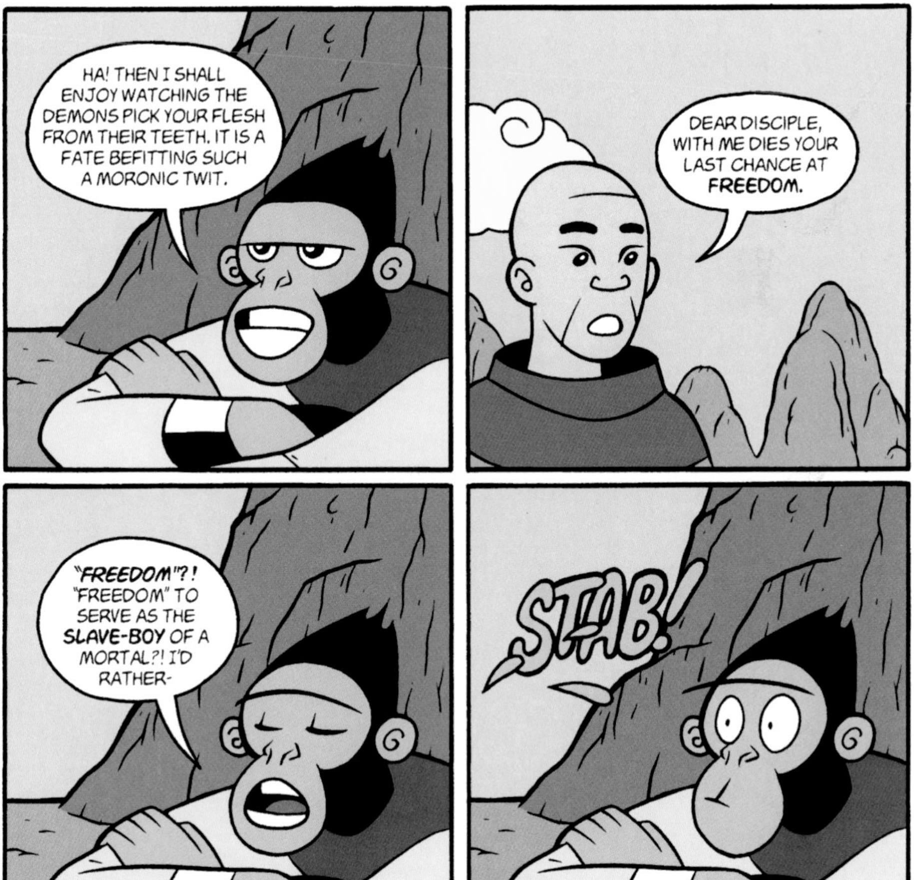
HA! THEN I SHALL ENJOY WATCHING THE DEMONS PICK YOUR FLESH FROM THEIR TEETH. IT IS A FATE BEFITTING SUCH A MORONIC TWIT.
DEAR DISCIPLE, WITH ME DIES YOUR LAST CHANCE AT **FREEDOM.**
"***FREEDOM***"?! "FREEDOM" TO SERVE AS THE **SLAVE-BOY** OF A MORTAL?! I'D RATHER-
STAB!

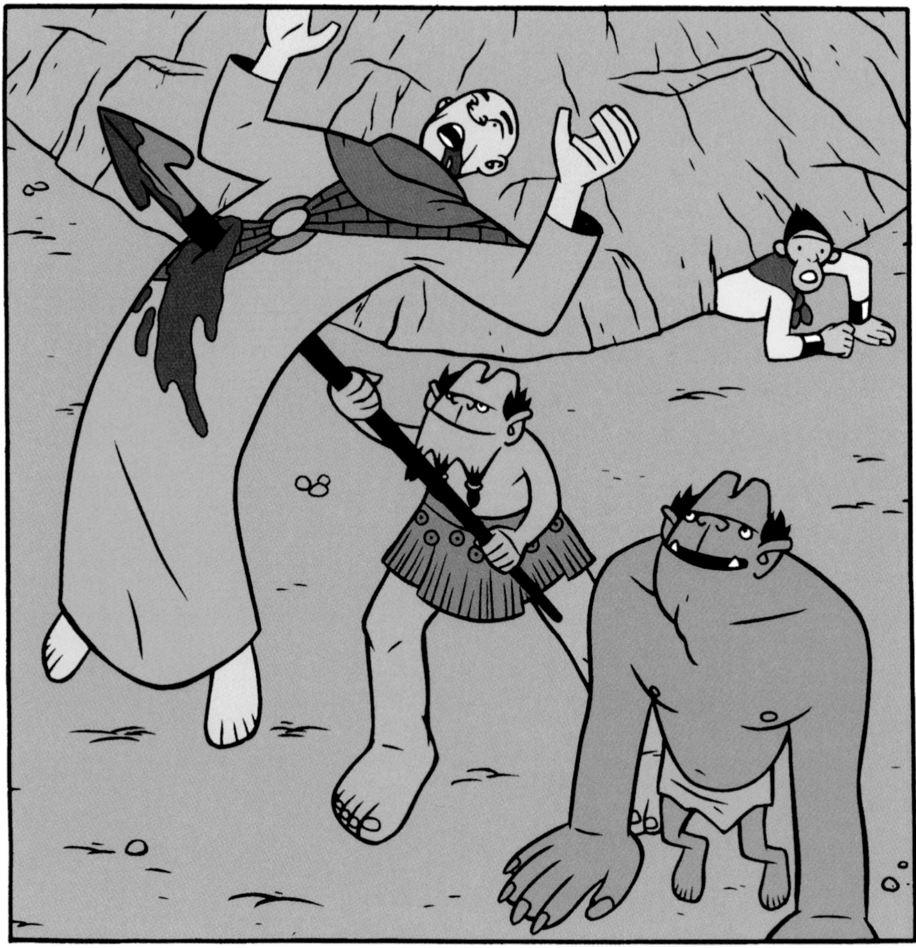

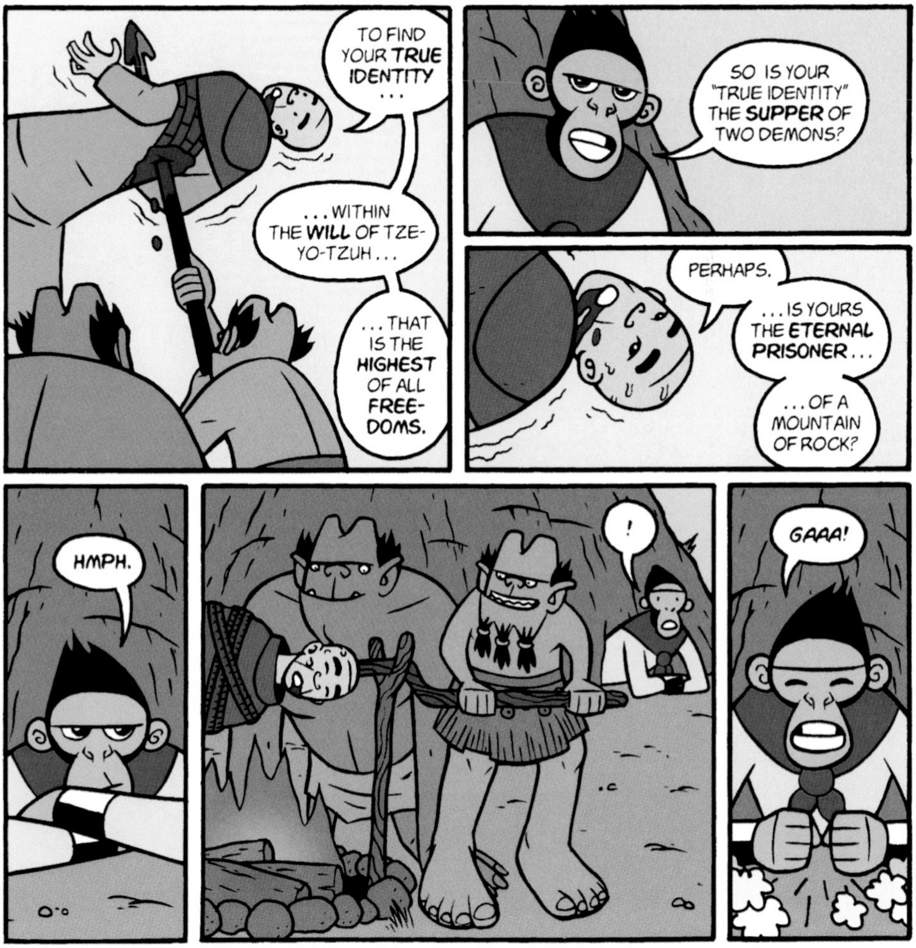

TO FIND YOUR TRUE IDENTITY . . .
. . . WITHIN THE WILL OF TZE-YO-TZUH . . .
. . . THAT IS THE HIGHEST OF ALL FREE-DOMS.
SO IS YOUR "TRUE IDENTITY" THE SUPPER OF TWO DEMONS?
PERHAPS.
. . . IS YOURS THE ETERNAL PRISONER . . .
. . . OF A MOUNTAIN OF ROCK?
HMPH.
!
GAAA!

150

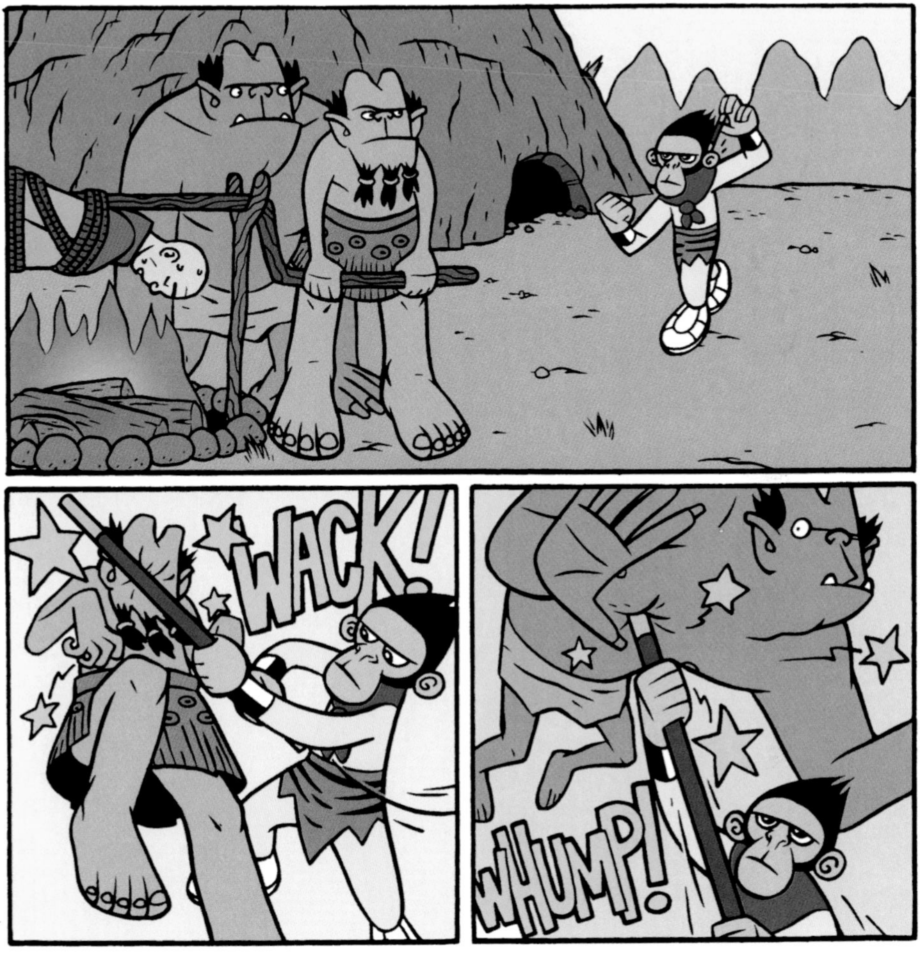
WACK!
WHUMP!

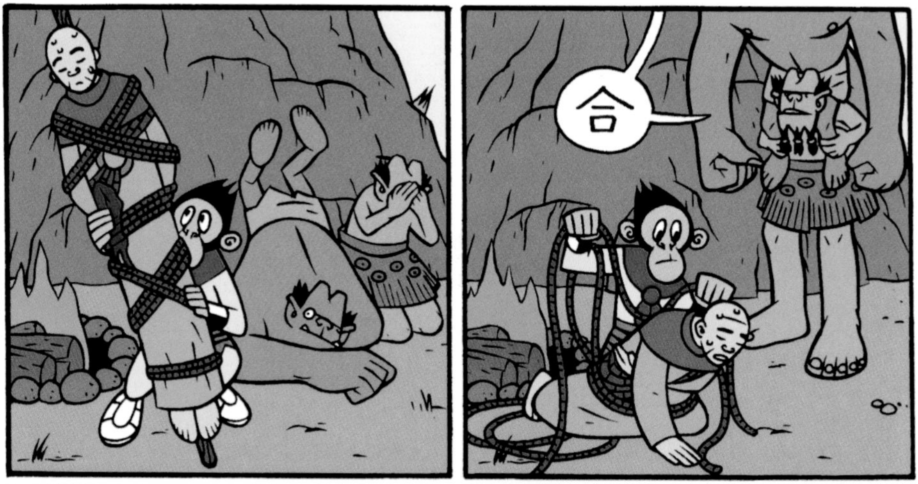
合
?!

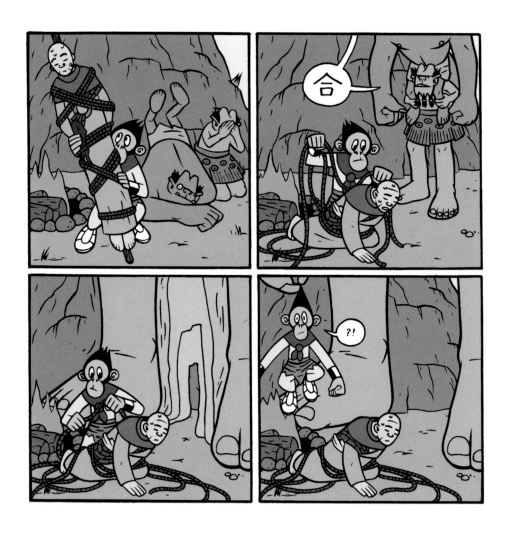

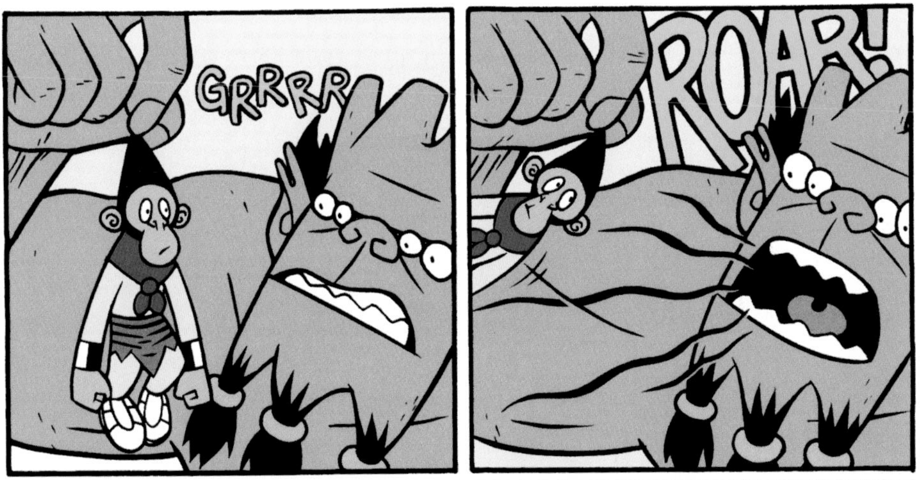
GRRRR
ROAR!
HUFF
HUFF
HUFF
swing
swing
!
ppft!

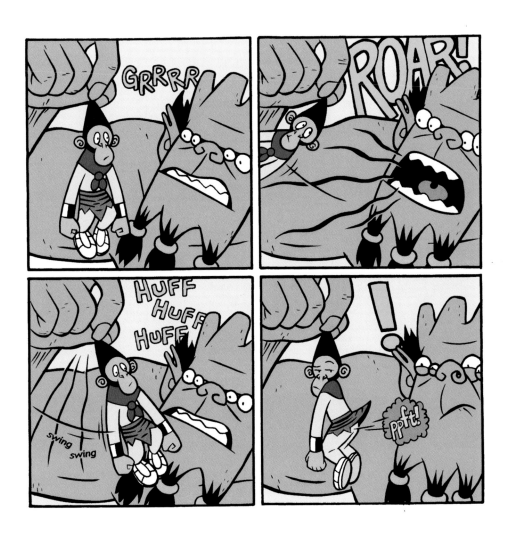

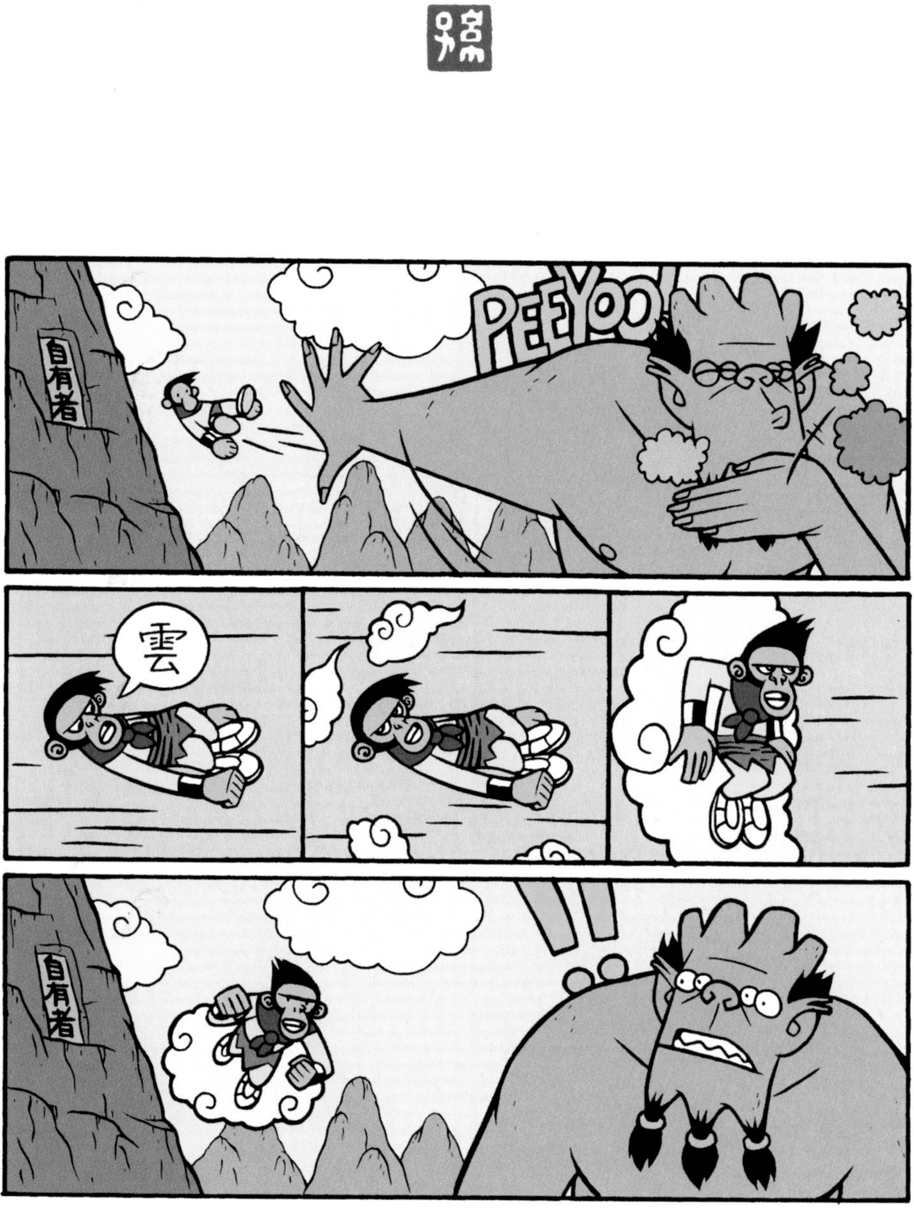
自有者
PEEYOO!
雲
自有者

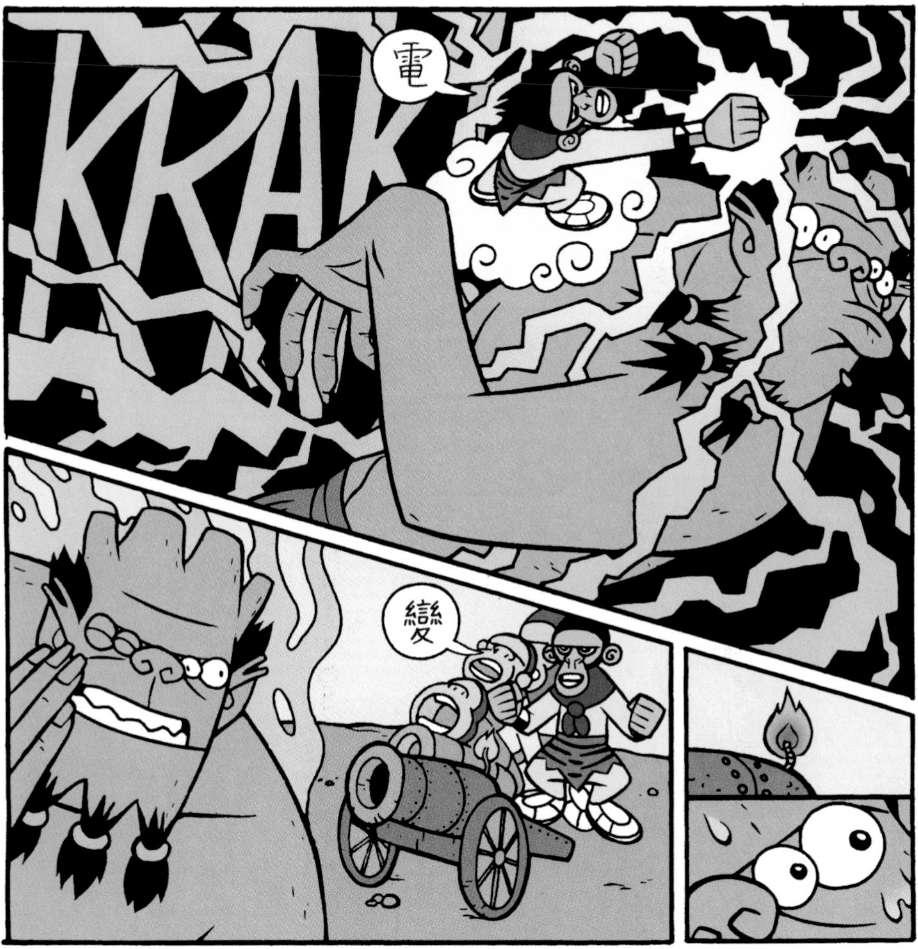
KRAK
電
變

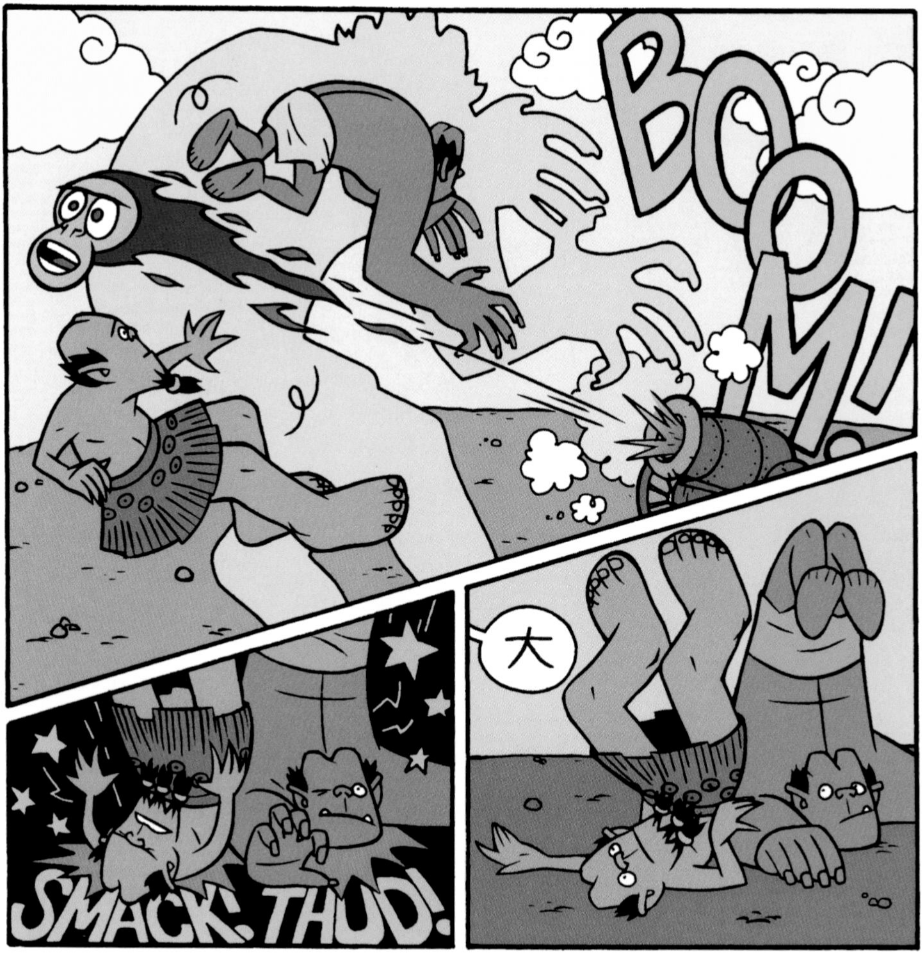
BOOM!!
大
SMACK! THUD!

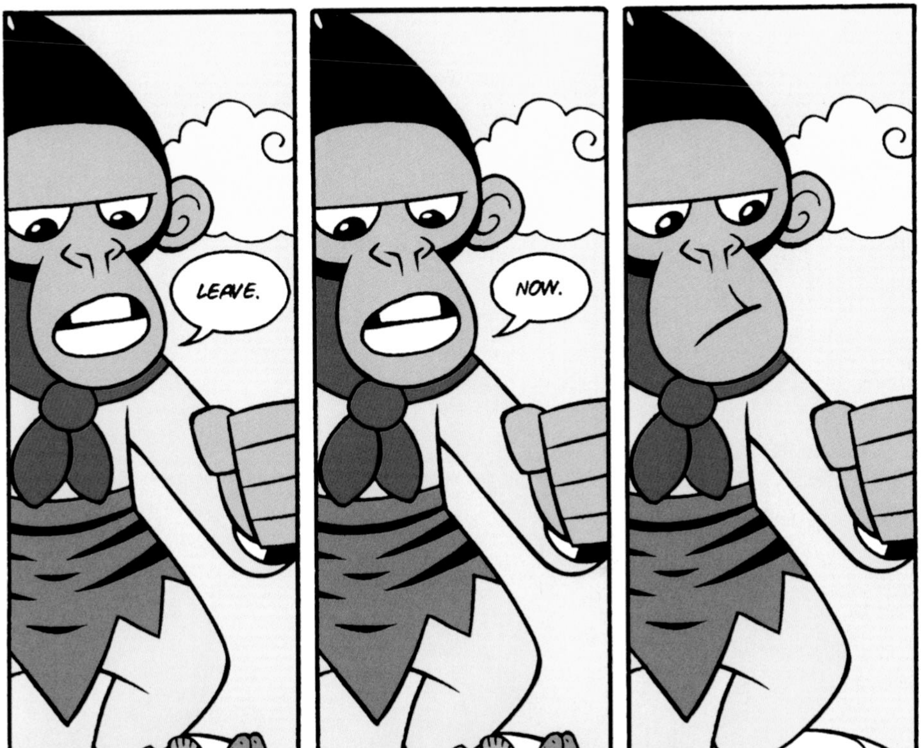
LEAVE.
NOW.
ZIP!
ZIP!

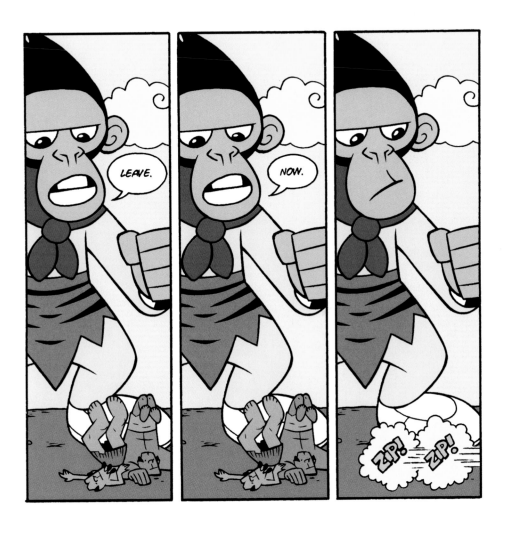

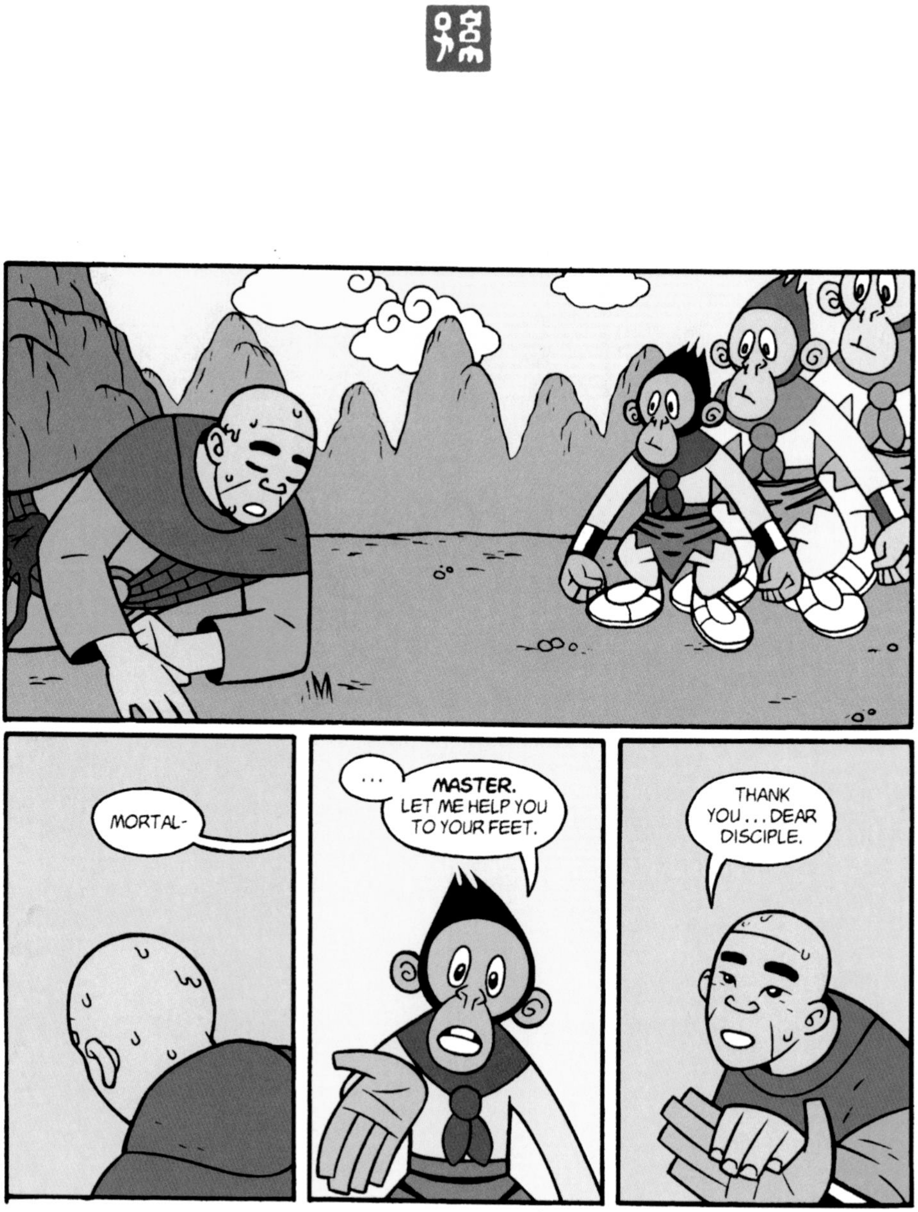
MORTAL-
... MASTER. LET ME HELP YOU TO YOUR FEET.
THANK YOU... DEAR DISCIPLE.

YOUR WOUNDS ARE HEAVY. I'LL FLY YOU TO THE NEAREST TOWN.
NO . . . NO SHORTCUTS. YOU CAN, HOWEVER . . . RETRIEVE THOSE . . . PACKAGES FOR ME.
THERE'S ONE . . . MORE THING, DEAR DISCIPLE.
ON THIS JOURNEY . . . WE HAVE NO NEED . . . FOR **SHOES.**
. . .

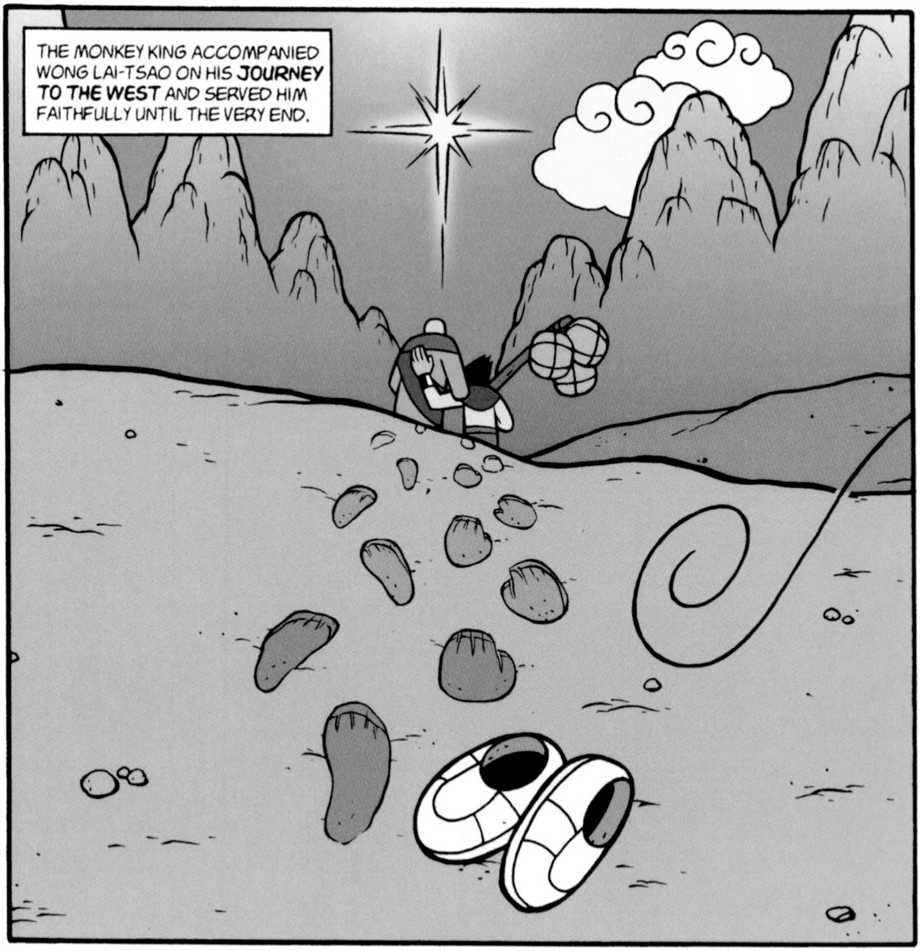
THE MONKEY KING ACCOMPANIED WONG LAI-TSAO ON HIS **JOURNEY TO THE WEST** AND SERVED HIM FAITHFULLY UNTIL THE VERY END.

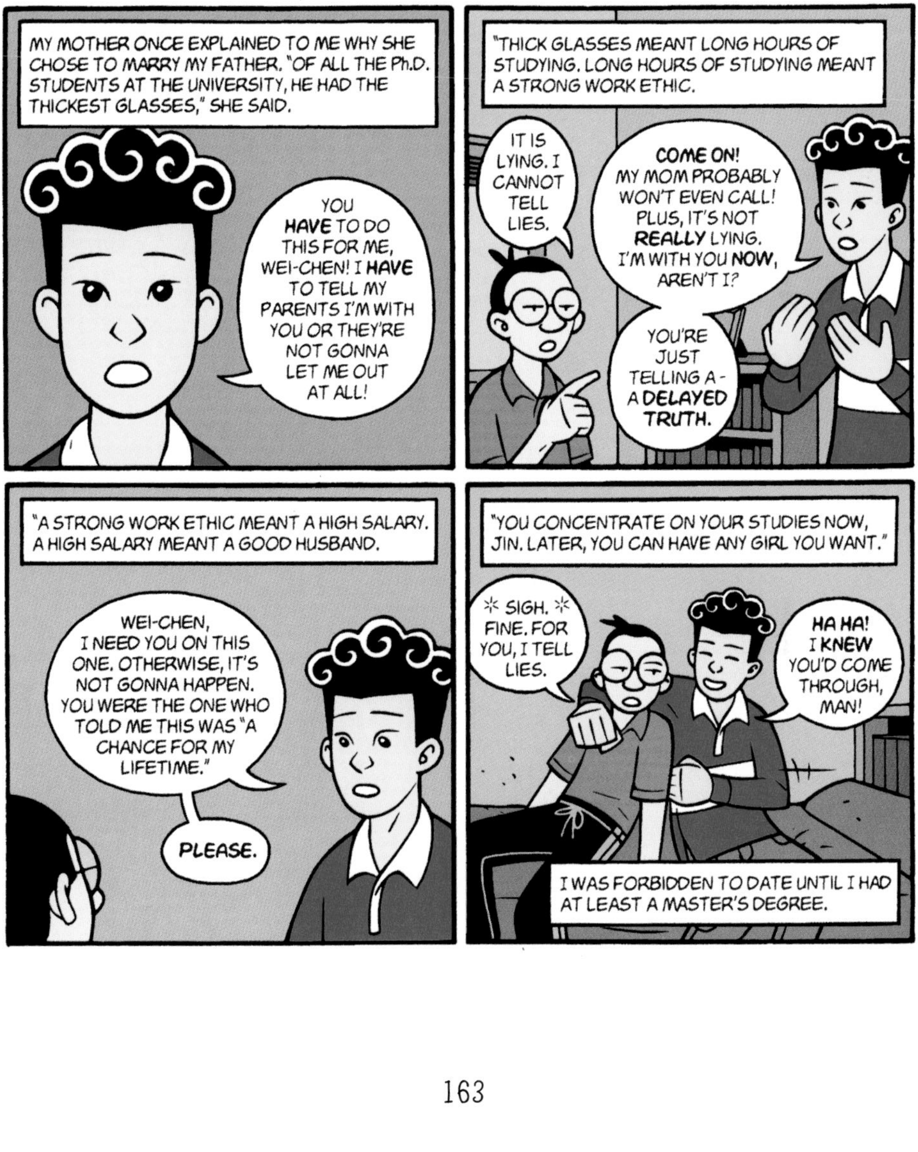
MY MOTHER ONCE EXPLAINED TO ME WHY SHE CHOSE TO MARRY MY FATHER. "OF ALL THE Ph.D. STUDENTS AT THE UNIVERSITY, HE HAD THE THICKEST GLASSES," SHE SAID.
YOU **HAVE** TO DO THIS FOR ME, WEI-CHEN! I **HAVE** TO TELL MY PARENTS I'M WITH YOU OR THEY'RE NOT GONNA LET ME OUT AT ALL!
"THICK GLASSES MEANT LONG HOURS OF STUDYING. LONG HOURS OF STUDYING MEANT A STRONG WORK ETHIC.
IT IS LYING. I CANNOT TELL LIES.
COME ON! MY MOM PROBABLY WON'T EVEN CALL! PLUS, IT'S NOT **REALLY** LYING. I'M WITH YOU **NOW**, AREN'T I?
YOU'RE JUST TELLING A- A **DELAYED TRUTH.**
"A STRONG WORK ETHIC MEANT A HIGH SALARY. A HIGH SALARY MEANT A GOOD HUSBAND.
WEI-CHEN, I NEED YOU ON THIS ONE. OTHERWISE, IT'S NOT GONNA HAPPEN. YOU WERE THE ONE WHO TOLD ME THIS WAS "A CHANCE FOR MY LIFETIME."
PLEASE.
"YOU CONCENTRATE ON YOUR STUDIES NOW, JIN. LATER, YOU CAN HAVE ANY GIRL YOU WANT."
* SIGH. * FINE. FOR YOU, I TELL LIES.
HA HA! I **KNEW** YOU'D COME THROUGH, MAN!
I WAS FORBIDDEN TO DATE UNTIL I HAD AT LEAST A MASTER'S DEGREE.

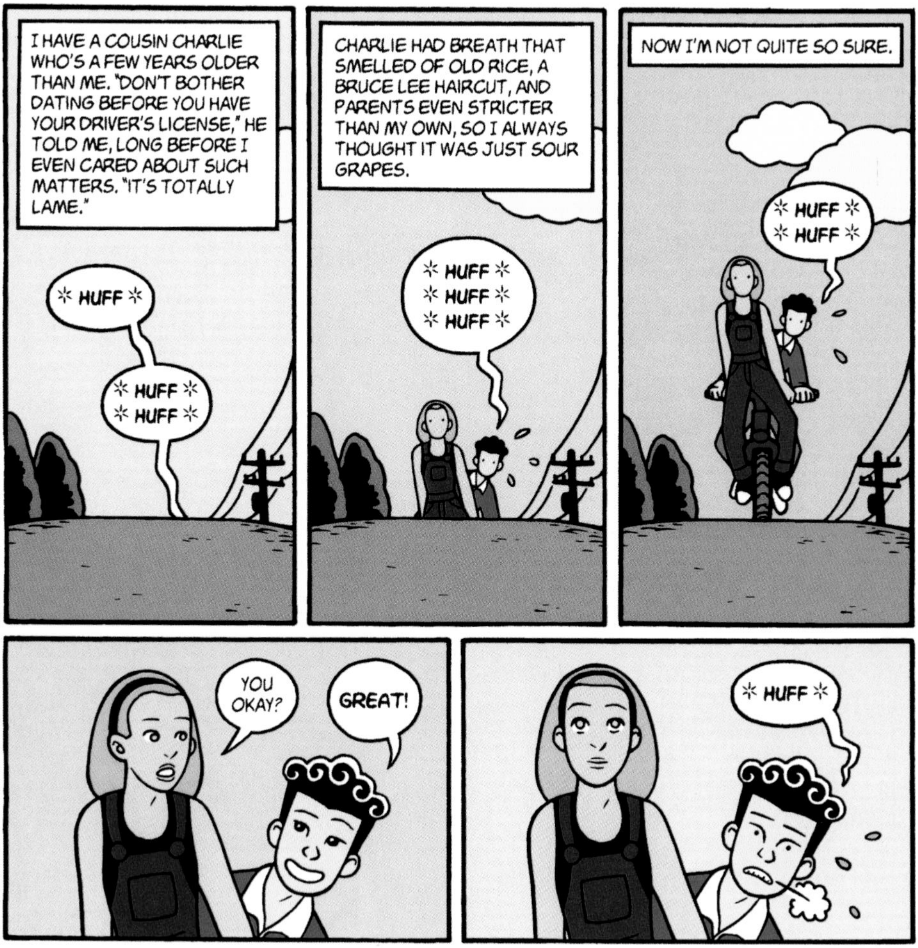
I HAVE A COUSIN CHARLIE WHO'S A FEW YEARS OLDER THAN ME. "DON'T BOTHER DATING BEFORE YOU HAVE YOUR DRIVER'S LICENSE," HE TOLD ME, LONG BEFORE I EVEN CARED ABOUT SUCH MATTERS. "IT'S TOTALLY LAME."
HUFF
HUFF HUFF
CHARLIE HAD BREATH THAT SMELLED OF OLD RICE, A BRUCE LEE HAIRCUT, AND PARENTS EVEN STRICTER THAN MY OWN, SO I ALWAYS THOUGHT IT WAS JUST SOUR GRAPES.
HUFF HUFF HUFF
NOW I'M NOT QUITE SO SURE.
HUFF HUFF
YOU OKAY?
GREAT!
HUFF

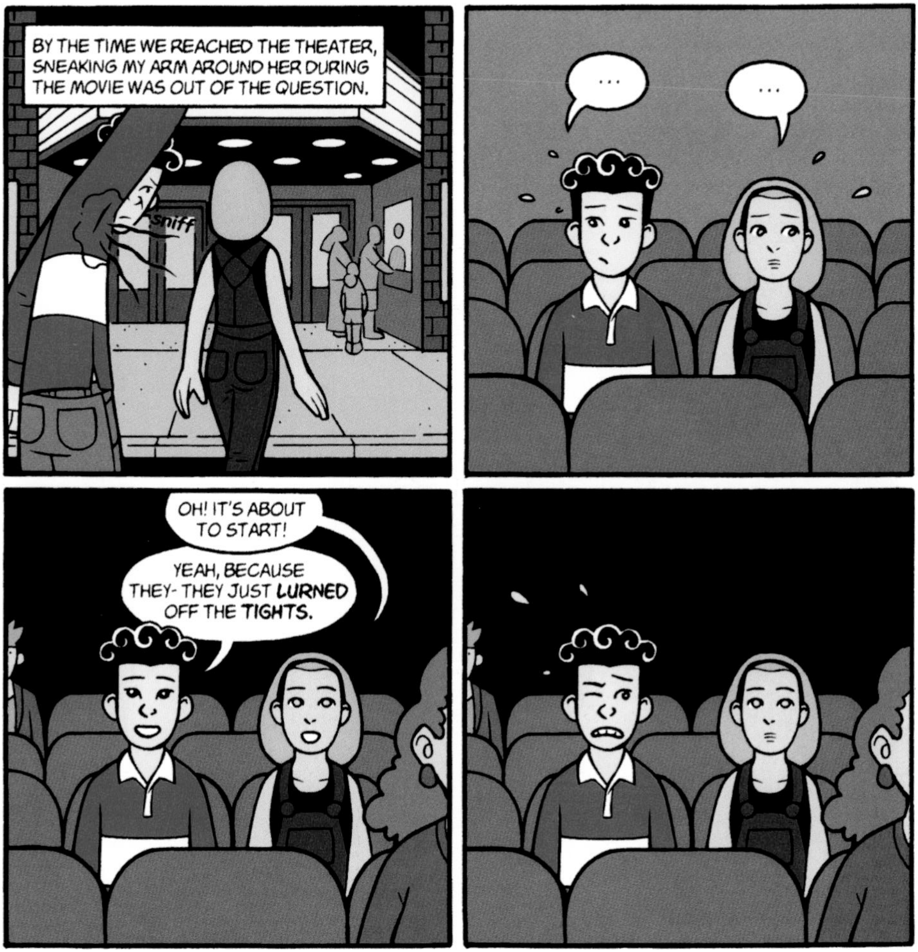
BY THE TIME WE REACHED THE THEATER, SNEAKING MY ARM AROUND HER DURING THE MOVIE WAS OUT OF THE QUESTION.
sniff
...
...
OH! IT'S ABOUT TO START!
YEAH, BECAUSE THEY- THEY JUST **LURNED** OFF THE **TIGHTS.**

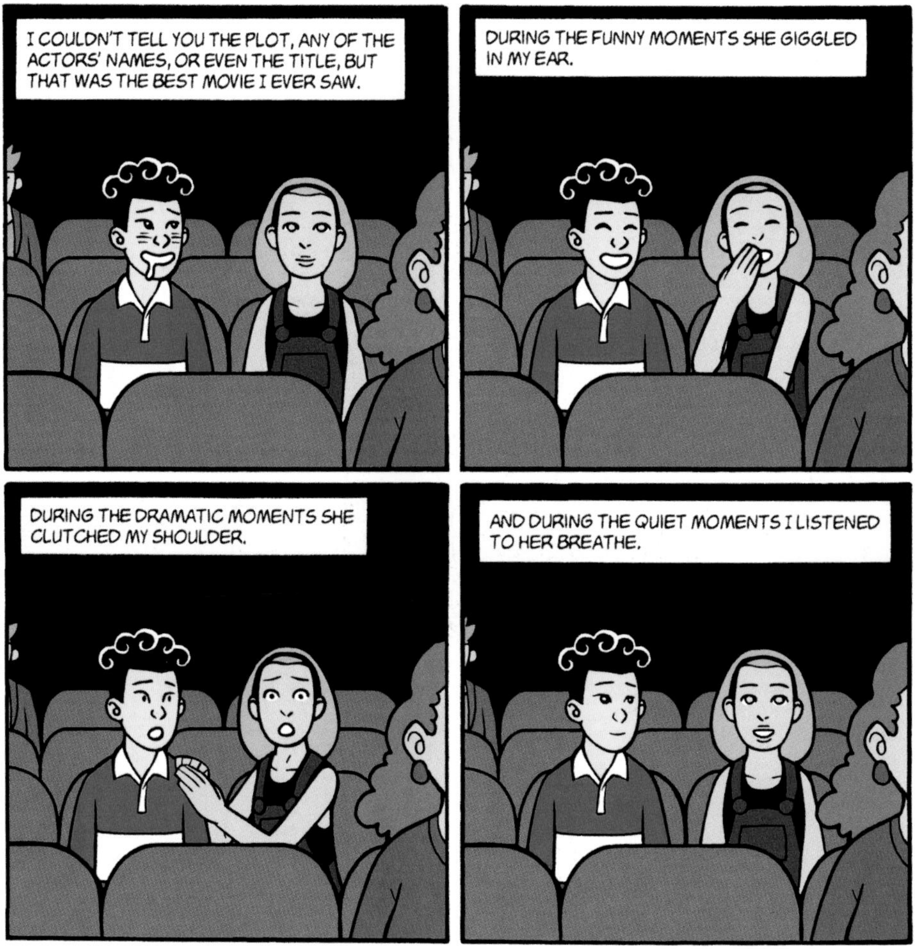
I COULDN'T TELL YOU THE PLOT, ANY OF THE ACTORS' NAMES, OR EVEN THE TITLE, BUT THAT WAS THE BEST MOVIE I EVER SAW.
DURING THE FUNNY MOMENTS SHE GIGGLED IN MY EAR.
DURING THE DRAMATIC MOMENTS SHE CLUTCHED MY SHOULDER.
AND DURING THE QUIET MOMENTS I LISTENED TO HER BREATHE.

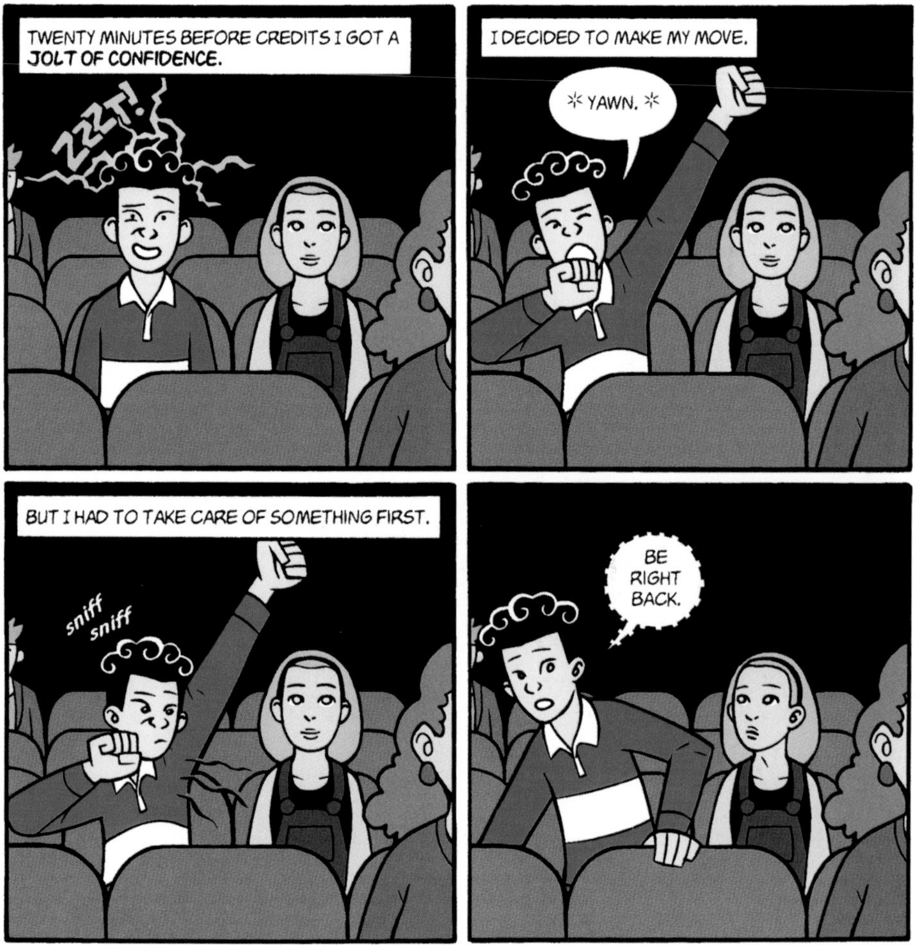
TWENTY MINUTES BEFORE CREDITS I GOT A JOLT OF CONFIDENCE.
ZZZT!
I DECIDED TO MAKE MY MOVE.
YAWN.
BUT I HAD TO TAKE CARE OF SOMETHING FIRST.
sniff sniff
BE RIGHT BACK.

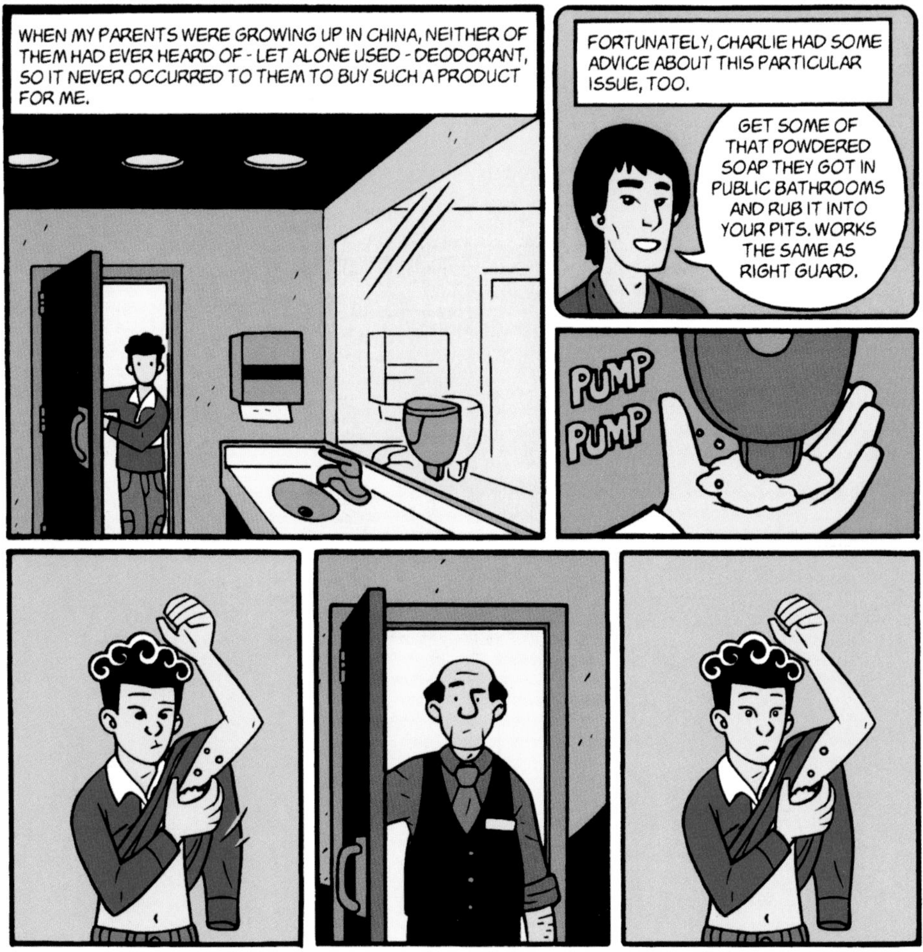
WHEN MY PARENTS WERE GROWING UP IN CHINA, NEITHER OF THEM HAD EVER HEARD OF - LET ALONE USED - DEODORANT, SO IT NEVER OCCURRED TO THEM TO BUY SUCH A PRODUCT FOR ME.
FORTUNATELY, CHARLIE HAD SOME ADVICE ABOUT THIS PARTICULAR ISSUE, TOO.
GET SOME OF THAT POWDERED SOAP THEY GOT IN PUBLIC BATHROOMS AND RUB IT INTO YOUR PITS. WORKS THE SAME AS RIGHT GUARD.
PUMP
PUMP

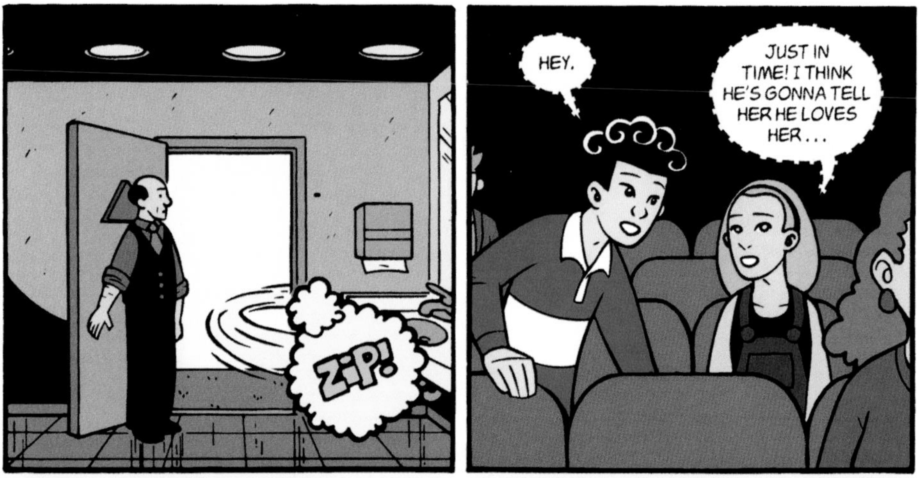
ZIP!
HEY.
JUST IN TIME! I THINK HE'S GONNA TELL HER HE LOVES HER . . .
ZZZT!
AWWW . . .

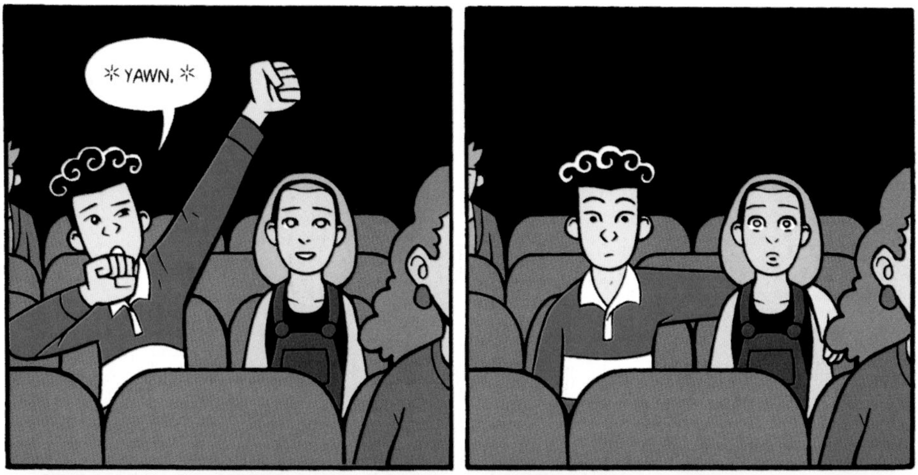
YAWN.

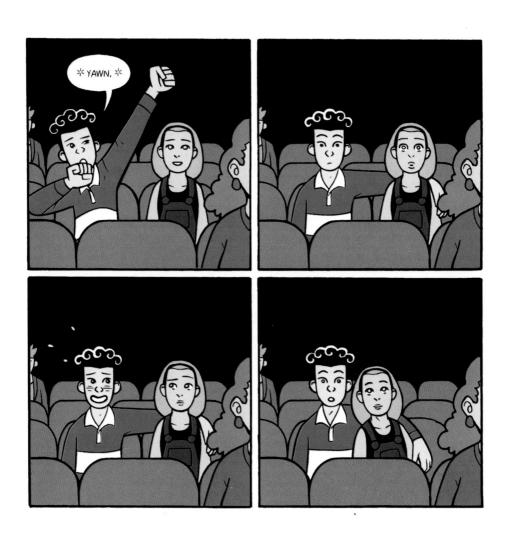

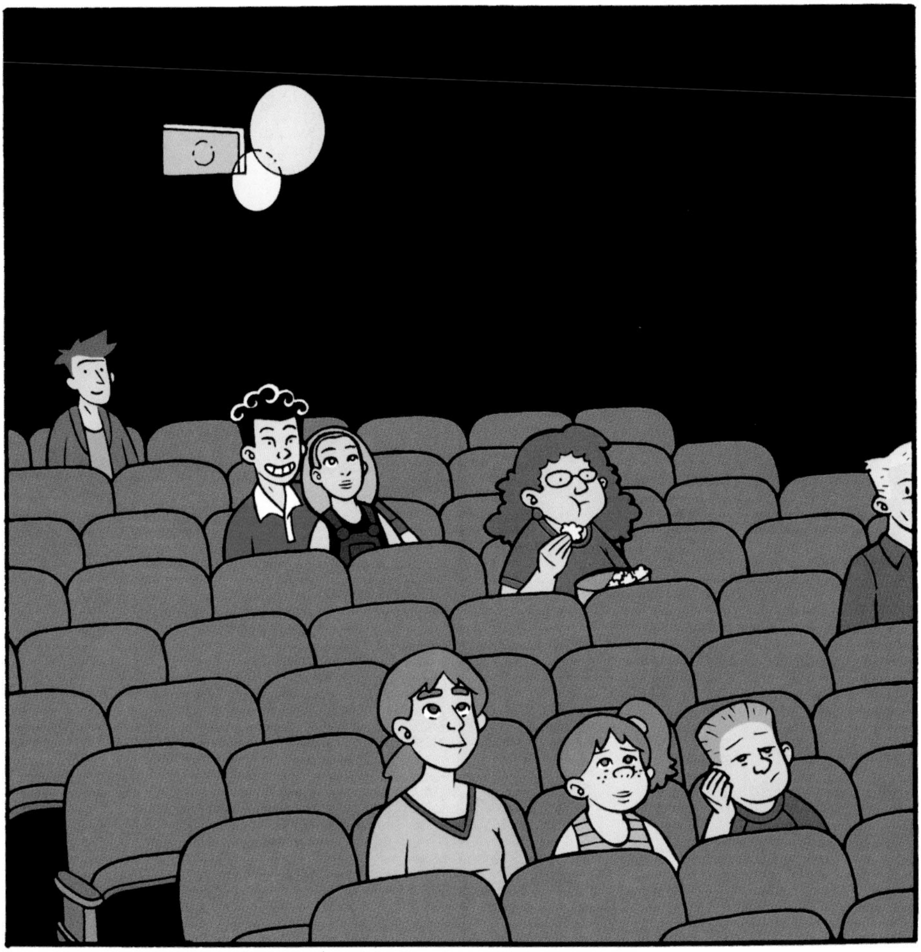

I DIDN'T SEE IT UNTIL AFTER WE'D LEFT THE THEATER.
. . . AND WHEN HER DAD FINALLY APOLOGIZED FOR FORGETTING HER BIRTHDAY, I ALMOST CRIED.
YEAH . . . UH . . . ME TOO.
WHAT'S THAT ON HER SHOULDER?
SOAP BUBBLES?!
SO YOU WANNA GO GET MILKSHAKES OR SOMETHING?
ACK!
JIN?
MILK-SHAKES! YUM!

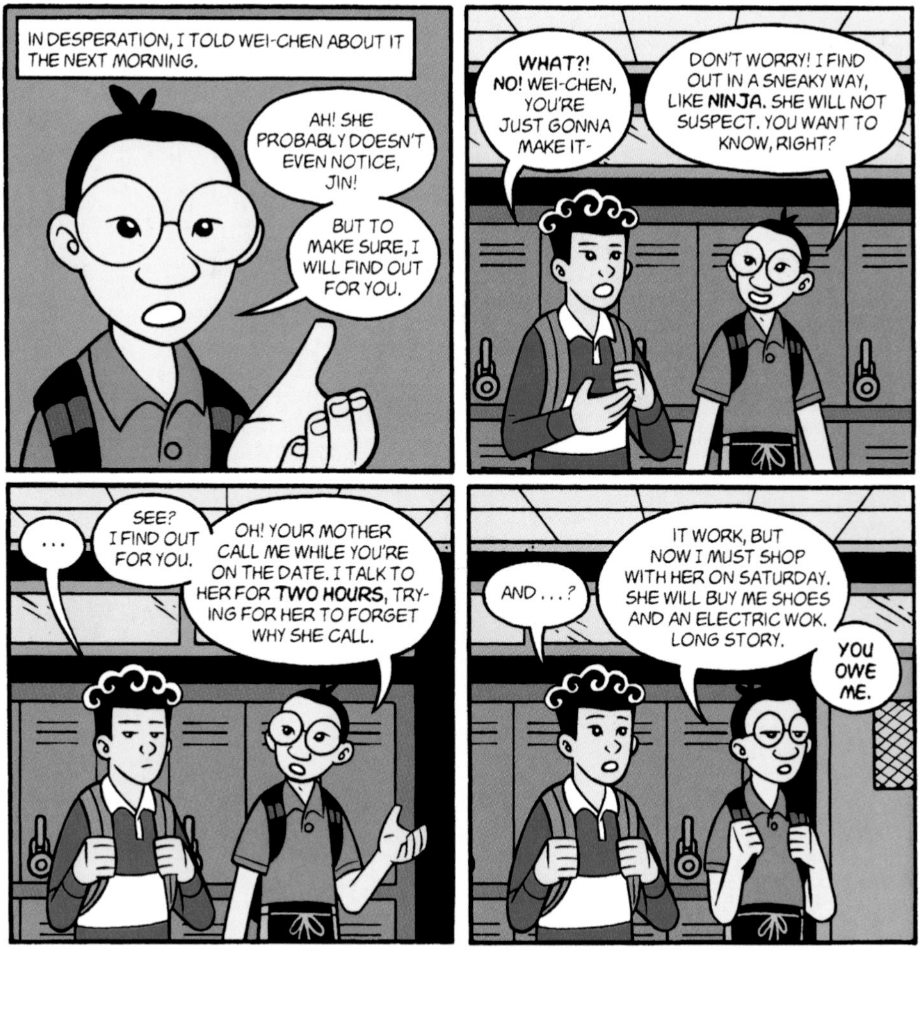
IN DESPERATION, I TOLD WEI-CHEN ABOUT IT THE NEXT MORNING.
AH! SHE PROBABLY DOESN'T EVEN NOTICE, JIN!
BUT TO MAKE SURE, I WILL FIND OUT FOR YOU.
WHAT?! NO! WEI-CHEN, YOU'RE JUST GONNA MAKE IT-
DON'T WORRY! I FIND OUT IN A SNEAKY WAY, LIKE NINJA. SHE WILL NOT SUSPECT. YOU WANT TO KNOW, RIGHT?
. . .
SEE? I FIND OUT FOR YOU.
OH! YOUR MOTHER CALL ME WHILE YOU'RE ON THE DATE. I TALK TO HER FOR TWO HOURS, TRYING FOR HER TO FORGET WHY SHE CALL.
AND . . .?
IT WORK, BUT NOW I MUST SHOP WITH HER ON SATURDAY. SHE WILL BUY ME SHOES AND AN ELECTRIC WOK. LONG STORY.
YOU OWE ME.

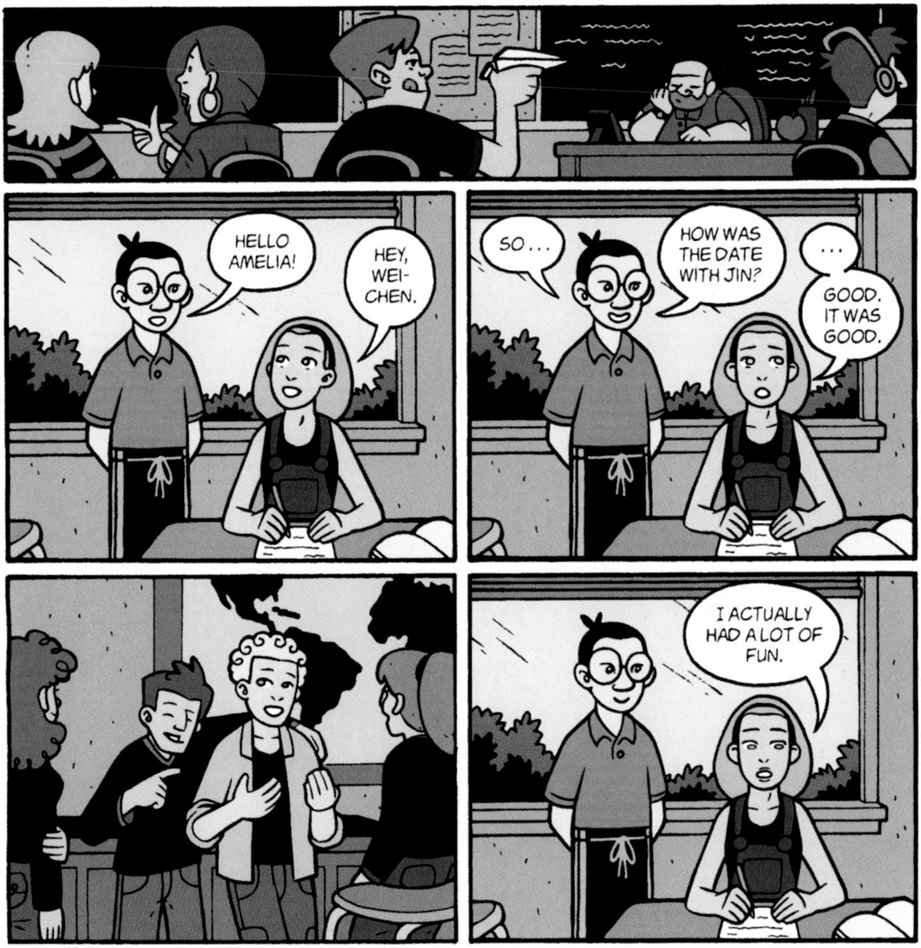
HELLO AMELIA!
HEY, WEI-CHEN.
SO . . .
HOW WAS THE DATE WITH JIN?
. . .
GOOD. IT WAS GOOD.
I ACTUALLY HAD A LOT OF FUN.

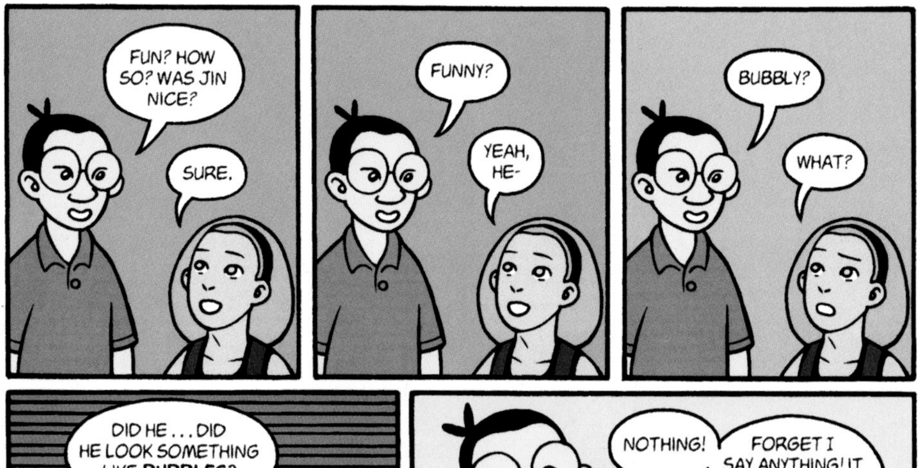
FUN? HOW SO? WAS JIN NICE?
SURE.
FUNNY?
YEAH, HE-
BUBBLY?
WHAT?
DID HE . . . DID HE LOOK SOMETHING LIKE **BUBBLES**?
WEI-CHEN, WHAT ARE YOU **TALKING** ABOUT?
NOTHING!
FORGET I SAY ANYTHING! IT WAS GOOD THAT YOU HAD FUN.

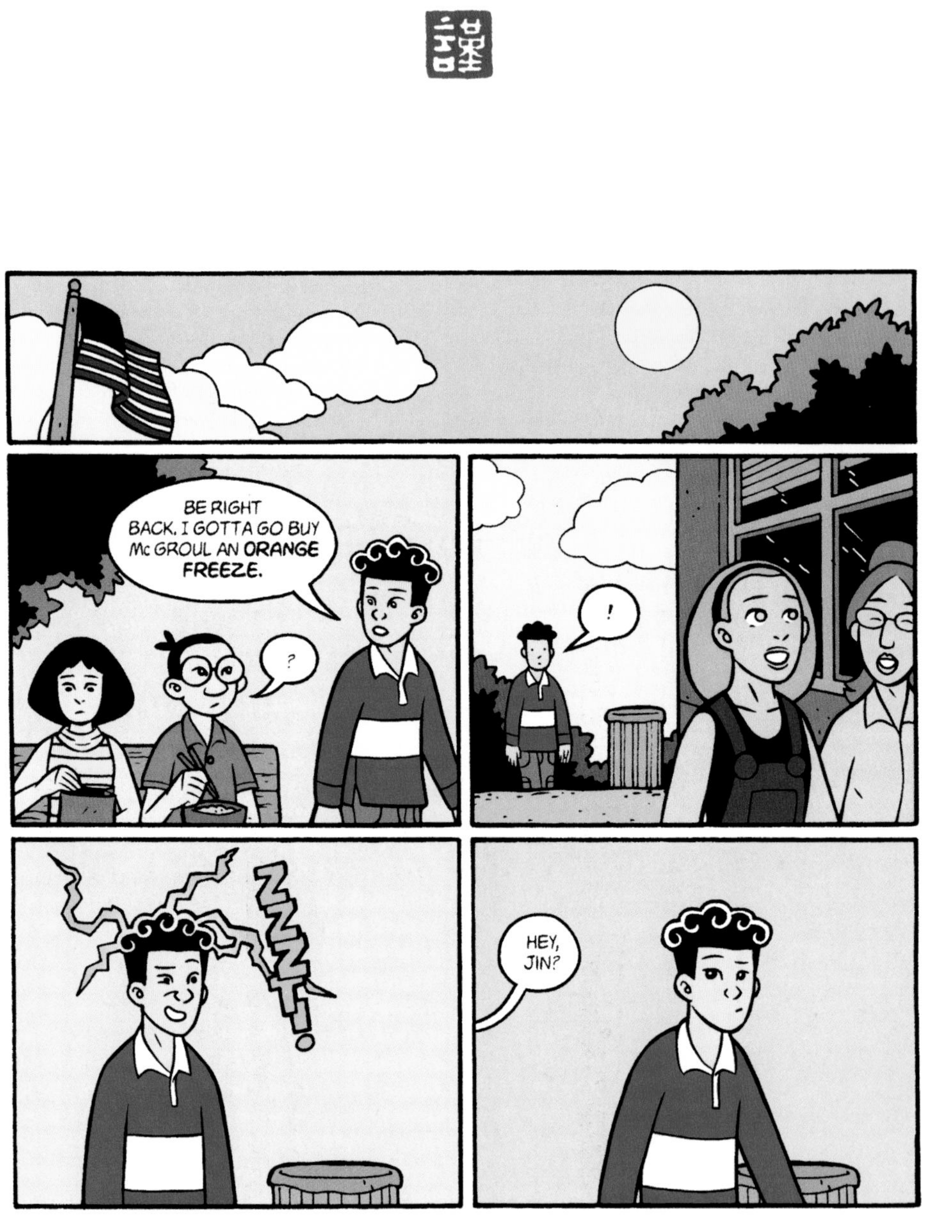
BE RIGHT BACK. I GOTTA GO BUY McGROUL AN ORANGE FREEZE.
?
!
ZZZT!
HEY, JIN?

謹

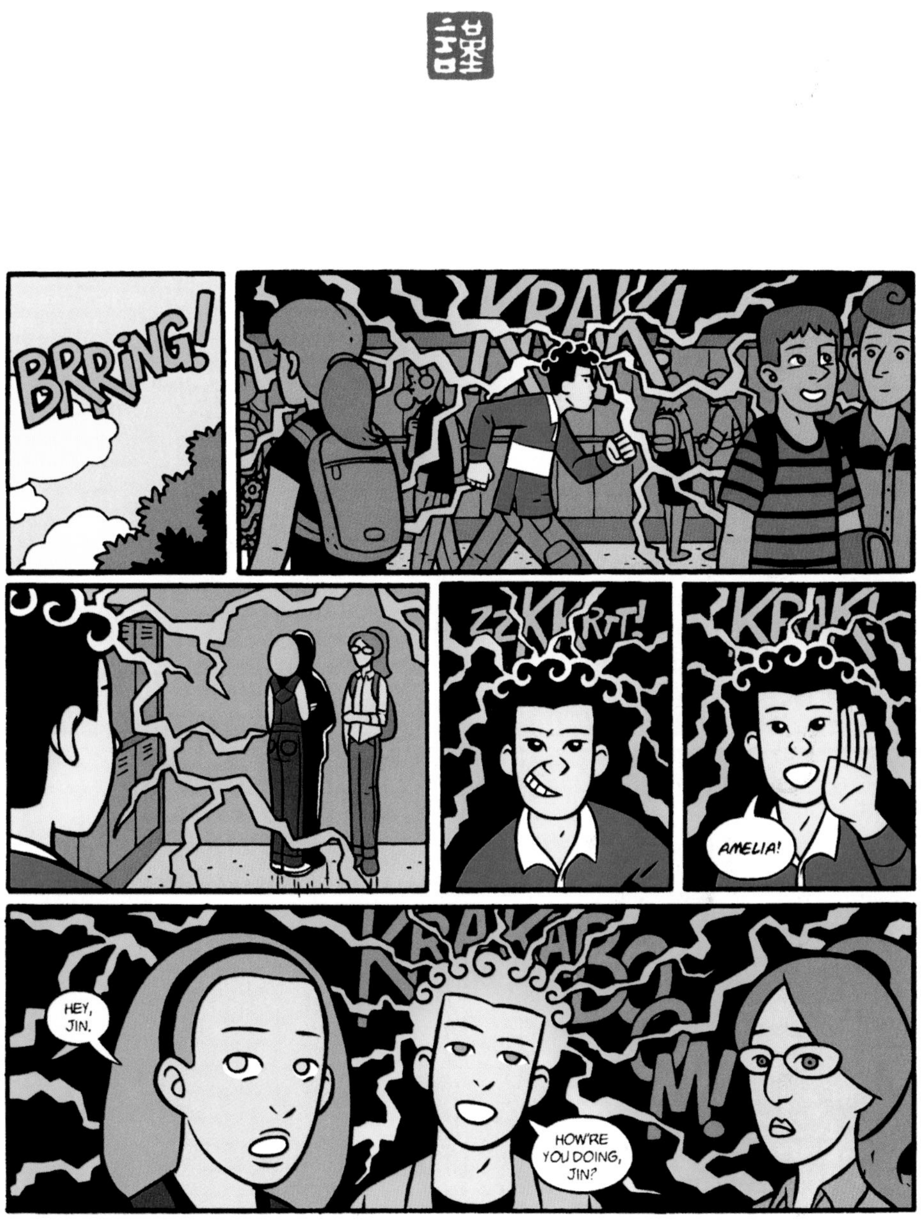
BRRING!
KRAK!
ZZKKRTT!
KRAK!
AMELIA!
KRAKABOOM!
HEY, JIN.
HOW'RE YOU DOING, JIN?

185

ABOUT TWENTY MINUTES INTO THE PARTY, THOUGH, I FIGURED OUT THAT LAUREN DIDN'T ACTUALLY INVITE ME. HER MOM WANTED TO HANG OUT WITH MY MOM, AND I SORT OF JUST GOT BROUGHT ALONG.

LAUREN AND HER NEW FRIENDS HAD THEIR OWN THING GOING, SO I SPENT THE REST OF THE PARTY WATCHING TV IN THE LIVING ROOM. I FELT SO **EMBARRASSED**.

...

TODAY, WHEN TIMMY CALLED ME A . . . A **CHINK**, I REALIZED . . . DEEP DOWN INSIDE . . . I KIND OF FEEL LIKE THAT **ALL THE TIME**.

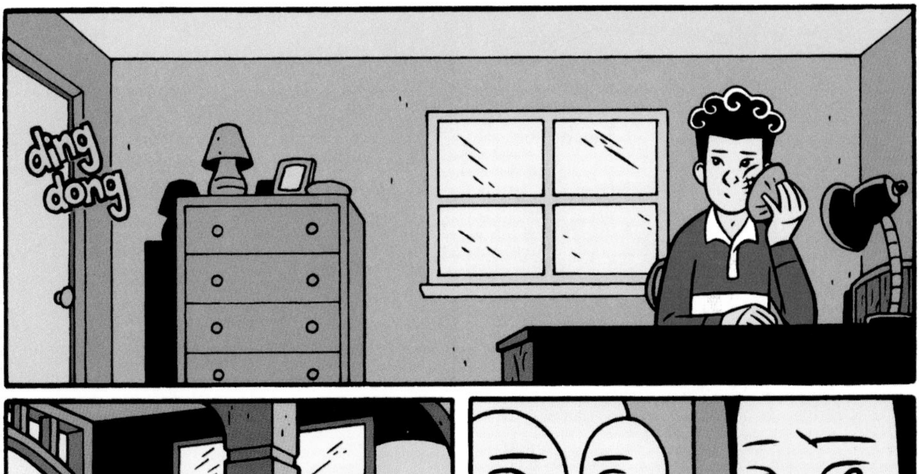
ding dong
WHY- WHAT IS A REASON . . . WHY YOU **KISS**-?
< JIN, HOW COULD YOU EVEN **THINK** TO DO SOME-THING LIKE THIS? HOW COULD YOU HAVE EVEN LET IT ENTER YOUR **MIND**?! >

190

I HAD TROUBLE FALLING ASLEEP THAT NIGHT. I REPLAYED THE DAY'S EVENTS OVER AND OVER AGAIN IN MY MIND.

AND AT AROUND THREE IN THE MORNING, I FINALLY **BELIEVED** MYSELF.

EACH TIME I REACHED THE SAME CONCLUSION: WEI-CHEN NEEDED TO HEAR WHAT I HAD TO SAY. IT WAS, AFTER ALL, THE **TRUTH**.

193

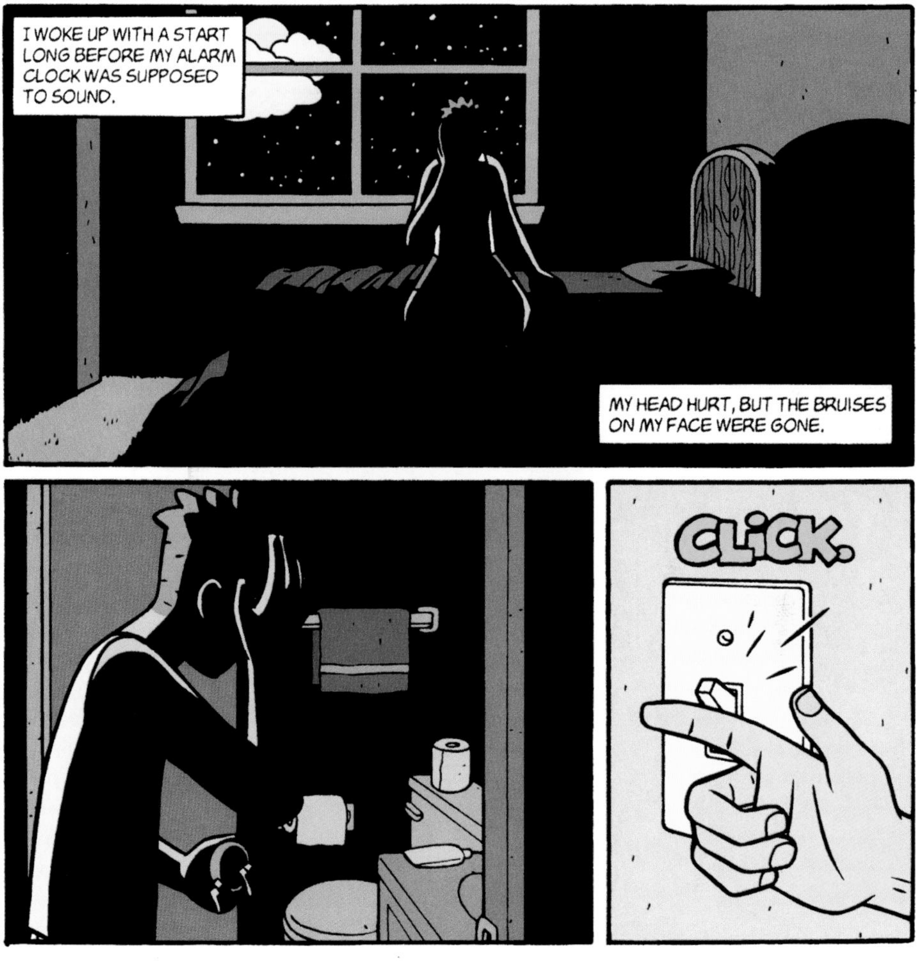
I WOKE UP WITH A START LONG BEFORE MY ALARM CLOCK WAS SUPPOSED TO SOUND.
MY HEAD HURT, BUT THE BRUISES ON MY FACE WERE GONE.
CLICK.

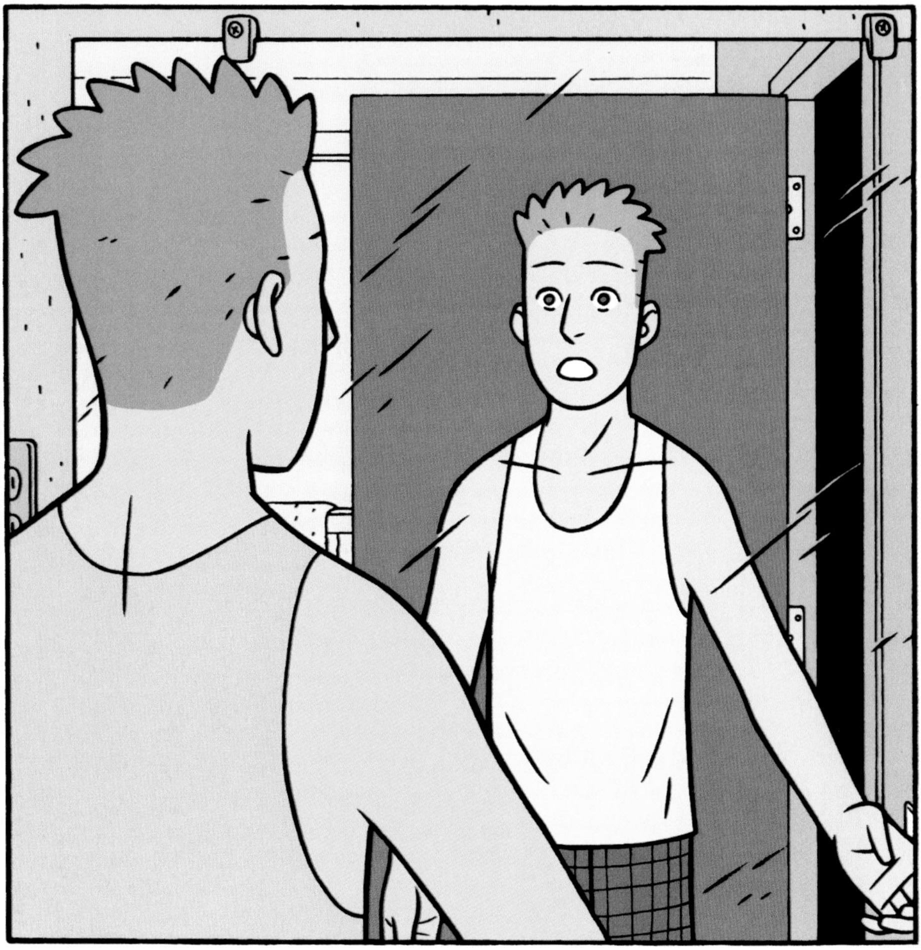

謹

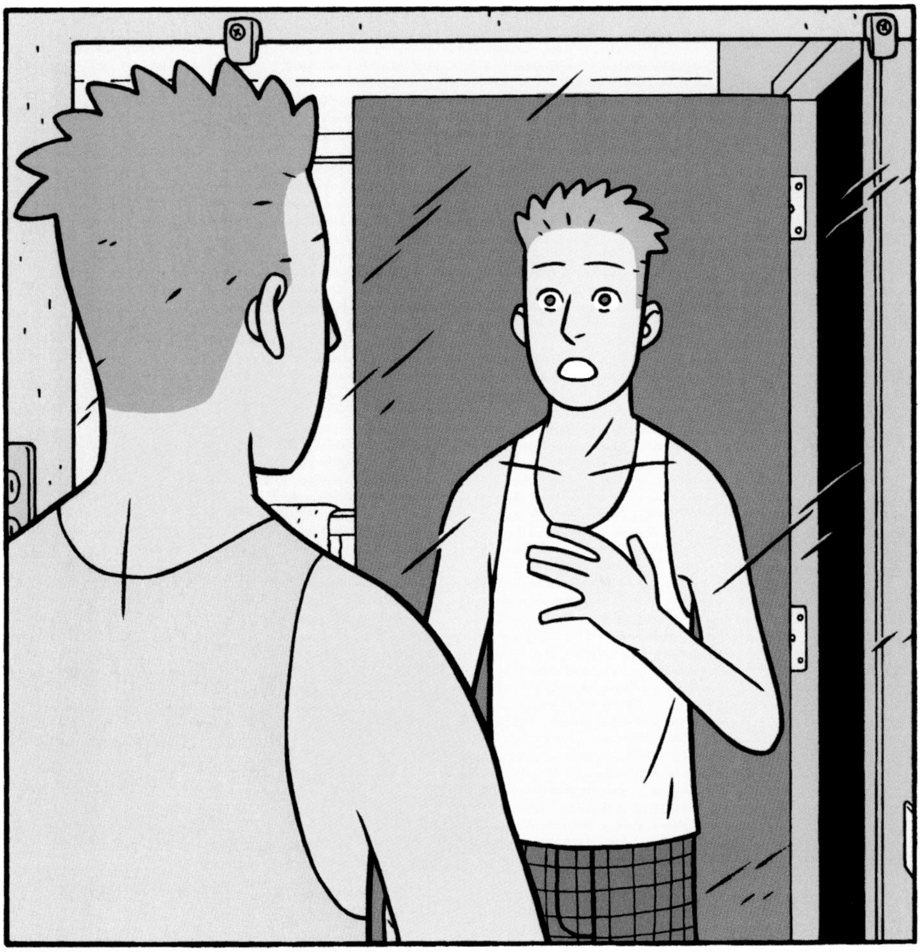

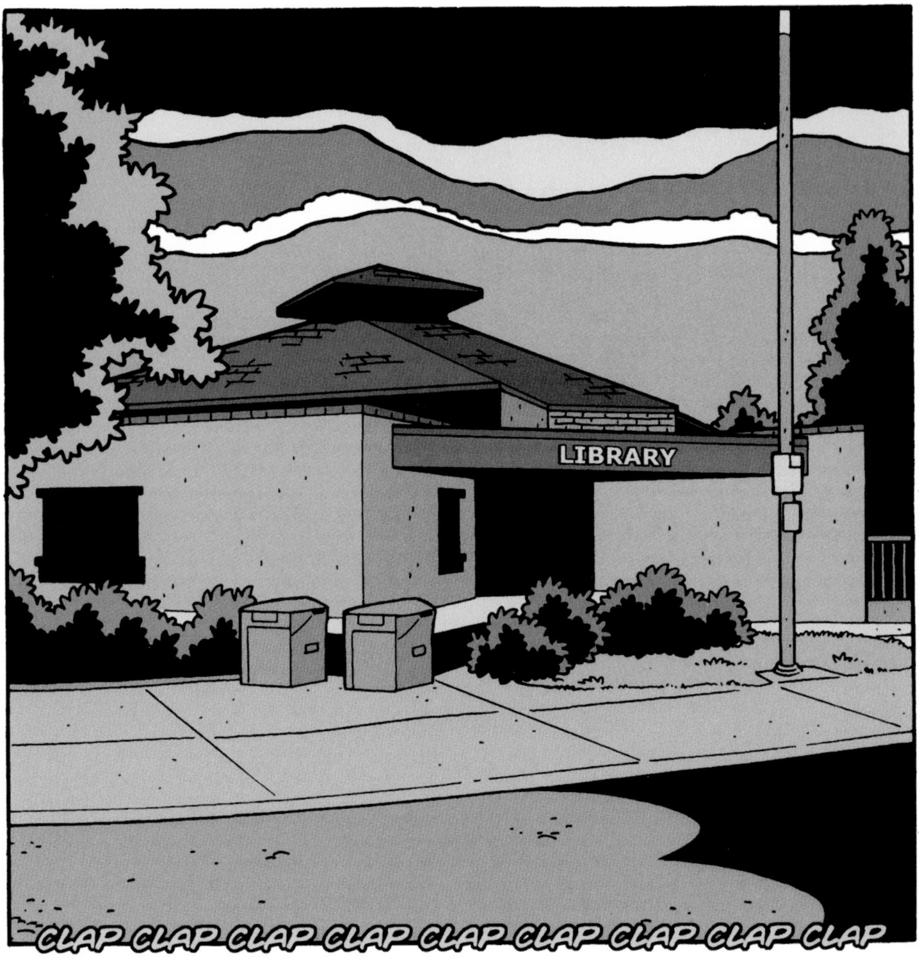
LIBRARY
CLAP CLAP CLAP CLAP CLAP CLAP CLAP CLAP CLAP

205

206

208

AAAA!
POP!
HA HA H-
bounce
bounce

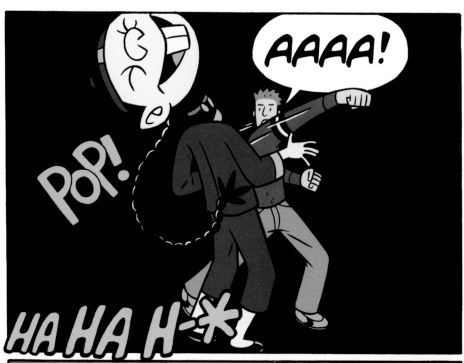

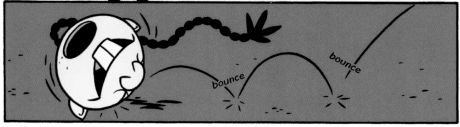

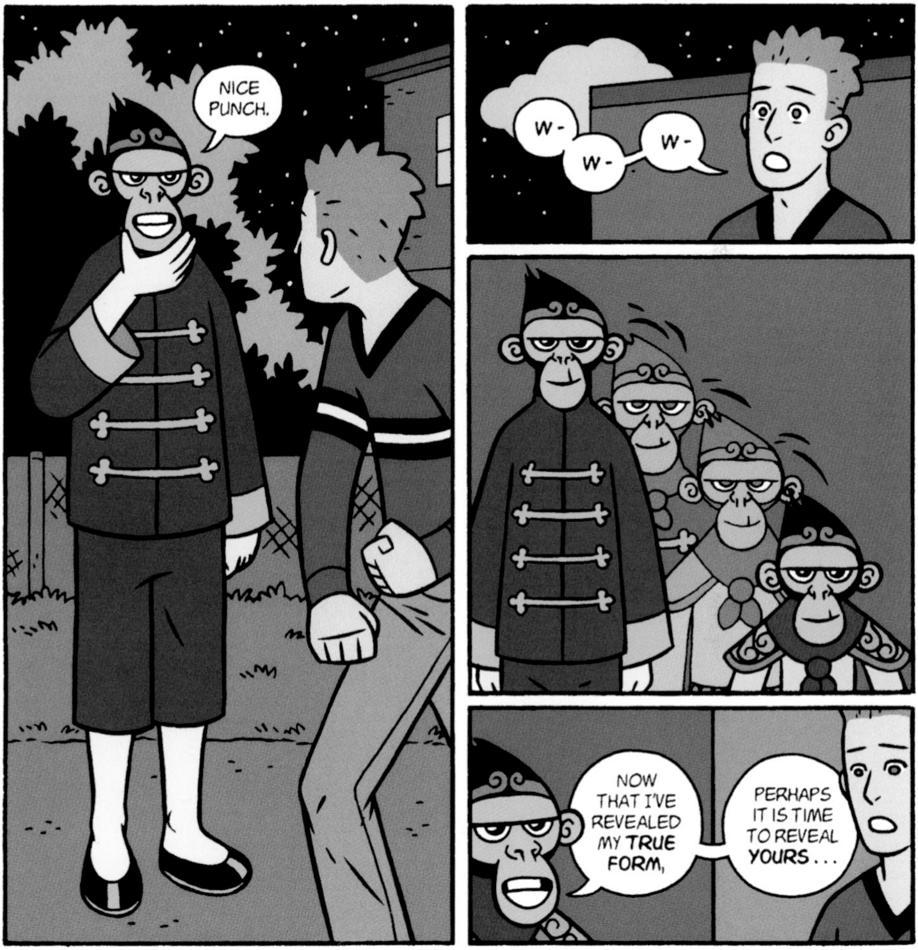
NICE PUNCH.
W-
W-
W-
NOW THAT I'VE REVEALED MY **TRUE FORM**,
PERHAPS IT IS TIME TO REVEAL **YOURS**...

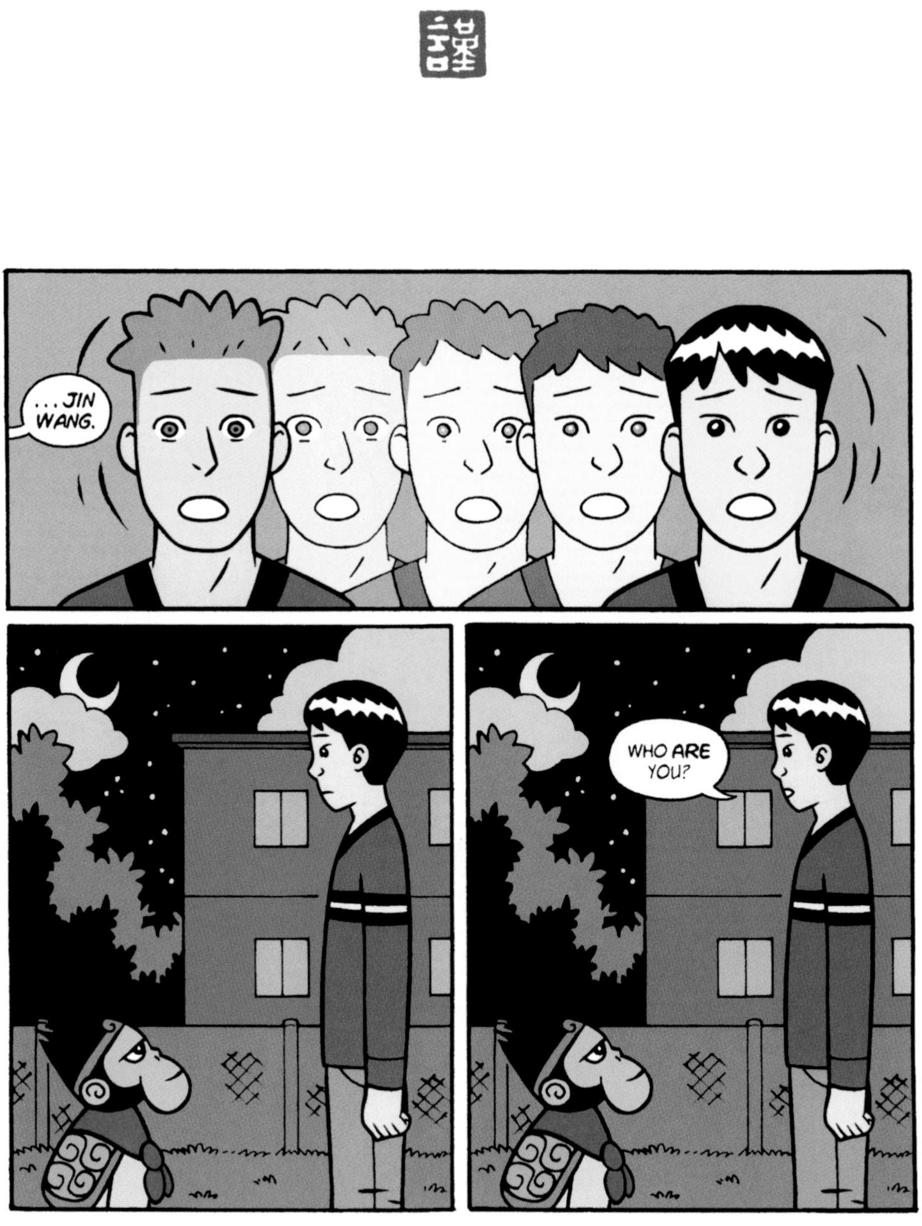
...JIN WANG.
WHO ARE YOU?

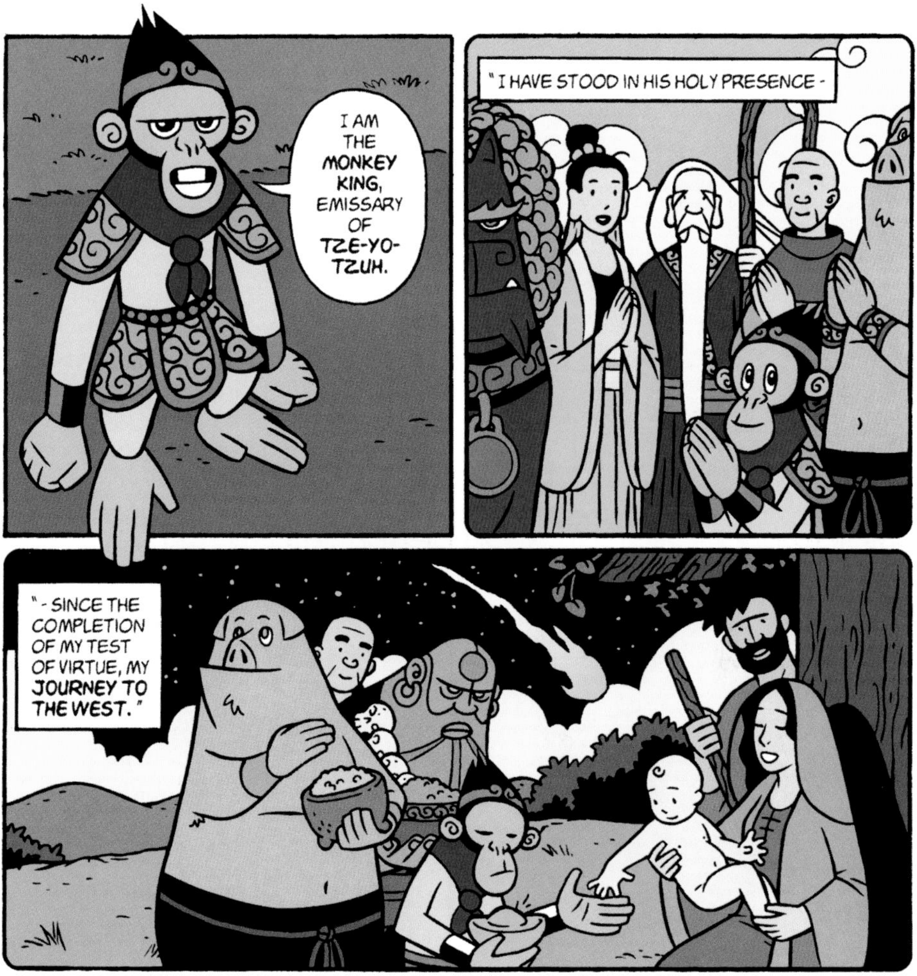
I AM THE MONKEY KING, EMISSARY OF TZE-YO-TZUH.
"I HAVE STOOD IN HIS HOLY PRESENCE -
"- SINCE THE COMPLETION OF MY TEST OF VIRTUE, MY JOURNEY TO THE WEST."

216

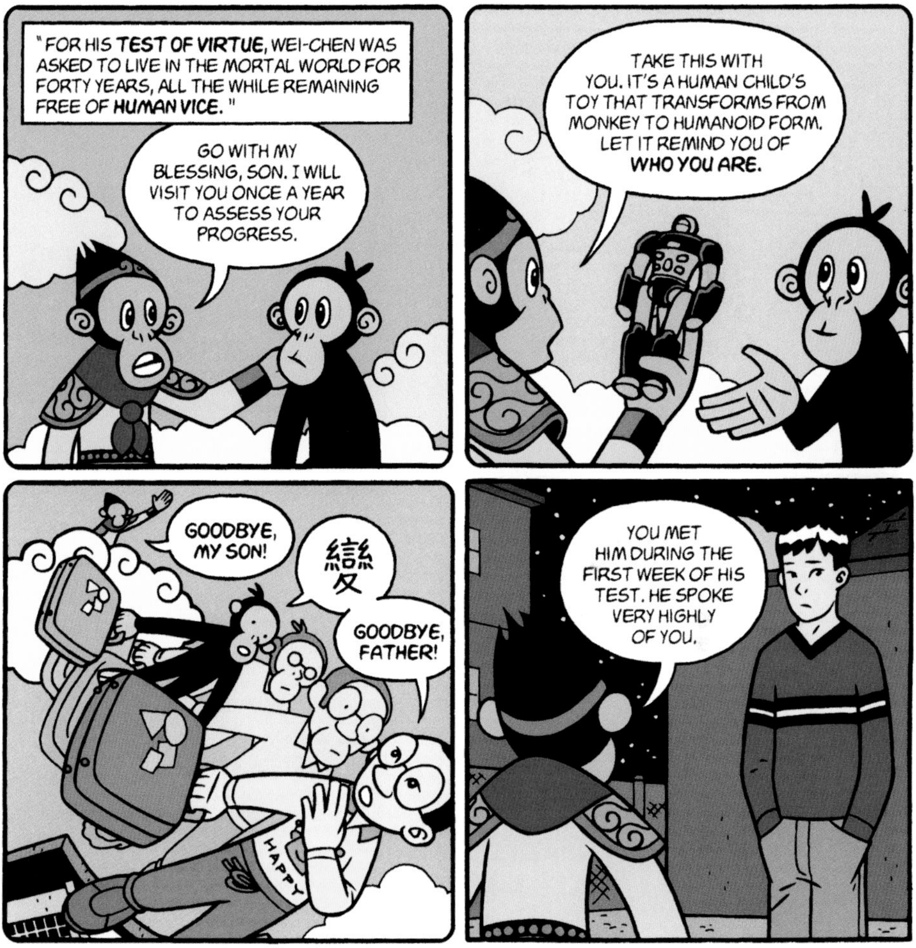

"FOR HIS **TEST OF VIRTUE**, WEI-CHEN WAS ASKED TO LIVE IN THE MORTAL WORLD FOR FORTY YEARS, ALL THE WHILE REMAINING FREE OF **HUMAN VICE**."
GO WITH MY BLESSING, SON. I WILL VISIT YOU ONCE A YEAR TO ASSESS YOUR PROGRESS.
TAKE THIS WITH YOU. IT'S A HUMAN CHILD'S TOY THAT TRANSFORMS FROM MONKEY TO HUMANOID FORM. LET IT REMIND YOU OF **WHO YOU ARE.**
GOODBYE, MY SON!
變
GOODBYE, FATHER!
HAPPY
YOU MET HIM DURING THE FIRST WEEK OF HIS TEST. HE SPOKE VERY HIGHLY OF YOU.

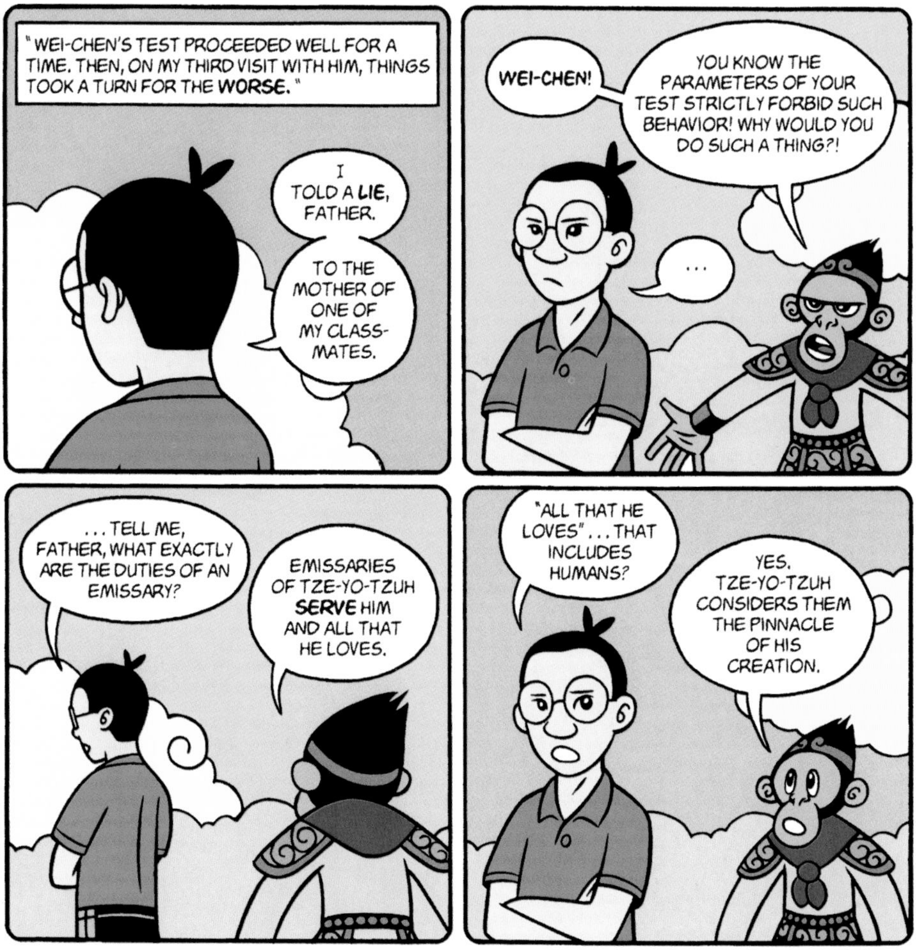
"WEI-CHEN'S TEST PROCEEDED WELL FOR A TIME. THEN, ON MY THIRD VISIT WITH HIM, THINGS TOOK A TURN FOR THE **WORSE.**"
I TOLD A **LIE**, FATHER.
TO THE MOTHER OF ONE OF MY CLASS-MATES.
WEI-CHEN!
YOU KNOW THE PARAMETERS OF YOUR TEST STRICTLY FORBID SUCH BEHAVIOR! WHY WOULD YOU DO SUCH A THING?!
...
...TELL ME, FATHER, WHAT EXACTLY ARE THE DUTIES OF AN EMISSARY?
EMISSARIES OF TZE-YO-TZUH **SERVE** HIM AND ALL THAT HE LOVES.
"ALL THAT HE LOVES"...THAT INCLUDES HUMANS?
YES. TZE-YO-TZUH CONSIDERS THEM THE PINNACLE OF HIS CREATION.

219

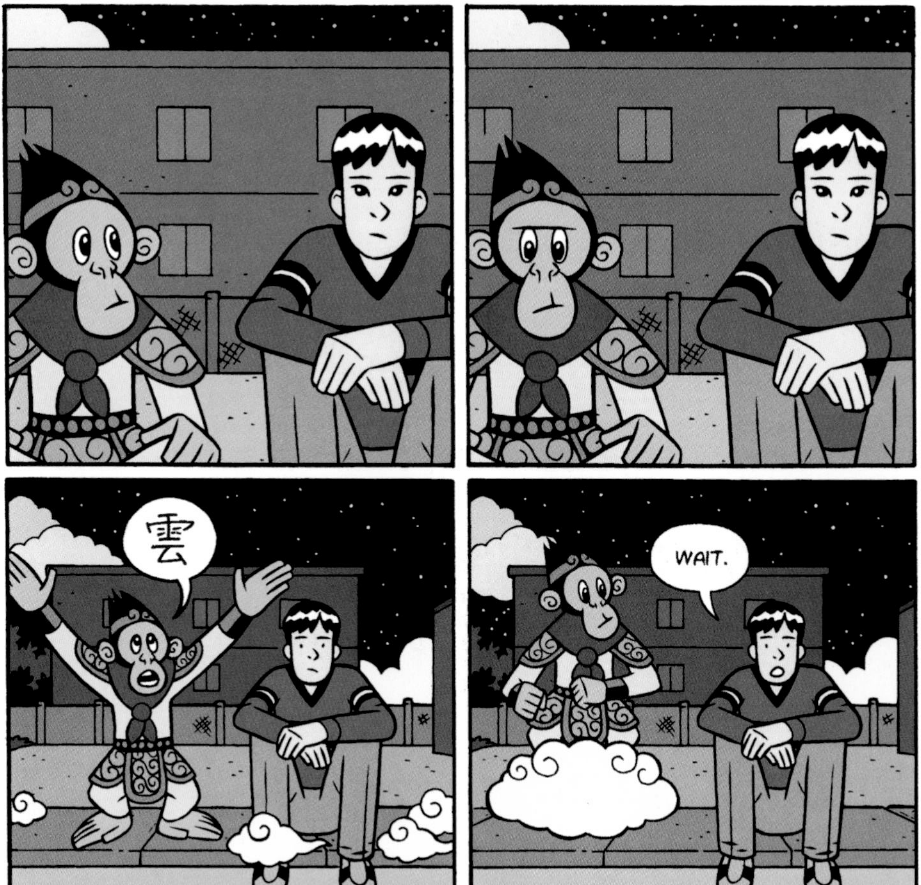
雲
WAIT.

223

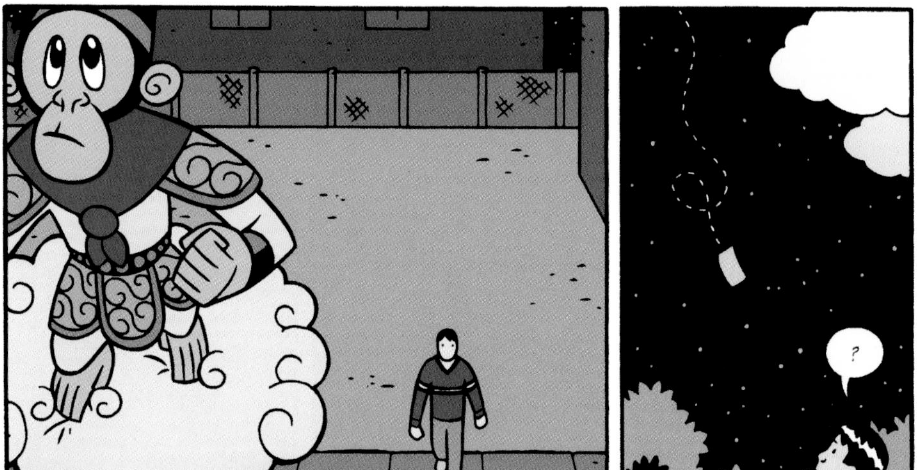
?
490
snatch!
490
餐廳餅家

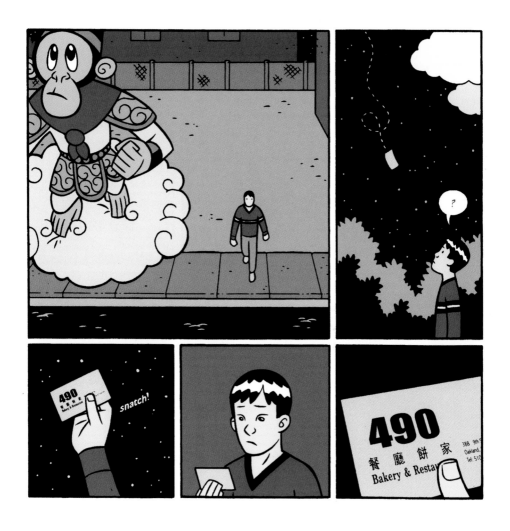

225

226

229

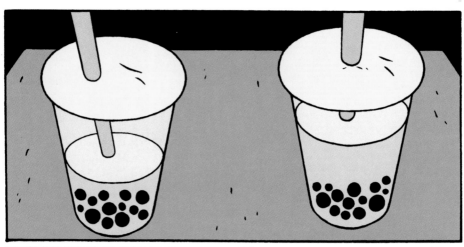

< WHY ARE YOU TELLING ME ALL THIS? >

I GUESS...

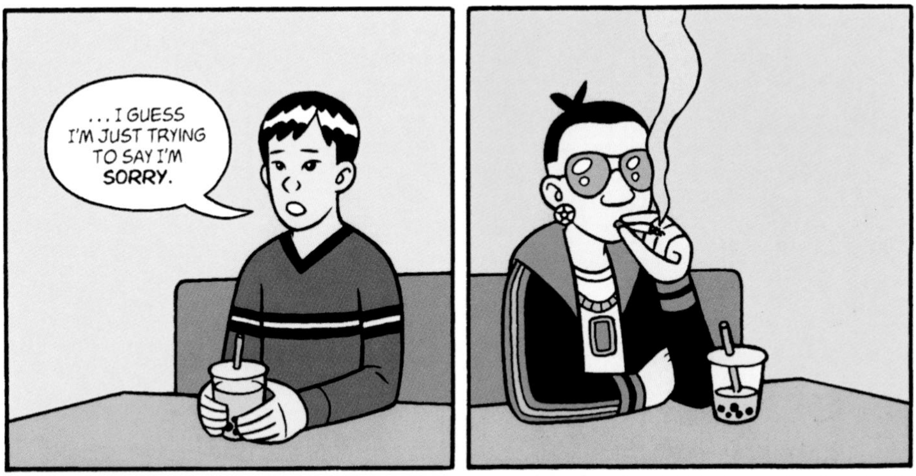
...I GUESS I'M JUST TRYING TO SAY I'M SORRY.
sip.

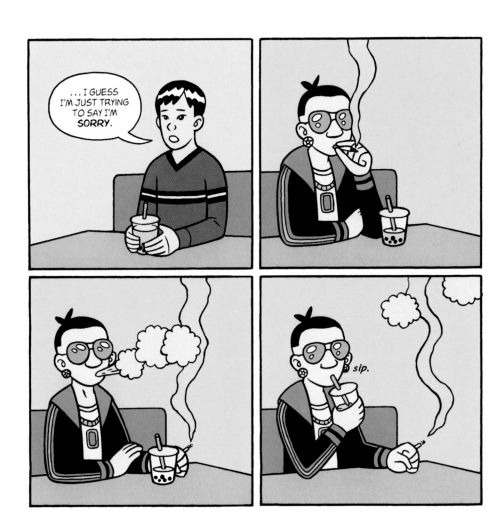

The End

Interview with
Gene Luen Yang and Kelvin Yu

Kelvin Yu is the series creator and executive producer/showrunner of the genre-hopping action comedy American Born Chinese *on Disney+. Recently, he and Gene Luen Yang sat down with First Second to talk about the process of adapting a graphic novel to the screen.*

FIRST SECOND: Kelvin, when did you first come across the graphic novel?

KELVIN YU: I was actually gifted this book by my older brother, Charlie Yu, who wrote the pilot with me. It was probably ten years ago. Because I'm an Asian American writer, the book has come up many, many times in my life. I was aware of its place as a seminal piece of the Asian American canon.

FS: Gene, when did you first think about adapting *American Born Chinese* for the screen?

GENE LUEN YANG: I've had a media agent since the book was first published in 2006, but back then, there wasn't a ton of interest in stories about Asian Americans. Shows like *Fresh Off the Boat* and movies like *Crazy Rich Asians* had to pave the way. They proved to Hollywood that our stories can have a wide appeal.

It wasn't just external resistance. I had a lot of internal resistance, too. There's a character in *American Born Chinese* who is essentially a walking, talking Asian stereotype. He's satire, but my greatest fear was that clips of this character would show up on social media, completely stripped of their context. Kelvin and his writing team addressed this fear brilliantly. Those social media clips I was so afraid of, they made them a part of the story.

FS: What are the challenges of adapting a graphic novel to a television series?

KY: The challenges dovetail with the benefits, I think. The basic unit of storytelling of a graphic novel, if you will, is like that of a film. The panels are like frames, so you can read the graphic novel as a storyboard, and there is a huge temptation to just make that.

At the end of the day, however, that isn't enough for an adaptation. In television, you need a cast of characters who are going to show up regularly, week in and week out, episode after episode. For instance, one of the first things I thought was, *Jin's parents have to be major characters*.

Then, specifically to *American Born Chinese*, the story is fractured. It's a structural innovation of the original book. One way to make that into a show would be to do one episode of Jin, one episode of the Monkey King, one episode of the sitcom, and then loop it, but you can't really present that to most networks.

So the conversation became, "What is the heart of what Gene Luen Yang was trying to get at? What does that look like and feel like on the screen within a series of thirty-five minute television episodes?"

I would say the most important thing for me to capture was the tone. That was more important than structure. The book is rightfully lauded for many reasons, but my favorite part is the tone. I'm a comedy writer and I think everything has humor, even our most tragic moments.

That was the biggest challenge, I think. Making sure the show had the heart, the profundity, and the humor of Gene Luen Yang's *American Born Chinese*, tonally.

GLY: On my side, I was thinking a lot about the strengths and weaknesses of comics versus television. That was the challenge. An adaptation can be very different so long as it takes advantage of the new medium's strengths while still maintaining the heart of the original. It just has to be good, you know?

The book has one beginning, one middle, and one end. I guess you could argue that it has three beginnings, middles, and ends for the three different storylines. But with the series, Kelvin and his team were creating an eight-episode season. That's at least eight different beginnings, middles, and ends, probably more if you count the B stories, so it becomes much, much more complicated.

You have to introduce more characters and plotlines, but you still want to keep that tone, that underlying foundation.

FS: What was the most fun thing that happened while working on the show?

KY: The most fun thing that happened? I have a few answers. The fourth episode takes place in Chinese heaven. I remember walking onto that set and just having to pick my jaw up off the floor.

I will also never forget walking into the Wang family home. Our production designers, Michele Yu and Cindy Chao, put so much attention and love into that set. Every single person of Chinese or Taiwanese descent who walked onto that set had a very profound reaction to it.

GLY: Including me.

KY: We couldn't believe a home like this was going to be on TV. Then I would also say casting our two main guys, Jimmy Liu and Ben Wang, to play Wei-Chen and Jin.

GLY: They're both perfect.

KY: If we hadn't found those guys, we'd be dead in the water. Lastly, I'll just say that working with Peng Zhang, our stunt coordinator, has been just really gratifying. He's a real storyteller and his language just happens to be fight choreography. He's really cool, so that's been fun.

GLY: For me, there were lots of surreal moments, like meeting Destin Daniel Cretton on Zoom, then shaking his hand in real life. On the first day of filming, I stood on a high school baseball field next to Michelle Yeoh and Daniel Wu. Ke Huy Quan gave me a piece of roast pork. Then I watched Ben and Jimmy do the scene with the toy robot. That was from a panel I drew almost twenty years ago.

KY: That must've been really surreal. This has been a "pinch me" project from the beginning, you know? We got to work with Destin Daniel Cretton and Michelle Yeoh and Melvin Mar and Lucy Liu, all these amazing people.

GLY: And for me, getting an up close view of Kelvin and this whole team of creative people working in another storytelling medium was a thrill. The whole thing has been super fun.

KY: Really, really fun.

FS: The show's time period is different from that of the book. Can you comment on that?

GLY: The book came out in 2006 and when I was working on it, I was actually thinking back to my own childhood in the 80s and 90s.

With the adaptation, we made the decision early on to set the show not in the 80s or 90s, but in present day. The conversation about Asian American issues has changed since then, right?

KY: Yeah. That should be the headline about the challenge of adaptations because the issues we're dealing with are such moving targets from year to year. Not only are Asian American issues different, but young people's issues are different.

How a sixteen-year-old or eighteen-year-old kid sees the world is different. America's relationship with China is different. Young people's relationship to America is different after Barack Obama, after Donald Trump.

It was a lot to juggle. It was difficult, but I will say this: Every once in a while, something in the news or in politics would serendipitously—and often unfortunately—affirm that we still have a lot of work to do. I would read some article about a hate crime against an Asian American and I would think, *This is all still true. It's different from how it was in '06 and '96, but it's still true.*

GLY: Yeah. What struck me during the adaptation process is a realization that things are K-shaped. They talk about how the recovery from the pandemic is K-shaped, how certain communities in America recovered quickly while others are still struggling. I think the same thing is true of Asian American issues. In some ways, things are better than we ever could have imagined. But in other ways, it's like we're falling backwards in time.

KY: That's true. While working on this eight-episode series, I had to find something that I wanted to say. And over the past several years, a theme that I continually go back to is confidence.

I had to ask myself early on, *Is confidence an idea worthy of all these hundreds of people coming to work every day, from the gaffer adjusting a light to the audio guy?* Then, *Is that a theme that resonates with the Asian American experience?* And finally, personally, *Did I have the confidence to tell this story about confidence?*

The answers for me were yes, all the way down the line.

Another word for *confidence* that has come up is *entitlement*. In the last ten or twenty years, we've had a big conversation about entitlement in this country. What are we entitled to? What are we not entitled to? What does it mean to have a toxic, unhealthy sense of entitlement? What does it mean to have a healthy, justified sense of entitlement? What are you worthy of?

It's very complicated for a fifteen-year-old Chinese American kid to have these different voices in your head, telling you to sometimes hold your head up high and be an American, and sometimes keep your head low and do your job and follow the rules. It's confusing, but I thought it was a story worth telling.

GLY: That part of the conversation about the Asian American experience has stayed consistent since the publication of the book. The question about entitlement or confidence is really a question about belonging, right?

KY: Yeah, that's another good word.

GLY: We Asian Americans sometimes feel like we are guests in America. We're often treated as foreign even if we've been here all our lives. And it's gotten a lot worse during the pandemic.

So a lot of us respond by trying to be polite. We try to be good guests and not make a fuss, because America feels like somebody else's house.

KY: And then you notice that other people don't have that problem at all.

GLY: Yeah. That's right. And maybe that's what we're trying to do with the book and the show. Convince people, including ourselves, that America is our home.

First Second

Published by First Second

First Second is an imprint of Roaring Brook Press,
a division of Holtzbrinck Publishing Holdings Limited Partnership
120 Broadway, New York, NY 10271
firstsecondbooks.com

Library of Congress Cataloging-in-Publication Data
Yang, Gene.
American born Chinese / Gene Yang; coloring by Lark Pien
p. cm.
Summary: Alternates three interrelated stories about the problems of young Chinese Americans
trying to participate in the popular culture. Presented in comic book format.

Our books may be purchased in bulk for promotional, educational, or business use.
Please contact your local bookseller or the Macmillan Corporate and Premium Sales Department
at (800) 221-7945 ext. 5442 or by email at MacmillanSpecialMarkets@macmillan.com.

Media Tie-In Edition, 2023

Edited by Mark Siegel
Interior book design by Danica Novgorodoff
Color by Lark Pien
Chinese chops by Guo Ming Chen

Printed in the United States of America

ISBN 978-1-250-89139-6 (media tie-in edition)
10 9 8 7 6 5 4 3 2 1

She Bangs
By Afanasieff & Child
© 2000 Sony/ATV Tunes LLC, Wallyworld Music, Desmundo Music, Warner
Tamerlane Pub. Corp., A Phantom Vox Publishing. All rights on behalf of
Sony/ATV Tunes LLC, Wallyworld Music and Desmundo Music, administered
by Sony/ATV Music Publishing, 8 Music Square West, Nashville, TN 37203.
All rights reserved. Used by permission.

Don't miss your next favorite book from First Second! For the latest updates go to
firstsecondnewsletter.com and sign up for our enewsletter.

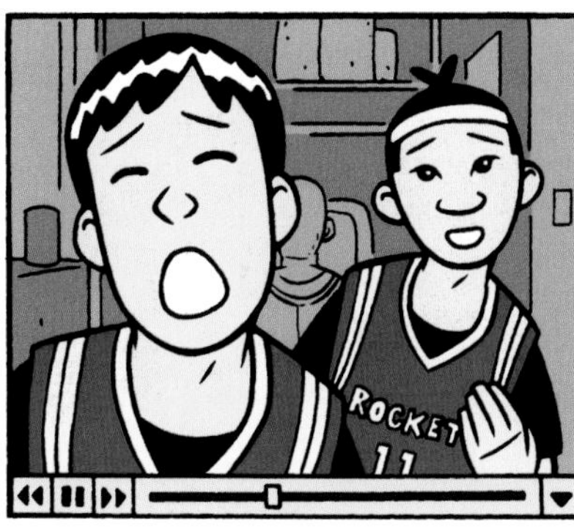
ROCKET
11